The Extraordinarily Ordinary Life of

Cassandra Jones

Southwest Cougars Year 1

Southwest Cougars Year 1

The Extraordinarily Ordinary Life of Cassandra Jones

Tamara Hart Heiner

print edition
copyright 2017 Tamara Hart Heiner
cover art by Tamara Hart Heiner

Also by Tamara Hart Heiner:
Perilous (WiDo Publishing 2010)
Altercation (WiDo Publishing 2012)
Deliverer (Tamark Books 2014)
Priceless (WiDo Publishing 2016)

Goddess of Fate:
Inevitable (Tamark Books 2013)
Entranced (Tamark Books 2017)

Kellam High:
Lay Me Down (Tamark Books 2016)
Reaching Kylee (Tamark Books 2016)

The Extraordinarily Ordinary Life of Cassandra Jones:
Walker Wildcats Year 1 (Tamark Books 2016)
Walker Wildcats Year 2 (Tamark Books 2016)

Tornado Warning (Dancing Lemur Press 2014)

Table of Contents

Episode 1: Growing Girl

Chapter One

Andrea's Birthday

"I can't believe we're about to start junior high," Cassandra Jones said, watching as her best friend Andrea pulled out a tray of different colored nail polishes.

The two girls sat in Andrea's bedroom, both perched on the bed with Andrea's white coverlet. Everything in Andrea's room was white, and Cassie always felt like she'd entered a serene fairy land when she came over. Nothing like the mad chaos that existed at her house, between her three siblings, their dog, and one cat. Their cat had a kitten a few years ago, but Mrs. Jones gave it away to another family and fixed the cat so it would never have another kitten.

"I know," Andrea said, pulling Cassie back to the conversation as she selected a bright red polish. Like Cassie, she wore glasses and kept her hair long. But hers was a wavy honey-brown with a hint of red, while Cassie's was dark, dark brown and very straight. "What do you think it will be like?"

Cassie shook her head, a nervous sensation bubbling in her stomach. She hated to admit how it frightened her, moving from elementary school to junior high. She chose a hot pink nail polish. She uncapped it and dragged the brush from the bottom of her nail bed to the top, glad she didn't bite her nails anymore. "I hope we have classes together."

"That's the scary part, right?" Andrea sighed. "We have no idea what classes we'll have."

Cassie squirmed. Just two years ago her family had moved to Arkansas from Texas, and it had taken this long for her to feel she had a place, a good group of friends. It hadn't been easy to make them. What would happen if she and Andrea didn't have classes together? Would she have classes with anyone she knew?

As if reading her mind, Andrea glanced at her and winked. "Maybe you'll have classes with Miles."

Miles. Cassie's lips curved upward as his face, complete with his friendly smile, appeared in her mind. A warmth flowed through her chest. Only to Andrea had she ever admitted her crush on their classmate. Miles, of course, had no idea, and Cassie never intended to tell him.

"Isn't your birthday party in a week?" Cassie asked, changing the subject before Andrea could pry her more. Andrea always urged her to tell Miles her feelings, but the thought terrified her.

"Yes, but I'm not having a slumber party. It's just for a few hours." Andrea capped the nail polish and blew across her fingers. "I'll text you the date."

"Great," Cassie said with a giggle. She and Andrea had both gotten phones after they graduated elementary school, and texting back and forth was enormous fun. Cassie didn't actually like to talk on it very much, though Andrea did. "I have soccer camp in a few weeks, and church camp a week after that, so as long as it's before then, we should be fine."

"I thought you decided you didn't like soccer?"

Cassie leaned back, waving her newly-polished nails to dry them. "I do like soccer. I'm just really bad at it." And she hated running, and the other kids on her team, especially Connor Lane, always made fun of her. "Hopefully a week of soccer camp will help me improve."

"Well, my party is next week. So you should be fine. But guess what!" Andrea pushed upward against the bed, her eyes lighting up with excitement. She grabbed Cassie's hands, careful to avoid her nails, and pumped them excitedly.

"What, what?" Cassie said, growing excited as well.

"Kitty's coming!"

For a moment Cassie just blinked at her, and then her memory jolted. She remembered Andrea talking about her old best friend Kitty, the one who moved away in the middle of fifth grade. Cassie had seen her once or twice, but she'd been in the other classroom, so they didn't know each other. But now a flash of jealousy rippled through her. If Kitty hadn't moved, would Kitty and Andrea still be best friends?

"Oh, that's nice," Cassie said, trying to hide her insecurities.

"I know you two will just love each other. You'll get along so great." Andrea squeezed Cassie's hands, the smile on her lips threatening to split her face.

"I'm sure," Cassie said, her heart starting to pound at the thought of spending time with Kitty. She pictured the other girl as she remembered her in her mind's eye: much taller than Cassie, skinny, with short brown hair. Glancing toward the mirror, Cassie frowned at her reflection. Large pink glasses framed her brown eyes, and the roundness to her face only emphasized her shortness. Her hands pulled away from

Andrea and went down to squeeze the pudge that had gradually built up around her waist over the past year. Her frown deepened.

It's fine, she told herself. *Andrea's your best friend.* And yet, she couldn't shake the feeling that this was an unwanted complication.

❦

Friday morning, the day of Andrea's birthday party, Cassie rushed through the required assignments her mom had given her so she could go to the party. She had just finished folding laundry and putting it away in the bedroom she shared with her sister Emily when she got a text from Andrea.

Can you come early to my birthday party and help set up?

Cassie lifted one eyebrow in surprise. The party started in just four hours. Her mom might not appreciate the late notice.

Cassie wandered out into the hallway, nearly tripping over her youngest brother and sister, Scott and Annette, as they built a large track out of wooden blocks. "Guys," she growled at them, but they merely glanced at her and then looked away, uninterested in her annoyance.

"Mom?" The door was open to her parents' bedroom, so she stepped in and sat across from her mom on the bed.

Mrs. Jones looked up from the envelopes she was stamping. "Yes, Cassie?"

"Andrea wants to know if I can come early and help set up for her birthday party."

"What time does she want you there?" Mrs. Jones put a stamp on another envelope and placed it in the stamped pile.

"I don't know."

"Tell her I can drop you off at noon."

That was an hour before the party started. Should be plenty

4

of time. Cassie's thumbs flew over the keypad as she texted, *I'll be there at noon.*

Great! Thank you! came Andrea's response.

Cassie hesitated, but she had to know. Quickly she typed out, *Is Kitty there?*

Not yet, Andrea said. *She'll get here when everyone else does.*

Some of the tightness went out of Cassie's chest. Andrea might be glad that Kitty was coming, but Cassie was still her best friend.

⚬ঌ৵ৎ৹

"This is the last year we'll be playing 'Pin the Tail on the Donkey,'" Andrea said as she and Cassie spread the plastic sheet across the wall.

"Why?" Cassie asked.

"Because we're too old for it." One of Andrea's eyebrows lifted. "We're going into the seventh grade. Next year we'll all be thirteen. No one will want to play this baby game."

"Hmm." Cassie nodded, though she wasn't sure it would be true. Could they all really change so much in one year?

Andrea let out a little giggle. "Remember your twelfth birthday, when your dog threw up on you? Hilarious."

Cassie remembered. Her face burned, and she was glad that her dark complexion would hide the blush. "Not really his fault. He's epileptic."

"Yeah, but still—and right before people started coming over!"

Andrea kept giggling, but Cassie tried not to think about the incident. Her birthdays lately hadn't gone all that well. This year she planned to forgo a party altogether. "Hopefully your party goes better than mine."

The doorbell rang, and Andrea swiveled around, dropping the pile of donkey tails onto the bookshelf. "Kitty!"

She raced for the door. Cassie lagged behind uncertainly, not sure of her role here.

Andrea threw open the front door. "Kitty!"

"Andy!" Kitty, even taller than when Cassie had seen her in fifth grade, squealed just as loudly as Andrea. Then they threw their arms around each other and swayed in a giant hug.

Cassie wrinkled her nose. *Andy? Since when?*

Since before Cassie, she guessed.

Andrea pulled out of the embrace first. "Kitty, do you know Cassie? She was in Ms. Dawson's class."

"Hi." Kitty smiled and waved, revealing braces with multicolored bands on them. She no longer wore glasses, either, leaving a clear line of sight to her light brown eyes.

"Hi," Cassie replied. Feeling awkward, she added, "Glad you could come."

"Come on, I want to show you a few things in my room," Andrea said, taking Kitty's hand. "Cassie, can you finish setting out the paper plates and cups?"

"You don't want me to come with you?" Cassie said, surprised at the dismissal.

Andrea brushed her off. "You were just in here. Kitty hasn't seen my room in almost two years."

Cassie forced a smile. "Of course. It's your birthday. I'll do whatever you need."

Andrea's mom joined Cassie in the kitchen, and they finished setting out the paper plates and cups. Even from here Cassie could hear Andrea and Kitty laughing and talking excitedly in the bedroom. Cassie's chest tightened.

The doorbell rang, and Mrs. Wall yelled, "Andrea! Your guests are arriving!"

"Coming!" Andrea shouted back.

A steady stream of kids showed up for the next several minutes, and Andrea spent all her time greeting them and directing them to Cassie, who seated them in the living room. Then they played musical chairs, and Andrea paid no more attention to Kitty than she did to all her friends. By the time they got to Pin the Tail on the Donkey, Cassie had relaxed. Kitty was only here for a few hours, after all.

"Presents!" Mrs. Wall shouted, bringing out the large stack that had collected by the front door. "Andrea, sit in the middle of the floor."

Andrea obliged, finding a spot facing everyone on the two couches.

Cassie spotted her present right away. Her mom had placed the straw hat in a hatbox and then wrapped it in shiny turquoise paper. A big green bow sat on top. Cassie just knew Andrea would love it.

"That one's mine," Kitty said, pointing to a massive pink box. "Open it first, please!"

Cassie frowned at Kitty. How dare she steal the show? Then she swiveled back to Andrea, waiting to see what she would say.

"Okay," Andrea laughed. She picked up the present and slowly peeled back the paper. Then she gasped. "Oh, wow."

Cassie craned her head, trying to see what it was. She needn't have bothered. Andrea undid the box and pulled out a large, light-pink crystal unicorn. The back legs were suspended on a pedestal while the front legs kicked up and out, as if the animal were about to take a flying leap.

Cassie's heart clenched. It was beautiful. Feminine and grown-up and expensive. Suddenly, she wanted to retrieve her hatbox and run from the room.

"Oh, Kitty!" Andrea gasped. "I love it!"

Cassie gritted her teeth while the two girls hugged—again. She wove her fingers together and watched as Andrea opened the other presents, finally getting to Cassie's.

"And this one's yours, of course," she said, flashing Cassie a smile. "I saved the best for last."

The words didn't comfort Cassie; instead, she only felt more embarrassed by her gift. "Don't get too excited. It's pretty lame." Especially compared to Kitty's.

"Never," Andrea admonished. She pulled up the bow, then peeled back the wrapping paper. Curiosity showed on her face as she lifted the lid to the box.

"This is beautiful!" she exclaimed, pulling out the straw hat, complete with flowers on the brim and a ribbon to tie it under her neck. "Thank you, Cassie!"

Cassie forced herself to smile while Andrea hugged her, but she felt like she was being patronized. The hat had looked so cute in the antique shop. Now, next to the other gifts Andrea had received, it looked like something for a little girl.

When the party ended, the guests began to clear out, except for Cassie and Kitty. Andrea thanked everyone as they left. Cassie sat stiffly on the couch, wondering when Kitty's mom would show up.

"Where's your mom, Cassie?" Kitty asked from the other end of the couch, as if thinking the same thing.

"Oh, I'm staying late," Cassie said, glad Andrea had asked her to stay after the party as well. "Andrea asked me to stay over after."

Kitty looked surprised. "I didn't know that."

"What about you?" Cassie glanced toward the door, where Andrea bade goodbye to the last guest. "Where's your mom?"

"I'm spending the weekend here. With Andrea."

A knot tightened in Cassie's stomach. Andrea had failed to mention that. "That will be so great. A chance for you two to catch up." *Without me.* Cassie pictured them forming a new, tighter bond than ever, replete with inside jokes and personal references that Cassie would never understand.

"Yeah. My parents are looking at houses. We might move back here."

The knot doubled up on itself. "Nice," Cassie said through gritted teeth.

Andrea rejoined them on the couch and sighed. "I couldn't have asked for a better birthday! I'm so glad you both were here and could help so much!"

"It was nothing," Cassie said, inexplicably close to tears.

Andrea picked up the hat Cassie had given her and placed it on her head. "How do I look?" She smiled and posed, batting her eyelashes at Cassie.

"Lovely, dah-ling," Cassie said, adopting a fake British accent. "I ah-dore you in that hat."

"I have to see." Andrea jumped up and ran to the bathroom. Kitty followed, and Cassie trooped along behind. Next to Kitty's tall, slender frame, all she wanted was to be taller and skinnier.

Giggling, Andrea took the hat off and pushed up on her hair. "It needs to be bigger. Hair spray, Cassie."

After more slumber parties over here than Cassie could count, she knew which cupboard had the hair spray. She handed it over to Andrea, who finished ratting her hair and then solidified it with the spray.

"Your turn, Cassie. Make it big."

Cassie held the can of spray and stared at her thick, straight hair. What could she possibly do with it? "I don't know how."

"I'll do it." Kitty took the hair spray and shoved almost all of her short golden hair to the side of her head. Then she sprayed it, waving the can back and forth as she pelted the hair with tiny droplets. When she finished, part of it fell into her face in a desperate attempt to return to its rightful place. She looked sexy and modern.

"Let me try." Cassie took the hair spray and swept her hair over to the side. Squinting her eyes, she held the spray tip down and coated her hair with the sticky wetness. Most of it held, only a small amount falling out of formation to form a wave across her forehead. She liked the look.

"We look so grown up," Andrea said, pulling out a container of make-up. "Now to finish it."

Kitty chuckled. "You've always thought yourself the make-up artist."

"Yeah," Cassie joined in, laughing. "And my mom makes me take it all off as soon as I get home."

Kitty looked at her, and they laughed together. Something loosened in Cassie's chest. Maybe there didn't have to be a competition between them.

Then she remembered that Kitty was spending the night. No, the sooner Kitty left again, the better.

Chapter Two

Soccer Camp

"I'm so excited for soccer camp," Cassie's younger sister Emily said. She quickly piled clothing into the suitcase spread wide open on her bed. "Isn't it great? Our coaches will all be professional soccer players from the university."

Cassie wasn't sure a student could be a professional soccer player, but she didn't correct her sister. Instead she stood by her dresser, eyes glazing over as she watched Emily.

Emily closed her suitcase and zipped it up, then shoved her long light brown hair out of her face. She looked at Cassie. "Aren't you going to pack?"

Cassie sighed and opened up a drawer, unmotivated in spite of the fact that they would leave for camp tomorrow after church. She'd asked for this. She'd begged her parents to let her play soccer, and they'd finally agreed, signing her and Emily up for it. The end result? She sucked at it. And instead of each practice getting easier, it only got harder.

"What are you afraid of?" Emily asked, as if reading her mind. "I thought you loved soccer."

"I do." Cassie dumped a pair of pajamas in her own suitcase. "But I don't think it loves me."

Emily giggled at that. "Well, after this week, I'm sure you'll be great at it."

Cassie appreciated her sister's vote of confidence, but she had her doubts.

When church ended on Sunday, Mr. Jones drove the two younger kids, Scott and Annette, home while Mrs. Jones drove the girls to the University of Arkansas in Fayetteville, just twenty minutes away. They pulled into a parking lot at the multi-leveled dorms. Cassie watched the other kids unloading their suitcases from the cars. Most of the girls were thick but muscular, with long hair trapped in ponytail holders and athletic shorts on. She looked down at her skirt and wished she'd had time to change.

"We need some cool shorts like that," Emily said.

"You want some?" Mrs. Jones asked.

"They're kind of nice," Emily said, a little sheepishly.

"Well, I have a surprise for you," Mrs. Jones said. "Let's check the trunk."

Intrigued, Cassie undid her seatbelt and followed her sister to the back of the van. Mrs. Jones popped it open, and next to the two suitcases was a large paper bag.

"Open it," her mother said.

Emily did, and she gasped as she pulled out a pair of bright blue shorts with a lime-green cuff. "These are awesome!"

Eagerly, Cassie pulled out another pair, this one purple with the same lime-green cuff. "I love them! Where did you get them?"

Mrs. Jones beamed at them. "Since Scott and Annette want to play soccer also, your dad's been searching everywhere for a good place to get your soccer supplies. He realized there just isn't one. So—he's going to start one."

Cassie's eyes widened. Her dad loved to take on new projects. The last one he'd done was a band at her elementary school. "Wow! That will be fun."

Mrs. Jones' smile weakened slightly. "Fun—and expensive and time-consuming."

Definitely time-consuming. "But he has a job," Cassie said. "How will he fit it in?"

Her mom's smile disappeared completely. "He's quitting his job. This is a venture he wants to embark on, and I'm supporting him."

Sounded great to Cassie. She loved how her dad was taking this leap of faith to pursue his dream.

"We'll need you girls to help out a bit in the store sometimes," Mrs. Jones went on.

"Like a job?" Cassie said, growing more excited.

"A very low-paying one, yes," Mrs. Jones said.

It had to be more than her measly allowance. Cassie picked up her suitcase, a little more pep to her step as she walked toward the dormitory.

A woman with short brown hair and a whistle around her neck greeted them in the foyer. She wore no make up, and her shirt stretched tight across her shoulders. The muscles on her arms flexed as she lifted her pencil. "Names?" she said, looking over her clipboard.

"Cassandra and Emily Jones," Mrs. Jones said, resting a hand on each girl's shoulder.

"Okay, you're rooming together on the second floor. Just take the elevator there—" she pointed behind her— "and go right. You'll see your names on the door. You'll be rooming with two other girls. Oh, and no elevators after today. We take the stairs." She winked at both girls.

They shuffled into the elevator, and as the doors closed, Emily leaned over and whispered, "That's what a real soccer player looks like."

Cassie nodded. Athletic. There was no other way to describe the woman. She looked down at the roll of skin around her belly, and the first word that came to mind was "portly."

"Hi," a girl with very curly brown hair and braces said when the girls dragged their suitcases into their room. She sat on the bottom bunk of one of the two bunk beds, her phone in her hands. "I'm Olivia."

"Cassie," Cassie said, choosing the bottom bunk of the bed closest to the door.

"I'm Emily."

"Our other roommate is Tara, but she hasn't come yet," Olivia said.

Cassie nodded. She turned to her mom with a big smile, suddenly eager to be on their own. "We got it from here, Mom."

"I guess it's time I headed home anyway," Mrs. Jones said. "Good luck, girls! We'll see you at the big game on Friday."

"Right," Emily said, already unloading her things on the top bunk. "I forgot we'd be playing for you."

"Yeah, all week we'll work on our skills. Isn't it cool that the actual Lady Razorback soccer players will be coaching us?" Olivia beamed.

"Bye, girls." Mrs. Jones hugged them both, then, with a final wave, she walked out.

Cassie barely glanced at her retreating back, focusing instead on arranging her things in the little space around her bed.

"Where are you from?" Olivia asked.

"Springdale," Cassie said. "You?"

"Where's that? I'm from Conway. It's about three hours from here."

"Oh. Springdale's only twenty minutes away."

"Nice! So do you go to a lot of the Razorback games?"

Olivia looked so eager, almost hungry in expectation, that Cassie felt bad admitting they weren't Razorback fans. "No."

Olivia leaned back on her bottom bunk, disappointment passing over her features. "I want to be one of the Lady Razorbacks one day. I've been playing soccer for five years. Next year I'm joining a competitive team."

"Really?" Cassie gave Olivia another look. "How old are you?"

"Eleven."

Cassie frowned. "So you're only going into sixth grade?"

"Yep. You?"

Cassie pointed at herself and said, "Seventh." Then she gestured to Emily and said, "Fifth."

"We've only been playing for a few months," Emily said.

"You must really like it to be coming to camp already."

"We hope to improve," Cassie said. "Have you come to camp before?"

"Yeah. This is my second year. I started coming as soon as I was old enough."

"What's your favorite part about camp?" Cassie asked. She put her suitcase under the bed, changing her mind about unpacking.

"The ice cream," Olivia said immediately. "We eat at a buffet in the cafeteria, and they have ice cream. Not the soft-serve kind, but the kind you have to scoop out. I have it with every meal."

"Every meal?" Emily echoed, her eyes widening.

"Yep." Olivia smiled and bobbed her head up and down.

Cassie pressed a hand to her stomach. She doubted she needed an ice cream with every meal.

"What else do you like?" Emily asked.

"Well, the soccer is fun, but it's grueling. Like super hard. Like you want to fall-on-the-grass-and-drown-in-your-water-bottle hard. But the final game is so worth it. They break us up into two teams and we play each other. No matter who wins, we all feel like winners. Because after five days with each other, we're one unit, you know?"

Cassie nodded, though she didn't know. She didn't really get along with anyone on her current soccer team. Some of the girls were friendly, but she knew no one really valued her. She hated running, and her foot missed the ball more often than it connected with it.

The more she thought about it, the more she really didn't know why she was here.

"But also Thursday night, before our last game, there's a talent show."

Her ears perked up again. "Talent show?" she asked. "Like who dribbles the best or who can pass the ball with the most control?"

Olivia laughed. "No, it doesn't have to be soccer related at all. Some people sing, play the piano, or tell jokes. Whatever."

"Cassie sings opera," Emily said.

"Ew, opera?" Olivia wrinkled her nose. "Nobody likes opera."

"No, really," Emily said. "It's fun. Sing something, Cass."

Cassie hesitated, then belted out the first two lines from a popular musical in full-on opera style.

"Ahh!" Olivia and Emily burst out laughing, holding their sides with mirth.

"Keep going!" Olivia shrieked. "Do some more!"

Grinning, Cassie obliged, singing the rest of the song like a star performer.

☙❧

Monday morning, the camp director, Carol, came around and knocked on all the bedroom doors.

"Socks and shinguards on, girls!" she shouted as she walked down the hall. "Ten minutes to eat your breakfast, and then meet me in the foyer!"

Cassie peeked one eye out from under her arm while Olivia groaned.

"We stayed up way too late last night," Olivia said.

"Yeah," Emily agreed from the top bunk, a yawn stifling her words.

Tara had come in later in the evening, after dinner, but the four girls had hit it off. They'd stayed up talking, and Cassie was pleased that the subject of soccer wasn't brought up at all. Now Tara lifted her blond head off the pillow just enough for Cassie to see it bob above the top bunk frame.

"Seven a.m.!" Tara groaned. "What are they doing to us?"

"It's like this every day," Olivia said. She'd already slipped on a soccer jersey and shorts, and now she pulled on her socks. "She's not kidding, either. We better run to breakfast or we won't get any."

Cassie hurriedly pulled on her t-shirt and new shorts, then her shinguards and knee-high socks. The four girls rushed out of the dorm room and down the stairs to the cafeteria on the first floor. Cassie grabbed a muffin and a banana and joined the group of girls in the foyer.

"The soccer field is just a few hundred meters away," Carol was saying. "And the best time of the day to be out there playing is right now, before it gets too hot. So put on your jogging hat and let's go!"

Cassie hadn't even eaten yet! She shoved half the muffin in her mouth and tossed the other half at a trashcan. The banana she held gently in one hand as the girls headed out the door, breaking into an easy jog.

Although Cassie started the run next to Emily, in about the middle of the group, between the chewing and swallowing and the actual running, she had to slow down. Before she knew it, she was at the back of the group. How much farther to the soccer fields? She squinted and looked down the sidewalk where they ran, two dozen other girls keeping pace in front of her. Brick buildings banked the concrete on one side, the road on the other. She didn't see any sign of a soccer field.

Her side began to cramp, and Cassie came to a halt. It would be easier to finish her food first and then run. She walked along behind, unpeeling her banana and keeping her eyes open for the fields. The pack of girls got farther and farther ahead. She ate her banana as quickly as she could, glancing around for a trashcan before shrugging and tossing the peel in the grass. She figured it would decompose.

When she looked up again, her heart gave a little leap. The camp of girls was about the turn the corner without her. Crapola! She'd never live it down if she showed up ten minutes after everyone else. Adrenaline surging her onward, Cassie broke into a jog again. The cramp in her side flared up even worse, and she pressed a hand to it, leaning heavily to one side with each step downward. Her breathing came in short, raspy gasps.

She turned the corner and saw the soccer field. Bleachers surrounded it on two sides, and red water coolers with plastic cups on top of them sat on top of tables nestled in the bright green grass.

Almost there! She told herself. She wanted to stop running. So badly.

Emily lifted her head and saw her, and her face lit up. "Cassie!" she called. "What happened to you?"

Almost as one, all the other girls turned to look at her. Some wore expressions of surprise, and others confusion. The confusion turned to derision, and a few girls huddled their heads together and whispered.

"Nothing happened to me," Cassie snapped, annoyed her sister had pointed her out. She stopped by one of the water coolers and poured a cup of water. "I had to stop a few times."

Carol's whistle blew. "All right, ladies! Every time we come to the fields, that's how we'll get here. When we head home after practice, we'll go the same way. By the end of the week, you'll be running a mile without breaking a sweat."

Cassie broke out in a sweat just hearing those words. Was this lady crazy? No way was she doing all that running.

Carol's eyes focused on another part of the field, and she smiled. Cassie followed her gaze as five tall, muscular young women walked onto the field, dressed in red and white shorts and jerseys, their hair tied back with red ribbons.

"And look!" Carol said. "Our Lady Razorbacks are here! I'll number you off into three groups. Each group will have two instructors." She counted them off, and Cassie broke off to join the group she was assigned to.

Carol called out, "We'll regroup in half an hour. Listen to your instructors, ladies!"

"Razorbacks!" shouted the instructors in the red and white jerseys. All of the campers looked at them, and Carol laughed before marching away.

So these were the Lady Razorbacks. Cassie scrutinized them. What was it about them that Olivia so admired?

It only took about two minutes of practice to figure it out.

"Hi, I'm Laine," the brunette with freckles across her nose said. "I'm a sophomore at the U of A, and this is my second year on the team."

"And I'm Rishika," the other girl said, a slight accent in her words. "I came on a soccer scholarship. This is my first year. If you play soccer really well in high school, you can earn a scholarship too."

"How many of you want to go to the U of A?" Laine asked.

Several of the girls cheered, waving their arms. Cassie didn't. She wanted to go to the same school her father had gone to.

"Fantastic! And how many of you want to play for the Lady Razorbacks?"

The cheers turned into screams, loud, excited, delirious screams.

"Then let's get on it, ladies!"

"Razorbacks!" Rishika shouted.

Laine tossed everyone a ball, and she and Rishika demonstrated how to steal the ball, make a feint, and pass the ball to a teammate in the back.

"Now everyone grab a partner and try these passes!" Laine said.

Passing wasn't too hard. Cassie paired up with Nikki, a redhead from West Fork who was also going into seventh grade.

"Hey, you've got good footwork," Nikki said.

"Thanks," Cassie said, feeling a bit more confident.

"You girls are doing good," Rishika said, walking around and watching everyone. "Looks like you know how to control the ball."

They went through the drills a few more times and then took a water break.

"Time for a scrimmage," Carol said, gathering the girls back together into one group. "All of you—against me and the Ladies."

"Razorbacks!" the Lady Razorbacks shouted. This time a few of the campers said it with them.

"Oh, easy!" someone said, and the campers laughed and jeered.

"We'll see how easy this is," Carol scoffed. "Olivia, you're team captain. I want three on offense, two on defense, and one in the goal. Decide who's playing first."

Olivia turned around. "Okay, who wants to play what?"

Cassie opened her mouth to claim defense, but two girls beat her to it. Emily and another girl claimed offense, and Olivia looked at Cassie.

"Cassie, do you want to play offense also?"

Cassie shook her head. "No, I do best on defense."

"What about goalie?"

"No way." It took a certain kind of player to be goalie, and it sure wasn't Cassie.

"I'll play goalie," another, much bigger, girl said.

"Thanks," Olivia said. "What's your name?"

"Gretchen."

"Okay, Gretchen's in goal." Olivia turned back to Cassie. "Want to try offense today, Cass?"

Cassie wanted to say no. But the way Olivia said her name, as if they were friends— "Okay."

"Great. Come on, everyone, let's scrimmage!"

Emily stepped up to the starting line, standing in the middle of the field. Cassie took the spot to her left. Even though she'd been playing soccer for a few months, she so rarely played striker that she wasn't quite sure what would happen next. The whistle blew, and Emily passed the ball to Cassie, catching her off guard. For some reason she'd expected Emily to kick it down the field. She hesitated a moment too long, and the other team barreled in and took the ball from her.

"Go get it, Cassie!" Emily shouted, already racing after it.

Crapola. Cassie spun on her heel and dashed down the field, slowing when her side began to cramp again. The girls on defense batted the ball back and forth with their feet for a bit before sending it out of reach of the opposing team. It rolled to a stop a mere few feet away from Cassie.

"That's yours, Cassie!" Olivia screamed.

Cassie summoned up a burst of energy and ran at the ball. She kicked it, feeling a jolt of pleasure when her foot connected. It shot across the grass and suddenly Emily was there, intercepting it and dribbling it toward the opposing goal. The other teammate on offense joined her, and they passed it back and forth, playing off each other. Cassie jogged behind, making an appearance at keeping up but not really.

Emily scored a goal, and Olivia shrieked and cheered. Cassie joined in, smiling and high-fiving her teammates as everyone gathered back behind the starting line. She hadn't done much—kicked the ball once—but nobody really seemed to notice. She let the other teammate take the kick-off, but she felt more prepared this time when the ball came her way.

After fifteen minutes, though, Cassie could no longer pretend to keep up. She lagged behind, walking down the field and clutching her side. Whenever Olivia screamed her name, she put on a burst of speed, only to let it taper off as soon as the ball was out of reach. When Olivia pulled her out so another girl could play, Cassie collapsed next to the red cooler and gulped down a cup of ice water.

"Are you okay, Cassie?" Olivia asked. "You were slowing down out there."

"I'm not used to this heat," Cassie lied. "I just need a break." It had nothing to do with that, and she knew it; but Olivia didn't.

Olivia nodded. "Make sure you drink lots of water, okay? That's what my coach always says. Don't want to get dehydrated."

Cassie bobbed her head and took another sip of water.

Cassie's legs ached by the time they ran back for lunch. Her muscles spasmed even after she sat down, and she was so tired she wasn't even hungry. She poked at her food before stealing up to her room for a rest. They got a two-hour break in the hottest part of the afternoon before hitting the sport hard again. Most of the girls went downstairs to the game room, but Cassie wanted to lay down in cool, air-conditioned silence.

A text from Andrea glowed on her phone screen when Cassie got back to her room. She grabbed the phone, anxious from anything from her best friend, something to make her feel more—valuable.

How is soccer camp? Miss you! Andrea wrote.

Cassie grimaced. How much should she reveal? She replied, *Harder than I expected, but still fun. Miss you like crazy.*

Andrea must've been at her phone, because the response came right away. *Guess what, guess what? I'm so excited, I can't wait to tell you!*

Cassie bounced up and down, grinning, Andrea's excitement contagious even through the phone. *What, what?*

Kitty's parents bought a house here! She'll be at Southwest Junior High with us next year!

Cassie's smile faded, and a rock settled in the back of her throat. Kitty would live here? She'd go to their junior high next year? Cassie swallowed hard. This was not good news. But Andrea wanted it to be, so . . . *Wow, how exciting! I know you're so glad!*

And that was all she could say. Cassie couldn't pretend to be happy about Kitty moving in, not when she felt insecure and threatened. She closed the phone and slipped it under her pillow, then stretched out on her bed and closed her eyes.

Chapter Three

Cassie the Fat Girl

After three days of camp, Cassie had to admit she could see definite improvements in her passing and blocking. But the running wasn't coming any easier. Though she didn't lose the other campmates again, she still ran at the back of the pack.

Gretchen usually ran with her. Gretchen was a short, heavy-set girl going into ninth grade who liked to be goalie.

"So I don't have to run," she told Cassie on the second day. "That's why I play goalie."

"That's why I play defense," Cassie said, her heart warming to the other girl.

That was yesterday. Today as they jogged along, Gretchen said, "Your sister Emily is doing really well."

"Yeah," Cassie said, straining to keep her feet moving forward. "She's good at everything." It was after lunch, and the afternoon sun beat down on her dark hair, making her head pound.

"Are you two really sisters? You look nothing alike."

"Everyone says that," Cassie said. Sweat beaded along her

forehead. "But we're sisters." Both girls had long hair, but that was where the similarities ended. Cassie's was straight and dark brown, almost black, while Emily's was a golden brown with a bit of a wave to it. Cassie's skin sucked up the rays of the sun, turning a nice olive in summer time, while Emily's fair skin had a tendency to burn. They both had brown eyes, though Cassie's were dark as night and Emily's the color of honey.

"Same parents?"

"Yep." She was down to one-word answers. It was all she could manage between panting breaths.

Gretchen fell silent as they rounded the corner to the fields. Then she said, "Some people say running is hard for me because I'm fat."

Cassie turned to study the other girl. While it was true that Gretchen was bigger boned and perhaps heavier set, Cassie would never have called her fat. "No, you're not."

Gretchen smiled at her. "I love your attitude. Us bigger girls have to stick together, right?"

Us bigger girls. Cassie just stared at her.

From the front of the pack, Carol turned around and shouted, "Hurry up, ladies!"

"Razorbacks," Gretchen and Cassie murmured dully.

They caught up to the other girls, and Rishika claimed Gretchen for their team. As Gretchen jogged toward the goal, Cassie tried to make sense of her words. Gretchen considered herself fat. Did she lump Cassie into that same category?

Cassie glanced down at her stomach, bumping out over the rim of her elastic shorts. Was she fat?

"Cassie," Laine called, "we need you over here!"

She shook off her ponderings and started toward Laine,

totally lacking the strength to run anymore. "I call defense."

Gretchen's words ran through Cassie's mind the whole time they scrimmaged. She played her hardest, telling herself to keep running even when she wanted to stop. She threw herself in the ball's path when it came at her, even when she wanted to cringe and duck aside. But ten minutes into it, after she came to a stop on the field and doubled over, hands on her knees and gasping for breath, Laine pulled her out.

"I'm worried you'll get heat exhaustion," Laine said, her pretty features creased with concern. "Your face is so red. Sit down and cool off a bit."

Cassie could only nod and flop onto the grass beside the water cooler. The heat lifted from her face in waves, and she fanned herself. "No one else is getting overheated," she complained when she caught her breath.

Laine turned from where she cheered and coached on the sidelines. "Everyone's different, Cassie. Some people are more built for running."

The words struck a sore spot for Cassie, reminding her of what Gretchen had said. "Are you saying my body's not fit for running?"

Laine just looked at her. Then she shrugged. "I'm sure you can work up to it." Then she went back to watching the team.

Tears stung Cassie's eyes, and she blinked them back. She was fat! How had that happened? When? Why was she just now noticing?

She didn't say anything after practice as she and Gretchen lagged at the back. She urged her legs to lift higher, her feet to pound faster, but no matter what she did, she couldn't seem to change her pace.

The campers entered the dormitory as one and then

dispersed, heading to their rooms to change clothes or the bathroom to shower. Cassie lingered in the shower stall, hoping everyone would have gone to dinner by the time she came out. She didn't want to eat. But as soon as she'd slipped into her clean clothes, her stomach growled, cruelly mocking her.

The door to the communal showers opened, and Emily came in, her room key swinging from the lanyard around her neck. "Cassie? Aren't you coming to dinner?"

"Yes," Cassie said with a sigh, wishing she didn't have to eat.

Emily fell into step beside her as they headed downstairs to the cafeteria. "Everyone's almost done. I wondered where you were."

"I didn't want to eat with everyone else."

"Why?"

Cassie shrugged.

They took the stairs to the cafeteria. Cassie counted each step, hoping they were making her thinner. *One, two, three, four . . .*

Just as Emily had said, most of the campers had already eaten.

"Did you eat?" Cassie asked, looking around at the vacant tables.

Emily shook her head. "No. I was waiting for you."

"Thanks."

The two girls started down the buffet line as the cafeteria emptied. Cassie considered the pasta, the cheesy broccoli, the meat in tomato sauce, the garlic bread. Were these foods good for her? She opted for a small spoonful of pasta and the cheesy broccoli.

"What's wrong?" Emily asked as they sat down. "You're quiet."

She didn't really know what to say. Cassie picked at her broccoli and sighed. "I'm not doing as well as I hoped I'd be."

"Yes, you are!" Emily exclaimed. "You're improving so much!"

Hot moisture wicked behind Cassie's eyes, and she widened them, willing herself not to cry. "I still can't even run that well. I'm always at the back with Gretchen."

Emily furrowed her brow. "I thought you liked Gretchen."

"I do!" Cassie said. "But—" She hesitated. How could she say she didn't want to be like Gretchen? "I think I need to work more on my endurance. I want to be healthier."

"But we're constantly running and exercising," Emily said.

"We are being healthier."

Cassie thought about that. "Yeah, I guess you're right."

"I mean, we don't run like this at home," Emily said. She gestured at Cassie's plate. "You're gonna need more food than that to keep up your energy."

Feeling a little better, Cassie nodded. "You're right." She finished her pasta and stood up. "Let's get ice cream!"

After the evening practice, the girls gathered in the common room to watch television and play games. Carol sat in a corner on her phone, there if they needed her but for the most part letting them be. This was the perfect chance for Cassie to curl up with a book. She breathed a sigh of contentment, her shoulders relaxing as she slipped into some much-needed down time.

"What are you doing for the talent show?" one girl asked Tara, Cassie's other roommate.

Cassie's eyes wandered over the rim of her book, curious in spite of herself.

Tara was an older girl with long hair and a slender physique. She took the time each morning to put on make-up, even though Olivia teased her there were no boys to impress around here.

Tara shrugged. "I don't know. I've been working on my footwork. I might do something with that."

"I like that idea!" the other girl said. "We could be partners and work off each other."

"Yeah, that could work," Tara agreed. She turned to Olivia, who sat beside her dealing cards. "What are you going to do?"

"Maybe tell some jokes," Olivia said. "I'm pretty funny." Raising her voice, she hollered across the room, "You're going to sing for us, right, Cassie?"

Cassie's face warmed, and she lifted her book up quickly to hide behind it. After reading, singing was what she most loved to do. But being the center of attention embarrassed her. "I don't know."

"What?" Tara exclaimed. "You sing all day long. In our room, in the shower, while you're reading . . ."

Cassie lowered her book just enough to frown at them. "I do?"

"Well, you hum," Olivia qualified. "Practically the same thing."

"Are you a good singer?" Gretchen asked.

"You should hear her," Olivia said, swinging her eyes around to the group. She spoke louder, aware that everyone watched her. "She can sing opera."

"Sing something for us, Cassie!" someone shouted.

"Not now," Tara said, tossing her ponytail behind her shoulders. "Wait until the talent show tomorrow night."

"So you'll sing?" Olivia picked up the deck of cards in front of her and shuffled them.

Cassie nodded. "Yeah. I'll sing." Which meant between now and tomorrow night, she needed to figure out what to sing.

⚬⚬⚬

All during practice on Thursday, Cassie tried to figure out what song she'd sing. She wasn't very good at pop music and couldn't remember the words to any song in its entirety. The ball bounced off her several time before she decided it wasn't the time to worry about the talent show. But truthfully, the thought of singing excited her way more than soccer did.

Just before dinner, it came to her: a song she'd learned at Girls Camp last year.

There was no evening practice because of the talent show. Instead, the girls cleaned up and put on costumes and make-up.

Cassie didn't have a costume, and she wasn't allowed to wear make-up. All she had was her Sunday skirt. She put it on and scowled at her reflection. She sucked in her gut, wishing she was skinny and tall like Tara.

"Time for the talent show!" Carol called, walking down the hall and knocking on doors. "Gather in the common room!"

"Here." Olivia grabbed Cassie's arm as she moved toward the door. "You need this." Pulling out a compact of glittery green eyeshadow, she spread it across the backs of Cassie's eyelids. "There. Now you're ready."

Cassie took a deep breath and tried to smile, but her stomach fluttered with nerves.

They sat by Emily and Tara in the common room. Several girls went on stage before Cassie, performing dances and soccer routines and even gymnastics. Cassie tried to enjoy each act, but all she could think about was her upcoming piece. She replayed the words over and over in her head, her fingers tapping out the rhythm on her leg.

Emily walked up the stage and played the piano in the corner, and Cassie's heart went into double-time. It was her turn next. Everyone clapped when Emily finished, and Cassie forced her feet to carry her onto the stage. She took two deep breaths to steady herself, tapped her fingers on her thigh, and started her song.

"Once I dreamt of magic . . ." she sang. Her voice trembled slightly, but the acoustics in the room bounced the sound waves back to her. The song sounded good, and she stood straighter, more sure of herself. She finished singing and smiled, pleased she hadn't forgotten any of the words.

Everyone clapped.

"But Cassie," Olivia called out, "we wanted opera!"

"Yes," Carol, the camp leader, said from the back of the room. "I was told you can sing opera."

Cassie blinked in surprise. Singing opera was a joke, something she did just for fun.

"Opera! Opera!" Olivia chanted, pumping her fists. The other campers joined in.

"Okay," Cassie said, her heart racing again. They quieted down and looked at her. Clearing her throat, Cassie launched into the familiar song of "Tomorrow," a song everyone knew. Only this time, she sang it as if she were dressed in a viking outfit with lots of fur and a metal helmet and long blond braids. She held her hands out in front of her in dramatic gestures, using her diaphragm to pump out the sound just like her music teacher had taught her.

Carol's face turned beet-red with laughter. She pulled her shirt over her head, her shoulders shaking. The other girls yelled and cheered. When Cassie finished, they all stood up, laughing and clapping for her.

Cassie beamed and made her way back to Emily and Olivia.

"You did superb!" Olivia said, wiping at tears in her eyes. "Oh my. So funny."

The rest of the acts finished up, and Cassie found herself enjoying them, laughing along with the rest of the campers now that her part was over. When it finished, Carol went on stage with a large bag of candy in her hands.

"Girls, that was a lot of fun!" she said, and her words were met with more cheers. "I've laughed till I've cried, and we've all been highly entertained. But one act shone out above the rest. Thus it is with great pleasure that I pronounce the best act of the night. Cassie Jones!"

"Cassie, that's you!" Olivia shrieked. Emily shoved her in the arm, and Cassie pulled herself to her feet. She climbed on the stage and accepted her bag of candy.

"Can we get one more song, Cassie?" Carol said. "One more opera?"

Crapola. She hadn't prepared anything. The campers fell silent, and while they stared at her, Cassie searched her brain. Only one song came to mind, and before she could over think it, she blurted out, in her best operatic soprano, "Happy birthday to you. Happy birthday to you." The rest of the words, though she kept singing, were completely lost in the raucous shouting and hooting erupting from her fellow campers. They didn't stop even after Cassie sat down, and it took Carol a few minutes to calm everyone again.

"Tomorrow is our big game," she said. "After breakfast, we'll all meet at the fields and break into teams. Your parents will be arriving to watch the final play off. This will be your chance to show your skills. With that in mind, even though it's our last night, don't stay up too late! Good night, ladies!"

"Razorbacks!" the girls chorused.

Chapter Four
Final Game

Cassie woke up in the morning with her heart a flutter, and it took her a moment to remember the source of the anxiety. Then she sat up in her bed with a little gasp. Today was the big game day!

"Good morning," Tara said as she shoved something into her suitcase. A quick scan of her bed showed she'd already packed. She also wore her soccer clothes, complete with cleats and shinguards. "Ready for the big game?"

Cassie's heartbeat quickened. Her whole family would be out on the bleachers today, waiting to see how much she'd improved during this camp. "I guess." She rubbed the skin between her eyebrows and then pushed out of bed.

Olivia yawned loudly and stretched her arms. "Morning, ladies!"

"Razorbacks!" Tara crowed.

"Razorbacks," Emily mumbled, still tucked in her blankets on the bed.

Olivia grabbed up her soccer things. "Hurry! We'll have to

skip breakfast if we don't eat now!"

Tara went down by herself, but Olivia waited while Emily and Cassie threw on their soccer gear.

"Do you think we'll be on the same team?" Emily asked as they trooped down the stairs together.

"Let's hope so," Olivia said, jumping the last two steps to the floor. "We'll want Cassie's mad defense skills."

Cassie's face warmed with pride as Olivia walked away, and Emily elbowed her.

"See?" she said. "You have improved."

Cassie powered up with eggs and sausage and a piece of toast for good measure. She avoided the pancakes and syrup, certain those foods would only slow her down. Carol entered the cafeteria and clapped her hands, quieting them.

"All right, ladies!" she shouted.

"Razorbacks!" came the expected response.

Carol grinned. "Today's the day to see what you're made of! We've pushed you all week. You've increased your endurance and honed your skills. Let me tell you that your families are on their way now, loading up the bleachers. When we leave this building and run out on that field, you are no longer campers but soccer players! Finish up your food and line up. I want to see what you can do!"

Chairs scraped back from tables as several of the girls jumped up and dumped their plates in the wash bin. Cassie's stomach did a little flip, and she regretted the eggs and sausage she'd eaten. "I think I'm going to be sick," she said, pushing her tray away.

"Then stop eating." Olivia stood as well, grabbing her long curly hair and forcing it back into a ponytail. "Let's play some ball!"

"Come on," Emily said.

Still Cassie lingered. "What if I'm tired by the time we run onto the field? What if I don't have any energy for playing after that?"

Emily looked toward the lobby, where the other campers were gathering, and tapped her foot against the ground. "Let's just go. We'll see what happens."

Emily was right. Cassie cleaned her plate, putting the food in the trash before letting the plate fall into the soapy water. "All right. I'm ready."

They jogged out of the dormitory as one unit, but it wasn't long before Cassie found herself falling behind. Gretchen fell in beside her, matching her pace with a smile.

"Gretchen," Cassie said, panting and trying to ignore the cramping in her side, "I don't want to be the last one on the field today. Do you think we could run a little faster?"

Gretchen pulled the edge of her shirt up and mopped her brow. "You can. I'm good here."

Cassie hesitated. A part of her really didn't want to leave her friend behind, but an even bigger part of her didn't want to be the last one on the field. "Okay. I'll see you there." With that, she put on a burst of speed. Her lungs ached as she forced herself to take deep breaths and catch up with the other girls.

Nobody spoke as they ran, and Cassie realized that even though they made it look easy, running was hard on all of them. The morning sun beat down on them. As they rounded the corner onto the fields, a loud cheer broke out. Cassie's eyes swept upward to the bleachers, and she saw people in shorts and brightly colored shirts standing there, clapping their hands and waving.

Carol blew her whistle, and Cassie focused on finishing

their jog around the field. They came to a stop on the white line in front of the bleachers, and finally the girls had the chance to yell and wave back to their parents. Cassie found her family. Annette and Scott stood on the seats, enthusiastically bouncing up and down. Her mom and dad stood close by, beaming down at them. Cassie waved and stood up straighter. This was her chance to make them proud. She'd show them what she'd learned.

Carol pulled them all back in a huddle. She numbered them off and assigned placements. "Cassie, team two, defense. But I want you to sit out first quarter." She handed her a blue vest, and Cassie slipped it on. "Emily, team one, offense." Carol handed Emily the yellow vest.

Cassie stole a quick glance at her sister, but Emily's eyes were honed on Carol, her expression serious. Cassie frowned. She hadn't planned on playing against her sister. How would her parents know who to cheer for?

Assignments made, Carol blew the whistle again, and the girls scattered. Cassie made her way to the sidelines and sat down on the grass, watching as Emily got into position behind the starting line. Olivia stood next to her, playing offense alongside her. Cassie turned to her own teammates. Tara was on defense, and Gretchen was in goal.

The other girls sitting out the first quarter settled in behind Cassie. They talked and whispered, but Cassie made no effort to scoot back and join them. Instead, she picked a blade of grass and shredded it while she watched the teams face off. Should she root for her sister, or her own team?

The whistle blew, Olivia passed the ball to Emily, and Emily took off down the field. Cassie straightened up as Tara ran to intercept. Emily's foot-work evaded her, and soon she was past Tara, streaming toward the goal.

"Come on!" Cassie shouted, wishing she were out there. She'd stop her sister.

Gretchen ran out of the goalie box and launched herself at Emily, but Emily passed the ball to Olivia. Before Gretchen could pivot, Olivia shot the ball over her head and into the goal.

Cassie sighed and stood up. "Carol," she shouted as the two teams lined up again.

Carol glanced toward her, squinting a little and shielding her eyes.

"Put me in," Cassie said. "I want to play."

"You'll go in soon," Carol said. Then she spun around and returned her attention to the field.

Cassie sat down again. She tapped her feet on the grass, watching anxiously as the teams started up. The blue team had the ball this time, and they quickly swept it past the offense and took it downfield. But as soon as they hit the defensive line, they met resistance. The yellow team blocked their passes and pushed them backward, until suddenly Olivia was there, taking the ball away from the blue team and driving it back to the yellow team.

Cassie groaned and tugged at her hair. Olivia and Emily played off each other like choreographed dancers, occasionally passing the ball to Nikki, who was also playing offense. Cassie stood up and paced in agitation. Once again, they approached the goal. The other defender ran out and met them, but Olivia quickly sidestepped her. They were going to score again!

Tara swooped in, blocking Olivia's pass. She kicked the ball high overhead, sending it into the safe zone on the other side of the field. Cassie exhaled in relief.

"Cassie!" Carol shouted, jogging over. "You're up. Defense. Tara! Come sit out!"

Cassie and Tara exchanged high-fives as they passed each other, but Cassie wished the other girl was staying on the field. She didn't really know Rachel, the other defender, and she didn't seem to be as good a player as Tara. They nodded at each other and then waited midfield.

Cassie steeled herself as the yellow team seized the ball and worked it back toward her. She rocked on the heels of her feet, waiting for the right moment to run out and intercept. This time it was Olivia and Nikki coming her way. Cassie waited—and waited—and now! She shot forward, getting between the two girls. Nikki had the ball and tried to outmaneuver her, but Cassie closed in, placing her feet next to Nikki's and stealing touches to the ball. Olivia and Emily drew near, and Cassie kicked the ball behind her, hoping Rachel would be there.

She was. In the open, with no one else around, Rachel knocked the ball away from their goal.

"Here!" someone on offense shouted, and Rachel passed it upfield.

Cheers from the stands erupted, and Cassie's shoulders relaxed a bit as the blue strikers ran the ball toward the other goal. And then she found herself holding her breath as they got closer and closer to the goal. The blue team kicked, the yellow goalie ran out to meet it, and then—

"We scored!" Rachel shouted.

Cassie threw her hands in the air and did a happy dance with her. Now they were tied, one-to-one. And she'd actually played. She'd done something valuable. Her heart swelled, and she readied herself for the next round.

The game finished five to four, with the yellow team

winning. Even though Cassie's team lost, she felt proud of their efforts. She'd played two straight quarters, taking a break at half-time but quickly coming back in for the third quarter. And she'd been a contributor, running and fighting for the ball instead of slugging down the field.

When the game ended, Carol gave a brief speech about how much they'd improved. Then she handed each girl a medal and sent them out to meet their parents.

"Great job, girls!" Mrs. Jones said, opening her arms to hug Cassie and Emily.

"We're sweaty," Cassie said, sidestepping the hug and sitting down next to Scott and Annette instead.

"Good hustle out there," Mr. Jones said. "Looks like you girls really learned some soccer skills."

Cassie nodded and took a sip of her water bottle. She had learned, and she was proud of how she'd played. But it wasn't quite enough. She needed to work on more than just her physical endurance. Her eyes slipped down to the bulge beneath her red shirt, hanging out over the elastic band of her shorts.

"Do you like your soccer shorts?" Mr. Jones asked.

"Yeah!" Cassie said, her eyes lighting up as she remembered what her mother had told them. "They're from your new soccer store, right?"

"It's not open yet." He grinned, a child-like excitement on his face that Cassie rarely saw. "The grand opening's right before school starts. I'll teach you how to do the register before then."

"I can't wait!" Cassie squealed.

"And me too?" Emily asked.

"When you're older," he said, tugging her ponytail.

"But first you have church camp," Mrs. Jones said. "Then you can worry about working for your dad."

Cassie held in a groan. She was not looking forward to church camp, with the snobby clique of girls who ignored her every Wednesday and Sunday. She'd prefer to do another week of grueling soccer camp over that.

Chapter Five

Wedding

Andrea texted Cassie on Sunday.

Ms. Timber's wedding is next Saturday. Want to spend the night and ride together?

Cassie's eyes widened. With soccer camp going on, she'd completely forgotten about their sixth grade teacher's upcoming wedding. She quickly texted back. *I'll ask my mom, but plan on it! What fun!*

Mrs. Jones said yes, and Friday night she dropped Cassie off at Andrea's house.

"Hi!" Andrea exclaimed, hugging her tight and rocking back and forth as if they hadn't seen each other in years. "I missed you! What are you, like a star soccer player now?"

"Hardly," Cassie said with a laugh. She followed Andrea to her room and dropped her overnight bag on the bed. "It was so much fun, but I just don't think I'm that good at it. I think — " Cassie hesitated to say these words out loud. The idea had been rolling around in her head for a few weeks now, but to say it out loud was a kind of commitment. She plunged onward. "I think I need to go on a diet."

Andrea blinked at her. "Really?" she said, her voice hushed. "To get skinny?"

Cassie nodded, placing her hands around her waist and squeezing the excess skin there. "I just feel like if I were a bit thinner, things like running would be easier."

"I think you look fine," Andrea said.

Cassie smiled at her. "Thanks. But I'm going to. My clothes will fit a bit better too, I think."

"What kind of diet?"

Cassie shrugged. She hadn't thought that far. "I don't know. Just eat less, I guess."

Andrea frowned and looked down at herself. "Do I need to go on a diet?"

Cassie appraised her best friend. She'd never thought Andrea needed to change anything at all. "I don't think so."

"I don't think you need to, either."

She didn't want to talk about it anymore. "So tell me about Kitty." She put on a smile and tried to look excited. "What's going on?"

Andrea perked right up. "Her family bought a house not too far from here. She's planning on going to Southwest with us!"

"Wow," Cassie said, still smiling.

"Yes! I can't wait until orientation. Maybe we'll have classes together."

"Maybe," Cassie echoed. She tried to shrug off her insecurities. The friendship she and Andrea had was strong enough to allow other good friends. As long as Cassie remained Andrea's best friend.

"I bought this heart paper." Andrea opened a drawer and pulled out thick card stock, white with red hearts on it. "I thought it might be nice for us to make a card for Ms. Timber."

"That's a great idea," Cassie said, happy for the subject change.

Andrea folded the card stock in half and wrote across the top,

To Ms. Timber. On your lucky day.

"What's Ms. Timber's new last name going to be?" Cassie asked.

"Something really weird. Let me find the invitation." Andrea left the room, and Cassie took the moment to survey it. She loved Andrea's room, with the full bed covered in a pink bedspread, to the closet with the sliding door, always overflowing with cute skirts and tops. A bookshelf next to the bed held a few books, but mostly old toys and cute knick-knacks. The white vanity pressed against the opposite wall, full of drawers and cubbies and a jewelry box on top. Countless hours Cassie had sat in that chair, staring at her reflection while Andrea curled her hair or did her make-up. Cassie sat there now, pushing her glasses up on her nose and staring at herself. Her round face, tanned from soccer camp and with a sprinkling of freckles across her nose, peered back at her. A plastic blue headband held back her long dark hair. What did other people see when they looked at her?

Andrea returned with the invitation and set it in front of Cassie. "Snodgrass." She giggled. "I knew it was something weird."

Cassie picked it up. From Ms. Timber to Ms. Snodgrass. "It's not such a bad name," she said. "Not if it's the man you love."

"Oh, of course." Andrea leaned in close, pressing her cheek against Cassie's and uttering a sigh as she stared at their reflections. "But of course, your last name will be Hansen."

She batted her eyes and puckered her lips.

Heat crept up Cassie's cheeks, rushing all the way to her hairline. "Miles and I are just friends," she said. "Though it is a nice last name," she added with a small smile.

Andrea burst out laughing and settled back on the bed. "Cassandra Hansen! I love it."

Cassie picked up a nail file and lowered her eyes to hide how much the sound of that pleased her. Maybe if she were skinnier, Miles would like her back.

Cassie and Andrea put on dressy clothes the next morning. Cassie had brought her black leather pin skirt, the one her mom said was too short to be decent. It just barely hit the tops of her knees. She paired it with a red blouse and imagined she looked grown up and sophisticated. However, a glance in the mirror said otherwise. The skirt pinched a little too tightly around the waist, making the blouse bunch up and wrinkle. Cassie tugged up and down and finally got the skirt in a place where it didn't pinch, but now it was two inches above her knee.

Andrea came into the room from the bathroom, already dressed in a sleeveless floral dress. "Wow, you look sexy," she said, eyeing Cassie's skirt.

"It's not supposed to be this high," Cassie admitted. "My mom would kill me."

"Good thing your mom won't be there," Andrea said. She opened her jewelry box and pulled out a gold chain. "Miles will love it."

Would he? Cassie frowned at her reflection. All she could see was a fat girl.

She forgot her concerns when Mrs. Wall dropped the two

girls off at the chapel. They found most of their classmates in the back and crowded into the pews next to them, whispering and gossiping excitedly. A quick survey of her classmates showed Miles wasn't among them. The groom stood at the front of the chapel in front of beautiful stained glass windows, a handsome man with dark blond hair and a black tux. He faced the aisle with an air of expectancy. Cassie craned her neck, trying to peer past her classmates and get a glimpse of the bride.

The organ music started, and everyone stood up. Cassie did as well. She'd never been to a wedding and didn't really know what was going on, but she wasn't about to sit when no one else was.

A moment later, Ms. Timber appeared. Her short dark hair had been piled on top of her head and trapped with a small tiara. Ringlets framed her face and escaped down the nape of her neck. Cassie took in a sharp breath at the sight of the dress. The fluffy, billowing skirt emphasized Ms. Timber's slender waist, and pink embroidery and pink pearls decorated the satiny fabric.

Beautiful, Cassie thought.

The man's face broke into a smile, and Ms. Timber beamed back at him, radiant in her happiness. Cassie closed her eyes, lost in a moment of euphoria. Would she someday feel such happiness as she walked down the aisle to marry a man who loved her as much as this man loved Ms. Timber? She opened her eyes and leaned forward, breathless with hope.

The vows passed by in a blur, and then they kissed. The whole ceremony was incredibly romantic, and Cassie clasped her hands together, trembling with anticipation. If only, if only, if only. Surely this would be her one day.

The guests filed out of the chapel and into a reception room, where the new Mr. and Mrs. Snodgrass cut their cake. As soon as that was done, everyone entered a line at the buffet. Cassie took a quick inventory of the available food. Meatballs in sauce, little pieces of cheese, bread slices, bacon-wrapped dates. It all looked exquisite and so not good for her.

She poured herself a cup of water and sat down, averting her eyes from the food line. Her mouth watered, and she wanted very much to fill a plate with her classmates.

"Aren't you going to eat, Cassie?" Andrea asked, sitting down across from her.

The aromas of cooked meats and melted cheese wafted toward her, and Cassie nearly caved. And then she spotted someone. Lingering against the wall, back straight and not talking to anyone, was Betsy Walker.

Betsy. Cassie hadn't seen her since child services took Betsy away from her parents last spring and placed her in a house with her aunt in Mountain Home.

"Maybe later," she said, pushing away from the table and heading toward her.

Before Betsy left, she had been a giggly girl who sat by Cassie on the bus every day, full of life and laughter and comfort. She'd come to Cassie's birthday when no one else had. She'd stayed by Cassie's side after the death of her beloved dog. And she'd cried out her fears to Cassie the one time her social worker arranged a visit between them.

None of those emotions showed on her face now. Her expression was closed and drawn, her eyes blank and hooded. She stood stiff, a drink in her hand, her lips in a rigid line. Her blond hair hung a little longer, flipping out just below her shoulder blades.

"Betsy?" Cassie said, suddenly uncertain.

Betsy's eyes turned toward her. "Cassie," she said, but she didn't smile. She still stood as stiff and rigid as before.

Cassie paused beside the wall. "How are you?" she asked. "Do you still live in Mountain Home?"

Betsy nodded and took a sip of her punch. "My aunt insisted I come to this."

"Oh." Cassie hesitated, then held an arm out to indicate her classmates. "But aren't you glad you did? Aren't you happy to see all your friends?"

Betsy shrugged. "These people aren't my friends."

"But I'm your friend," Cassie said.

Betsy finally looked at her, and some of her hard façade cracked beneath a brief smile. "Yes. You're my friend."

Cassie relaxed and slid closer, leaning against the wall beside her. "Are things going all right?"

Betsy didn't reply, and Cassie supposed that was answer enough. They stood there in silence, and then Cassie reached over and squeezed Betsy's hand.

"I miss you," she said.

Tears sprang to Betsy's eyes, and her lips moved, murmuring something. Cassie didn't catch the words.

"I've got to go," Betsy said. She turned and wrapped her arms around Cassie, squeezing her tight. "Thank you." She let go and slipped out the door, and Cassie turned to watch. Her own eyes burned, and she blinked back the moisture that gathered there.

෴

"So disappointing," Andrea said as Mrs. Wall drove them home after the wedding. "Miles wasn't there."

"I know," Cassie said. But maybe that was a good thing. She

didn't like how she looked in this skirt.

"How was the ceremony?" Mrs. Wall asked.

"Beautiful," Cassie said, just as Andrea said, "Dreamy."

The girls looked at each other and giggled.

"Some day that will be us," Andrea said.

"To be loved like that," Cassie sighed.

"Her dress was exquisite," Andrea said.

"The pink!" Cassie exclaimed. "I could barely breathe!"

"I know," Andrea agreed. She grabbed Cassie's hands and squeezed them. "I want a dress just like hers."

"With a sparkling tiara."

"And my hair done in soft curls."

"Piled on top of my head."

They both sighed loudly, relishing in their delicious fantasies.

"All right, girls," Mrs. Wall chuckled, pulling the car into the driveway. "At least we have it set in stone that you both want beautiful weddings one day. Now let's settle back into reality. You're only twelve with many years ahead of you. Don't forget to enjoy life right now."

"We won't," Andrea said.

"Yeah," Cassie agreed. Besides, she wasn't ready to get married yet. There were too many things she needed to do first.

"Do you want to come over again next week?" Andrea asked as Cassie changed out of the tight black skirt and into the jeans she'd worn the day before.

"I wish," Cassie said with an unhappy sigh. "I have church camp."

"Won't that be fun?"

"No." Cassie shook her head. "I don't like any of the other girls. And they don't like me."

"You could skip it," Andrea suggested.

"Would love to, but my mom won't let me."

A car honked outside, and Cassie shouldered her overnight bag. "That's my mom. I'll see you later."

Andrea hugged her. "Text me."

"Oh." That reminded Cassie of another reason she wasn't excited about church camp. "No electronics. I won't be able to talk to you until next Saturday."

Andrea looked disappointed, but she nodded. "That's all right. I'll see what Kitty's doing."

Cassie gritted her teeth. Like salt to the wound. "Glad you'll have someone to hang out with," she said instead. Then she turned and headed for the front door.

Episode 2: Lost in School

Chapter Six

Girls Camp

There were very few times that Cassandra Jones wished her sister Emily was with her, but as her mom pulled into the primitive campsite for church camp, Cassie suddenly wished she wouldn't be attending alone.

"Why couldn't Emily come?" she asked, not budging from the passenger seat of the van. She pulled the ponytail holder off her wrist and secured her long dark hair, careful not to dislodge her glasses in the process. Tall deciduous trees, covered with green leaves and the vines so typical in Arkansas, shaded the grassy field. A few green portable toilets hung around the periphery. Yuck.

Mrs. Jones put a shocked look on her face. "You actually want your sister here? That's a first."

Cassie didn't feel like pointing out how much Emily stuck up for her whenever they attended camp together. "I just don't know anyone."

"Emily's only ten. You get to come because you're twelve, but church camp is only for kids twelve and up. And what do you mean you don't know anyone? You've been going to Wednesday night activities with these kids since March."

Thus the root of the problem. Cassie frowned, watching the girls from church as they wandered around the four or five dome tents set up on the grass. In the five months since she'd joined the youth group, none of the girls had friended her. Cassie didn't know them, and they didn't care.

"Come on." Mrs. Jones undid her seatbelt and slid out of the car. "Let's get your things."

Cassie heaved a sigh and joined her mom, retrieving her duffel bag and sleeping bag from the trunk of the car. They made their way over to Sister Lofland, the girls' youth group leader, where she knelt in front of a fire pit and worked on the logs. Cassie recognized the A-frame formation from the lesson they'd had on fire building in Girls Club, though she wondered why anyone would be trying to build a fire in this heat and humidity.

She wished she was at Girls Club camp instead of church camp.

"Hi, Cindy," Mrs. Jones said.

Sister Lofland looked up, shoving a strand of black hair out of her face that had escaped her bandanna. Her skin, olive-toned even in the winter months, had darkened to a chocolatey brown in the summer sunshine. "Well, hello there!" she said with a cheerful smile. "Hi, Cassie! So glad you could make it!"

"Hi," Cassie said, wishing she were pleased to be here.

"You're in that tent over there," Sister Lofland said, pointing to a small orange dome. "You're sharing with Michelle."

"Thanks." Cassie hefted her bags and headed over to the tent, wishing more than ever that she could get back in the air conditioned van with her mother and go home. The hot August sun beat down on her brown hair, and sweat beaded along her face. The humidity sucked the oxygen right out of her lungs. She threw opened the tent door and groaned as the stifling air wafted out.

Michelle's stuff was already in a corner, with her sleeping bag unrolled and laid out across the tent floor, but Michelle was nowhere to be seen. She would be with her best friend Sue Copper. The two of them didn't have room in their friendship circle for anyone else.

"Cassie!" her mom called.

Cassie rolled out her sleeping bag and exited the tent, removing her glasses to wipe more sweat from her face. She rejoined her mom at the campfire, where Sister Lofland had succeeded in lighting it.

"Why are you building a fire?" Cassie asked, curiosity winning over her reluctance to speak.

"We'll be cooking our dinner on this," Sister Lofland said with a beaming smile. "It might take a few hours to get the coals we need, so it's best to get started now."

"Oh," Cassie said. All sorts of negative thoughts flitted through her head, but she resisted. She didn't need her mother accusing her of murmuring.

"I'm leaving now, Cass," her mom said, giving her a big hug even though Cassie did nothing to encourage it. "I hope you have a wonderful time."

Cassie met her mom's eyes as Mrs. Jones pulled back. "Please don't make me stay," she whispered. "None of these girls like me."

Mrs. Jones brushed back a strand of Cassie's dark hair. "Then make new friends, sweetheart."

If only it were that easy.

She watched the light blue van drive away from the campsite, then turned back to Sister Lofland. "Where are the other girls?" she asked.

"I told everyone once they finished unpacking, they could explore, meet the campers from the other units. There are units here from Rogers, Bella Vista, Bentonville, and Fayetteville. You can go look around. Just don't get in the river."

River? Cassie wandered away from the campsite, searching for the forewarned river. She found it just beyond the trees. It wasn't huge, maybe ten feet across, with a small divot just passed the bank were the water ebbed and swirled around a protruding rock. Grayish-green in color, Cassie had no trouble heeding Sister Lofland's advice to stay out.

She went back up through the trees, passing the campsite where her unit, the Springdale one, had set out their tents. She'd only taken a few steps when she bumped into two girls. They both wore shorts and matching green t-shirts that said "Rogers Rabbits."

"Hi," the shorter one said. Her long blond hair was pulled into a ponytail, and her striking blue eyes crinkled in a smile. "I'm Elise. Who are you?"

Cassie hunched her shoulders, instantly intimidated by the other girl's prettiness. "I'm Cassie."

"I'm Tesia," the taller one said. Her curly brown hair was cut short, just below her chin, and freckles adorned her wide, friendly face. "We're from the Rogers unit. What about you?"

Gathering her courage, Cassie said, "Springdale." She gestured to their shirts. "What's with the rabbits?"

Elise groaned and Tesia giggled. "The theme this year is

animals," Tesia said. "So our leader thought rabbits would be perfect. You know, because we're from Rogers?"

Cassie frowned. "But it sounds like the cartoon." Cassie had never seen the cartoon *Roger Rabbit*, but she'd heard of it, and she knew it involved a very sexy bunny.

"Oh, we know," Tesia said as Elise buried her face in her hands. "But I guess our leader didn't. By the time we told her, it was too late. Now we all have matching Roger Rabbit shirts."

"It's kind of funny," Cassie admitted.

"Yeah," Tesia giggled, and even Elise laughed, pulling her hands from her face and shaking her head.

"What's your unit's animal?" Elise asked.

Cassie shrugged. "I haven't heard anything about it."

"Want to see our campsite? We're right next to Springdale," Tesia said. Without waiting for a response, she turned and walked away.

"Come on, then," Elise said, tossing her long ponytail over her shoulder. "We can hang out."

I'd love that, Cassie thought, the tension rushing out of her in a whoosh.

The Rogers campsite looked very different than her own. Instead of five individual tents, the unit had one giant tepee. Cassie's mouth fell open as she circled it.

"You all fit in there?" she asked.

"It's so fun." Elise took her hand and pulled Cassie inside. "Look."

Laid out in a circle like spokes to a wagon wheel were fifteen sleeping bags. Elise tiptoed over several and sat on one. "This one's mine."

"And this one's mine." Tesia sat down next to her. "Come

sit."

Cassie sat between them, wondering why they were being so nice to her.

"How old are you?" Elise asked.

"Twelve," Cassie said.

"Us too!" Tesia said. "It's our first year. Isn't it great? Aren't you so excited?"

Before Cassie could respond, the tent flap opened, and four older girls came in. Seeing them, the older girls switched directions and walked over.

"Hi," one said. "Who are you?"

Cassie glanced at Tesia. Would the other girls be mad she was in here?

"She's Cassie," Elise supplied. "She's from the Springdale unit."

"Awesome!" the girl exclaimed. "I'm Laurie."

Several other introductions followed, but Cassie lost track of them. Her head spun. Nobody in Springdale was ever this nice to her.

"Girls!" A woman who Cassie assumed was the leader poked her head in. "Let's make dinner!" Spotting Cassie, she smiled. "Hi. You're more than welcome to join us, but you should probably check with your unit first. They probably have food for you."

"Okay," Cassie said, getting up.

Tesia and Elise followed her out.

"Come see us after dinner," Elise said. She lowered her voice and added, "And wear your swimsuit. We found this super awesome swimming hole."

"Sure," Cassie said. "See you later!"

"There you are!" Sister Lofland said when Cassie stepped

into her own campsite. "I've got your dinner stuff ready. Just take a foil and add the food you want."

The other girls already stood in a line, adding food to their foil meals. Some were older, girls in high school that Cassie didn't know. Michelle, Sue, and Jessica, a small girl who always followed them around, glanced at her and went back to their foils. Lily, Sister Lofland's daughter, gave Cassie a small wave. Cassie waved also, but Lily had already turned back to building her dinner. With a sigh, Cassie grabbed up a piece of foil and started doing the same.

"Once your dinners are made," Sister Lofland said, "come place them in the coals over here. You don't want them to burn, so don't put them in the fire. They should be done in about half an hour."

"What do we do while we wait?" Michelle asked, settling on a log next to Sue.

"Talk about that boy you like," Sue teased, hitting her with her shoulder.

"No talking about boys," Lily objected.

"It was a joke," Sue grumbled.

"We can sing songs," Sister Lofland said. "Michelle, this is your second year here. I bet you know some."

"I can't think of any," Michelle said.

"I know some," Cassie said. "We learned a bunch at Girls Club camp last summer. They're really fun."

"Those aren't the kinds of songs we sing at church camp," Michelle said.

"How do you know if you haven't heard them?" Cassie said.

"I've been to Girls Club camp before." Michelle looked at Sue and rolled her eyes.

"I can lead us in some," one of the older girls said. "I'm a fourth year." She started up a fun and energetic song, one that Cassie knew and would normally enjoy, but she didn't feel like singing.

Standing up, Cassie slipped away from the campsite. Nobody noticed her. She crossed the distance between the Springdale unit and the Rogers one. The laughter and hooting reached her ears before she saw them, and then she came around the tent. The fifteen girls were crowded around a picnic table, shrieking with laughter as they ate something out of a large black pot.

"Cassie!" Elise said, spotting her. She ran over and looped an arm around her. "Are you already done eating?"

"No," Cassie said as Elise pulled her to the table. "My food is cooking. So I came over." She eyed the black pot. "What are you eating?" She could see peas and carrots and white meat, all in a thick gravy with some kind of breading on top.

"Chicken pot pie," their leader said. "Only I guess it's dumplings instead of pie."

"It's so good," Elise said with an exaggerated eye-roll. "You should try it."

"We cook all our meals in the dutch oven," Tesia said. "It's so easy."

It smelled amazing, and Cassie's stomach growled. "I don't know. My food is cooking with my unit."

"Just have a little, then." Elise took a small tin bowl and dumped a spoonful in it. The other girls scooted over at the table and made room for Cassie.

"A little," Cassie agreed, then slid into the spot. She closed her eyes as she took the first bite. "Oh, so good." She finished her food, and then before she even realized what she was doing, she got herself another bowl.

"We're having blueberry cobbler for dessert," Tesia said.

While that sounded wonderful, Cassie suddenly remembered her own foil dinner, cooking away at her campsite. "I better get back." She put down the bowl. "Thanks so much for the food."

"Anytime," Elise said.

"Bye," Cassie said, walking away. The girls from Rogers echoed the farewell.

"Where did you go?" Sister Lofland asked when Cassie returned. "Your food is done."

"I made friends with the Rogers unit," Cassie replied. She dumped her foil dinner on a plate and frowned at it. The carrots and potatoes looked flavorless and the chicken very dry. Black charcoal clung to the bottom of the vegetables. She glanced at Sister Lofland and saw she wasn't watching. Cassie stood and threw her foil dinner in the trash. Going to her tent, she changed into her swimsuit, then went back to the Rogers unit.

☙❦❧

"Are we allowed to go here?"

The sun still hung high in the sky, even though everyone had eaten dinner and the frogs had started their evening chanting.

"Sure," Tesia said. "Our leader showed it to us. She said they used to come here when she was a kid."

"But we can't come alone," Elise added. "So don't come back here without us."

"I won't." Cassie followed the two girls through the underbrush.

Only a few minutes later, they came to what looked like a

well. It was circular, about the size of a round table for four, with a one-foot high rock frame around it. Water was visible just a few inches below the rocks, which were level with the dirt. Tesia dropped her towel on the ground and jumped in. Cassie gasped, but before she could become alarmed, Tesia's head popped back out.

"It feels great!" she said.

Elise yanked her t-shirt over her head, revealing a pale, skinny body in a sparkly blue swimsuit. "Incoming!" She grabbed her knees into a cannonball and plummeted into the water.

Cassie looked down at her own purple and black giraffe swimsuit and scowled. She looked like a short pregnant lady. Then she remembered the two helpings of chicken pot pie she'd had and scowled even deeper. At least she'd skipped dessert.

Elise's head appeared as well, and Tesia squealed when Elise splashed her.

"Is it deep?" Cassie asked, sticking a toe in. The tepid water warmed her foot, just like a bath.

"I think so," Tesia said. "We never go all the way down. There's a rock ledge all around the inside. You can sit on it."

Placing her towel on a rock, Cassie lowered herself into the warm water. She closed her eyes in contentment. Finding the rock ledge, she sat down. The water came up to her shoulders.

Tesia and Elise climbed on the ledge opposite her, and Elise poke Cassie's leg with a bare toe.

"What do you think of it?"

"Fantastic," Cassie said, marveling. "I love it." And she was having a really great time, thanks to these two girls. "What is this?"

"It's a water cistern," Elise said. "It's always got water."

"What's everyone doing back at your unit?" Tesia asked.

Cassie shrugged. "I don't know. They don't include me. I wanted to teach them some songs, but they didn't want to hear them."

"Oh," Elise said, her eyebrows shooting up. "I wondered about that. Everyone says the girls from Springdale are really snobby. But you're so nice."

Cassie didn't even know what to say to that. She simply shrugged.

Tesia scratched at a bug bite on her arm. "You can teach us songs."

Cassie brightened. "I learned some really awesome ones at Girls Club Camp, and I love to sing."

"Us too," Elise said. "Sing something for us."

Cassie only hesitated a moment, and then she launched into "Magic," her favorite song from Girls Club Camp.

"You have such a beautiful voice," Elise breathed when she finished. "Sing us another one."

Sheepish but pleased, Cassie started in on another.

It started to get dark, and just when Cassie wondered if they should leave, several flashlights bounced through the trees.

"There you are!" Laurie, one of the girls Cassie had met in the tepee, said. She quickly shed her clothes, revealing a tight one-piece, and climbed into the water.

"Isn't this great?" another girl said, sliding in as well. Soon seven bodies were crammed into the little cistern, all splashing and talking at once.

Cassie relaxed on her rock wall, feeling content and included. Then their leader appeared, her large flashlight blinding them as she swept it over their faces.

"It's time for devotional," she said. "You're Cassie, right?"

Cassie nodded.

"Your unit is looking for you. Come with us to devotional, and you can meet up with them there."

ᏮᏮᏮᎧ

Nobody said a word as Cassie slipped in with the Springdale girls during evening devotional. Sister Lofland led them through a skit that Cassie had apparently missed learning, and they were introduced as the Springdale Sheep. She "baaed" along with everyone else, thinking they would be more aptly named the Springdale Snakes.

"Were you with the Rogers girls again?" Sister Lofland asked after the song and prayer of devotional ended.

Cassie trudged along with her unit back to their campsite. "Yes." Even now she wished she could join Elise and Tesia.

"She thinks she's too good for our unit," Jessica murmured to Sue, who let out a quiet laugh.

"She just knows we're too good for her," Michelle said, with a glance over her shoulder at Cassie.

Even though Cassie knew better than to let it bother her, the words still stung. She looked at Sister Lofland to see if she'd heard, but she was busy talking to Lily. Cassie sighed. And she had to share a tent with Michelle. Maybe she could just sneak over to the Rogers unit at night.

Cassie burrowed into her sleeping bag and pretended to be asleep when Michelle came in.

"She's asleep," Michelle whispered.

The tent flap rustled, and Cassie heard someone else entering the tent. A giggle slipped out, and she knew it was Sue.

"Don't step too close to her," Michelle murmured. "You

might break her glasses."

"I'd be doing her a favor," Sue said.

Michelle laughed. "You're mean."

"I am not."

Cassie peeked through her closed eyelids. Sue sat on Michelle's sleeping bag, and Michelle propped her flashlight open like a lantern, casting them into an eerie shadow. Sue glanced toward Cassie, then faced Michelle again.

"I'm just saying. She could be pretty."

Michelle snorted. "Yeah, with a total body makeover."

"There's more to people than looks, you know."

"Spoken like a true hypocrite."

Sue changed the subject, and they started talking about people from their school that Cassie didn't know. Her school, she realized. Michelle and Sue both went to Southwest Junior High. Cassie closed her eyes and sang songs in her head to tune them out. Didn't look like she'd be able to sneak out tonight.

Chapter Seven

Stuck

The next day Cassie went over to the Rogers unit right after breakfast. The whole group welcomed her, and Cassie paired up with Elise and Tesia for their daily activities. They played crafts together, swam together, and ate meals together. Only at night after the evening devotional did Cassie rejoin her own unit. She hadn't missed them at all.

On the third day, everyone gathered at the pavilion after lunch. Sister Mecham, the camp leader who led them all in evening devotionals, stood at the front.

"Okay, girls," she said, and Cassie fought back the urge to yell "Razorbacks!" like they had at soccer camp. "Tomorrow morning is our long hike. Today we'll pair you up with your hiking buddy, and then we'll go over some of the skills you'll need during the hike."

Long hike. A prickle of nervousness pierced Cassie's heart. Hopefully it wouldn't be as bad as running.

"Today we'll teach you the basics you'll need for tomorrow. Find your buddy. We have three stations set up: using a compass, first-aid, and the dead-man carry. Go with your buddy to each station and learn your skills."

Cassie froze, her heart pounding in her ears. Who would be her buddy? Elise and Tesia would pair up together. That would leave her with who?

A hand touched her arm, and she turned around to see Elise. Elise smiled, her blue eyes crinkling. "Want to be buddies?" she asked.

"You want to be my buddy?" Cassie said, her eyes widening. "What about Tesia?"

"Oh." Elise looked around. "She's over there. Should we ask her to buddy up with us?"

They could have two buddies? The idea had never occurred to Cassie. She nodded, too surprised to speak.

Tesia spotted them and came over, grinning. "So are we a trio?"

"If that's okay with Cassie." Elise looked at her.

"Of course!" Cassie exclaimed.

Tesia hooked an arm through each of theirs. "Then let's go find station one."

Cassie worried she wouldn't get her skills passed off, but the stations turned out to be incredibly easy. The leaders worked with her and Tesia and Elise, sometimes amidst laughter, until they got each skill signed off.

"I still don't know that I'd be any good at carrying someone," Tesia remarked as they headed back to the campsite.

"Unless it's Elise," Cassie joked. "She's as small as my little sister."

"Yeah," Tesia said with a laugh. "I think she and her eight-year-old sister even share clothes."

"How trendy," Cassie said, pleased when Tesia laughed harder.

Elise gave them a mock glare. "Just better hope I don't have to carry either of you."

"I'll ask Cassie to do it, not you," Tesia said, earning another glare and a shove from Elise. Tesia responded by grabbing Cassie's arm and throwing her against Elise. Cassie shrieked and grappled for something to help her keep her balance but only succeeded in taking Elise down with her.

Tesia stood back, doubled over and laughing so hard she could hardly breathe.

"Cassie," Elise said, pulling her to her feet. "We can't let her get away with that."

"Absolutely not," Cassie agreed.

"Let's get her!"

Tesia yelped and took off running, and Cassie scrambled behind Elise, breathless and sweaty and more content than she could remember being in months.

⌒ↅↄ⌒

The next morning Sister Mecham lined everyone up in their buddy groups and made them fill their canteens before the hike.

"It will get hot," she said, "and you don't want to get dehydrated. Believe me, the nasty salty fluid we have to give you if you do is a whole lot worse than the water you get to drink right now."

Cassie believed her. She took a giant swig of her canteen, making a face at the metallic flavor.

"Ew," Elise said, watching her.

"Yeah," Cassie agreed.

"There will be four stations on the hike," Sister Mecham

said, raising her voice to be heard over the chatter of the girls. "The first will be orientation, where you'll need to show us how well you can read a compass. Hopefully you remember what you learned yesterday. That will get you to station two. At station two, you'll practice knot tying. From there you'll move to station three and practice first aid carries. Finally at station four, you'll meet up with the other hikers, and everyone will climb down the hill together. Get your compasses out and line up over here behind station one."

"Do you remember how to do this?" Tesia asked, flipping open the little metal disk.

"I think so," Cassie said, pulling hers out. "You hold it flat in your hand and turn the top part until the red needle matches up with the north marking."

"Oh, that's right." Tesia nodded. "Because the red needle doesn't move and we have to make the north marking agree with it."

"Yep."

Elise pulled hers out as well. "I'm ready."

They waited their turn, then stepped up to the table.

"All right," Sister Mecham said, "here are your coordinates." She handed Elise a sheet of paper. "To get to station two, you must head north for thirty feet. Then go east for fourteen, and north again for twelve. Don't try to remember it, it's all written on your paper. Then you'll see station two."

That didn't sound too hard. Cassie looked at her friends, who also looked confident in those directions.

"Right," Elise said. "Let's do this."

"How far is thirty feet?" Cassie asked as they stepped out of the pavilion and into the woods.

"I'll count it out," Tesia said. "You lead us north."

"And it's really hard to get lost," Elise murmured, leaning close to Cassie. "Look." She pointed into the trees ahead of them, and Cassie could make out the other campers following their compasses.

"Oh, yeah," Cassie said with a giggle. "I guess that's true."

"Let's try and do it the right way anyway," Tesia said.

Cassie led the way, going straight and then right and then straight again while Tesia counted out the steps. When they finished, they could see the second station, but they were still several feet from it.

"Close enough," Elise said with a shrug, and they headed over.

"Good job!" the Bentonville leader said to them when they arrived. "That's excellent for your first time. Now I'll show you how to tie knots."

The knots were too difficult for Cassie, and no matter how hard she tried, she only succeeded in doing the square knot. She gave up and watched Elise and Tesia. In the end, only Elise mastered all of them.

"I win!" she crowed, thrusting her arms over her head.

They went to station three, manned by Sister Lofland from Springdale, and practiced the dead man's carry, as well as learning the two-armed hold. Then they carried each other around for a bit, laughing hysterically, until Sister Lofland told them to finish the hike.

The path meandered along a small creek, several giant rocks causing small waterfalls to form as the stream tumbled down the hillside. The air grew hotter and more stifling, and sweat made Cassie's glasses slide down her nose. She stopped several times as they hiked upward, pressing her hand to her chest and trying to catch her breath. She could see the rest of the campers in a little pool at the top, some of them stepping into the water and splashing while others took pictures.

"That wasn't too bad at all," Elise said when they reached the top. The few remaining girls came up the hill behind them. Elise pulled out her phone and used the camera function to take a panorama shot of the woods and waterfall.

"Yeah, it was fun," Tesia agreed.

"Yeah," Cassie echoed, though her chest felt tight and swollen. Her head pounded like a drummer had taken up residence. One hand massaged the area just above her heart, and the other pressed against her scalp.

"Are you okay?" Elise asked, looking up from the pictures.

"Just hot," Cassie said.

"Drink more water." Tesia uncapped the canteen and handed it to her.

Cassie took a drink, and a little shudder ran through her. "I'm fine," she said. She sat down on a rock and took her shoes off, letting her feet rest in the water. Tesia and Elise started jumping along the rocks, leaning over to peer at the water tumbling down the hill.

"Ah!" Elise shrieked when Tesia gave her a playful shove. She turned around and pushed Tesia backwards into the shallow creek. Tesia landed on her bum, laughing.

"Everyone out of the water!" Sister Mecham marched through them, a frown etched on her face. "I said we'd meet up here, not go swimming up here." She looked at the older girls as if they were responsible. They climbed out, and the younger girls followed.

"Good job on your stations," she said, facing them all. "When we get back to the campsite, get your camp books and have your leaders sign off your requirements."

Cassie put her shoes back on and stood up. Her feet felt
good, but the rest of her body seemed to be emanating heat.
She poured some water from her canteen into her hands and
splashed it on her face.

"That was so fun," Elise said, joining her. Tesia came as
well, and the three of them started down the hillside behind
the other campers.

"You're quiet, Cassie," Elise commented.

Cassie didn't answer. It took all her concentration to put
each foot in front of her and not stumble.

Tesia touched her arm. "Do you need to rest?"

Cassie hesitated and then came to a stop. "Yes. Let's rest just
for a minute."

The three girls stood in silence, watching the campers in
front of them move down the hill. Cassie took several deep
breaths and another sip of her water.

"Okay," she exhaled. "We can go again."

They started forward, and then Cassie's head grew so hot

she thought it might explode. She sank down to the ground and sat on the compacted dirt. Tesia and Elise crouched next to her, exchanging worried looks.

"Are you okay?" Elise asked.

Cassie closed her eyes and laid her head back.

"Let's just hurry up and get her back to camp," Tesia said, her voice anxious.

"Come on, Cassie." Elise picked her up under her arms. "We have to keep moving."

Cassie opened her eyes and tried to help, but she couldn't seem to get her legs under her.

"At least we learned how to do the dead man's carry," Tesia joked.

"Humph," Elise grunted.

Tesia took another arm, and together they dragged Cassie over the rocks and sticks bumping out of the ground.

"I don't remember the way back to camp," Tesia panted.

"It's down the hill," Elise said. "Just keep going."

Cassie felt the moment they left the worn path beside the creek and entered the heavy underbrush of the forest. Bushes snagged her hair and plants caught themselves in her clothes.

"How far is it?" Tesia gasped.

"I can't keep going like this," Elise moaned.

"I'm sorry," Cassie murmured, opening her eyes to squint at them. Sunlight dappled their clothing as it attempted to pierce the thick foliage above.

"Don't you even worry," Elise said, stroking her arm. She turned to Tesia. "I have to go to camp. I have to get help."

Tesia nodded. "We'll wait right here. Be careful."

"Give her water." Elise unhooked her own canteen and handed it to Tesia. "Keep her cool." With that, she turned around and darted off, ducking and dodging branches as she ran through the plant life.

Tesia crouched beside Cassie and chewed on her fingernail. "Hurry, Elise," she murmured.

Chapter Eight

Closing Doors

Cassie blinked up at the blue sky visible between the leaves. It felt better here in the bushes, not as hot. Her head seemed to be cooling off. Tesia wiped her brow with water.

"Close your eyes, Cass," Tesia said. "Just rest."

Cassie did.

Time seemed to pass very slowly, but finally the underbrush rustled with the sound of someone approaching. Tesia jumped up.

"Here!" she said, waving her arms above her head. "We're over here!"

Elise parted the bushes, her ponytail disheveled and her eyes puffy and red from crying. Behind her came Sister Mecham and Sister Lofland.

"Cassie, what happened?" Sister Lofland asked, her face a mask of concern.

"Looks like she got overheated." Sister Mecham bent as if to pick her up, and then backed away. "Girls," she said, a rebuke in her voice, "you laid her in poison ivy."

"We did?" Tesia squeaked. She surveyed the plants around Cassie, her eyes widening.

"Oh no!" Elise gasped.

"I'm severely allergic," Sister Mecham said. "You'll have to get her, Cindy."

"I'll need help," Sister Lofland said. She knelt beside Cassie and tried to lift her. Elise and Tesia joined her, and together the three of them managed to get under her.

Cassie felt a bit better now, and she helped place her feet on the ground. "I think I can walk a bit."

"We'll move together. Ready? Walk."

They shuffled forward as one body, inching along the ground a step at a time. It was slow going, with Sister Lofland encouraging them every few paces. Finally the end of the forest came in sight, and a moment later they found the pavilion.

The other campers all sat under the shaded building, speaking quietly to each other. When they spotted Cassie, they clapped and cheered. The girls from the Rogers unit ran forward and wrapped them in a hug.

"Okay, Cassie," Sister Lofland said, "we're taking you to the camp nurse."

Cassie groaned. She had lots of experience with camp nurses. Last summer she'd been bit by a snake, and the camp nurse gave her rides to all the activities around the camp. It wasn't that she didn't like the nurses; she just didn't want to be the invalid camper anymore.

"Her tent has an A/C unit in it," Sister Lofland continued. "I just want you to rest and drink lots of fluids and cool off."

"Is she okay?" Michelle, Sue, and Jessica popped in front of Cassie, the perfect picture of worry marring their faces.

"She will be."

Tesia and Elise didn't leave Cassie's side until after the nurse got her tucked into a cot with a light blanket on her.

"What are you scratching?" the nurse asked Tesia as she raked her fingernails down her bare legs.

"Ugh, I'm just itching like crazy."

Elise took another look at Tesia. "You have little bumps everywhere."

The nurse came closer and examined her. "You've got poison ivy all over you. What did you do, lay in it?"

Tesia glanced at Cassie. Cassie gave a little smile, and Tesia giggle.

"Kind of," she said, and Elise laughed also.

Tesia stayed the night in the nurse's tent, covered in medicine to help with her poison ivy. Though Cassie felt completely fine after several hours of sleeping in the frigid air, she decided to stay with Tesia. Elise joined them after dinner, and the three girls told stories and sang songs until the nurse sent Elise back to her unit. When morning came, she kicked Tesia and Cassie out as well.

"It's time to go home," she said. "Your parents will be here soon. Go pack up."

Cassie followed Tesia out the tent flap, the hot humidity and sunlight hitting her like a slap in the face. "It's over," she said, not quite believing it. Even more, she couldn't believe how much fun she'd had. She turned to Tesia and grabbed her arm. "I don't want to leave you!"

"I know!" Tesia exclaimed.

They separated to go and pack their things, planning to meet up as soon as they finished.

"You're back," Michelle said when Cassie entered the tent. "Are you okay?"

Cassie didn't even look at her as she rolled up her own sleeping bag. "Fine." She stuffed the few belongings she had into her duffel bag.

"We were so worried about you. We just kept thinking, what if something happened to you?"

Cassie stood up, sleeping bag in one hand and duffel on her shoulder. "I'm sure." She exited the tent and deposited her things on the grass. Then she hurried over to the Rogers unit.

Cars were beginning to arrive, parents driving up to campsites to load up their daughters. Cassie quickened her pace, afraid Elise or Tesia might leave before she got to say goodbye.

"Cassie!" Laurie said when she saw her, and the girls from the Rogers unit quickly welcomed her with a big hug. Cassie's heart warmed. Maybe she could convince her mom to attend church in Rogers.

The girls pulled away from her, and Tesia and Elise stood there waiting. Cassie fell into their arms, and the three girls clung to each other.

"I'll miss you both so much!" Cassie said, suddenly realizing she was crying.

Elise wiped at her own eyes. "I wrote my phone number down. You have to call me."

"Me too!" Tesia said. "We only live half an hour from you. We can get together, hang out."

Cassie nodded, taking their phone numbers and wishing she'd written hers down. "Yes, of course! We'll definitely see each other!" She spotted a familiar blue van driving past the Rogers unit. It came to a stop several yards away, just outside the Springdale campsite. "That's my mom. I have to go."

They hugged again, and Cassie didn't want to let go. They shared a special bond. Tesia and Elise accepted her and loved her just the way she was.

Finally she slid out of the embrace. "I'll see you soon."

"Call me!" Elise cried.

"Very soon!" Tesia said.

They waved goodbye to Cassie until she was forced to turn her back on them and hurry to her mom's van.

꙳꙳

The first thing Cassie did when she got home from camp was take a long shower. She rinsed out the bug spray, the sweat, and any lingering poison ivy juices. At least she hadn't had a reaction to the plant like Tesia.

After the shower she stood in the mirror and examined her body. The summer sun had tanned every inch of her exposed skin and freckled the bridge of her nose. She turned sideways and inhaled, sucking in her pale belly. Though she'd tried to eat smaller portions at church camp, it didn't look like she'd really made a difference.

She needed to be a little stricter with her diet.

She texted her best friend Andrea to say she was home, and she'd barely put her clothes on before her phone rang.

"I'm so glad you're back!" Andrea exclaimed. "Was it as awful as you feared?"

Cassie lay back on her bed and stared at the ceiling. "It actually wasn't so bad at all. I made a few new friends, and they made it worth it."

"That's good!" Andrea said. "My mom's taking me clothes shopping for school tomorrow. Want to come?"

"I'll ask my mom," Cassie said. While she wanted to spend

time with Andrea, she didn't actually enjoy shopping. Everything that looked cute on the hanger looked painfully tight and round on her.

"It's okay if you can't," Andrea said. "I can ask Kitty. I've seen her a lot this week."

The familiar undercurrents of jealousy swirled in Cassie's heart, and she frowned. Kitty had been Andrea's best friend a few years ago, but after Kitty moved away, Andrea and Cassie became best friends. Now Kitty was back, and Cassie had this horrible fear that she would lose Andrea to her.

"I'm sure my mom will let me come," Cassie said, crossing her fingers.

"Great! Come over around ten, and we'll go to the mall."

Mrs. Jones did not like having plans sprung on her last minute, and she made that clear to Cassie as she drove her to Andrea's house the next morning.

"You need to ask me before you agree to something," she said.

"I know," Cassie said. She didn't want to explain to her mom how important this was.

"Next time you tell me I have to take you somewhere, I'll say no."

"Okay, Mother," she said, irritation flashing in her voice.

They pulled up to Andrea's house. "Be good," Mrs. Jones said. "I'll pick you up at three."

"Look how dark you are." Andrea examined her in the entryway, holding Cassie at arm's length. "You got really tan."

Though Andrea and Cassie were about the same size and both wore glasses, the similarities ended there. Andrea's wavy brown hair had a reddish tint to it, and her fair skin burned and freckled before it tanned.

"We were outside a lot." Cassie squirmed a bit under the scrutiny.

"Did you eat breakfast?" Andrea went into the kitchen, and Cassie followed. "We've got donuts." Andrea picked one up and took a bite.

Cassie shook her head. "I ate before I came." Her stomach growled. Even though she'd eaten, it had been a very small bowl of cereal.

Andrea's eyes widened. "Are you still on your diet?"

"Yeah." Cassie shifted a bit. "It was hard to stick to it at camp. So I'm doing better now."

"We'll find you a cute outfit for the first day of school. So you can look good for Miles."

Not that again. "Seventh grade orientation is next Monday," Cassie said. "Want to go together?" She prayed Andrea wasn't already going with Kitty.

"Of course. I already planned on it."

Andrea and Cassie wandered around the mall with Mrs. Wall trailing behind them. Cassie fingered clothes on the hangers and tried things on when Andrea did, but nothing fit right. She finally chose a glittery blue and gray shirt with a matching gray skirt. But no matter how she sucked in her gut and tried to button it, she couldn't make the size she wanted fit her. Giving up, she picked the next size up, quite irritated. Her mind flashed back to Elise and her tiny little body. They were the same age. Why was Cassie so much bigger?

They made their purchases and headed home. Andrea performed the usual hair and makeup ritual on Cassie, but Cassie's heart wasn't in it. All she could think of was that she wanted to be skinny.

Chapter Nine

Soccer Store

Mrs. Jones dropped Cassie off at the junior high Monday morning for orientation. Cassie slowly walked down the concrete path leading to the four-door entrance, her eyes on the orange awning waving in the breeze. She sat down on one of the benches outside and texted Andrea, keeping her face toward the phone while surreptitiously studying the other students walking past her. Anxiety made her skin crawl, and her heart beat nervously. New place. New faces. Like moving all over again.

I'm here, Cassie texted. *Sitting outside. Where are you?*

Almost there, came the reply.

A moment later Andrea's mom pulled up, and Andrea hopped out. She'd curled her hair and put on cute clothes. Cassie glanced down at her jeans and t-shirt and wished she'd done the same.

Andrea's eyes glittered excitedly behind her glasses frames. She looked behind Cassie toward the entrance. The building continued on either side of the awning, windows like eyes systematically scattered down the length of it.

"Junior high!" Andrea breathed. "We're growing up!"

"Yep," Cassie said, though she wasn't nearly so excited. The upcoming school year scared her more than anything.

They went up the walkway together and stopped at the table just inside the doors. A few kids were in front of them, scanning the papers on the table.

"Find your names on this sheet of paper," a woman said, looking at Andrea and Cassie. "Peel your name off, put it on, and go to the library." She pointed toward a room just behind her.

Andrea went first, and Cassie leaned over her shoulder, searching out her own name. She found it and pried off the sticker.

The entryway door opened, and other kids Cassie didn't know came in. A little flutter batted against her heart. So far, Andrea was the only familiar face. Would she know anyone here?

Andrea found her name tag, and they went into the library. Several kids already sat there, and Cassie noted with relief that she recognized some of them. She greeted her old classmates and followed Andrea to the back. Her fists unclenched and she exhaled, feeling her body relax. Junior high. She wasn't a little girl anymore. She scanned the backs of heads for Miles Hansen, her crush since the fifth grade. She realized with disappointment that he wasn't here. Maybe he was out of town. Oh well. Hopefully they'd have at least one class together. She smiled and waved at a few more people, feeling more comfortable with each passing minute.

And then Kitty walked in. She was easy to spot, taller than most seventh graders with short, light brown hair. Cassie held her breath and looked at Andrea. She hadn't noticed yet.

But Kitty noticed her.

"Andrea!" she called. Then she began climbing over students to get to the back.

"Oh, Kitty, there you are!" Andrea stood up and hugged her, then they sat down.

"I've been texting you," Kitty said. "I thought you were going to wait out front for me."

"I didn't see your texts. I came in with Cassie."

Kitty saw Cassie then and nodded at her. "Hi, Cassie."

"Hi, Kitty," Cassie said, shifting in her spot on the ground.

A woman came in and cleared her throat, saving Cassie from having to make small talk with Kitty.

"Hi, seventh graders!" she said, and the group of kids quieted down, all facing forward to hear what she'd say. "Welcome to Southwest Junior High! We are so excited to have you. Behind me I have all of your schedules and your locker assignments. I'm going to discuss some of the clubs we have, then you'll want to get your schedule, find your classes, and try your locker. Memorize your combination and make sure you can open it."

Cassie sat up straighter, the first stirrings of eagerness in her chest. Clubs? That could be fun. She made a mental list of the clubs that interested her as the woman rattled them off. Drama, poetry, Youth for Christ. Many of the other girls murmured excitedly when the pep club, the precursor to cheerleading, was mentioned, but Cassie had zero interest in cheerleading. That wasn't something she aspired to.

Finally the woman finished talking and called them up to get their schedules. Immediately Cassie's heart started its nervous pitter-patter. She crossed her fingers, praying she and

Andrea would have some classes together.

Cassie found her schedule first and waited while Andrea sorted through the Ws.

"Here it is!" Andrea turned around and smiled. She hooked her arm through Cassie's and pulled her off to the side.

Cassie read over her schedule. English, health, math, science, geography, life skills, and art. The classes sounded kind of fun.

"What did you get?" Andrea asked, and she held her paper next to Cassie's to compare schedules.

Cassie's heart sank. Though they had the same math teacher, they had it at different periods. Everything else was completely different. "We don't even have the same lunch," she said.

"It's okay." Andrea brandished the paper with her locker assignment. "I bet our lockers are next to each other."

"Let's see your schedule!" Kitty popped over, scooting next to Andrea and peering at her classes. "Hey, we have geography together! And we both have A lunch!"

Another stab to the heart. Cassie blinked back the sudden stinging in her eyes. Why would fate collaborate against her and put Andrea and Kitty together?

"Let's go find all our classes," Andrea said. "And then we'll check out our lockers."

They wandered the halls searching out room numbers, all the way around the gymnasium to the math wing and back by the cafeteria to the science and English wings. To Cassie, the enormous school just went on and on. None of her classes were close to each other, and she started to panic. She'd be lost before she ever made it to lunch.

"How many minutes do we have between periods?" she

asked.

"I think they said four," Kitty answered.

Four minutes. Cassie licked her lips. That didn't seem like very long.

They finally located all of their classes, though Cassie had serious doubts she'd ever be able to find them again. Especially since she'd have to go to her locker at some point in between. They made it to the seventh grade locker hall, separate from the rest of the halls.

"I bet they're in alphabetical order," Kitty said. "Which means Tucker and Wall will be close to each other, right?"

"Oh, good thinking!" Andrea said.

Cassie hung back, scanning the locker numbers closest to her, as the other two girls continued down the hall. It looked like Kitty's theory was right, and Jones was nowhere near Tucker or Wall.

The week before school started, Mr. Jones took Cassie to his new soccer store. Tucked into the corner shop in a small shopping center, the store only had room for a few racks of clothing and a wall of shoes. Her dad hustled about with an excited energy, showing her trinkets like a soccer ball piggy bank and a soccer ball calculator.

"You're playing soccer again in the fall, right, Cassie?" he said. He sat behind the register and used the key to turn it on.

Cassie hesitated. At first she hadn't liked soccer camp, but by the end of the week, she felt like she'd learned a few things and even improved. She enjoyed soccer. She just didn't feel very good at it. She went for the white lie.

"I'm kind of nervous about school," she said. "I want to see how well I do in my classes first. When I feel comfortable with them, I can venture out into other activities."

"Fair enough." He nodded. "Come over here and let me show you how to do the register."

Cassie went to the store with her dad every day for the next week, getting familiar with the brands and the prices. The grand opening was on Saturday, and her dad had a big banner made for the occasion. He took out an ad in the newspaper, and phone calls began coming in, asking about the hours.

It all sounded very promising.

"How many people do you think will come?" Cassie asked him on Friday as they set out the baskets of doorbuster prizes.

"It's hard to guess, isn't it?" her dad said. "I shared the news at the soccer association. We've gotten plenty of calls about it. I'd say a couple hundred. Maybe two or three."

Cassie had nothing to compare it to, but that sounded like a good number to her. "Can I sell my friendship bracelets in here?" Last year in Girls Club they'd learned how to make bracelets. Cassie had recently gotten a book with different bracelet designs, and she made several bracelets a month while watching movies with her family.

"Sure. Put a price tag on them and stick them right there." He pointed to a spot next to the register.

"Great!" She brightened at the idea of people buying her bracelets.

Saturday morning, her dad woke her up early to set up for the grand opening. Cassie stopped long enough to open her box of completed bracelets and grab several. While her dad unlocked the doors and set up the banner, Cassie priced the bracelets.

"Do you think one dollar is a fair price?" she called to her dad where he stood on the ladder.

"Sounds good to me," he said.

She hummed a little and put the tags on the bracelets, then put them in one of the tiny baskets of impulse-buys.

"All right, it's time." Mr. Jones popped over to the side of the open door and waited, fidgeting with his hands.

Cassie sat up straighter behind the cash register. Her eyes went to the door, scanning the sidewalk and the parking lot beyond. So far the only car was her dad's tiny Acura.

"They're coming," Mr. Jones said.

"Of course," Cassie said.

After about ten minutes, she started to feel bored. Glad she'd brought a book, Cassie reached under the cash register and pulled it out.

"Welcome!" her dad's voice boomed out.

Cassie lifted her eyes and put away her book. A woman with three little boys came in.

"Hi," she said. "We saw your ad in the paper and need to get soccer stuff for the fall season. What have you got?"

"Everything!" Mr. Jones beamed and scurried around the store, finding shinguards, socks, cleats, and shorts for all her boys.

"This is a really nice store," the woman said as Cassie rang up her purchases. "You have so many things."

"Yes, we do." Cassie put all the items in a bag and smiled at the woman. "Did you get a door prize?"

"Oh, no." The woman sifted through the bowl of prizes on the counter.

"Hey, can I have one of these?" One of the little boys picked up a friendship bracelet.

Cassie hesitated. They were supposed to be a dollar.

"I love these colors," he said, showing his mom.

"Are these door prizes?" the woman asked, looking at Cassie.

She faked a smile. How could she say no? At least someone wanted one. "Yeah. Go ahead. He can have one."

"Thank you." She gathered up all her bags, and the boy pocketed the bracelet. "If we need anything else, we know where to come."

Cassie watched as they walked out, and then Mr. Jones hurried over.

"How did it go?" he asked. "What did they spend?"

Cassie pulled up the receipt log. "One hundred and thirty-four dollars."

"Our first sale!" her father cheered. "We just need ten more like that!"

A few more people wandered in and out of the store for awhile, but after lunch it slowed down. Cassie ate her sandwich and read her book, then went outside for a bit.

"Hey," she said to a boy in a baseball cap as he walked down the sidewalk.

"Hey," he replied, stopping by her.

"Are you coming into the store?" She gestured behind her.

He looked up at the banner across the top with the store name. "Do you have football gear?"

"No." She shook her head. "It's a soccer store."

"No thanks, then. I only like football." He put his hands in his pockets and continued down the sidewalk.

Cassie scowled after him. Sport snob.

⚬⚭⚬

Right before the store closed, Mrs. Jones came by. She brought Cassie's younger sisters Emily and Annette and her younger brother Scott. The younger kids immediately ran off to browse through the store, and Mrs. Jones sidled up to Mr. Jones at the counter, where he rifled through papers.

"Well, how did it go?" she murmured.

"We made a thousand dollars." He grinned at her. "It wasn't a huge crowd, but we had steady traffic. I think it was a good start."

"And Cassie?" Her mom lifted her eyes to Cassie, sitting behind the register. "Was she a good help?"

"Fantastic. Couldn't have done it without her."

"I ran the register and cleaned up after people left," Cassie said. And sometimes, people's small children tore clothing from the racks and knocked things off the shelves. It wasn't always an easy clean up job.

"Good for you, Cassie. That's great." Her mom looked at the bowl of friendship bracelets. "Did you sell any?"

Cassie's smile slipped a bit. "No. I did give one away. Just because the little boy thought they were door prizes and I didn't have the heart to tell him no."

Mrs. Jones laughed. "Well, I want one. Do you have any with purple?"

Cassie brightened. "Absolutely." She pulled out the purple ones and displayed them on the counter. Her mom bought one, and Cassie beamed as she rang her up.

"I sold a bracelet," she whispered to herself. "I sold one."

Chapter Ten
New Frontiers

"Emily!" Cassie banged on the bathroom door Monday morning, her first-day-of-school clothes in her arms. "Come out of the bathroom! I have to get ready too!"

"Hold your horses!" Emily shouted back.

"Just use the other bathroom!" Mrs. Jones yelled from the kitchen. Usually she stayed in bed and let Cassie wrangle the children, but the first day of school was special. She'd been up early making breakfast for them all.

Giving up, Cassie followed her mom's advice. She ran down the hall, through the kitchen, and into the guest bedroom. In the back was a bathroom. Cassie dumped her clothes on the floor and used the toilet with a sigh of relief. Grabbing her clothes back up, she stood in front of the mirror and stared back at the same face she'd seen yesterday. Dark brown eyes, straight brown hair, pink glasses. Checking carefully to make sure she put the clothes on straight, Cassie tugged the gray skirt up over her hips. She sucked in her breath to button it and lifted one eyebrow in surprise when she realized she didn't have to. She pulled off her pajama shirt and examined her reflection. Was she imagining it, or had she actually gotten skinnier? She had no problems buttoning her skirt; in fact, there was definite space between the skirt and her stomach. She remembered having to buy the next size up at the store because the other one was too tight.

Excited now, she pulled on her sparkly shirt. Instead of catching at her waist the way her clothes normally did, the shirt went straight down, adding some nice curve appeal that hadn't been there before. Cassie pulled half of her long hair into a clip and let the other half fall around her shoulders. Then she adjusted her glasses and slipped out of the bathroom.

Instead of a backpack, Cassie now had a binder with all her folders in it. Today she'd receive books and carry them around to her classes, or dump them in her locker if she thought they were too heavy.

She eyed the pancakes and syrup on the kitchen table warily and opted for an apple instead. She ate quickly and waited impatiently for her younger siblings to finish.

"We ready?" she said when they'd cleared their plates and gathered by the front door. Annette and Scott nodded, backpacks on their shoulders and lunch boxes in their hands. Lunch. Her mom had given her lunch money yesterday. Cassie checked her binder. There it was. "Where's Emily?"

"Here." Emily ducked out of the bathroom, her honey-brown hair pulled up like Cassie's, half up and half down.

Cassie shrugged it off. Emily could dress like her, wear the same clothes as her, the same hairstyle, it didn't matter anymore. They went to different schools now. "Bye, Mom!"

Mrs. Jones gave them all a hug. "Have a great first day of

school. Cassie, you'll love it."

Junior High. Kitty. Classes. A knot formed in Cassie's stomach, and she wasn't so sure she'd love it. She opened the front door and ushered everyone out to the bus, trying not to worry about anything yet.

⚬⤳⟜⚬

The bus dropped the elementary school kids off first. Cassie watched them leave the bus circle and walk up the familiar sidewalk, and for the first time she felt a pang of nostalgia. She'd gone to Walker Elementary for two years after they moved to Arkansas from Texas. She'd made a lot of friends and learned a lot of things about herself. There was a part of her that would miss it.

The bus pulled away from the circle and drove the short distance to the junior high. Several other buses already crowded the drop off zone. Cassie took a deep breath, grabbed her binder, and climbed off. Her heart hammered in her throat as she walked through the back doors and toward the locker hall at the opposite end of the school. She avoided the ninth graders by their lockers and the eighth graders in the next hall over. When she saw the seventh grade locker hall, she breathed a sigh of relief.

A boy bumped into her and gave a start. "Cassie, hey," he said.

Cassie looked at him and smiled when she saw her friend from elementary school. "Emmett! How are you?"

"Great! How was your summer?"

"So busy!" She laughed, more at ease now that she'd found someone she knew. "This place is crazy big."

"Sure is. What do you have first?"

For the life of her, Cassie couldn't remember. She pulled out

93

her schedule and checked. "English."

"Cool. I have math, and it's in the other building, so I better go."

"See you."

Cassie continued to her locker and paused. Even from the back, she recognized Miles Hansen where he stood, swirling the combination of his locker. He had the same haircut, the front spiked just a bit. She took a deep breath, gathering her courage to say hi when someone barreled into her.

"Cassie!" Andrea squealed, breathy with excitement. "Look at us in seventh grade!"

Kitty came with Andrea, standing just behind her shoulder, towering over the other seventh graders.

Cassie nodded, her own excitement bubbling over. "Yeah! We made it!"

Andrea looked her up and down. "You look really nice. Your diet must be working."

"I think so," Cassie agreed, a little timidly. Out of the corner of her eye, she saw Miles turn around and look at them.

"Hi, Cassie," another girl said.

Cassie turned toward her and saw Riley Isabel, only a few lockers down from her own. When Cassie moved to Arkansas in the fifth grade, Riley had been her best friend. But the girls drifted apart in the sixth grade. Riley still wore her blond hair short, right about her ears. But over the summer she'd traded in her slender frame for a more mature, developing figure.

"Hi, Riley," Cassie said politely. "Nice to see you."

"We want to get to our classes early." Andrea took Cassie's elbow. "Come on."

Cassie's class was closest, so Andrea dropped her off with a hug and continued on with Kitty.

First class. Deep breath. Cassie stepped inside and chose a desk against the wall. Nicole, a friend from soccer, came in and waved at her, followed by Leigh Ann from Girls Club and a few other friends. Leigh Ann slid into the desk in front of Cassie with a smile and a hello.

Then the bell rang, and the teacher marched herself to the front of the room. She was a little lady with short black hair, and she quickly explained that they were in the advanced English class, and she expected no excuses from them.

No excuses. Cassie nodded. No forgetting her homework or not doing an assignment. She could do this.

When she stepped into her health class second hour, the first thing she noticed was a nervous undercurrent in the room. Cassie recognized a few kids but didn't see any friends, so she sat down in an empty desk near the front. The tardy bell rang, and the teacher, a tall woman with a bob cut and a long nose, came in.

"Good morning, class," she said in a dry voice. "I'm Ms. Hanks. I am, obviously, your health teacher."

Nobody spoke. Nobody reacted at all.

She pulled out a stack of papers and tapped them on the palm of her other hand. "I'm sure you've all heard about what to expect out of a health class. I want to let you know that while yes, we will be talking about sex—" she waited a moment for the nervous giggles to disperse— "we will also be covering other areas related to health. So your young teenage sensitivities won't be constantly shocked." Now she smiled. "Though these days it's getting harder and harder to shock people.

"I've got two sheets of paper here. One is for you to take home and have your parents sign; it pertains to things we'll be discussing in class. The other is a worksheet for you to do to help us get to know each other."

Ms. Hanks started the papers down the rows. Cassie took one of each. The permission slip she stuck in her binder, and then she examined the worksheet. At the top was a place for a name, so she wrote her name. Then she saw a long list of instructions.

Cassie remembered being taught in Girls Club that before she started on step one of any project, she should always read the steps through to the end. Unexpectedly, something from step five might pertain to step two, and it was better to know that up front. So Cassie put her pencil down and started reading the instructions. They were rather odd things, like, "stand up and pat your head," and "say your name out loud." As other classmates stood up and down and voices rang out in the room, Cassie hoped she wasn't getting too far behind. Then she read the last instruction.

Don't do any of the above. If you haven't already written in your name, do so now. Turn your paper over and sit quietly.

Cassie blinked, astounded. It was a trick! She turned her paper over and sat, marveling at how many kids had fallen for it. A few, like her, already sat with their papers over.

The first kid who had followed each step reached the end and exclaimed, "What? Oh, come on!"

Cassie bit her lower lip to keep from giggling. She heard them all come to an understanding, some laughing, others sheepish.

"Okay," Ms. Hanks said, standing up and smiling. "I'm sure you saw what I did there. This was a test to see if you would read all the instructions before acting on them. Some of you did, most of you didn't. The good news is, this didn't count as a grade, and you probably learned a lesson. Anytime you start to build something, follow a homework assignment, or cook a recipe, it's important to read all the steps through first."

Cassie sat up straighter and braided her hands together, pleased she'd done it right.

"Now please pass in your papers, and we'll do a little getting-to-know-you game."

All of her classes had similar activities, with Cassie seeing a few people she knew in each one. One girl, Farrah, was in two of Cassie's classes.

"You were in my math class last hour," Farrah said in fourth hour, depositing her binder next to Cassie at the geography table. Pretty with shoulder-length blond hair and an intriguing scar on her chin, Farrah looked older than twelve.

"Yeah," Cassie said, surprised Farrah noticed.

Emmett came in. He spotted Cassie and switched directions to sit at her table. "How are your classes so far?" he asked her.

"So far so good. I haven't been late to any."

"Not like that time in fifth grade when you got lost going to P.E." His brown eyes sparkled as he tease her.

Cassie's face warmed. "I stopped to tie my shoe."

"I'm Farrah," Farrah interrupted, resting her chin in her hands and starting at him. "Who are you?"

He looked at her now. "I'm Emmett."

They quieted as the teacher began talking, and when the bell rang for lunch, the three of them walked out together.

"Where's Andrea?" Emmett asked Cassie. "I thought you two were joined at the hip."

Cassie sighed. "She has the other lunch."

He nodded. "So does Miles."

Cassie turned to him, her curiosity piqued. "How do you

know?"

"Because he's one of my best friends."

Cassie arched one eyebrow and shook her head. It was so hard to tell with boys. With girls, she knew right away who was friends with who. "Bummer, huh?"

"Major."

They walked into the cafeteria, and Cassie scanned the lunch lines. There was the tray line that many people stood in, and then there was the sandwich and salad line, and finally an a la carte line with pizzas and muffins and cheese sticks. Her stomach growled at her, but she remembered her vow to eat less. She decided to get a salad.

"Someone's waving at you," Farrah said, nudging her.

Cassie turned her head to see Riley, practically dancing on the table to get her attention.

"Should we sit with her?" Farrah asked.

Cassie hesitated. She wasn't sure she wanted to. But she had nowhere else to go, and it would be rude to ignore Riley. "Sure. Let's sit there. But let's get food first."

"Hi!" Riley greeted, her face breaking into a huge smile when Cassie and Farrah sat by her. "How's your first day of school going?"

"It's going fine." Cassie unwrapped her sandwich, and Farrah bit into a cheesy, gooey mozzarella stick. "Yours?"

"Good. I have some fun classes. How come you're not in choir?"

Cassie vaguely remembered the option in elementary school to sign up for the seventh grade choir, but it was during first hour, and that was the only time the advanced English class was offered. "I'm busy with the Children's Chorus through the art center." Which was the truth. Between the biweekly practices on Mondays and Thursdays, and her private voice lessons on Wednesdays, her voice got plenty of practice.

"Oh." Riley nodded, looking slightly disappointed. "Does that mean you're not doing Girls Club this year?"

"Of course I am!" Cassie stirred her salad around with her fork. "How will it work, now that we can't meet at the elementary school?"

Riley shrugged. "I don't know. I haven't seen Maureen. I'm sure her mom's still in charge. Maybe we'll just meet at her house every week."

"What's Girls Club?" Farrah interrupted, opening her soda.

Her lunch didn't look very nutritious, but Cassie wasn't one to mention that. Besides, Farrah was skinny. She could eat junk. "It's a club where we get together and learn things that will help us with life. Sometimes we go outside and do survival skills."

"Neat. I'd come if there were boys in it."

"That defeats the purpose, doesn't it?" Riley said. "It's a *Girls Club*."

"Yeah, I caught the name," Farrah said, raising one eyebrow. She shot Cassie a humorous look.

They fell into an uneasy silence, and Cassie shoveled her lettuce leaves into her mouth. She remembered now why she and Riley weren't close friends anymore.

❧

Cassie found a table in her life skills class and set her binder down just as Farrah walked in. Farrah took one look at her and laughed.

"Are you stalking me?" she teased, joining Cassie's table.

Cassie smiled back. "I was so scared I wouldn't know anyone today. I didn't realize I'd meet you."

"Lucky, huh?" Farrah tossed her blond hair behind her shoulder.

The teacher stood up and explained they'd be learning about budgeting, wise-spending habits, social skills, etiquette, and other equally boring things. Cassie pulled out a notebook paper and doodled. Her parents had already taught her these things. What did she need to learn them at school for? She checked the school clock. One more class to go, and she would have survived her first day of junior high.

Her last class was art. Cassie dabbled in drawing and thought she could be good at it if she practiced. She noted with disappointment that Farrah wasn't here. Instead she sat by a thin, dark-complected girl with spiral curls in her brown hair and big brown eyes.

"Hi," Cassie said. "I'm Cassie."

The girl smiled, displaying dimples on both sides of her face. "I'm Jaclyn."

Cassie was instantly taken with her friendly smile and timid manner. She settled back in her chair and listened to the teacher talk, feeling very comfortable in this new setting.

Watch out, Southwest Junior High, she thought. *Here I come.*

Chapter Eleven

Boy Trouble

School had barely been in for two weeks when Cassie's parents told her they had to go out of town for a few days.

"We've already found places for your sisters and brother," Mrs. Jones explained to her. "Do you think Andrea's parents would let you stay with her while we're gone?"

"Oh, yes!" Cassie exclaimed, ecstatic with the idea. Though she and Andrea always met up before school, she didn't see her much otherwise. Their classes were different, they weren't usually at the lockers at the same time, and as soon as school was over, Cassie had to run out the back doors to get to the bus. Sometimes she saw Andrea from a distance, walking with Kitty or Cara Barnes, a girl from their elementary school, or other girls Cassie didn't know. Cassie hated feeling so helpless, as if they were drifting apart and she couldn't do anything about it.

"Why don't you call her and ask her?" Mrs. Jones said. "Just to make sure."

Cassie retreated to the room she shared with her sister

Emily. "Did Mom and Daddy tell you?" she asked her sister.

"About what?" Emily sat on her bed by the window, a notepad across her legs, doodling.

"That they're going out of town." Cassie pulled out her cell phone.

"Oh, right, yeah. I'm staying with Jenni from Girls Club."

"Cool. Mom said I can stay with Andrea." Cassie pressed Andrea's number and lay back on her bed, phone against her ear.

"Hey, Cassie!" Andrea answered. "How's it going?"

"Great!" Cassie responded. "What are you doing?"

"Just hanging out with Kitty. She's over here."

Cassie deflated. Of course she was. While the Joneses lived out in the country, twenty minutes from town, all of Cassie's friends lived near each other, five minutes by car at the most.

"That's nice. Hey, I have a question for you. My parents are going out of town next week. They want to know if I can stay with you and go to school with you."

"That sounds great!" Andrea squealed, and Cassie smiled, glad she still wanted her over. "Let me ask my mom!"

A moment later Cassie handed the phone to her mother, and Mrs. Jones and Mrs. Wall made quick arrangements. Then Mrs. Jones returned the phone to Cassie.

"It's all set!" Andrea said. "You come over after school Wednesday and stay here until Saturday! One giant slumber party!"

"I can't wait!" Cassie said, bouncing on the bed. *Take that, Kitty*, she thought.

Monday and Tuesday passed as slowly as they could. When Wednesday morning arrived, Andrea cornered Cassie in the locker hall and bounced around.

"You're coming over today!"

"Yes!" Cassie said, bouncing with her.

"You're fidgety," Farrah commented in geography after telling Cassie for the fifth time to stop tapping her pencil. "What's going on?"

"My parents are going out of town," Cassie began.

Farrah gasped, her eyes going wide. "Are you having a party?"

Cassie just blinked at her, and then she laughed. "Are you crazy? No way."

"Oh. So why are you anxious?"

"I get to spend the night at my best friend's house for three days."

Farrah looked suitably impressed. "Who's your best friend?"

"Andrea Wall."

"Oh, I think I know her. But I thought she was best friends with Cara Barnes."

Cassie frowned at that. Last year in sixth grade, Cara had been the first girl to start wearing makeup and a bra. She'd had a boyfriend and a first kiss while the rest of them were still figuring out how deodorant worked. Beautiful and aloof, Cara had been the subject of much gossip but never the source of friendship. It was true Cassie had seen Cara and Andrea together, but there was no way they were really friends.

"No. It's me. I'm her best friend."

"Well, good for you, that sounds fun!"

Riley wasn't nearly so excited when Cassie told her at lunch. "I didn't think you guys were friends anymore."

Cassie scowled. Why did everyone think that? "We're definitely friends. She just has a totally different schedule than me."

"You could have stayed with me."

Cassie kept quiet. While it was true, her mom would've let her stay with the Isabels, she didn't want to. She couldn't wait to spend time with Andrea.

⚜

"So." Andrea giggled as she settled on the bed across from Cassie. "Tell me everything. All about your first two weeks of school. New friends? Boys?"

Cassie exhaled, relishing the delicious friendship between them. Although they texted almost every day, they hadn't had a serious conversation in two weeks. "It's been super fantastic. I hang out a lot with this girl Farrah."

"Who do you eat lunch with?"

"Farrah and Emmett and Riley."

"Oo, Emmett!" Andrea wriggled her eyebrows. "Is he the new guy in your life?"

"Definitely not," Cassie said with a laugh.

"So are you still stuck on Miles?"

Cassie let out a sigh. Though Miles' locker wasn't far from hers, they hadn't done more than say hi to each other in the hall. Every time she saw him, her heart beat a little faster. She searched for more words, something to keep the conversation going, but all ideas fled the moment he smiled at her. It was like they barely knew each other.

"I take that as a yes," Andrea said.

Cassie groaned and pulled a pillow over her head. "I don't even know what to do."

"Tell him you like him."

"No. Way." She could never do that. She lifted the pillow and eyed Andrea. "What about you? Hanging out a lot with

Kitty?"

"Yeah, we hang out a lot. She lives so close to here." Andrea shrugged like it was no big deal. Then she grinned, a mischievous glint coming into her eye. "And there's this guy."

"A guy?" Cassie sat up straight. Last year Andrea had a boyfriend, but it didn't last long.

"Yes. His name's Jake. He got my phone number last week, and we text all the time. Look." Andrea hauled her phone out and showed the messages to Cassie.

Cassie scanned them and nodded. They were all friendly, kind of teasing, nothing too serious. "He seems nice."

"Here's a picture of him." Andrea flipped through the phone and pulled up a new screen, then handed it to Cassie.

Cassie studied the boy. He had glasses, a round face, and bowl cut on his light brown hair. But the smile looked fresh and friendly. "Nice."

"Yeah." Andrea pulled it back and smiled at his photo. "What do you think? Should he be my boyfriend?"

"Sure." In sixth grade a boy had asked Cassie out, but she hadn't liked him, and honestly, she hadn't felt ready for that. Now she did.

"Girls." Mrs. Wall poked her head into the bedroom. "I know you're having fun, but remember it's a school night. I want you to get all your homework done and go to bed."

"Yes, Mom." Andrea made a face at her as she left.

Cassie pulled out her binder. "We better get our work done."

"Let's curl our hair for school tomorrow."

"That sounds great." Cassie opened up her English assignment. "But I've got to get homework done first."

Andrea sighed. "If you insist."

The next morning before school, Andrea put hot rollers in both their hair. Andrea's hair took to the curls, large voluminous waves flowing around her face and shoulders. Cassie's hair weighed them down, leaving just a slight wave on the edges.

"You can't even tell I did anything," she said with a sigh.

"It did something." Andrea pushed a strand of hair with her hand. "Let's hairspray it. That will help."

Andrea's phone dinged while she worked on Cassie's hair, and she checked the message. "Oh, that's Jake! He wants to meet before school."

"Great," Cassie said, actually excited to meet him.

He wasn't the only one waiting for Andrea. As they walked up the sidewalk after Mrs. Wall dropped them off, a girl with long wavy blond hair and designer jeans turned around. Her brown eyes crinkled when she flashed Andrea a smile.

Cara Barnes.

"Hi, Andrea," she said.

"Hi, Cara!" Andrea said.

A boy approached them, ambling forward with his hands in his pockets. Andrea spotted him before he spoke.

"Jake! This is my friend Cassie. Cassie, meet Jake."

"Hi, Jake," Cassie said, giving a small wave. Wait. What had Andrea said? A numbness spread outward from her chest, and she had a hard time breathing. Just friend? Not best friend? Surely that was a slip.

"This is Brad," Jake said, pulling another guy up to them.

"Hi, Brad," Cassie said, barely noticing him. Where was Andrea? She'd turned back to Cara, and now Kitty and two other girls had joined them. Cassie recognized Maureen from her Girls Club. She stepped back toward Andrea, anxious to be included. But though Maureen scooted over and made room for her to join them, Cassie had no clue what they were talking about. The conversation bounced around about boys and church and something funny that had happened at lunch the day before. Cassie forced the smile to stay on her face, but all the comfort and security she'd felt the night before with Andrea was gone.

The warning bell rang, and Andrea retreated to Cassie's side as they walked into the school building.

"What did you think of Jake?" she asked.

"He was nice," Cassie said, though she had no thoughts about Jake.

"And Brad?"

Who was Brad? "Yeah, him too."

"I'm so glad!" Andrea grabbed her arm, grinning. "I told Jake all about you and he brought Brad to meet you! Did you think he was cute? Did you like him?"

Andrea's words barely made any sense to Cassie. She wanted to go back to Andrea's house, where it was just the two of them in their safe, secure friendship. "Yeah. Really great."

Andrea squealed and ushered Cassie inside.

The school day continued as normal, but the tight feeling in Cassie's chest didn't ease up. She wished she at least had lunch with Andrea. How could she immerse herself in Andrea's life and compete with her new friends if they never saw each other?

Ms. Caraway had them drawing shapes in art class, but Cassie couldn't concentrate enough to make her sphere round. It kept coming out oval. She erased and erased so many times that the paper grew dark and cloudy. With a frustrated sigh, she dropped her pencil on the desk and leaned back in her chair.

"What's wrong?" Jaclyn asked, lifting her eyes from the paper.

"I can't get this stupid circle." Cassie scowled at the mess she'd made.

"I think you need a new piece of paper."

"Probably." Cassie sniffed and blinked hard, hoping she wouldn't cry.

Jaclyn reached into the center of the table and handed her a new sheet. "Is something else wrong?"

"I don't know." Cassie sighed again. "I think I'm losing my best friend."

Jaclyn's brown eyes softened in understanding. "I'm so sorry. What's happening?"

"We don't see each other anymore." A tear slipped down her cheek, and Cassie blinked rapidly, trying to dissuade any others from falling. "She's making all new friends, and I don't know them. When she's with them, it's like I don't exist."

Jaclyn gave a sympathetic murmur and stroked Cassie's arm. "I know exactly what that's like. But you're making new friends too, aren't you?"

Cassie considered Farrah and Jaclyn and the other kids she'd gotten to know in the past two weeks. As much as she liked them, she didn't feel the same bond that she did with Andrea. "Yeah," she said softly.

Jaclyn hugged her shoulders. "You'll find other people you'll connect with."

Not like with Andrea. Cassie knew their friendship was special. But she just nodded her head.

"Can I borrow your blue pencil?" The boy from the desks

behind them came over and rummaged through their colored pencils.

"You don't have one?" Cassie asked.

He looked at her. He had short brown hair and very pale skin. He gave her a sheepish grin. "Not the right shade of blue."

"Okay," Cassie said, though she couldn't understand why that made a difference.

"I'm Luke," he said, selecting one of her pencils.

"Cassie." Cassie glanced at Jaclyn, who had already gone back to coloring. "That's Jaclyn."

Jaclyn lifted her head, gave a brief smile that highlighted both of her dimples, and bent her head again.

"Thanks for letting me borrow this," Luke said, giving a wave.

One more friend, Cassie thought, watching him walk away. She needed to be more grateful.

Chapter Twelve

Peer Pressure

Andrea met Cassie at her locker after school, just as happy as she had been that morning.

"Ready to come over?"

Cassie closed her locker and juggled her books. A sense of relief flooded her at the reminder that in a few minutes, it would be just her and Andrea at Andrea's house. "So ready."

"Hey, Cassie."

Both Andrea and Cassie turned at her name, but Cassie knew from the thudding of her heart that it was Miles.

"Hi, Miles," she said, her tongue suddenly thick. Proper words fled her mind, as they always did when he said hi.

He pushed his glasses up on his nose, his short brown hair spiked in the front. "Are you going to Andrea's house today?"

"Yes," Cassie said.

"She's staying with me for the week," Andrea added. "Until Saturday."

"That's cool." He hesitated a moment more. "Well, I'll see you later."

"Bye," Cassie said.

Andrea grabbed her arm and spun her around. "He so likes you!" she whispered.

"He does not!" Cassie whispered back, but she giggled right along with Andrea.

Andrea looped an arm through hers, and they walked toward the school doors.

"Hey, Andrea." Jake and his friend—Brad?—appeared, taking up residence on Andrea's other side.

"Hi, guys," Andrea said, shooting Cassie a grin.

"Andrea!" One of the girls from this morning, the one Cassie didn't know, hurdled into the midst of them. Wrapping an arm around Andrea's neck, she whispered into her ear, "Call me as soon as you get home. Stop talking to Jake."

Andrea pulled back and frowned at her. "What?"

The girl backed away, miming a phone with her hand and mouthing, "Call me."

"Um." Andrea looked at Jake as the three of them walked out the doors. "I've got to go. I'll text you."

"Okay. Sure. Bye."

"What was that about?" Cassie asked as soon as the boys had left.

"Who knows?" Andrea shrugged. "That's Amity Stafford. She just moved here. Sometimes she's a little weird."

Andrea's mom pulled up, and they climbed into the car. Andrea texted away the whole drive home, and as soon as they got into her bedroom, she closed the door and made a phone call.

"Hey, Amity, what's up?" she said.

Cassie settled herself on the bed with her homework and tried not to eavesdrop.

"What do you mean? What?" Andrea sounded frustrated

now. "Says who? That hasn't happened. Nuh-uh. Okay. I'll call you. Bye." She hung up. "Argh!"

"What?" Cassie asked, looking up from her homework. "What happened?"

"I guess Jake told some kids he's going to ask me out."

Cassie pressed her hands together. "That's a good thing, right? You like him!"

"Well, I do, but, Amity kind of freaked out. She said it's not a good idea."

Cassie frowned. "Why is it any of Amity's business?"

"She said she heard some rumors from Jake's friends about last year. I guess he got in trouble at his old elementary school."

Cassie rolled one hand. "So? We were just kids then. It doesn't matter."

"Yeah, well." Andrea averted her eyes and shrugged. "Amity says if he asks me out, I should definitely say no. She said it wouldn't be good for me and it would say something about the kind of people I hang out with."

Cassie narrowed her eyes, not liking where this was going one bit. "Is Amity in charge? What if next she tells you not to be friends with me?" Just saying the words out loud hurt, but Cassie held her ground.

Andrea's eyes widened, and she lifted her gaze. "No way! No one could ever make us stop being friends."

That made her feel a little better, but not much. This Amity girl had way too much influence on Andrea. "What does Kitty say?"

"Everyone seemed to like him. I'll ask her." Before Andrea could text anything, though, the phone rang. "It's Jake," she whispered, staring at it.

"Answer it," Cassie said.

Taking a deep breath, Andrea did. "Hello?" she said, her voice instantly more chirpy and girly. "Uh-huh. Yep." She made a face at Cassie, and Cassie leaned closer, wanting to hear the other side of the conversation. "Oh. I don't know, Jake. Can I think about it? Sure. I'll call your right back." She hung up and met Cassie's gaze. "He asked me out!" she squeaked.

"What are you going to do?" Cassie breathed.

"I don't know!" Andrea wrung her hands together. "Amity said to say no. What should I do?"

"What you want to do!" Cassie exclaimed. "Don't you like him?"

"Yes—but—but—" Andrea grabbed her phone again. "I'll ask Kitty."

She started texting, and Cassie rolled her eyes.

"Okay." Andrea exhaled. "Kitty says I should say no. I'll tell him no."

Cassie didn't say a word as Andrea called Jake back. Andrea fluffed her hair up, expression agitated.

"Jake, hi! Yeah. Yes, I was thinking. The thing is, Jake—I can't." Andrea let her breath out in a whoosh. "I'm so sorry. No, I like you a lot. I'm just not—it's not the right time for me to have a boyfriend." Andrea shot Cassie a desperate look. "I'm focusing on school right now. Yeah, we can be friends. Sure. Of course." Putting the phone down, she threw herself back on the bed. "Oh, I'm glad that's over."

"What did he say?" Cassie asked. "How do you feel?"

"I think he understood. He seemed okay." Andrea's phone rang, and she picked it up. "That's Kitty. Let me take this."

"Don't let me stop you," Cassie grumbled, annoyed. Why

did Andrea's new friends have so much influence over her? Cassie continued with her homework and did her best to tune out Andrea and whatever was going on.

"Kitty says I did the right thing." Andrea put the phone down and paced at the foot of the bed. "I hope so. I mean, I just feel—" Her phone dinged. "Hang on, someone just texted me."

Cassie pulled out her own phone, wishing it would do something so she didn't feel so left out.

"It's Brad, Jake's friend. He wants to know if he can call me." Andrea bit down on her thumbnail. "Do you think he's with Jake? Is he going to try to convince me? Or!" She brightened and looked at Cassie. "Maybe he wants to talk about you!"

"Me?" Cassie couldn't see what she possibly had to do with this.

The phone rang, and Andrea answered it. "Hello? Hi, Brad! Yeah, I'm here, just hanging out with Cassie. Say hi, Cassie."

"Hi," Cassie said toward the phone, resisting the urge to pull her hair out.

"Did you want to talk to her? Oh? Oh, okay. What? Um, I don't know." Andrea gave a weak laugh. "Sure, I'm a little surprised. I'll call you back, okay?" Andrea hung up and looked at Cassie, her brows knit together in worry. "Cassie, I'm so sorry."

"For what?" Sure, all this drama was irritating, but Cassie couldn't figure out why she'd need to apologize.

"Brad asked me out." She bit down on her lower lip.

"He did what?" Cassie straightened, shocked by this turn of events.

"Are you mad?"

"But he's Jake's friend! And he's had a crush on you this whole time?"

"Yeah, I was surprised too. But you're not mad?"

"Why would I be?"

"Because—" Andrea hesitated. "Didn't you like him?"

Cassie guffawed. "I met him for a minute! No, I didn't like him!"

"Okay, good." Andrea looked relieved and picked up her phone again. "I've got to ask Amity."

"Ask Amity what?" Cassie stared at her friend, baffled by this behavior.

"If I should go out with him, of course."

"You don't need Amity for that." Cassie closed her book and grabbed Andrea's arm. "You don't like him. You liked his friend, Jake. Which, duh, he's Jake's friend! You can't go out with him after you just told Jake no."

Andrea blinked once, chewing on her lower lip. "I'll just call Amity real quick."

Cassie sighed and let go. "Can you go out in the hall? I'm trying to study."

"Oh, sure, sorry." Andrea got up and went out.

Even with the door shut, Cassie could hear Andrea's excited chatter. And then she hung up with Amity and called Kitty. Her voice got louder, more enthusiastic, and finally she came back in, her face flushed.

"Okay." She beamed at Cassie. "Both of them said it would be fine to go out with Brad."

"That doesn't mean you have to do it."

Andrea cradled her phone and hesitated. "But they said I should."

"Do you even like him?"

She shrugged. "I could like him. He's cute. I just don't know."

"Maybe you should get to know him first."

"I'll just—give him a call." Andrea stepped back out into the hall, but she left the door open. "Hi, Brad? It's Andrea. Okay, yes. Yes, I will. Uh-huh. Yep. Sure. See you tomorrow."

She came back into the room and put the phone down on her vanity. "That's done! I'm Brad's girlfriend!"

"Yay," Cassie said, but she didn't bother to feign excitement. "Why would you go out with a guy you don't even like?"

"Because—" Andrea paused and searched for the right words. "Because it's, like, important, you know, to be liked. To have a boyfriend. It means you're like, important."

"Oh." Cassie considered those words. "So if you don't have a boyfriend, you're not important?"

"Well, it just says something. About how attractive you are, and how into you people are. You know?"

"No," Cassie said softly. "I don't know." She turned back to her book, wishing she didn't feel such a deep ache in her heart. If that was how Andrea judged someone's value, it wouldn't be very long before she didn't think Cassie was good enough to be her friend.

Or maybe it would be Andrea's friends deciding Cassie wasn't good enough to be her friend.

Chapter Thirteen

Mean Boys

Cassie pulled out the dining room chair in Andrea's kitchen. She had been so excited for these three days together. But the more time Cassie spent with Andrea, the more she realized her best friend was changing. And Cassie was pretty powerless to stop it.

"You're not eating much, Cassie," Andrea's mom said. "Don't you like the food?"

"Oh, sure," Cassie said, nodding. She hadn't really been paying attention. Now she looked down at the food on her plate. The potatoes and chicken looked delicious, but Cassie had been working really hard for almost two months to lose weight. She couldn't allow herself to overeat now.

That, coupled with the weirdness of Andrea and Brad, left her without much of an appetite. Not even an hour ago, the boy Andrea liked had asked her out. But because her new friends didn't think she should go out with him, Andrea turned him down and decided to go out with his best friend.

Like that wasn't asking for trouble.

Cassie sighed and picked at her food some more.

"As soon as you're done, you girls clear your plates and go to bed," Mrs. Wall said, standing up and moving into the kitchen. "Remember you have school tomorrow."

"We know, Mom," Andrea said with an eye roll and a wink at Cassie.

"Thanks, Mrs. Wall," Cassie said. She found herself annoyed with Andrea and didn't return the wink. Instead, she stood up and carried her plate to the sink. Andrea followed her, and then they went back to her room.

"How's your diet going?" Andrea asked, closing the door behind her.

"Good, I think." Cassie glanced down at herself. "My clothes are fitting looser."

"Yeah, you look really good." Andrea pinched the skin around her belly. "I think maybe I should go on one too."

Cassie took a good look at her. Her reddish-brown hair still had the voluptuous waves in it from when they curled it this morning. Like Cassie, she wore glasses, and her face was a bit round. "I don't think you're fat at all." Cassie pulled her own long dark hair in front of her face, checking to see if any wave remained. Andrea had curled it for her this morning also, but Cassie's rebellious, stubborn hair refused to hold the curl.

"You weren't fat either, but you look better now."

Cassie lifted her face and straightened her shoulders, some of her earlier irritation falling away under the praise. "Thanks."

Andrea's phone rang. She picked it up off the vanity and frowned. "It's Jake."

Uh-oh. Jake was the boy she liked, the one she'd been so excited about yesterday and this morning. And yet, when he finally asked her out, she'd rejected him. "Are you going to answer it?"

Andrea just stared at it. "I don't think so."

It stopped ringing. And then a moment later, it started up again.

"It's him again. What do I do?" Andrea asked.

"Just answer it. You're friends, right?" But Cassie felt the same trepidation in her chest that Andrea must.

Andrea took a deep breath and opened her phone. "Hello?"

Jake's voice, loud and accusing, echoed from the tiny speaker. Cassie caught the words "Brad" and "liar" and a few words she wouldn't repeat, even in her head.

"No, no, it's not like that," Andrea said, blinking rapidly as tears filled her eyes.

Jake rode right over her, still yelling into the phone.

Enough was enough. Cassie took the phone from Andrea. "Jake? This is Cassie, Andrea's friend. Don't call again. If you do, I'll hand the phone to her dad." Then she closed it.

Andrea burst into tears, her breathing coming in ragged gasps. "He was so mean! The things he said to me—that I'm a liar—and a player—that I was just using him!"

Cassie could totally understand why Jake felt that way, but seeing Andrea so distraught brought tears to her own eyes. "He just doesn't know you, Andrea."

"I have to call Amity," Andrea choked out. Before she could, her phone rang again. "Oh, it's Brad. Hello?" Though her voice trembled, she put a smile on her face. A smile that rapidly faded when Brad started talking. "No, no!" she said, breaking into sobs. She hung up the phone and crumpled to the carpet. "Brad broke up with me. He said he knows what I did to Jake and he's going to tell the whole school that I'm a skank!"

Cassie didn't know exactly what a skank was, but judging from Andrea's reaction, she had a pretty good guess. "I'll call him."

"No, don't, Cassie!"

Cassie ignored Andrea and grabbed the phone. She pressed redial.

"What do you want, Andrea?" Brad's voice came on the line.

"This is Cassie," she said, holding her voice firm. "You're wrong about Andrea. She is not a skank. And if you tell people that about her, I'll report you for bullying."

There was a momentary pause, and then Brad said, "I remember you. If you're friends with Andrea, you must be a skank too. You probably knew about this and told her go out with me."

Cassie's blood boiled, and her timid nature fell away, giving way to anger. "Want to talk about friendship, Brad? You knew Jake liked Andrea. But you asked her out anyway."

"What was your name again?"

She straightened her shoulders. "Cassandra. Cassandra Jones."

"You're going down, Cassandra Jones."

"Bring it," she hissed.

༄

It took hours for Andrea to calm down. She cried and cried and cried, and then she called Kitty and Cara and Amity and cried some more. Cassie couldn't understand why she wasn't enough, since she was right there, but apparently Andrea needed more than one sympathetic ear for this mess. Then finally she put her phone away and lay on the bed next to

Cassie, still crying.

"Brad's just as mean as Jake," she said. "I never should have said yes."

"You should have done what you wanted to do. What did you want?"

"To go out with Jake!" she moaned.

"Why didn't you?"

Andrea didn't directly answer that question. Instead, she sobbed, "It's too late now!"

It pretty much was. Still, Cassie rubbed her shoulders and said, "Let's see what happens tomorrow."

She didn't have much hope for tomorrow.

❦

Andrea was not her usual bubbly self when they got out of the car Friday morning. They walked up the long sidewalk, Andrea shirking behind Cassie as if hoping Cassie could shield her somehow. Cassie saw Amity and Cara and Andrea's other friends in their huddle, but Andrea made no move to join them, so Cassie continued toward the entry.

"Let's just go to the lockers," Andrea whispered when they got inside.

The halls were mostly empty, since the majority of the students preferred to hang outside the building until the bell rang. They switched out their books, and Andrea took a deep breath.

"Okay," she said, "to the bathroom."

"Are you doing all right?" Cassie asked, following her.

"Yeah. All right."

They were almost to the bathroom when suddenly Jake was there, blocking their path. Brad stood beside him, the two boys making an effective wall.

"Excuse us," Cassie said, holding her chin up. "We need to use the bathroom."

"She's a skank," Jake said. "She used me to get to my best friend."

"No, she didn't," Cassie said, turning glaring eyes upon Brad. "Your best friend used you to get to her."

"I did not!" Brad protested, his voice cracking. "Don't listen to her. She's a skank just like her friend."

Cassie faced Jake instead. "He's not your friend. But Andrea really likes you."

Jake's brow crinkled with confusion. "Then why did she say yes to him and no to me?"

Andrea tugged on Cassie's arm, tears dripping down her face. "Let's just go back," she whispered.

"Liked you," Cassie corrected. "Until you went off on her on the phone. Come on, Andrea." Cassie grabbed Andrea's arm and yanked her between the boys, forcing them to separate for her.

The rest of the school day passed without much incident, in spite of Jake and Brad's threats. Of course, Cassie had made her own threats, and maybe they'd taken her seriously.

She didn't see Andrea all day, but this time she didn't worry. She'd defended Andrea, helped her when no one else was there. She couldn't protect her all the time, and for once she was glad Andrea had other friends. They would make sure she was all right.

She found Andrea at the lockers after school, and Andrea gave her a wan smile as she put away her books.

"Well, I survived the day," she said.

"Yes, you did." Cassie only had math and English homework. She shoved the other books into her locker. "Did anyone give you a hard time?"

Andrea shook her head wearily. "No. Cara and Amity kept everyone away."

They walked outside together and waited at the end of the sidewalk for Andrea's mom.

"I made a mistake, didn't I?" Andrea ventured finally.

Cassie exhaled, glad Andrea had reached that conclusion herself. "Yes. I'm pretty sure you hurt Jake's feelings and made Brad break bro-code."

Andrea laughed softly. "What should I have done?"

Cassie shrugged. She didn't really have the answer for that. If Andrea had said yes to Jake, she never would've known what a jerk he could be. Then again, maybe everyone had the potential to be a jerk when wounded and provoked. "You should have done what you felt was right."

"It can be so confusing sometimes," she murmured.

Cassie faced her. "You don't have to rely on other people to make decisions for you. You have a head. A brain." She tapped Andrea's forehead with her index finger. "You're the one who would be Jake's girlfriend, not Amity or Kitty or Cara. So you get to decide."

Andrea sighed and leaned her head on Cassie's shoulder. "I'm so glad you came over. I needed to spend time with you."

"I'm glad too," Cassie said. But something stirred restlessly in her heart. She couldn't be by Andrea's side always, and she wouldn't be staying at her house anymore. Somehow, she doubted Andrea would stand her ground the next time one of her new friends told her what to do. And Cassie wouldn't be there to be the voice of reason.

Episode 3: Of Life and Limb

Chapter Fourteen

Goal

The sound of a doorbell chiming penetrated Cassandra Jones' dreams, lulling her from her sleep. But she didn't recognize the chime. The doorbell at her house didn't sound that way. She must be dreaming still.

The doorbell chimed again, and someone groaned beside her. Someone was in her bed! Cassie opened her eyes and sat up, and then laughed when she realized she was at her best friend Andrea's house, in Andrea's bed. For a moment she'd forgotten.

The front door opened with a creak, and adult voices carried down the hall. She recognized her father's voice. Cassie fished around the side of the bed for her phone, then pulled it in front of her face to check the time. "What?" she hissed. Not even eight in the morning! What was he doing here?

A soft tap came on the bedroom door, and then Mrs. Wall opened it and poked her head inside.

"Cassie," she whispered, "your dad's here."

"Thanks," Cassie murmured. She rolled out of bed and

grabbed her clothes.

Andrea stirred and opened one eye. "What are you doing?"

"My dad's here."

Andrea pushed up on an elbow. "Are you leaving?"

"Yeah." Cassie tossed on her clothes and threw her pajamas into the duffel bag. She leaned over and hugged Andrea. "Bye, Andrea."

One arm came up and hugged her back. "Thanks, Cassie. You were so great this week."

Cassie slipped out the door, having very serious doubts about that. Andrea had made some poor decisions, and Cassie hadn't been able to talk her out of them.

"Ready to go?" Mr. Jones said when she got to the front door. He wore navy blue soccer shorts and a colorful green jersey.

"Why are you here so early?" Cassie said, not bothering to speak quietly as they stepped outside. "We were still asleep."

"You're lucky you got to be here today at all. Your mom and I got in from our trip last night, and we could have come to get you then."

Cassie doubted her parents let her stay one more night for her sake. More likely, they weren't quite ready to have four additional people under foot at home after a few quiet days of just the two of them. But she thought it in her best interest not to mention that. "So what's going on today?"

"I need you at the store. Should be a big day. Lots of teams start up next week, and last-minute shoppers will be looking for things."

"Oh, okay." Her dad owned a soccer store, and Cassie didn't mind hanging out there. "Any friendship bracelets sell?" She made bracelets for the store, but so far she'd only managed to sell one and give one away.

"Not yet." He took another look at her. "Did you have a nice time?"

"Sure." She settled into the passenger seat and flipped the visor down. Her face looked less round every time she checked, proving her diet was working. She pinched the skin around her waist and was pleased to see there wasn't so much to grab. No one would call her the fat girl now.

She helped her dad organize the new clothes shipment, and then he switched the sign in the store from "closed" to "open." Cassie settled behind the register and pulled out her book. She'd worked here enough to know that some days were busy, with lots of people flowing in and out, and other days were completely dead, with just her and her dad to keep each other company.

The bell rang as two customers come in, and she straightened up. While they shopped, another family came in. Soon the store was hopping, and a line formed at the register as people waited to check out. Cassie rang them up as fast as she could, not liking to have people wait on her.

It continued that way for most of the morning, then died down around lunch time.

"Well, that was great," she said, turning to her dad.

"Yes," he said, looking quite pleased with himself. "The store seems to be doing well. Soccer's a really big sport right now, and the community supports us."

"I was thinking I need some new pants," Cassie said. She pulled at the waistband of her jeans, noticing how loose they were.

"You can get new shorts here." Her dad gestured to one of the racks of clothing. "Go ahead, pick a pair. Any you want."

That wasn't what she had in mind. She thought of Cara Barnes with her skinny legs and fancy jeans, the ones with the glittering gems on the back pockets. She wanted jeans like that. "I'll just ask Mom to take me shopping."

Something like hurt flashed across her dad's face. "You don't want one of these shorts? I have some really nice brands here."

She hated to disappoint him. "Okay, sure." Standing up, she came around the counter and examined the satiny soccer shorts, with all bright colors. These shorts were great for a flashy game, but nobody wore stuff like this to school. She picked out a purple pair just to please her father. "I'll take these."

"Wonderful." He beamed behind his mustache, apparently happy to contribute something to her wardrobe. Cassie smiled back, deciding not to worry about it. At least she'd made him happy.

After lunch it picked back up again. A few more families came in, and then a group of teenage boys burst in, chattering and laughing boisterously. Cassie hunkered down behind the register and examined them. They didn't look much older than her, maybe thirteen or fourteen. All four of them wore baseball caps and flip flops. They didn't notice her as they picked out shoes and laughed at the soccer ball calculators and soccer ball whistles.

One of the boys wandered over to the register and plopped his box of soccer cleats on the counter. "Hi," he said, his eyes sweeping over Cassie.

"Hi," she said, standing up and starting to ring up his shoes.

"Are you from around here?" he asked. The other boys stepped up behind him, holding onto their purchases.

"Yes," she said, pushing back a strand of her dark brown hair. "I go to school at Southwest Junior High. You?"

"We're from Fayetteville," he said. "We got to Ramey Junior High."

"Oh, okay." She handed him his bag, and he gave her cash. "Are you an eighth grader?" he asked.

She straightened her shoulders, for some reason pleased he thought she was older than she was. "No. Seventh grade."

They all kind of laughed a little, and he smiled, his eyes friendly. "Bottom of the food chain."

Cassie smiled back, and then another boy shoved his way forward to buy his things.

"What was your name?" the first one asked, standing off to the side.

"Cassie." She finished ringing everyone up, and they headed for the door.

"Bye, Cassie," he said, holding his bag in one hand and pushing open the door with the other. The bell chimed, and he said, "See ya next time we come in."

"See ya," she echoed, her whole body humming with an excited energy.

Her dad came out of the back and frowned at her. "Did those kids buy anything?"

"Yes." She checked the register. "They all spent about forty dollars."

"Humph." He still didn't look happy. "Don't spend so much time talking to the customers."

"What?" That went against everything she'd ever heard him say about customer service. "I was being friendly."

He grumbled under his breath and disappeared into the stock room again.

As they closed up the store for the day, Mr. Jones said, "Any more thoughts on soccer this year, Cassie? You've missed the registration deadline, but I might be able to pull some strings."

She had thought about it. She really liked the sport. And soccer camp had been so much fun. But she hated running. Passionately. Every part of her body, from her neck to her lungs to the balls of her feet, hurt when she ran. She wondered briefly if she might be better at it now that she'd lost some weight, but she didn't want to spend the time trying.

"I think I'm going to sit this season out, Daddy," she said, as gently as possible. "I still love the sport. I'll help out a lot with the store."

"Well, that's too bad." He shrugged it off. "We'll use you at the fields, then. I want to set up a booth during the games in case anyone needs something."

"That sounds great." She exhaled, relieved he'd accepted her answer so well.

Chapter Fifteen

Drifting

Cassie texted Andrea several times over the weekend to make sure she was okay. After the drama with Jake and Brad, Cassie expected her best friend to still be heartbroken. But Andrea always responded cheerfully, as if nothing had ever been wrong.

Cassie didn't see her at the lockers before school Monday or Tuesday. On Wednesday morning, Cassie went outside to the sidewalk after the bus dropped her off, searching for her friend.

Masses of students crowded the sidewalk and stood under the orange awning. Cassie's eyes surveyed the small groups. She saw Andrea next to Cara and her friend Amity, leaning in close and peering at something on Cara's phone. Kitty sat on a bench beside them, talking excitedly. Cassie hesitated, not sure she wanted to interrupt, but then she braved the group and stepped over to Andrea.

"Hey," Cassie said, tugging on Andrea's sleeve.

"Oh, hey." Andrea turned toward to Cassie. "What's up?"

"I just wanted to see how you're doing."

"I'm good."

Amity and Cara burst out laughing, and Andrea's eyes slid back toward Cara's phone.

"Everything okay with Jake?" Cassie moved her head, trying to catch Andrea's eye.

"Hm? Jake?" Andrea blinked. "Oh. Yeah, every thing's good. I like someone else now."

It was Cassie's turn to be startled. "You do? Who?" And how? How had Andrea found a new guy to like so quickly?

"His name's Clay. You don't know him, he goes to Central Junior High."

"Look at this!" Cara interrupted, swiveling to Andrea and waving the small screen.

Andrea's attention turned away from Cassie completely, and her small group of friends closed in, shutting Cassie out. Cassie stood there for a moment, then she turned around and walked back into the school. She opened her locker and stared into it, her thoughts a muddled mess.

Andrea was, apparently, just fine.

۞

Cassie texted Andrea on Friday to see if she wanted to come over. Andrea sent a quick response, saying she couldn't but Cassie could come over on Saturday.

I'll be there! Cassie responded.

Great! See you tomorrow! Hugs!

Clinging to that hope, Cassie dressed quickly in the morning, attempted to tame her long hair, and cleaned her room. Then she did her chores in the kitchen and even took care of Pioneer, the family dog.

"You're being awfully helpful," Mrs. Jones said, eyeing her

suspiciously. "What's going on?"

Cassie took a deep breath. "Andrea wanted me to come over today. I thought if I got all my chores done quickly, I could go."

Her mom studied her a moment before saying, "Your dad was hoping you'd help out in the store today."

Cassie's shoulders slumped. "But I haven't really seen Andrea all week."

Mrs. Jones relented. "All right. Go ahead and give her a call. But when you're done at her house, you'll need to go help your dad at the store for a few hours."

"Yes!" Cassie perked right up, rocking forward on the balls of her feet. "Thank you!"

Hurrying to her room, Cassie pulled her phone out and dialed Andrea's number. It rang several times before going to voicemail. Cassie tried one more time. When the same thing happened, she sat on her bed with the phone in her hands, staring at it.

A moment later, her mom knocked on the open bedroom door. "Are we going to Andrea's?"

"She didn't answer the phone," Cassie replied, still looking at her hands.

Her mom came in and sat down on the bed next to her. "Maybe she's in the shower or something."

It was possible. It was only a little after ten in the morning, after all. "I'll try again in a few minutes."

"Is everything okay between you two?" Mrs. Jones asked.

Cassie could feel her mom's gaze on her, and she deliberately kept her face forward, afraid of what the warmth behind her eyes might mean. "I don't know." It was the most honest answer she could muster.

Her mom patted her on the shoulder and then got up and left the room. Cassie picked up a book and tried to concentrate, but even *The Babysitters Club* held no interest for her right now. After ten minutes, she picked up the phone and tried again. Still no answer.

Mrs. Jones let her try for a full hour. Around eleven, she came back into Cassie's room. "If you're not going to Andrea's, we need to head to the store. Your dad needs your help."

"Can we just swing by her house?" Cassie begged. "See if she's home?"

Mrs. Jones hesitated, and then nodded. "Sure. We can stop by."

Cassie jumped up and jammed her feet into her shoes, excited again. She just knew everything would be fine if she made it to Andrea's house. Andrea would let her in, and they'd talk, and clear the air, and they'd be best friends again.

They pulled up to the curb of Andrea's house half an hour later. Cassie had tried calling one more time, with no answer. She shoved open the passenger door as soon as they came to a halt and ran up the steps to the front door. She rang the doorbell and rocked on her feet anxiously.

Mrs. Wall opened the door, one eyebrow arching over her clear blue eyes. "Cassie! Hi. What are you doing here?"

"Can I talk to Andrea?" Cassie said breathlessly.

"Well, Andrea's not here. She spent the night at Kitty's house. I think they went to the mall. Why don't you try calling her? You can probably meet up."

The words stabbed Cassie in the heart. "Okay. Thank you." She turned around and tromped back down to the car, willing herself not to cry.

"She wasn't home?" Mrs. Jones asked.

"No." Cassie slouched down in her seat and stared out the window. Her mom put the car into gear and pulled away from the curb, and Cassie allowed the tears to slide down her cheeks.

⁊꙳

Cassie didn't try to text Andrea all weekend. On Monday, she sent a nice "hello" text and received a "hi!" in response. Encouraged, Cassie typed out, *How was your weekend?*

No response.

Cassie couldn't help but check her phone every time class ended, since they weren't supposed to have them out during class unless the teacher told them they could. Nothing.

On Tuesday her mom took her to the first children's chorus practice of the year. Cassie stepped into the community center timidly. She recognized a handful of kids from the chorus last year, but most were new faces. Ms. Vanderwood stood at the piano next to a long line of students, her pretty red hair curled around her shoulders. She checked off names and put the singers in their assigned places. Cassie got in line at the back and waited her turn.

Ms. Vanderwood looked up as Cassie stepped up to the piano.

"Cassie!" she said, a pleasant smile transforming her face. Her eyes traveled Cassie up and down. "You've lost a lot of weight. Have you been sick?"

"Um." Cassie looked down, her face warming under the compliment. "No. Just trying to be healthier."

"You look great." Ms. Vanderwood eyed her. "Just don't take it too far."

"Okay."

135

The choir teacher consulted her chart. "First soprano, right there." She pointed with her pen to the second row.

Cassie gladly took her spot. Her voice was one of the few things she took pride in. At least other people recognized her talent.

Chapter Sixteen

StuCo Issues

Three days went by with no response from Andrea, even when Cassie texted her.

"Who are you expecting a text from?" Farrah teased her on Wednesday as they walked toward lunch. "Some hot guy? Every time I look at you, you have your phone out."

"No one." Cassie's face warmed, and she slipped her phone into her back pocket. Something ached deep in her chest, and she fought a constant urge to cry. She liked Farrah fine, and she got along well with Jaclyn, her friend in art class. But neither of them came close to replacing Andrea.

Riley and Emmett were already at the lunch table.

"We should have a slumber party," Farrah said, popping open her can of soda. "At my house."

"That sounds great!" Riley said, her face lighting up.

"What am I supposed to do?" Emmett joked.

"We'll call you and include you in the party," Farrah teased back.

A slumber party. Cassie resisted a sigh. She pulled her

phone out and checked it again. Still nothing.

"I'll call you, okay?" Farrah said, taking their numbers.

Maybe it would do Cassie good to hang out with other people.

Farrah called that night after Cassie got home from voice lessons.

"I was thinking we could do the slumber party at your house," Farrah said excitedly. "Would your mom be okay with that?"

"Yeah, I think so," Cassie said, trying to drum up some excitement for the event. "I'll ask her."

"Are you really good friends with Riley?" Farrah added. "Because I'd rather just hang out with you."

The flattery warmed Cassie's heart, but she knew all too well what it felt like to be left out. "Let's invite her this time. We kind of planned it in front of her. Next time we can do something and not mention it to her."

"Okay. You're right."

Cassie tried not to, but as she started down the seventh grade locker hall Thursday morning, her eyes moved of their own accord toward Andrea's locker. Not that she was there. Cassie exhaled and felt her shoulders slump, though she couldn't be sure if it was relief or disappointment. Andrea would be outside right now, hanging out under the awning with her new friends. Cassie opened her phone, her thumb pausing over a new text message. Then she closed it and put it away. What would be the point? Andrea had ignored her other texts.

"Hi, Cassie," a boy said, and she turned around. She nearly dropped her binder when she saw Miles, shooting her a smile before opening a locker close to hers.

"Oh, hi!" she said, forcing the words out of her mouth before she could clam up. Her face grew hot. What was wrong with her? She and Miles had been such good friends last year. This year, they'd hardly spoken at all.

"How are your classes going?" he asked, stuffing a few books into his backpack. He pushed his wire-framed glasses higher on his nose and focused on her. "Do you like school so far?"

"Yeah." She bobbed her head several times. "It's great. Do you like it?"

"It's fun. I've made lots of friends." He hooked his backpack on his shoulders. "Are you running for student body next week?"

Student body. Her mind flashed on an announcement earlier this week about student president and student government elections being held next week. Anyone wanting to run just needed to fill out an application by Friday—tomorrow. "I hadn't really planned on it."

"You should. I'm going to. You'll vote for me, right?"

How could she not? His serious brown eyes were melting her into a puddle of goo, and she wanted to hold onto this moment of conversation forever. "Of course I will."

"I'll vote for you too." He smiled again and gave a small wave. "See ya, Cassie."

That did it. Cassie watched him go, her heart thumping in her chest. She was going to run for student body.

"That's a great idea!" Farrah said in math before the tardy bell rang. "I'd vote for you! In fact, I think I'll run!"

"You should." Cassie smiled, encouraged by Farrah's

response. Farrah knew everybody, was beautiful and well liked. "We'd have so much fun together." And Miles, too. She shifted in her seat, jittery with anticipation of spending extra time with him during the school year, planning events and school socials.

"Let's put a campaign together at your house tomorrow." Farrah pulled out a piece of paper and started brainstorming. "Do you have the applications?"

"No." Cassie drummed her fingers on the desk, feeling ignorant. "Where do you get those?"

"At the counselor's office."

"Okay." Cassie nodded. "I'll pick some up before lunch."

"Great." Farrah opened her mouth to say something more, but then the bell rang and Mr. Adams came in, silencing them.

Cassie found her homework and sat up straighter. Though Mr. Adams, an older man with white hair and a large belly, always addressed them with a gruff voice, the smile lines around his eyes and their constant twinkle made him one of her favorite teachers. Sometimes the kids could get him off on a tangent, talking about war stories, and he'd completely forget their homework assignment.

Farrah pulled her brainstorming paper back out at lunch, when they finally had time to talk again. "Okay, let's discuss running for StuCo." Farrah referenced the popular acronym for student council.

"Who's running for StuCo?" Emmett asked, shoving half his pizza in his mouth.

"We are." Farrah gestured at her and Cassie proudly.

"Cool," he said, though it sounded like, "kumf." He took a drink and swallowed, then added, "Andrea's running too."

"She is?" Cassie stared at him. "I mean, I know." Why did

that thought worry her so much? If they both made it, they'd have more time together. But what if Andrea made it and Cassie didn't?

Oblivious to Cassie's dilemma, Farrah had just started to explain her campaign plan when Riley dropped her tray on the table and sat down beside them.

"Oh, are you planning our slumber party tomorrow?" she asked, craning her head to see the paper.

Farrah covered it up with one hand. "No, just going over my math homework." She folded the page in half and shoved it in her purse.

Emmett, who had been watching silently from across the table, snickered.

"Oh." If Riley noticed, she didn't react. She opened her box of juice and took the lettuce out of her chicken burger. "What are we doing for the slumber party?"

"It's going to be at Cassie's house," Farrah said. She tossed her shoulder-length blond hair over one shoulder. "Right, Cass?"

"Yep." Cassie still couldn't muster up any excitement about this. Out of habit, she pulled her phone out. Nothing, of course.

The conversation moved on to discussing how hard the class assignments were becoming and who had the stricter mom. As soon as Riley got up to put away her tray, Farrah grabbed Cassie's hands, directing her attention.

"What are you doing after school today, Cassie? We could get together and plan our election strategy."

"I can't today," Cassie said. "I have the children's chorus practice."

"Maybe I can stay late on Saturday after Riley leaves,"

Farrah said. "I don't want to talk about this in front of her, you know? She might decide to run also."

Riley might decide that. Not that Cassie thought it was any big deal. Anyone was allowed to run.

"Shouldn't talk about it in front of me, either," Emmett said. He flashed a smile, his bluish-green eyes crinkling. "I might decide to run."

"Go ahead, you're not competition," Farrah returned. "It's five girls and five boys, remember?"

"Miles is running," Cassie told him.

"Yeah, I know," Emmett said. "He told me." He gave her an odd look. "Is that why you're running?"

Crapola. Cassie didn't like the way his gaze probed hers. She couldn't have one of Miles' friends figuring out she liked him. "No. I just thought it would be fun."

"Who's Miles?" Farrah asked, her eyes switching back and forth between Cassie and Emmett.

"Just a friend we went to elementary school with." Cassie pasted on a smile and swiveled to face Farrah.

"Did you get the applications?" Farrah asked.

"Oh, yes." Cassie had almost forgotten. She pulled them out of her back pocket, all folded up and crinkled. "We have to turn these in by tomorrow."

"I'll get mine in as soon as school's out."

"Good idea." Cassie returned her blank application to her pocket. A spark of eagerness lit in her chest. With Farrah's help, she might have a good chance of making it.

The bell rang, and the three stood up just as Riley rejoined them.

"I'll call you tonight," Farrah said, motioning to Cassie. "Don't forget!"

"Don't forget what?" Riley asked, following Cassie out of the cafeteria.

"Nothing," Cassie said, feeling a flash of irritation. Why was Riley always following her? "She's going to help me run for StuCo."

"You're running for StuCo?" Riley squealed, excitement lighting her features.

Cassie bit down hard on her tongue. Why had she said that?

"Oh, I want to also!" Riley grabbed Cassie's arm and did a little jig. "We can run together!"

༄

Farrah called Cassie after her children's chorus practice. She had been less than thrilled when Cassie told her Riley was running now also, and Cassie braced herself. Farrah probably wanted to complain some more.

"Hi," Cassie said, balancing the phone on her shoulder and working on her math homework. She sat at the kitchen table, the rest of her family scattered throughout the house. Cassie was the only one still doing schoolwork. Choir always put her a little behind. She juggled the tiny phone with her chin and attempted to concentrate on the equations.

"Hey," Farrah said. "I've got bad news."

"What's up?" Cassie scowled and erased the number. Crapola, she'd gotten the answer wrong.

"I won't be able to come over tomorrow for our slumber party."

Cassie paused, pencil still in the air. Finally she put it down and gave the conversation all of her attention. "But elections are next week, Farrah. We were going to work on our campaign together."

"Don't you think that would be a bit weird, with Riley there too? Or were we going to help her with her campaign?"

Cassie gritted her teeth. "We all have a fair chance here, right?"

"We shouldn't get her hopes up. She'll just be more upset when she loses."

Cassie sighed. "That's fine. Don't worry about the slumber party. I'll just work on it by myself."

"We can still brainstorm tomorrow in school!" Farrah said, false cheer entering her voice. "And who knows, maybe you and Riley will come up with something awesome!"

"I don't want to hang out with Riley," Cassie snapped, more frustrated than she wanted to admit. She'd been counting on Farrah's popularity to help her ride the wave. "I'm going to cancel the sleepover. I'll get more done by myself."

"I totally understand," Farrah said, her tone all congenial. Not even remorseful, despite the fact this was her fault. "I'll see you tomorrow, okay?"

"Kay." Cassie snapped the phone shut and resisted the urge to snap her pencil in half. She knew better than to count on anyone besides herself.

On a random impulse, Cassie opened her phone up and called Andrea. She thought of all the times her best friend had listened to her vent, helped her through an emotional situation, just been there for her.

"Hello?" Andrea said.

Cassie straightened, pleased Andrea had at least answered the phone. "Hey."

"Hey."

The silence echoed between them, and Cassie hurriedly searched for words. "Want to come over tomorrow night?" she blurted. Instantly she winced. That's not what she'd meant to say.

"Oh. Um, that's really nice. But I have plans."

"Of course you do," Cassie said.

"What?"

"Nothing, nothing." Time for a subject change. "You're running for StuCo, aren't you?"

"Oh, yeah!" Andrea's voice brightened. "You're voting for me, right?"

"Definitely," Cassie replied without hesitation, her loyalty toward Andrea igniting against her will. She would always support her. "I'm running too, did you know?"

"You are?" Andrea made a noise in the back of her throat. "Wow, that's great, Cassie! Maybe we'll be on it together!"

Hope flared at the excitement in Andrea's voice. Maybe she really did want to spend time with her. "Yeah! What are you doing for your campaign?"

"Well." Now she hesitated. "I can't exactly tell you, can I? It's like, a campaign secret."

"Oh." Cassie's face flamed with embarrassment, and she was glad Andrea couldn't see her. "No, that's not what I meant. I wasn't trying to steal your ideas. I just thought . . ." She trailed off, not even sure what she'd thought.

"I better go," Andrea said. "Lots of work to do."

"Yeah, me too," Cassie said softly. "Bye." She hit the End button and stared morosely at her math homework. Her dislike for the subject was the only constant in her life right now.

May as well call Riley and let her know the slumber party was off. Her night wasn't going to get any better.

Chapter Seventeen

Competition

"Cassie." Farrah dropped into the chair beside Cassie in third hour on Friday and beamed at her. "I told you I wouldn't leave you hanging." She unrolled a large white poster board, displaying a hand-drawn caricature of a cute, petite brunette in glasses with the words "Vote for Cassandra Jones!" written underneath in big bubble letters.

Cassie's mouth dropped open. Her eyes roamed over the poster board, shocked. Never mind that the girl looked nothing like Cassie. "You did this for me?"

"I made one for myself, too." Farrah unrolled a second poster board, revealing a curvaceous, sexy blond with sparkling braces, also urging classmates to vote for her.

Cassie arched an eyebrow. "These are amazing."

"So." Obviously quite pleased with herself, Farrah leaned back on her chair and gave Cassie a smug smile. "Now just work on your fliers this weekend. We can put these up today. You're still on track." She rolled the poster back up and handed it to her.

"I don't even know what to say," Cassie sputtered, staring at the thick white paper.

Farrah jabbed her in the arm. "I told you I'd come through for you."

"You really did."

The two girls were late for lunch because they stopped in the seventh grade hallway to put their posters on the wall. Afterward, both girls stepped back to admire their handy work. Cassie couldn't help wishing she looked like the girl Farrah had drawn. She glanced down at herself and had to admit she wasn't chubby like she had been a few months ago, but she was far from curvy and pretty.

Kids don't put girls like you on StuCo, a nagging voice said in her head. *They put girls like Farrah and Andrea. Cara. Pretty, outgoing, popular.*

Popular. There was that word again, searing its way into Cassie's mind. A year ago, she hadn't given it much thought, but now that Andrea was leaving her behind, clearly joining the popular crowd, Cassie felt like an ugly duckling watching the swans fly by. And she had to admit, she'd do anything to be a swan right about now.

StuCo would be her ticket in. She just had to win this election.

Cassie walked into the locker hall from the east entrance after math and drew up short. There was Andrea, standing at her locker and laughing as she poked a boy in the arm. Amity and Cara stood around her, giggling with every word Andrea said. Andrea wore a pair of tight, dark jeans and a long frilly blouse. Cassie realized with a start that Andrea looked a lot skinnier than the last time Cassie had seen her. Maybe even skinnier than Cassie.

Andrea hadn't spotted Cassie. Cassie waited until Andrea faced her locker and Amity and Cara weren't looking, and then Cassie slipped up behind her. She stood a moment, expecting Andrea to turn around, to see her and say something, but Andrea was busy with her books, and then checking her phone. Cassie reached out and pulled back Andrea's wavy hair. She braided the ends of it, feeling like a timid stranger rather than the best friend who had stayed up countless nights watching movies and looking through yearbooks while they did each other's nails.

Andrea finally swiveled around, a smile on her face. The smile froze in place when she saw Cassie. "Oh, hi, Cassie."

"Hi," Cassie said, taking a step backward. Suddenly she wanted to flee. A hard lump formed in her throat, making it hard to swallow.

Amity and Cara were turning toward Andrea, their eyes already sweeping along the lockers. In a moment they would see Cassie. Cassie ducked her head and hurried past, not about to be the newest source of giggles and gossip.

☾☽

Cassie spent Friday night working on her fliers, finding the right digital image and messing with the words until she had what she thought was an appropriate slogan.

Vote for Cassandra Jones, the girl who gets the job done!

It sounded professional and promising. She could do it.

Cassie stood with Farrah outside of the school building Monday morning and handed out fliers. On the far side, she watched Andrea and Cara handing out their own pamphlets. She noted with a flash of alarm that their fliers had a piece of candy taped to them.

"We need candy," she told Farrah.

Riley looked at them with red eyes at lunch. "I didn't have time to turn in my application. So I'm not running."

Farrah made a sympathetic noise in the back of her throat. "That's too bad."

"I'm sorry," Cassie added.

But when Riley stood up to throw her trash away, Farrah sent Cassie a triumphant smile.

Tuesday Farrah showed up with several packages of gum. She and Cassie spent all of lunch hour taping the gum to a new flier that had both Farrah's and Cassie's names on it. Then they went around and stuck the fliers in every seventh grade locker.

Finally Friday, the election day, rolled around. Cassie couldn't even eat breakfast, her stomach was so tight. It rolled around on the bus ride to school, and Cassie worried she'd be sick.

"Are you ready?" Farrah asked, finding her at her locker before first period.

"I'm trying not to vomit," Cassie replied. She pressed a hand to her face, wondering if she had a fever.

"Good luck today, Cassie," Miles said, popping out of nowhere beside Farrah. "You know I'm voting for you."

Cassie straightened, her heart pounding just a little faster. "Me too. I mean, I'm voting for you too."

"And voting for yourself, right?"

She bobbed her head. "Yes. Of course."

"It's like flying a paper airplane." He moved his hand like a plane and winked at her. Then he gave a small wave, and Cassie stared after him as he went down the hall.

"Whoa," Farrah said, following Cassie's gaze. "You like

him."

Cassie didn't bother responding. Even if she didn't win, at least she knew Miles had voted for her.

All she heard all day were different kids talking about the election. Several wished her luck, and Cassie beamed at them, her confidence growing. She had friends, and many people knew her. As she changed books after second hour, she overheard two boys on the other side of her open locker talking about the candidates. She leaned closer, eavesdropping.

"Who are you voting for?" one boy asked.

"Farrah and Cara, of course. They're both hot."

"Yeah. Definitely voting for the hotties."

"Then I know who you're not voting for."

They both laughed, and Cassie drew back, her face flaming. They hadn't mentioned her name, but she couldn't help feeling she already knew which list she was on.

The ballots were handed out during third hour geography. Cassie drummed the eraser of her pencil on the desk, knowing the voting was coming and hardly able to listen to her teacher. A glance at Farrah showed her twirling a strand of blond hair around and around her finger, her eyes glazed over.

Finally, her teacher announced the election and handed out long strips of paper with all the student body candidate names on them. Cassie's eyes scanned the list, her heart in her throat. She breathed a soft sigh of relief when she saw her name. There was also Farrah, Andrea, and Cara, along with a dozen other names. She swept over the boys' names, but the only one she noticed was Miles'. None of the others really mattered. She checked off his name, then considered the other ones and chose those she recognized.

Back to the girls. Of course she voted for herself, and Farrah, and Andrea. She voted for Janice, a friend from Girls Club. One more girl. She didn't know the other girls, but she picked one anyway, not voting for Cara out of spite. She crossed her fingers and toes that soon she would be in StuCo with Andrea and Miles.

Seventh hour was almost over when the intercom buzzed.

"Students and teachers, we would like to announce the results of today's student body election."

The teacher stopped her demonstration on proper shading techniques, and all eyes focused on the intercom, as if watching it could make the words appear faster.

"We'll start with the seventh grade results," the nasalized voice said.

Cassie squeezed her fingers together under the desk, pinching the skin until it hurt. She held her breath. Jaclyn, the pretty olive-skinned girl who sat next to her, flashed a smile.

"Jeremy Grey, Michael Collins, Joey Wright, Miles Hansen, and Chris Tarren."

Miles had made it. She squeezed her fingers harder, heart thumping so violently in her chest she feared she'd have a heart attack.

"Congratulations to these boys."

On with it! Cassie screamed in her mind.

"For the girls, we have Cara Barnes, Farrah McKenna, Janice Seidelbacher, Rachel Smith, and Amanda John. Congratulations to these girls."

For several moments, the thudding of her heart in her ears was the only thing Cassie heard. Then slowly, the words filtered through, perforating her mind and coloring her mood like a can of blue dye. An awful, cold sinking feeling began in the top of her head and drifted down to her toes. She hadn't made it. Her fellow students hadn't voted for her.

Hot tears of disappointment blurred her vision, and she pulled her hair in front of her face and ducked her head, embarrassed to be sitting in class. Now everyone around her knew she'd tried and failed. It was worse than not trying.

In the back of her mind, a dark part of her realized with vicious satisfaction that Andrea hadn't made it, either.

Chapter Eighteen
Community Service

"Cassie."

Cassie turned around as Riley caught up with her after school. Cassie didn't really want to talk to her former best friend. She didn't want to talk to anyone, actually. Only moments before she'd found out she hadn't made the student body council. All she wanted to do was curl up in her bed and cry. Since that wasn't an option, she'd hoped to escape to her bus and hide in the back before anyone tried to talk to her.

Apparently she couldn't be so lucky. Waiting a heartbeat for Riley to catch up, Cassie continued toward the bus lot. Riley jogged slightly to keep pace.

"I'm sorry you didn't make StuCo," she said. "I voted for you, you know."

"Thanks," Cassie said flatly. It didn't matter that Riley had voted for her. The majority of her peers hadn't. Not only had she lost the election, but it was a huge blow to her ego. If only she were prettier. More popular. Skinnier.

"Do you want to come over tonight?" Riley asked as they

reached the buses parked by the soccer fields.

They got on the same bus with several other kids Cassie knew, including Cara Barnes and Janice Seidelbacher, two girls who had made StuCo. Cassie studiously avoided their eyes and went to the back. They would ride the same bus together to Walker Elementary. The elementary school operated like a bus station, and they would all get off and catch separate buses to their houses. If she could just hold it together until then, she could cry all by herself on her bus.

"Well?" Riley continued, plopping into the vinyl-clad seat next to Cassie.

"Well, what?" Cassie snapped, turning to glare out her window.

"Do you want to come over?"

Scowling, Cassie swiveled to face the other girl. Riley's wide greenish-gray eyes blinked, apparently unfazed by Cassie's bad mood. Cassie sighed, some of the anger going out of her. "Thanks, but no." She swallowed hard, hoping Riley wouldn't notice the moisture welling up in her eyes. Cassie adjusted her glasses and returned her attention to the window.

"If you change your mind, just call, okay?"

"Thanks," Cassie mumbled. She swiped at her eyes beneath her frames.

They rode in silence to the elementary school, and Cassie breathed a sigh of relief when the bus came to a stop. Without a second glance at Riley, she bolted from her seat and rushed for the door, clutching her binder of schoolwork to her chest. Her arms shook with the effort of holding in her emotions. She marched herself down the sidewalk to the correct bus and hurried on, keeping her head down as she rushed to the back.

Finally alone. Cassie collapsed into a seat and let out a long, slow breath. Readying herself for the onslaught of emotion, she replayed the election results in her head. Miles Hansen, the boy she'd had a crush on since the fifth grade, had been voted in as one of the five boy representatives. She'd been so happy for him, and she'd crossed her fingers that her name would be next, voting her in to represent the seventh grade girls. As each name was called, her heart dropped a little bit more. First Cara Barnes, a stunningly beautiful and stuck-up Barbie doll. Then Farrah McKenna, one of Cassie's new friends. Even Janice had made it, a larger but friendly girl from Cassie's Girls Club group.

Two other names had been called, girls Cassie didn't know. But not her name.

She let the bitter tears run free now, sliding down her face in a hot torrent of rage and disappointment. For a few days, she'd actually believed she had a chance. But no, she was still just frumpy Cassandra Jones, not anyone special, not good enough to rise above the other seventh graders and be on the student body council.

The worst part, the worst part of all, was that Miles would spend all year getting closer to girls like Cara.

She pulled her glasses off and dropped her head into her hands, letting her long dark hair fall over her face so she could sob in seclusion.

❧

Cassie's younger sisters, Emily and Annette, cast worried glances at her the whole walk home from the bus stop, though their little brother Scott, a third-grader, didn't notice at all. He stopped every few feet to gather up rocks and exclaim that he thought he found a crystal.

Mrs. Jones called Cassie to her room as soon as Cassie

walked through the front door. Cassie knew there was no hiding the fact that she'd been bawling; even Scott had commented when he finally looked up at her, saying her face and eyes were red and poofy.

She entered her parents' master bedroom, across the hall from the room she shared with Emily.

"Yes?" Cassie mumbled, not lifting her head.

"Honey, what happened?" her mother asked, and then her brow furrowed in understanding. "Oh, Cassie. You didn't make StuCo, did you?"

Cassie squinched up her nose, but it did nothing to stop the unwelcome tears that filled her eyes. Mrs. Jones came to her and wrapped her arms around her, and Cassie gave in, shoulders shaking as the tears made their escape.

The whole time, her mom made soothing noises and said consolatory phrases like, "You should've won, sweetheart" and "there's always next year." Each sentence sent another blade of bitterness into her heart. She would never try something like this again.

"Do you want to talk about it?" Mrs. Jones asked when Cassie pulled away.

Cassie shook her head. Her failure wounded her more than she cared to explain.

Her mom stroked the top of Cassie's hair. "Take some time to yourself. But don't mope too long, Cassie. You have the youth service trip tomorrow."

Cassie reared back. "What service trip?"

Mrs. Jones blinked, brown eyes exactly the same as Cassie's. She even wore glasses like Cassie. But her mom had short, curly hair, while Cassie wore hers long and straight. And boring. With a flash of impatience, she knew she had to change her appearance.

"Your youth group has been planning this service trip to Dallas for a month. You should already know all about it."

Dimly, Cassie remembered some talk about the upcoming trip. She hadn't realized it was now, though. The stupid StuCo election had taken up all of her time. "What time tomorrow?"

"You meet up with everyone at the church at five in the morning."

"Five!" Cassie groaned. No way. Not on her Saturday.

"Yes. All the kids from Fayetteville and Springdale will be there. You guys are taking a charter bus to Dallas, and it's a seven-hour drive. If you don't leave that early, you won't get there till late."

"Do I have to go?" Cassie said, turning whiny. She didn't even really like the kids at church. None of them were her friends. Now if the kids from Rogers were also going, it would be different. She had friends in that group.

Her mom's expression went from sympathetic to disapproving. "Of course you do. Honestly, I expect more of you. I'm surprised you'd be more concerned with nursing your injured ego than helping people in need. Besides, it's Texas. You love Texas."

She did love Texas, and a part of her still missed the state and the friends she'd left behind when they moved to Arkansas two years earlier. But she wasn't delusional enough to think going on a service trip to Dallas meant she'd get to see her old friends. Cassie turned away, knowing she'd go out of a sense of obligation if nothing else, and that angered her. "I'm just going to bed, then."

"Eat some dinner, at least," her mom called after her as

Cassie crossed the hallway to her room.

"Not hungry," Cassie called back.

Chapter Nineteen

Doing Time

Cassie stood outside the church building in the dark morning hours before the sun rose, bracing herself against her mom's van and holding her light jacket close around her. Late September in Arkansas still meant warm sunshine and air conditioning during the day, but at night it cooled off. She wore jeans, tennis shoes, and a t-shirt, clothes that she didn't mind getting dirty. Those had been the instructions.

Brother Abrams, the youth leader from the Fayetteville group, called out names from a clipboard and herded the youth onto the big bus. Cassie didn't know him personally. He seemed nice enough, but between the pre-dawn wake up and yesterday's crushing blow, she was in no mood to be charitable.

"Cassandra Jones?" he shouted, and her dad poked her. Not even her mom had gotten up for this.

"I heard," Cassie snipped. She grabbed her purse from the front seat of the car and threw it over her shoulder.

"Have a nice time," her dad called. "Text any time!"

She considered not replying, but couldn't bring herself to be that rude. "Bye," she answered.

He waved at her, and she climbed onto the bus. A quick search revealed familiar faces, but none she considered friends. With a sigh, Cassie plopped down beside a girl with short brown hair. At least she wouldn't be expected to make conversation. She leaned into the headrest, closed her eyes, and went to sleep.

She woke a few hours later to a rumbling stomach. A glance at her phone showed it was only seven-twenty in the morning. "Oh, man!" she groaned out loud. "We're not even halfway there!"

"I know," the girl next to her said. "It's such a long drive."

Cassie rolled her head toward the girl, appraising her for the first time. She had a plump face and friendly brown eyes. She held out a granola bar.

"Want one?" she asked. "I brought a whole box."

Cassie considered it a moment before accepting. Granola bars had to be healthy, since they were made with oatmeal and dried fruit. "Thanks."

"I'm Crystal," the girl said. "I live in Fayetteville."

"Cassandra." Cassie unwrapped her bar and spoke around a mouthful of food. "I'm in Springdale."

"How old are you?"

"Twelve," Cassie answered.

"That's why I've never seen you before. I'm thirteen."

Cassie nodded. Twelve was the age that children were allowed to join the youth group. This was her first service excursion, but she knew the church group went on at least one a year.

Talking to Crystal helped the drive go by, and when the

conversation lulled, Cassie pulled a book out of her purse and lost herself in the fantasy world. Her spirits lifted, and she found herself looking forward to getting out and doing manual labor for someone else.

The bus pulled into a school parking lot in a quiet suburban neighborhood a little after noon. Brother Abrams handed out bagged lunches as they got off the bus and explained the assignment while everyone ate, sitting in a mass of kids on the concrete pad.

"Last month the rain left many sections of Texas flooded and under water," he said. "While they weren't hit as badly here as in other parts of the state, many houses had standing water in them for days. What we're going to do is go into these houses and shovel out mud, pull off molding, and help tear out drywall."

Cassie glanced down at her thick-soled shoes and baggy jeans, appreciating the clothing instructions now. She finished half of her sandwich and put the other half back in the bag, then took a big swig of water to stave off any remaining hunger.

"Find a partner. I'll assign teams of six people to a house, so make sure your partner is someone you work well with."

Cassie turned to Crystal, glad she'd made a friend on this trip. "Want to be partners?"

"Sure," Crystal said.

Each team had at least two boys on it to help with the heavy lifting, and Cassie felt a pleasurable tug in her chest when she and Crystal were assigned to Tyler and Jason Reeves' team. Jason, the older brother, had always been kind to her. Tyler was her age, and even though he was always arrogant and snotty to her, something about his blue eyes melted her into a puddle of wordless mush whenever he looked at her.

Luckily she wouldn't have to talk. All she and Crystal had to do was work.

None of the homeowners were living in their houses, but they were around to help supervise. A heavyset man with a thick Texas accent put Crystal and Cassie to work in the kitchen, mucking out the mud and pulling up broken pieces of tile.

"How awful," Cassie said, digging her fingers into a crack in the floor and pulling up the loose ceramic. She tossed it into the trash bin next to them. "I wonder how much they lost."

"My mom keeps all kinds of things on the floor," Crystal said. "Piles of books, photos, clothes. All of it would be ruined."

"Not too mention things like the couches, the beds, the carpet."

They worked in a companionable silence, imagining how much these people must have lost. Realizing how fortunate she was, Cassie ignored the uncomfortable heat in the house and the way the mud hardened to her face after she accidentally brushed her hair back.

The man stepped into the kitchen and handed them each of glass of water. "When you finish with the tile in the kitchen, you can work in the hall bathroom. The wallpaper is peeling on the bottom. There are scrapers to help you get it off."

"Sure," Crystal said, and Cassie nodded.

"Let's take the trash bin with us," Cassie said when they finished. She stood up to push it and paused when something twinged painfully in her abdomen. She waited a moment, expecting it to go away, but it didn't. It did lessen, however, so she stepped up to the bin and pushed it into the hall. She heard the other two groups in the house chatting as they worked, and she and Crystal stepped into the bathroom.

The linoleum had already been ripped up, revealing the particle board subfloor. Grabbing one of the metal scrapers, Cassie sat herself down in front of a wall and poised the metal edge at the seam in the wallpaper.

The twinge came in her abdomen again, a sharp twisting that magnified until it diminished into a dull throbbing. Cassie didn't move. She hesitated, waiting to see if the pain would intensify again. When it didn't, she shoved the scraper under the wallpaper and began to pry it off. But the whole time, her mind remained aware of the ache below her belly button. No, not quite below her belly button. It was in her right side, just to the inside of her hip bone. The sensation remained tolerable, however, and she worked on ripping off sheets of paper instead of thinking about how her body felt.

She was able to almost ignore the feeling until she stood up, and then a stabbing pain pulsed through her side. Cassie doubled over, dropping the scraper as her fingers ran along her skin, searching for the source of the pain.

"What's wrong?" Crystal asked.

"Something hurts," Cassie managed to reply. But that was all she got out. She pressed her fingers against her flesh, pushing where it hurt. She felt nothing. Whatever it was wasn't on the surface of her body. It was inside.

Even as she thought it, the wave of agony subsided. Cassie straightened up, breathing a little heavier but otherwise okay.

"Do you need something?" Crystal asked, her brown eyes wide.

Cassie shook her head. "I'm fine now. It was just a cramp."

"Are you sure?"

Cassie thought of Jason and Tyler in the other room, and her face flushed. No way would she admit to them that she had some weird girly pain. "Yeah. I'm great now." Which wasn't entirely true; though nearly gone, her insides still ached like someone was twisting them into a rope. She gathered the cleaning supplies in her arms and walked into the living room. Each step brought a small stab to her side, but she could minimize it with ginger movements. She put the cleaning supplies on the table and took her time organizing them, letting Crystal drag the trash bin out to the curb.

"Time to head back to the bus," Jason said, gathering the teams into the front room.

"Thank you so much for your help," the owner said, shaking each of their hands. "It really helps get us back on track."

"You're welcome," Jason said with a smile.

Cassie tried to add her own smile when the man shook her hand, but the warm glow of helping paled next to the worsening ache in her abdomen. She gritted her teeth and fell into step with the other kids. She didn't contribute to the conversation, afraid that if she did, her voice would give away how much pain she was in.

Brother Abrams greeted them all cheerfully in the parking lot. Cassie leaned against Crystal, feigning sleepiness while Brother Abrams called roll, making sure they had all returned.

"We did good service today," he said, consulting his clipboard again. "Cleaned out twenty-three houses, hauled off three truckloads of garbage . . ."

Cassie closed her eyes, disinterested in the statistical outcome of their day. All she wanted was to get on the bus and sit down.

Finally, he ushered everyone back on. "We'll stop for dinner in two hours. Good work, kids!"

Cassie pulled out her phone and checked the time as she settled into the seat next to Crystal. Just after four p.m. Seven more hours until they got home. Crystal chattered for a little bit, but Cassie's lack of responses eventually killed the conversation. Cassie retrieved her book from her purse, hoping to lose herself so fully in the made-up world that she didn't notice the throbbing in her side.

The bus gained momentum as it started up the twisting pretzel of on-ramps to the interstate. The cramping in her side increased as well, much like how Cassie imagined it would feel to have a screwdriver bearing into her skin. She drew in a breath and bit down on her lower lip, trying hard to conceal her pain.

"Are you okay?" Crystal asked again, swiveling her head to look at Cassie.

A tear snaked its way down Cassie's face. She sniffled and tried to hold the others in, but another crept after it. "It hurt," she said, her voice wobbly.

"What hurts?" Crystal asked, her voice loud with alarm. Some of the kids around them turned their faces in their direction.

Cassie wished she could sink farther into the chair. She hated all the curious eyes on her. "My side hurts." She pressed hard on the spot next to her hip bone. The pressure helped, momentarily relieving the pain.

"I'll get Brother Abrams." Crystal crawled over Cassie and hurried to the front of the bus. Cassie lowered her gaze, pretending like she didn't notice everyone staring at her.

Chapter Twenty
Doctor Visit

"Cassie?" Brother Abrams came to her seat, his expression a mask of concern. "What's wrong, hon?"

"I don't really know," she admitted, wishing the listening ears would disappear. "It just started to hurt."

"What did?"

"My side." She touched the spot on her abdomen.

"When did it start hurting?"

"I don't know. I noticed it a few hours ago."

He looked at Crystal. 'Thanks for watching out for her. Cassie, come on up front with me."

Cassie stood, shouldering her purse and keeping her eyes on the aisle beneath her feet. Brother Abrams put a hand on her shoulder, holding her steady as they marched to the seat in the front. He conferred with another leader, then sat down next to her.

"You tell me when the pain gets bad, okay? For now I just want you to sit up here with me."

"Okay," she mumbled. She averted her eyes, certain he must

think her immature or dramatic.

"You live in Springdale?"

She nodded.

"How old are you? Is this your first service project?"

It looked like she wouldn't be able to avoid a conversation with him. "Yes. I'm twelve."

He smiled, kind lines crinkling the corners of his light brown eyes. "I have a daughter just a year younger than you. Next year she'll be able to join us on our service project. Won't that be nice?"

"Yes," Cassie said, because she wasn't sure what else to say. She sucked in a breath as another wave of pain hit her.

"Do you want to squeeze my hand?" Brother Abrams asked.

Cassie hesitated, and then the pain hit again, and she nodded. He offered his hand and she gave it a tight squeeze. She squeezed her eyes shut against the tears.

"I'm sorry," Brother Abrams said. "It looks like it hurts."

The pain subsided, and she opened her eyes, blinking them to clear them. "It's okay now."

"What can I do to help you?"

Cassie leaned her head against the back of the seat and sighed. Exhaustion weighed heavy on her eyelids, and her skull pounded like ping-pong balls were bouncing off of it. "Maybe it's okay now." How stupid she must look. She imagined all the other kids on the bus whispering about her, pointing at her and giggling at how childish she was. Great.

At that moment, the stabbing pain started up in her side again. Cassie gasped and then bit her lip. She pressed the palm of her hand against the pain, tears leaking from her squinted eyes. "Ow! It really hurts."

"I know, hon." Brother Abrams squeezed her shoulder, then

leaned over and conferred with the other youth leader. Clearing his throat, he settled back next to Cassie. "Cassie, because we don't know what's wrong and we're afraid it could be serious, we're going to stop at a local hospital."

"Okay," Cassie whispered. Her body flushed warm with embarrassment at the thought of going to the hospital. Anyone who didn't already know about her condition would figure it out soon. She'd be the center of attention, like it or not.

Jason and Tyler were sure to notice.

"We need to contact your parents. Do you have a phone?"

"Yes." Cassie reached into her purse and pulled it out. Her hand trembled as she pushed the button for home.

"Hi, sweetie, how are you?" her mom answered.

"Mom," Cassie said, and she started to cry.

"What's wrong? What is it?" Mrs. Jones' voice rose in alarm.

"May I?" Brother Abrams asked, holding his hand out for the phone. With a nod, Cassie handed it over.

"Hi, Sister Jones, this is Brother Abrams. I'm the youth leader on this trip. Yes, hi. Well, we don't know, exactly. She's got a sharp pain in her side. We're worried it might be appendicitis, so we're going to stop at a nearby hospital."

Appendicitis! Last summer Cassie spent a week in the hospital from a snake bite. She remembered one of the other patients there, a young girl who'd had her appendix removed. The girl had hobbled around the common room area with a pinched, pained look on her face. Cassie's anxiety doubled. She sure hoped that wasn't what she had.

Brother Abrams handed the phone back. Cassie cleared her throat. "Mom?"

"It's okay, sweetheart. You call me whenever you can. It's all going to be okay."

Cassie clenched her hand, wishing her mom was with her. "Yes."

Her mom said a few more words, then they hung up. Another wave of pain hit her, and she choked back a moan.

"Try to breathe through it," Brother Abrams encouraged. "That's what my wife did when she was having babies." He gave her a brave smile, but Cassie could see the concern on his face.

She followed his advice, taking slow, deep breaths. Her head cleared, if nothing else, and she could focus a bit better.

She flipped her phone open and stared at it, wanting more than ever the support of her best friend. Her chest ached. She pressed the button for Andrea's number, her eyes already filling with tears.

"Hello?" Andrea said, surprising her by answering.

"Andrea," Cassie gasped out. "Something's wrong with me. I'm going to the hospital."

"Really? Oh no!" Concern and interest piqued in Andrea's voice. "Where are you? What happened?"

"I'm in Texas. I don't really know what happened. I just started feeling this pain. So I'm going to the hospital."

Andrea made sympathetic noises on the phone. "I hope you're okay! Call me and let me know!"

"I will," Cassie said, some of her fear easing. At least Andrea still cared.

It was less than half an hour later, but seemed like forever before they pulled into the ER. The other youth leader passed out the sack dinners and Brother Abrams lifted Cassie up, carrying her down the bus steps. She wanted to protest, to tell him she could walk herself, but she knew putting her feet on the ground would only exacerbate the pain.

Nobody waited in the emergency room. The attendants placed Cassie in a wheelchair and quickly moved her through the door leading to the hospital rooms. Brother Abrams and the other adult leader stayed at the check-in window, filling out paperwork and talking on the phone with Cassie's mom. Then someone closed the door, and Cassie couldn't see them anymore.

"Can you stand?" a man with a scruffy beard and a clipboard asked her. "We need to weigh you."

Weigh her? Why was that necessary? Even in her agonized state, the thought of someone seeing her weight brought a rush of warmth to her face. "I can try to stand."

The man stood her on a scale, and Cassie tried not to look as he toggled the weights around. "All done," he said, and she couldn't help lifting her eyes.

A hundred and six. She felt a flush of victory, pleased that she'd dropped ten pounds since last summer started. He helped her sit down in a chair and took her blood pressure.

"I'm going to draw some blood," a woman in polka-dotted scrubs said, right before she poked Cassie.

"Oh!" Cassie exclaimed, trying not to jump.

"We've got to check your white blood count," the woman said by way of conversation. She filled a vial and started on another. "If your appendix ruptured, the numbers will be high."

Cassie stared at the second vial filling with her crimson blood, spots dancing before her eyes. She started to slump over, and the woman grabbed her shoulder.

"Don't watch if you have a weak stomach."

Crapola. Now on top of it all, she had a weak stomach. She closed her eyes.

"Cassie."

She opened her eyes at her name. Brother Abrams came in, his forehead wrinkled. She smiled, and some of the creases disappeared as he smiled back.

"I talked to your mom and dad, and they know you're here. As soon as we know something, we'll let them know."

"Thanks," she said, then sucked in a breath as another wave of pain hit her.

"Can you get on this bed, Cassie?" the woman asked.

Cassie focused now on the bed in the room, just a thin mattress on a metal frame. It didn't look as nice as the one she'd slept in last year when she got a snake bite. A hospital gown lay folded in a neat pile next to the pillow. "I think so." Cassie only whimpered a little, putting most of her weight on the woman as she moved from the chair to the bed. The throbbing in her abdomen increased when she lay flat, however, and she curled into a ball.

"I need to ask you a few questions," the woman said, getting in Cassie's face. "On a scale of one to ten, how bad is the pain?"

How was she supposed to know that? It felt bad now, but it could get worse, and then she wouldn't think this was so bad. "A five?"

"When did it start?"

"After lunch."

"Has this ever happened before?"

"No." The pain subsided a bit, and she straightened up.

"Do you have any pain in your shoulder?"

Cassie furrowed her brow. What an odd thing to ask. "No."

"We need to rule out an ectopic pregnancy. Is there any chance you could be pregnant?"

Chapter Twenty-One

Safe and Sound

Cassie nearly choked. She couldn't even look at Brother Abrams, knowing her face must be flaming scarlet. Pregnant! "No." *Absolutely not. No way. Not possible.* But she kept her lips shut, letting her "no" suffice.

Brother Abrams looked at her and winked, giving her shoulder a squeeze.

"We're going to do an ultrasound, okay?"

Cassie blinked at her, not quite sure what that was.

"Why?" Brother Abrams asked. "She said she can't be pregnant."

The woman gave him a look. "That's not the only thing we'll check for."

"Oh," he said, apparently mollified. "Okay."

Cassie glanced at him for reassurance, but he didn't seem too alarmed. She tried not to be too nervous as the woman wheeled her bed out of the room and down the hall.

"Brother Abrams?" Cassie called.

"I'm right here."

The next room was darker with a small television screen hanging from the ceiling. The polka-dotted lady handed the clipboard to a girl with a long brown braid hanging over one side of her shoulder.

"Hi," the girl said. "I'm gonna do your ultrasound, okay?" She pulled out a device that looked like a microphone. "Have you ever had one of these before?"

"No." Cassie hoped it wouldn't hurt.

"This will be easy peasy." The girl stood beside Cassie's bed. "I'm gonna smear this goop on your tummy. Can you unbutton your jeans? Just a bit. Good job." She squirted a warm gel on Cassie's belly and then pressed the head of the microphone device into Cassie's skin.

"Ow!" Cassie cried out as the wand ran over her side. She was distracted from the pain, however, when a black and white image appeared on the television screen overhead. "What is that?" she asked, suddenly fascinated. When the device moved over her belly, the image on the screen changed. She knew that somehow what she saw was connected to the wand on her stomach, but she couldn't identify anything she saw.

"Well, these are your internal organs," the girl said. "This black blob is your bladder."

Again the embarrassment crept up her face, hot and sweaty. "Oh."

"And these are your ovaries."

She pointed out a swirly blob, but it didn't look like how Cassie imagined an ovary looked. She redefined her mental idea of her internal organs. Weird.

"Do you see anything significant?" Brother Abrams asked.

"I can't say," the girl said with a bright smile. "But a

radiologist will interpret the ultrasound and let you know what he finds."

"Wait," Cassie said. "So you don't know what you're looking at?"

"No, I know," the girl said, a bit hesitant now. "I just can't say."

That didn't make any sense. The girl knew what she was seeing, but someone else had to tell Cassie?

"That's just the way hospitals work, Cassie," Brother Abrams said with a short chuckle. Somehow, it didn't seem like he actually thought it was funny.

☙

"Cassie?" The same woman in the polka-dotted scrubs opened the door to Cassie's room and pushed her way in.

Finally, Cassie thought, glancing at the clock. She'd been wheeled back to this room after the ultrasound. Though she and Brother Abrams had only been in here for about fifteen minutes, the total hospital visit so far neared an hour and a half. They still had six hours to get home. She could only image how frustrated everyone back on the bus was.

"Yes?" Cassie said, trying to sound polite and not impatient.

"We have all your results back. Your white blood count was normal, so we were able to rule out appendicitis. However, your ultrasound revealed extra fluid around your right ovary, which may indicate that a cyst recently burst. We're going to give you some pain medication. Otherwise, there's not much you can do for it. But some people seem to be prone to cysts, so if you ever feel this pain again, that might be what it is."

"Okay," Cassie said weakly. She didn't really know what a cyst was, but it didn't sound like a very big deal. Now she felt even more foolish. Would everyone think she was nothing but

174

a big baby?

"We're releasing you now." The woman picked up the unused hospital gown on the bed and placed it in a plastic bag. "You never put this on, but it's yours, so go ahead and take it home."

Cassie accepted the plastic bag, belatedly wondering what on earth she was going to do with a hospital gown.

It turned out that she didn't need to worry about her long stay at all. When she made her way gingerly up the bus steps and sat down, everyone cheered for her, including the girls from church that Cassie didn't really get along with. She fielded their questions the best she could, but then the pain meds kicked in. Her eyes slid shut almost mid-sentence. When she opened them again, she was in her room, her mom leaning over her.

"It's all over now, Cassie," her mom whispered, smoothing back her hair. "Just sleep."

Cassie did, all her other worries vanishing behind the medically induced peace.

⁖

Mrs. Jones asked Cassie if she wanted to stay home from church on Sunday, but Cassie felt almost normal now. She worried everyone would only think she was a bigger baby if she skipped church, too.

"No, I'm fine. I'll bring my pain meds in case I need them."

That appeased her mom, but Cassie didn't need them. She wasn't in any pain. It was as if nothing had happened. The kids greeted her kindly, asking how she was. Even Tyler was nice.

But what Cassie couldn't wait to do was get home and call Andrea. Somehow this incident had opened a connection between them, and Cassie knew she had to take advantage of it.

Andrea was laughing when she answered the phone. "Shut up! No, really? I can't believe it!"

Cassie knew from the distant quality of Andrea's voice that she wasn't speaking into the phone. Her voice became clearer, still giggling. "Hey, finally! I've been waiting for you to call! When are you coming over?"

Elation flooded Cassie like a drink of hot chocolate, pulling a smile from places she didn't know could smile. Andrea was waiting for her! Andrea wanted her to come over!

"Oh, I didn't know I was supposed to," Cassie said, hoping she didn't sound too breathy.

"Wait." Andrea said. "Oh. You're not Amity. Hi, Cassie."

Instantly the warmth in Cassie's body vanished, replaced with a shocking chill. "No," she said as the implications became clear. "It's me."

"Hi," Andrea said, but now she sounded distracted again. "No, stop," she giggled at someone off phone. "It's just Cassie."

Cassie cleared her throat, hoping to direct Andrea's attention back to her. "You told me to call when I got out of the hospital."

"Hospital? Oh yeah, I forgot you were in it! Are you okay?"

Cassie swallowed hard against a painful swelling in her throat. Andrea hadn't cared. She hadn't even remembered. "I'm fine," she mumbled. "It turned out to be nothing serious."

Andrea laughed loudly, and then said, "I'm so glad. Hey, can I call you later? I'm in the middle of something here."

"Sure," Cassie said, and hung up before Andrea could.

She knew better than to expect a phone call.

Chapter Twenty-Two

On the Outside

"So Halloween's coming up."

Cassandra looked up in third hour at Farrah but didn't respond to the statement.

Not that Farrah needed a response. She tossed back her layered blond hair, exposing the unique scar on her chin, and said, "What are you going to be?"

"I don't know," Cassie said. "I haven't thought about it at all, actually." Halloween should be easy for someone like Farrah: skinny, pretty, and popular. She could pull off the princesses and witches and fairies. Not Cassie. "You?"

"I'm going to be a fairy," Farrah said, twiddling her pencil between her fingers. She paused a moment, waiting for their geography teacher to turn back to the white board. "You should be one with me. I've already got the fairy wings and the glitter. Lots and lots of glitter." Farrah smiled, her scar crinkling. "And you should see my costume. It's like a glittery swimsuit."

That definitely ruled out being a fairy. No way was Cassie

ever parading around in a swimsuit-like costume. She might have lost weight, but she was no pixie. "I'll think of something."

Farrah pursed her lips out in a pout. "Come on, you don't want to be a fairy?"

The teacher turned around, sparing Cassie the need to defend herself. She'd been in a bad mood for the past week—past month, actually—and she needed a costume that would reflect her current mental state of being. She raked her mind through the rest of class, trying to think of what she could be.

Suddenly it came to her. She still had that unused hospital gown from the service weekend. She could use makeup to create a gruesome injury, and the hospital gown would be the final touch.

Farrah didn't miss a beat. As soon as class let out and they entered the hallway, she said, "I have an extra swimsuit you can use. The wings are easy to find online. You can come over, and we'll put the costumes together so we match."

"I have a costume," Cassie said, stopping Farrah before she got going too much. "I forgot."

"Oh." Farrah looked disappointed. "What are you going to be?"

"A zombie." Cassie hadn't known for sure until the words blurted out of her, but now she grinned. A zombie was perfect.

⋘⋙

The days leading up to Halloween, Cassie tried to be excited about her costume. Mrs. Jones had eagerly agreed to do the makeup, and a few quick internet searches revealed a few truly gruesome effects. But as grateful as she was for her friendships with Farrah and Emmett and Riley, what she really wanted to do was find an excuse to talk to Andrea again. Last year she and Andrea had been best friends, but this year they hardly spoke. Cassie didn't dare call, not after the last disastrous phone call.

The opportunity came by an unexpected means on Thursday. Cassie had an early rehearsal with her children's chorus at the community center. Cassie waited just inside the school doors by the choir room for her mom to pick her up. She'd specifically asked her mom to come to this entrance, where she knew there wouldn't be other students.

"Cassie?" a male voice said.

Cassie spun around, so lost in her thoughts she hadn't heard anyone approach. "Miles," she said, unable to keep the surprise from her voice when she saw Miles Hansen. Immediately her heart started doing a tap-dance, in spite of her attempts to tell it she was over him. After all, they hadn't talked since she didn't make StuCo a few weeks ago. Whatever friendship—or more—she had thought there was between them, it had obviously fizzled out the moment her fellow students voted her un-cool.

He gave her a smile, his brown eyes crinkling behind the wire frames. He didn't appear to know they weren't friends anymore. "What are you doing here?" He glanced around the empty entrance. "Why are you alone?"

She couldn't admit to him that she avoided the main entrance because she didn't want to watch Andrea play with her new friends. "I'm waiting for my mom to pick me up. I have a music thing."

He nodded. "That's great. You're such a good singer."

"Thanks," she said, and the heat rushed to her face against her will. In an effort to draw the attention off herself, she said,

"What are you doing here?"

"I'm on my way to a StuCo meeting. We have to plan the Halloween dance."

"Halloween dance," Cassie stuttered. She'd known about the dance, of course, but considered it lame compared to trick-or-treating and had no intentions of going. Until now. Suddenly all she could think of was standing next to Miles at the aforementioned dance, holding his hands while he spun her in a circle across the gym floor. She shook the fantasy off, reminding herself she'd be in a zombie costume. Yikes. "Fun."

"Yeah, it kind of is. Want to come in with me for a bit while you wait for your mom?"

Absolutely, she did. "But I'm not in StuCo."

"That's okay, no one will care if you're there for a little."

Who was she to resist? "Okay." She followed him willingly through a hallway and into the gym. Three tables had been set up, and StuCo members from each grade gathered around them. But Cassie's interest in what they were doing dissipated when her eyes landed on Cara Barnes, best-friend-stealer and nemesis. Cara giggled hopelessly as she attempted to cut something out, while beside her, cracking jokes, stood Andrea.

Cassie froze, torn between wanting to interrupt them and wanting to turn and flee.

Miles made up her mind for her. "Look, Andrea's here. She's your best friend, isn't she?"

How was it that the rest of the school had realized weeks ago their friendship was dying, but Miles hadn't noticed?

"Yes," Cassie croaked out of a suddenly dry mouth. "But I'm not friends with Cara."

"Oh, she's really nice. Just go say hi."

What choice did she have? Cassie stepped forward, placing

a huge smile on her face as she came to a stop in front of Cara and Andrea.

"Hi, Andrea!" she said. "And, Cara."

Both girls looked up and blinked at her in obvious surprise.

"Hi," Cara said. She looked a little confused, as if she wasn't quite sure who Cassie was. Which irritated Cassie, because they had, after all, gone to the same elementary school for two years.

"I'm Cassandra," she supplied, helping her out. "I'm Andrea's best friend."

Cara turned to look at Andrea, the confusion not leaving her face.

"What are you doing here?" Andrea asked, her brows pinching together. "You're not in StuCo."

"Neither are you." The words slipped off Cassie's tongue accusingly, and she winced.

"I'm with Cara." Andrea cocked her head toward the other girl and lifted her chin.

"I—Miles invited me." Cassie glanced over her shoulder at him, but he was already talking with some other guys.

"Miles?" Andrea gave Cassie a questioning look. "Is he your —?"

"No," Cassie blurted, not wanting Andrea to get the wrong idea about them.

"Why not?" Andrea said.

"What's going on?" Cara asked, looking back and forth between the two of them.

Andrea waved a hand breezily. "Cassie's had a crush on Miles for years. But she's too embarrassed to tell him."

"Oh, you should tell him," Cara said. She wore her blond hair in a clip, but a few pieces fell around her face, framing her large brown eyes. "He's so nice."

Cassie looked down, wishing Andrea didn't know so much about her. She had never considered that the private things she shared with her closest friend could be used against her. "I better go. My mom's probably waiting for me."

Andrea didn't hear her. She'd gone back to whispering in Cara's ear, and Cara's shoulders trembled as she bit her lower lip. At least both of them were staring at somebody besides her.

Gripping her bag tightly, Cassie didn't bother saying bye to Miles as she found an exit and left the gym. She made it all the way to the outside walkway before she broke into tears.

⚬⚭⚬

Normally singing had a way of cheering Cassie up, of distracting her from whatever plagued her mind. Not today. All through the practice with Mrs. Vanderwood and the other singers, Cassie replayed the dreaded conversation between her and Andrea again. How could Andrea treat her that way? Last year they'd been the best of friends. Andrea had even broken up with her boyfriend when he spread rumors about Cassie. She'd stood up for Cassie when the new girl treated her badly.

And now Andrea acted like they barely knew each other, unless she was divulging secret information.

Every time Cassie thought this she got teary-eyed, so she tried not to let Miles slip into her thoughts.

"Cassie."

Cassie stared at the chalkboard with the musical staff drawn on it. Her head felt stuffed with cotton, her eyes itchy.

"Cassie."

Giggles and whispers around her finally drew Cassie's

attention to the piano, where Ms. Vanderwood frowned at her.

"Oh," Cassie said, and titters erupted around the choir room. "Yes?"

Ms. Vanderwood sighed and tossed her curly red hair impatiently. "I'm moving you to second soprano. Please go stand next to Dani."

"What?" Cassie's gaze narrowed as she fully focused on her teacher. Was this a punishment because she hadn't been paying attention?

Behind her, RyAnn Spencer, a beautiful seventh grader with a hooked nose and long wavy black hair, snickered. "You're singing off-key. Move to the seconds."

Others laughed behind her, and Cassie's face burned. She climbed down the bleachers and moved to the left, fuming with indignation. She wasn't singing off-key. Ms. King, her elementary school music teacher, said she had a very high range for her age. This wasn't fair. She blinked rapidly, working hard not to cry. Ms. Vanderwood led them in song again, but this time Cassie only mouthed the words, not finding the heart to sing along.

Chapter Twenty-Three

Separation

Cassie climbed into the van after practice and let her siblings' conversation cover her silence. At dinner, she picked at her food, which wasn't so unusual, but apparently even her mom could tell she was a little mopier than usual.

"Was choir practice all right, Cassie?" Mrs. Jones asked, her eyes on Cassie's fork as it deftly shifted the rice kernels around the edges of her plate.

Cassie lifted one shoulder in a shrug.

"Something happen at school?" Her mom tried again.

"No, it's a boy," Scott said, making an obnoxious kissing noise and crossing his eyes.

"It is not," Cassie snapped, lifting her head to glare at him. Eight-year-old brothers were so irritating. There was too much truth in his words for comfort. It did involve a boy, though Miles' part in the event had been rather innocent. She trembled, afraid of what Andrea might have said to him after Cassie left. Would he ever talk to her again?

Mrs. Jones cleared her throat, and Cassie glanced up in time to catch her mother shooting a significant look at her father. He didn't seem to get it, though, just frowned at her mom and resumed eating.

From the couch where Cassie had dumped her backpack, her cell phone began to ring. Cassie twisted in her chair and looked at it. Her heart began to pound as if it knew something about this call that she didn't.

"Do you need to get that, Cassie?" Mrs. Jones asked.

Cassie spun around, hoping her eyes revealed the desperation she felt. "Yes."

"Go ahead."

Scooting her chair back so fast it nearly tipped over, Cassie dashed into the living room. She fished her phone out of her backpack. The blood ran cold in her veins when she saw the name: Andrea.

It had been weeks since Andrea called her. Maybe even a month. Coming right on the heels of their strained conversation at school, the call had to be important. Cassie rushed to her bedroom, flipping the phone open to answer as she went.

"Hello?" she said into the speaker as she closed the bedroom door. Her bed beckoned to her, and she moved to it, but she couldn't lay down upon it. She was too tense.

"Cassie?" Andrea said.

Who else would it be? "Yes. It's me."

"Oh. Hi."

Silence reigned in the wake of that profound sentence, and Cassie wondered if she was supposed to be the one to break it. Before she could, Andrea spoke.

"Cassie, I wanted to talk to you about something you said in the gym."

Cassie's stomach knotted up, and she thought she would puke. "What did I say?"

"You said I'm your best friend."

Her heart plummeted. Why would that be something to talk about? She squeezed her eyes shut. "Yes?"

Another pause, and then Andrea said, "I don't think we're really best friends anymore, Cassie."

"We're not?" Cassie squeaked out. Somewhere, she had known that already. But a part of her had hoped that maybe, on some level, they still were. "But why?" Her voice cracked, giving away the depth of emotion she felt. She could do nothing to stop it. She rubbed her chest with the palm of her hand to try to ease the ache. Her eyes burned, and the room shimmered before her.

"Well." Andrea sighed. "Well, I think we just changed. We're hanging out with other people, doing other things."

The knots in her stomach hardened into a rock. Other people like Kitty and Amity and Cara. She blinked, and the hot tears ran down her face. "I haven't changed," she protested.

"I'm sorry, Cassie," Andrea said, and she sounded sincere. "We had some fun times, didn't we?"

The best. Another blink sent more tears cascading down her cheeks, and she sucked in a sob. "Yes."

"You can call me anytime, okay? And you should talk to Miles. He's really nice."

The statement was like rubbing salt in her wound. The new Andrea with her new friends got to hang out with Miles, while Cassie, as unchanged and the same as she'd been in sixth grade, didn't have anyone. "Sure."

"You can still come over too. We'll hang out."

For a moment, that vicious hope flared, but then it died out. These were empty words, spoken to make her feel better. Andrea was better than Cassie now. There was a hierarchy, and Andrea had moved up, leaving Cassie behind.

"Thanks for calling, Andrea," Cassie said. She hung up and collapsed on her bed, sobbing into the pillow.

There was only one way to regain Andrea's friendship. Cassie had to move up too.

Episode 4: Season of Grace

Chapter Twenty-Four
Lonliest Number

The forecast for Halloween called for clear skies and nice, balmy, sixty-degree weather. Cassandra Jones checked over the costume laid out on her bed, complete with hospital gown, a white shirt and pants to wear underneath, and a makeup kit to transform her into one of the Undead. Perfect, since her heart felt dead.

In spite of all the emotional trauma she'd endured this month, the thought of getting dressed up and collecting gobs of candy stirred something to life within her. This was a holiday, and she planned to indulge. She wanted chocolate. Lots and lots of chocolate.

But right now, she needed to get to the bus. She darted out the bedroom door, clutching her binder and calling as she hurried down the hall, "Let's go! Time to catch the bus!"

"I see it, it's coming!" her little sister Annette yelled, throwing open the front door.

Not a good sign. If she could see the bus, it would reach the stop before they got there. "Run!" Cassie shouted, practically throwing Scott and Emily out the door after Annette.

Rhonda, the bus driver, had just started to close the bus doors when Cassie and her siblings appeared in the street, waving and yelling. The doors halted in their motion and swung back open. Cassie exhaled in relief. She would hate to explain to her mom that they'd missed the bus because she'd spent so much time admiring her costume.

"Thank you," Cassie said to the bus driver.

Rhonda rolled her eyes and gave a quick nod, tossing back her short, wavy blond hair. "I won't always wait," she warned, but Cassie knew it was an empty threat. She always waited.

She scanned the bus seats, hoping as always that she might spot a friend. There was no one. For a moment, dark thoughts threatened her mood, reminding her that it wasn't just on the bus she didn't have friends. She brushed the thought aside, refusing to let it bring her down. She had Farrah. Maybe someday they would be best friends.

She settled into the seat behind Emily and pulled out a book, excusing herself from having to make conversation with the second grader sitting beside her.

Cassie stopped in the bathroom before school and brushed on some lip gloss, the only makeup she felt comfortable wearing. Then she smiled at her reflection. "Operation: Become Cool" had gone into effect this week. Cassie was trying to dress trendier, not wear her hair in a ponytail, and smile at everyone she saw. But so far she hadn't noticed any changes. Not in her appearance nor in the way kids treated her. She glanced down at her clothes, pleased to see how loosely the jeans fit her. And the t-shirt was cute enough, gray with a smiling sunshine on it.

She stepped out of the bathroom and forced the smile to stay as she went to her locker. Friendly, confident, likable. That was the air she wanted to give off. That she was someone everyone wanted to be friends with.

She just wasn't sure how on earth to accomplish it.

She put away the books she'd brought home for homework and pulled out the ones she'd need for first and second hour. She turned around and came to an abrupt halt.

Andrea, her former best friend, stood in front of her, so close that Cassie took a step backward. Andrea clutched her binder to her chest and smiled at Cassie, a great big smile that stretched across her face.

"Hi," Cassie said, startled. She recovered quickly, her own smile timidly touching her lips. Her heart beat a little faster, afraid to hope Andrea might be re-initiating their friendship. She seemed different. Had she changed her mind about only needing her new friends? "How are you?"

Andrea just smiled at her, so big both top and bottom rows of teeth showed.

And then Cassie realized what was different. "You got contacts!" she gasped out, her eyes going wide as she took in Andrea's new visage without her glasses.

"Yes!" Andrea squealed, clutching her books to her chest and bopping up and down.

"I love them," Cassie said, basking in Andrea's attention. "They really bring out—"

"Andrea!" Kitty appeared from behind, laughing so hard she sagged against Andrea's shoulder. She looped her arm through hers. "You won't even believe—"

Kitty couldn't finish her sentence, she was laughing so hard, but that made no difference. Andrea was already giggling, laughing without knowing why.

"What? What is it?"

Kitty just laughed, and Andrea continued to pester her.

Cassie's heart sank into her toes. She felt like a cloud of invisibility had just descended on her. She turned around and made her way to first hour, filled with bitterness. What was wrong with her? Why didn't Andrea want to be her friend anymore? What made Kitty and Amity and Cara so special?

Cassie didn't know what they had that made the seventh grade class flock to them, but she was determined to figure it out. And she was determined to get it. She took her glasses off and glared at them before slipping them back on. Suddenly she hated them. And she hated her jeans, which hung awkwardly from her frame, and the t-shirt that she'd tucked into them with the stupid smiley face. And her stupid zombie costume that she knew for a fact neither Andrea, Kitty, Amity, or Cara would be caught dead in, pretend or not.

❦

That evening at home, Cassie took out the trash without being told, then helped her youngest sister Annette do the dishes. She made sure the table was set and her homework done before she plodded down the stairs to her mom's office in the basement.

"Hi, Cassie," her mom said. She had the hot glue gun out and several different colors of felt. "Remember tomorrow you're riding with Riley to Girls Club."

Girls Club met once a week, though Cassie had very little interest in the club right now. Or anything, really. "Okay," she said. She didn't ask what her mom was working on. It probably involved a new chore chart. "Can I get contacts?"

Mrs. Jones glanced at her briefly before returning to her

work, placing the felt blocks in a prearranged pattern on a piece of fabric. "Why?"

"I'm tired of my glasses. They make me look childish."

"You're too young for contacts."

Well, that simply wasn't true. "No, I'm not! Lots of my friends have them already."

Her mom shook her head. "Contacts are too expensive. And you're just not ready for them."

Cassie stomped her foot, frustration forming a heavy lump in her throat. "I do all my chores, all my homework, I shower and get dressed by myself, I'm twelve years old! I'm ready!"

Mrs. Jones heaved a sigh, a sign that she was tired of this conversation. "Not now, Cassandra. Ask again when you're fourteen."

Cassie swallowed hard, past the lump in her throat. "Can I get my hair cut, then?"

"Your hair's so long and beautiful. Why would you do that?"

"Because I'm tired of it!" Cassie shouted.

Now she had her mom's attention. Mrs. Jones looked up and narrowed her eyes, and Cassie regretted her outburst.

"That's enough, young lady," Mrs. Jones said. "The answer is no. I'm not discussing this again."

Cassie turned on her heel and charged up the stairs, letting each step feel the weight of her fury. As soon as she reached her room, she slammed the door and collapsed on the bed. Then she burst into tears. She threw her glasses across the room and buried her hands in her dark hair, tugging at the roots. Boring. Plain and boring. That's what she was.

The only thing she had any control over was her weight. Cassie stood up and pulled her jeans away from her hips, pleased at least by the inches of space between the fabric and her skin. If she could be just a little skinnier, maybe she would be special enough to join Andrea's group of friends.

Cassie's bad mood continued all through dinner, even with her younger brother and sisters excitedly talking about trick-or-treating.

"Which neighborhood are we going to this year, Mom?" Emily asked.

Since the Joneses lived in the country, they always went into town for Halloween. Few of the neighbors put candy out. Cassie held her breath, hoping it wouldn't be Andrea's neighborhood.

"We'll go over by Walker Elementary," Mrs. Jones said. "Just like last year."

Right by Andrea's neighborhood. That did it. Cassie pushed away from the table. "I'm too old for trick-or-treating."

Both of her parents looked at her in surprise. "But you've been looking forward to it all week," her mom said.

"No, I haven't," Cassie said, not wanting to explain her change of heart. "I just pretended to be excited for the kids."

"Well, I guess you can just walk with Annette," Mrs. Jones said. "Keep her safe."

"Fine," Cassie said. "As long as I don't have to dress up." No way would she risk Andrea and company seeing her in her lame zombie outfit.

Cassie threw herself on her bed and moped, staring at the ceiling and feeling sorry for herself. Her phone beeped, and she picked it up to see a text from Farrah.

Hey! she said. *We meeting up tonight? Want to see your costume!*

Cassie rolled over onto her belly and texted, *Not going.*

Decided to help my sister instead. Sorry.

Farrah didn't respond, and Cassie didn't care.

༄

Halloween slipped past, and October morphed into November. And all around her, Cassie's friends seemed totally unaware of how unhappy and lonely she was.

"Who remembers me mentioning at the beginning of the year that we would do two major projects in here, one each semester?" Ms. Talo, Cassie's first-period English teacher, asked.

Cassie glanced around. Only a few hands were up, including Jimmy and Nicole's. Her shoulders sagged in relief that she wasn't the only one to forget. It was November, after all. Who could be expected to remember something mentioned months ago?

Ms. Talo frowned and ran a hand through her short dark hair. "You all are seventh graders now, and this is an advanced English class," she said, chiding. "When I mentioned something at the beginning of the year, you should have been paying attention. Those of you who did will have an advantage on the others."

Several heads, including Cassie's, swiveled to Jimmy. He lowered his face, a pink hue creeping over his cheeks. Nicole had also raised her hand, but she was one of those super-smart kids who remembered everything and got perfect scores every time.

"I want you to tell me a story with this project," Ms. Talo said. "But just writing a story on paper won't be good enough. No, you have to find a way to show it to me. What are some different ways we can show a story?"

While the kids shouted out ideas, Cassie brainstormed. She

couldn't make a movie; she had no skills with that. She couldn't draw well enough to do a cartoon flip book, but maybe it was enough to do a slide show. She opened her folder and drew several boxes to represent slides. But first she needed to write the story.

Her mind flashed back to Andrea and the latest blow off in the hall. She tightened her grip on her pencil and started to write, the words of Ms. Talo and her classmates fading into the distance. The sentences flowed forth from her pencil, and Cassie found herself so riveted to the fictional—yet not-so-fictional—world she was creating that even after the bell rang to dismiss to second hour, she still sat there, pencil flashing across the paper as quickly as it could, transposing her thoughts and emotions and feelings into an object outside of herself. Only when she was the last person in class did she shove the story aside and rush out the door.

But the story didn't leave her. All through second and third hour, her mind replayed what she'd written. She wouldn't allow herself to imagine past that point, afraid she'd envision a beautiful scene now but be unable to recreate it later.

Cassie would've forgotten about Girls Club if Riley didn't remind her at lunch.

"Don't forget you're riding with me after school," Riley said.

"Why?" Farrah asked, adding extra pickles to her burger.

"For Girls Club," Riley sniffed, lifting her chin in the air.

"What are we doing today?" Cassie asked, eyeing the fries on Riley's tray and wishing she could ask for them. Instead, she ate her apple slices.

"I don't know." Riley shrugged. "It's at Maureen's house. I think we're learning to crochet."

"Crochet!" Farrah laughed loudly. "Sounds like something my grandma would do!"

Cassie couldn't help agreeing. "I have a lot of homework. I think maybe I should just go home."

"It's already arranged," Riley said, frowning at her. "Why would you miss?"

Why, indeed? Why was she even in Girls Club? Cassie wasn't sure what value it added to her life anymore. She turned away from Riley and ate another apple slice, not wanting to talk about it anymore.

After school she went to Girls Club and sat and crocheted with the other girls, but she couldn't remember a word they talked about. All she could see in her head was a fictional little girl who couldn't seem to make the other fictional little girl see they were meant to be best friends forever.

On Thursday Cassie walked over to her dad's soccer store from school to help him before he took her to her choir practice. The bell chimed when she pushed open the door.

"Hello!" his voice boomed out, cheerful and anxious. He came out of the back room, a smile on his face.

"It's just me," Cassie said, dumping her binder on the table in the stock room and glancing around. The store was empty besides her father. "Been busy today?"

His smile dampened. "It's been a quiet day. Actually, it's been a quiet week."

"Well." Cassie walked out to the store and clocked in at the register. "Maybe that will change."

"I don't need you at the register unless people come in," her dad said, following her. "I have a bunch of new shirts that just arrived. Can you sort them, then tag them and hang them?"

"Yes," Cassie said, groaning inside. She hated opening boxes and sorting things. Too much like cleaning.

No one came in the first hour Cassie worked.

The bell chimed around four o'clock, and Cassie shoved aside the clothes, ready to greet the customer. "Oh, hello, Elek!" she said, recognizing the tall, dark-haired boy from church.

"Hi," Elek said, his olive skin crinkling in a grin. Several years older than Cassie, Elek always greeted her respectfully. His family was Greek or Italian or something Mediterranean, and always very nice and shy. Today he wore an official soccer referree uniform. "I have a game to coach in twenty minutes and need some cards."

"Sure." She led him to the official supplies and handed him the packet of red and yellow game cards. "So you ref now?"

"When I'm not playing soccer." He paid for his purchase with another smile and left.

Less than ten dollars. Cassie sighed. This would not be a money-making day.

"Daddy," she said as the time slipped closer to five, "I have to leave for my choir practice soon."

He glanced at the clock with a frown. "I hate to close the shop. What if someone comes while we're out?"

No one was going to come. Even Cassie could see that. Still, she didn't want to make him feel bad. "I can just walk. It's probably only a mile."

He brushed her comment aside with a wave of his hand. "No, you'd be late. Let's just go quickly."

He didn't say much on the short drive over to the community center. Cassie imagined he was thinking about the lack of customers.

"Well, at least you won't have to pay me much," she joked, trying to make him feel better. "I didn't stay very long."

"Oh, about that." He brightened slightly. "Instead of paying you with cash, I thought I'd just let you pick out a few new outfits from the store. Some soccer shorts or nice jerseys, even shoes. Your mom said you could use new clothes."

Cassie slid down in her seat. Yes, she wanted new clothes. She wanted tight leggings and long tunics like Andrea wore. She wanted contacts and a new hair cut. She wanted cash so she could buy these things without asking her mom. She didn't want baggy shorts with drawstrings and neon-colored soccer jerseys. But he looked so excited, like finally something was going right. "Sounds great, Daddy," she said, stifling a sigh. She pushed the door handle and hopped out of the van before it came to a complete stop in front of the community center.

꧁꧂

"I have no idea what to do with this," Cassie announced to her younger sister Emily.

The two girls sat at the kitchen table on a sunny Saturday afternoon, but it was anything except relaxing. Cassie had a plastic slide strip in front of her, and somehow she had to turn it into a story-showing project—not to be confused with story-telling—before Monday. Though Cassie had her story written by Friday morning, she hadn't done anything else with it.

Emily picked up the plastic strip on the table. "I guess you just draw the pictures of your story."

"But which pictures?" Cassie tapped her fingers on the table apprehensively. The short dialogue in her story expressed the hurt and betrayal Cassie's fictional character felt when her best friend decided she wasn't pretty, popular, or trendy enough to hang out with anymore. And somehow, Cassie felt just a little bit better when she wrote it, as if by putting the emotions outside of herself, she relieved herself of some of her own pain.

Drawing it, however, was a different matter. How was she supposed to draw a story that was mostly raw feeling?

"What are they doing while they talk?" Emily asked. "Maybe imagine that first."

Cassie closed her eyes and pictured a scene. In front of Andrea's house, arriving to spend the day, only to find Andrea had left already with someone else. Or standing behind Andrea at her locker, playing with her hair, desperate for her to turn around and acknowledge Cassie. Or the worst one of all—bumping into Andrea in the gym and Andrea mocking Cassie about her crush of two years, Miles, while he and Cara stood nearby.

The heat rushed up behind her eyes, and Cassie swallowed hard. *Focus on the story,* she told herself. *Make it fiction.*

Make it fiction. That's all she had to do.

Since her estranged characters seemed to be alone with no other audience, she decided an encounter at the lockers would fit best. On a sheet of paper where she had drawn several squares to represent the slides, Cassie wrote in what she planned to draw. Standing at locker. Taking out books. Facing each other. walking down the hall.

She realized as she wrote that her story, while emotional, had very little action. It wouldn't hold her audience's attention. If the assignment wasn't for a grade, she wouldn't care, but it was, and she did. With a sigh, she pulled back out the sheet of paper with her story. What action could she do?

Twenty minutes later her story had morphed from two girls

talking to two accident-prone girls who tripped over a bench, lost a shoe, and knocked someone out with a purse while talking. It made absolutely no sense to her, but at least she had something to draw now. With a sigh, she used a fine-tipped permanent marker to begin sketching images meant to represent her short story.

Emily plopped down beside her and watched her doodle. "What is that?" she asked, pointing to the image of one girl falling over the bench.

"A bench," Cassie said, not bothering to hide the annoyance in her voice.

Emily giggled. "Are you going to tell your class what it is so they don't have to guess?"

Cassie scowled at her. Emily was only two years younger, but she could be so irritating. "Like you could do better."

Emily raised an eyebrow and Cassie groaned. They both knew Emily excelled at art. She could freehand draw cartoon characters just from looking at them.

"Want me to help?" Emily said, as if reading Cassie's mind.

Cassie picked up the hair spray bottle meant for erasing permanent marker. "May as well."

Half an hour later Cassie admired the artfully created slide show. She hoped letting her sister help was considered outsourcing and not cheating. The result was so much nicer than the stick figures she'd been planning on drawing.

"These look really great," she admitted.

"Now what?" Emily propped her chin up in the palms of her hands, a decidedly pleased look on her face.

"Now I have to record the story, complete with a chime to notify when it's time to move to the next slide." Cassie picked up her dad's phone, the one with a voice-recording option.

"Want to be one of the parts?"

Emily dropped her hands, her eyes widening. "Sure! Do I just read it?"

"I have a script written." Cassie pulled it out of her folder. She scribbled the action parts into the margins next to the corresponding dialogue. "You can be Girl Number One."

"What's her name?"

Cassie hadn't given her one. She liked the idea of these girls being nameless, without any real identities. They could be any girl anywhere, fit any situation, any description. She looked again at the girls on the slides that Emily had drawn, examining the long dark hair of Girl #2 and the wavy brown hair of Girl #1. She hadn't meant to, but she'd pictured herself and Andrea and described them that way to Emily.

"She doesn't have a name," Cassie said. "Neither one does. I want the audience to be more engaged by their conversation than who they are. We just have to make sure they have very distinct voices."

"Sure!" Emily said, her tone excited. "I can do that."

She could. And she would be the perfect character for Girl #1, the one who represented Andrea. Girl #2, the melancholy, sad, rejected one, would be played by Cassie.

Cassie set up the recorder on the table in front of them, her own phone in her hand to make the chime between slides. "Okay. Let's do this."

Cassie tried to be serious and somber while they recorded, but Emily kept switching from cheerful and peppy to giggling so hard she couldn't talk. Pausing the recorder, Cassie gave her a stern look.

"What's so funny?"

Emily's eyes grew large. "I'm just not sure what kind of

story this is. It's written like it's supposed to be sad, but then they keep doing stupid things that make it seem like it's supposed to be funny, like taking someone out with her purse. I'm just not sure how to read this."

Cassie scowled. "It's a serious story!"

"Okay." Emily wiped at her mouth as if to remove the grin. "I'll be serious."

Chapter Twenty-Five
Taking a Hit

Cassie checked three times Monday morning to make sure she had all the slides and the recorded story in her binder. She could recall too many times when she'd gone to school without her assignment.

Having everything with her didn't calm her nerves, though. She kept remembering the way Emily giggled as they recorded. Was she right? Was it a confusing mixture of humor and sadness that wouldn't make any sense at all? She knew it was too late to worry about it, but during the ride to school, that was all she did.

She skipped the pleasantries in the hall and slipped into first hour. Around her, Cassie's other classmates assembled their various projects on their desks. Cassie pulled her slides out and checked to make sure the slide projector was still on the teacher's desk. It was. She put her dad's phone with the recorded script next to the slides and sat up straight, pleating her hands together in front of her.

The tardy bell rang, and the class quieted as Ms. Talo moved to the front of the room.

"Are we ready?" she said with an enthusiastic smile. "I can't wait to see what mediums you used to tell your stories!" She looked around the class. "Nicole. Can you start?"

Nicole stood up, her frizzy blond hair pulled back in a ponytail. "Yes," she said with a smile.

Cassie had met Nicole in soccer last year. She liked Nicole, even though the other girl outsmarted her in every task. Cassie wasn't surprised when Nicole pulled the TV stand to the center of the room. She excelled at making movies and often posted her homemade videos online for people to see.

Nicole didn't disappoint today. Her flawless story about entering the unknown new world of junior high, told in an epic space opera manner complete with a rousing soundtrack, left Cassie feeling a bit sick to her stomach. What little confidence she had in her dramatic narrative melted away. There was no choice now; she had to carry on.

"Fantastic approach, Nicole," Ms. Talo said when Nicole finished. "Any immediate feedback, class?"

"I really liked it," Jimmy said.

"It reminded me of Star Trek," Leigh Ann said.

"Great editing," another boy said. "Really smooth transitions."

Murmurs of agreement followed, and Ms. Talo turned her attention to the next student.

A few other kids went, and then Ms. Talo's gaze fell on Cassie. "Your turn, Cassie."

Swallowing hard, Cassie slid out from her desk. Keeping her back to her classmates and her eyes on the slide projector, she carefully inserted each numbered block into the slot. Then she hooked her dad's phone into the audio port. Her heart hammered in her throat as she moved to the white board and grabbed the string to pull down the projector screen. She gave a soft tug, but it didn't move. She tugged a little harder. Still nothing.

A few giggles came from behind her, and sweat beaded on her forehead. What if she pulled too hard and the whole thing came down? She brushed the thought aside and yanked on the screen. It finally rolled down, but so fast that it bounced at the bottom and recoiled back to the top. The quiet giggling turned into laughter.

Cassie bit her lower lip.

"Let me help," Ms. Talo said. She stepped up to the board and pulled the screen down with practiced ease. Then she stepped to the projector and powered it on, shining the light directly on the white surface.

"Need me to get the lights?" she asked Cassie.

Cassie's head jerked. Was her teacher making fun of her? Then she saw the sparkle in Ms. Talo's eyes as she winked at Cassie.

"Oh, no," Cassie said, her voice shaky. "I'll get them." She wished she could keep her gaze down and avoid looking at anyone. But then she'd likely run into a desk and make a bigger fool of herself than Girl #2 in her slide show. She forced her eyes up. She had expected her classmates to be laughing, but she wasn't prepared for the friendliness behind the grins. All of them watched her, relaxing in their chairs, smiling, but not mockingly. They were waiting. Accepting. Like she was one of them, and this was all part of being a team.

Maybe it was.

Some of her confidence restored, Cassie stepped to the back of the room and hit the light switch. Then she returned to the slide projector. She put her finger on the trigger and hit play on her prerecorded script.

Her stomach tightened as hers and Emily's voices filled the classroom, ringing out with nonchalance and angst. And then Girl #1 tripped over the bench, and the whole class laughed. Cassie bit her lip and focused on the slide show. Silence fell again as they watched, and then when Girl #2 stepped in gum and lost a shoe, the class roared.

Oh, no, Cassie thought. Emily had been right. The story wasn't a drama and it wasn't a comedy. It was nothing.

The slide show finished, and Cassie hurried back to flip the lights on.

"Thank you, Cassie," Ms. Talo said. "Any feedback for her, class?"

No one said a word. And then Leigh Ann said, "I really liked how you interspersed the heavy drama with comic relief. It was like, just when I felt super depressed, you lightened it by making me laugh."

"Yeah," Emmett said. "It was a great way to lessen the tension."

"But the feelings were so real," Nicole said. Her eyes shone as she stared at Cassie. "I could totally imagine what she was going through."

Cassie swallowed hard, nearly moved to tears. It had worked. They could feel the emotion she'd put into the narrative. She'd made it real to them. And somehow, the corny accidents she'd put in had only served to enhance the unfolding drama.

⚭

Cassie's joy over her classmates' reaction to her slide show carried her through her morning classes. They couldn't know how personal the story was, but she felt as though she had shared something intimate with them. She walked on a cloud, euphoric—until she entered the lunch room.

The cacophony of noises and the clashing aromas of food crashed into her, and with an impatient snarl, her stomach demanded its share.

"Hi, Cassie," Farrah said, scooting her basket of fries over to make room at the table. Cassie dropped down beside her and waved hello to Riley and Emmett.

"What are you eating today?" Riley asked.

"Nothing," Cassie said, urging her stomach to shut up. She was in control, not her belly.

"Nothing?" Riley repeated. "That's what you ate yesterday, too."

Cassie stared at the Farrah's fries. Grease glistened on the golden strands, and they bent slightly beneath the pressure of Farrah's fingers. They smelled amazing.

"I'm not hungry lately," Cassie said, not taking her eyes from Farrah's fries.

"Want a mozzarella stick?" Riley asked.

Cassie's attention turned to the steaming breaded piece of cheese in Riley's fingers. Cassie swallowed as water accumulated in her mouth. She could imagine the gooey cheese inside, the salty flavor of the deep-fried coating mixing with the warm cheese.

Deep fried. Her mind honed in on those words, and she remembered why she wasn't eating. She couldn't put that trash into her body. It would make her gain weight, and she was trying so hard to be skinny.

"I just remembered I have something to do in the library," she said, standing up and extricating herself from the bench.

She could feel their eyes on her, inquisitive, curious, confused. "Some—homework." She hurried out the door and made her way to library, heart beating rapidly. It only calmed when she let herself into the quiet room full of books and settled herself on the carpet in front of a shelf.

Perhaps she would start spending lunch in here every day.

Cassie was surprised when she walked into art class and saw several groups of kids clustered together, some whispering and shooting furtive glances toward the door, others crying softly. Cassie walked over to her spot next to Jaclyn, her friend with the super curly brown hair and large brown eyes. Normally composed and mellow, even Jaclyn had a wild expression about her, eyes darting around the room, one finger tugging on the brown locks.

"What's going on?" Cassie asked.

"It's Luke," Jaclyn said.

Cassie thought back to the pale, quiet boy who sometimes came over to their desks to swap pencil colors. He wasn't a close friend, but he always acted friendly. Cassie's heart gave a tremor of worry. "What's happened?"

Before Jaclyn could answer, Ms. Caraway came in. Her face had a pinched look as if she smelled something nasty, and her eyes were rimmed in red.

"Class," she said, "I'm sure some of you have heard about Luke."

Cassie fidgeted restlessly in her chair. Yes, she'd heard about Luke, but what?

Ms. Caraway continued. "For those of you who haven't, Luke was—in a fight after lunch. Except what happened to him is nothing short of criminal. Two eighth graders cornered him, and while Luke huddled on the ground trying to protect himself, they kicked him and punched him over and over again."

Cassie gasped and her hand flew to her mouth. Fire flashed in Ms. Caraway's eyes, and she lifted her chin as she continued.

"Luke's been rushed to the hospital and those students suspended. I'm sure there will be legal proceedings. What those boys did was malicious and cruel and horrible."

Cassie's body hurt at the thought of being beaten while she lay in a fetal position. What kind of a person would do that?

"I don't know what their problem was with Luke, but it doesn't matter. They had no right to do that. Bullying is against the law, and if you feel threatened, you need to tell someone. Don't keep it a secret. That just gives them permission to keep bullying you." She met each of their eyes, and then she wilted, the fire going out of her. She waved a hand at the mess of art supplies in front of her.

"Instead of an assignment today, I want each of you to make a card for Luke. I'll take it to him at the hospital after school."

"Who did this to him?" Cassie whispered to Jaclyn.

"I do not know," Jaclyn whispered back. "But I hope they go to jail."

Chapter Twenty-Six

Entrepeneur

Luke didn't return to school on Tuesday. He wasn't there Wednesday, either.

Cassie walked to the soccer store after school, where she'd help her dad before he took her to voice lessons and then to church.

"Come on to the back, Cassie!" he called when she walked in. He looked up as she entered the stockroom and beamed at her.

"Got some new clothes in. Look at these." He held up a fitted black ensemble, complete with pants and a long-sleeved jacket. Bright red and blue stripes angled down the arms and legs of the suit.

"What is it?" Cassie asked. She fingered the fabric, liking the feel of the soft stretchy cloth.

"It's a tracksuit. Want one? I got a size small."

"I'm not a small," Cassie started to say before remembering all the weight she'd lost this year. Maybe she was a small now. Suddenly curious, she said, "Sure. I'll try one on."

"Here." He dug around in the box. "Take this one."

She stepped into the bathroom. She slipped off her school clothes and pulled the tracksuit on. It fit. It fit! In fact, it fit her loosely. She turned in the mirror, admiring the shape of her frame beneath the black jacket.

"I did it," she whispered to herself. "I'm small." Her heart suddenly lighter, she realized she'd reached her goal. Now, instead of trying so hard to get skinny, she could work harder on staying skinny.

Luke did not come back to school.

Everyone had stopped talking about him. But Cassie couldn't help thinking of him every time she stepped into art class. She wondered how he was and how she could see him but didn't know who to ask.

"We have another project coming up," Ms. Talo said Tuesday morning in English class.

"Another one?" Jimmy said. "But we just finished our story shows two weeks ago."

Two weeks. Cassie's mind flashed back to that critical day. It had been two weeks since Luke was beat up.

"This is an advanced class," Ms. Talo admonished, fixing her steely gaze on Jimmy. "It might say English on the curriculum, but this is much more than that. This is a class to mimic real life, where you finish one project at work and immediately begin another. Or you have to juggle two projects at one time for different clients. And you have to fulfill them to the exact letter, or you don't get paid. You might even get fired."

"We already have to do that," Nicole said. "We have seven different teachers who all give us different projects at the same time."

Ms. Talo's eyes turned to her. "But I guarantee none of them will challenge you the way this class will."

That was for sure. Ms. Talo said it as if being the most challenging subject was a good thing, instead of cause for concern.

"Any more objections?"

Cassie tapped her pencil on her desk and waited to see if anyone else would speak up. No one did.

"Excellent. You have plenty of time to prepare for this project. It won't take place until February. We are going to have a market day. Your job is to create an item you can sell at the market. This is not a play market, students. All of Southwest Junior High's students will be able to come to market and shop your items. Any money you make is yours to keep. But you need to plan out very carefully the expenses, what you will make, and how you can make a profit."

An excited murmur rippled through the class, but Cassie only felt a twisting of worry. Create something? Sell it? What could she possibly do?

"You can do this with a partner or by yourself. I want you to spend the rest of class brainstorming. If you want to do it with a partner, figure out who that will be."

The noise level elevated, and students sprang from their desks, hurrying to find a collaborator. They spoke in animated voices, hands gesticulating madly as they conveyed their ideas. Cassie tried not to panic. Ideas? She had none.

"Cassie." Nicole squatted beside Cassie's desk.

"Hi," Cassie said, swiveling to look at her.

"Want to be partners?"

Cassie exhaled in relief. If she didn't have to bear the burden of all the creativity, it would go much better. "I'd love to be."

"Great." Nicole grabbed the empty desk next to Cassie and slid it closer. "Let's start talking."

Sunday evening after church, Mr. Jones gathered the family together. They crowded on the couches and on the floor in the living room, Cassie and her sisters, Annette and Emily, and her brother Scott.

"There are a few things we need to discuss as a family," Mrs. Jones said, folding her hands in front of her. "But before your dad and I speak, I want to hear from you guys. Is there anything on your mind? Anything you want to talk about? Annette, since you're the youngest, we'll start with you."

"Well." Annette took a deep breath, her brown eyes wide as she searched for a topic. Cassie tried not to laugh. At six years old, there was no telling what Annette might come up with.

"At recess today," Annette said, fired up now, "I climbed the zip line by myself. And the second grade boys said their dad was stronger than mine." She crossed her arms over her chest and shook her head. "And I said, no, he's not, my daddy is the strongest." She looked at Mr. Jones, wanting his validation.

He chuckled and patted her on the head. "You're very sweet to stick up for me that way."

"But can you come to school, Daddy?" She latched onto his hand. "Can you show them you're the strongest?"

"But what if I'm not?" he said, the twinkle still in his eyes.

"Just come and show them. You are."

"How about I come and eat lunch with you next week instead?"

At Annette's excited nod, Mrs. Jones turned her attention to

Scott. "Scott? Anything you want to share?"

He poked at a pillow, the moodiest eight-year-old Cassie ever saw. "I missed five minutes of recess every day this week."

Mr. Jones opened his mouth, but Mrs. Jones silenced him with a look. "Was it someone else's fault again?" she asked Scott.

He shrugged. "Chris always gets me in trouble."

"And I've been telling you for years to stop playing with him. You're old enough now to take responsibility. If someone else is doing something that will get you in trouble, you need to get away. Have you heard that before?"

"Yes," Scott grumbled, not looking at all pleased with the response.

Mrs. Jones turned to Emily. "How about you, Emily?"

"I was the only one not to miss any on my science test. And my teacher said I'm one of her brightest students."

Cassie rolled her eyes. That wasn't a surprise. What was Emily not good at?

"That's fantastic, Emily. I hope you'll keep that attitude with school. Cassie?"

Both of her parents turned to face her. Cassie thought about the different worries on her plate. Not having a close friend, being careful what she ate, worrying about how to get her homework done when she had music practices three times a week. But one concern leapt out at her, one that had been bothering her for weeks. "A boy in my class was beat up a few weeks ago. It was really bad. I'm not sure how to help him. And I'm not sure what to do if something like that happens to me."

Silence fell over them, and Cassie lifted her eyes toward her mother, waiting for the response.

Mrs. Jones looked at her husband, and Mr. Jones cleared his throat. "That's a very hard situation, Cassie. Did this boy know these kids were going to hurt him?"

"I really don't know," Cassie said.

"I don't know what happened with this boy. But I want all of you to listen to me." He caught each of their eyes, making sure they were looking at him. "If anyone ever threatens you or makes you feel scared, you tell an adult. You tell a teacher, a friend, me or your mom. We can't help you if we don't know. And if you see someone threatening another person, get an adult."

"What if you don't know they're going to hurt you?" Scott asked. "What if they just attack you?"

"Then you fight back with everything you have," Mr. Jones said, a fire gleaming in his eye. "And you fight for each other. Never let someone hurt one of your family."

The silence hung there a moment while they internalized his words, and then Mrs. Jones took another deep breath. "My turn." She glanced at Mr. Jones, then faced the kids. "The soccer store is not bringing in the money we need it to."

Cassie's eyes shot to her father, who looked grim. She knew the store was his dream child, his treasured hobby. She turned back to her mom. "What does that mean?"

Her mom sighed. "It's draining us as a family. Instead of being an additional income, it's an additional expense. We have some decision to make regarding it, and I want the family's input."

They were going to close the store. She just knew it. Cassie's heart sank, and she couldn't look at her dad, afraid to see the disappointment on his face. He'd put so much time, and love, and energy into it.

"Either we can close the store—"

"No!" Emily and Scott chorused.

"There must be another way," Cassie chimed in. "I'll work more hours with no pay."

"We'll all help out," Emily agreed. Unlike Cassie, she had stayed in soccer. And Scott had just started. The two of them were thriving in the sport.

"It won't be enough," Mrs. Jones said, her voice weary. "The store is just too much money."

"So there's no other option?" Cassie said.

"Yes, there is," Mr. Jones said. "But it requires some sacrifice on our part."

"On my part," Mrs. Jones said, casting him an indecipherable look. "The other option is that I get a job."

Chapter Twenty-Seven
In the Red

Cassie could not remember her mom ever having had a job.

"What kind of job are you looking for?" Cassie asked, drumming her fingers on the legs of her jeans. It had been two days since the ominous family meeting when Mrs. Jones announced she'd have to get a job. Cassie had volunteered to spend her Tuesday evening with her mom after children's chorus, helping her look for one. She sat in the passenger side of the car, trying to lend moral support. She couldn't think of what else she had to offer.

Mrs. Jones sighed and pulled into a fast food parking lot. "Anything I can get. Stay here."

Cassie pulled out a book but couldn't concentrate. Instead she watched cars line up at the drive thru and inch forward, disappearing around the building. Other vehicles slid into diagonal spots and families meandered out, strolling across the parking lot. Finally Mrs. Jones came back and climbed into the car.

"Did you get the job?" Cassie asked.

"I filled out an application." She pulled the van out of the lot and drove ten feet into the next fast food joint parking lot. "Stay here."

"Shouldn't I come in with you?"

"No. It'll just take a second."

Cassie fidgeted. "Why did I come with you if I'm just going to stay in the car?"

"Because you were the one who wanted me to get a job."

Cassie pondered that statement after her mom closed the door and walked away. It wasn't like it had been just Cassie's decision. Everyone wanted to try and keep the store. They had all agreed that Mrs. Jones' getting a job would be the best thing to help make ends meet. Was there something else Cassie was supposed to do?

When her mom came back in, Cassie said, "Do you want me to get a job?"

Mrs. Jones laughed. "You're only twelve, Cassie. No one would hire you."

Ouch. "Well, what am I supposed to do to help, then?"

"You're doing plenty. You help out at the soccer store, you babysit your siblings every time I ask."

That was true. And Cassie didn't get paid for it.

They pulled into another fast food restaurant.

"Why are you applying at all these fast food places?" Cassie asked.

Mrs. Jones put the car into park and stared out the windshield. Then she turned to face Cassie. "I'm not really qualified to do anything else, Cassie. I never went to college, never got a degree. I haven't been in the workforce since before you were born. If I wanted a real job, a good job, I would need to go back to school."

That didn't sound like fun. "Do you want to do that?"

Mrs. Jones smiled. "Not really. I don't really want a real job. I want to be home with you kids. I like being a part of your days. But you remember, Cassie, if you want a real job, or even just the option of having one, you need to go to college. You need to be educated and prepared."

Cassie nodded. She already planned on college, and she already knew she never wanted to work in fast food.

Mrs. Jones undid her seatbelt. "Be right back."

That night, Wendy's Old-fashioned Hamburgers called them.

Mrs. Jones took the call in her bedroom, away from the noises of the TV blasting out in the family room. When she came out of the room, she muted the television and stood in front of it, a reluctant smile on her face.

"Well?" Mr. Jones said, looking at her expectantly.

"I got the job," she said, her face flushed with pleasure in spite of herself. "I'm the new breakfast manager at Wendy's."

"Congrats, Mom!" Cassie exclaimed. Mr. Jones stood up and hugged her.

"When do you start?" he asked, stepping back.

"Monday. And I have to be there at five-thirty in the morning." This time she shot a glare his way. "I'm doing this for you."

"I know." He pulled her over to the couch, and Scott turned the TV sound back on.

But not before Cassie heard her mother whisper, "It won't be enough money, Jim."

❦

On Wednesday, Ms. Talo had them sit with their partners again so they could discuss their market project for February.

"Thanksgiving break starts next week," she said. "I want you to think about this during the break. In December, you should start working on prototypes of your projects and pricing them out, see how long it takes to make them. By the time February comes along, you should be experienced in your craft."

"What do you think we should do?" Nicole asked, settling next to Cassie.

"I don't know," Cassie admitted, doodling on her paper and avoiding Nicole's eyes. "I'm not very good at these things."

"My mom makes beaded jewelry. Maybe we could do that."

"Yeah, that might sell really well." She remembered a necklace she'd seen at a fair once, made out of magazine paper. "I can make beads."

"Okay, so jewelry." Nicole wrote it down. "What else? That might get the female crowd, but we still have to get the guys."

"I have no idea what guys like. I never even know what to get my brother for Christmas."

"Sports. Cars. Food."

Cassie nodded. She didn't see how any of that helped, though.

Nicole tapped her pencil on the paper, then said, "We'll think of something. Let's keep our minds open all week, see what we come up with."

"Sounds great," Cassie said. "Hey, how's soccer going?"

Nicole's face lit up. "Fantastic, I love it. You should play again." She launched into a description of the fall season, which had just ended, and Cassie nodded along. It did sound like fun. She had enjoyed soccer. But she was so, so horrible at it.

When Cassie walked into art class seventh hour, she was

shocked to see Luke sitting at his desk. She did a double take. He didn't look the same. His face was paler, thinner. He had his eyes down, dark brown hair falling over his face. Cassie waved a greeting at Jaclyn and then slid into the spot next to him.

"Luke, hi," she whispered. "I'm so happy to see you!"

He lifted his head, and she saw the scar around his eye where a wound had been stitched. His face was hollow, the skin slightly yellow. He pressed his lips together, but they never quite made it into a smile.

Cassie's throat ached, and she knew tears weren't far behind. Leaning over, she gave him a shoulder hug. "I'm so sorry. And I'm so glad you're back." She left his desk and sat down next to Jaclyn before she could get emotional.

"Is he okay?" Jaclyn whispered.

Cassie slid a glance Luke's direction. "I don't think so," she whispered back. She wasn't sure if he ever would be again.

She kept an eye out for Luke in the school hallways. She spotted him sometimes between classes, sticking to the lockers or edges of the hallways as if afraid to bump into anyone. But kids gave him space, and a few people greeted him or walked with him. She relaxed a bit when she realized no one was threatening him.

She wasn't sure if Luke realized it. He looked ready to bolt at any given moment.

Chapter Twenty-Eight
Blessed Peanut Butter

Cassie wasn't quite sure when things began to change. It happened so gradually, she almost didn't notice. But Mrs. Jones began finding excuses not to pay them allowance. And then she gave them less money for lunch, until finally she said they were going to start bringing lunches from home. Cassie wanted to tell her mom not to bother, that she didn't eat lunch anyway, but she knew that wouldn't go over well.

More than once, she overheard her parents arguing. It was unavoidable, since their bedroom was across from hers, and she had to pass it every night on her way to bed.

"Christmas is coming," Mrs. Jones said, "and we don't have any money."

"We will by then," her father promised.

Cassie closed her bedroom door, their words replaying in her mind. What did it mean, to not have money for Christmas?

On Thursday at her choir practice, Mrs. Vanderwood handed out order forms. "We're doing a Christmas program this year, and I need everyone's sizes for our special uniforms.

Please have your parents fill this out and bring the check after Thanksgiving."

Cassie glanced over it. Nothing exciting. White shirts, black skirts, something called a cummerbund. She put it aside while they practiced their music, then took it out to her mom.

"We're ordering uniforms for Christmas," she said, handing the paper to Mrs. Jones. Cassie slid into her seat and pulled her seatbelt on. "I need to bring a check after Thanksgiving."

To her surprise, tears filled her mother's eyes. Mrs. Jones got out of the car and walked toward the community center.

"Mom?" Cassie said in alarm. She let go of her seatbelt and hurried after her mother.

"Go back to the car, Cassie," her mom said.

"But—" Cassie began.

"Now!"

Cassie slowed her walk but didn't go back. Instead she waited until her mom went inside, then she hurried after her. Lingering at the corner, she heard her mother knock on the open door to the practice room.

"Hi, Vanessa?" Mrs. Jones said.

"Karen, come on in!" Ms. Vanderwood said.

"I'm sorry, I—Cassie just brought me that order form. For the uniforms? And I'm sorry, I hate to do this, I hate to say this —" Her mom's voice broke, and even from where she hid around the corner, Cassie could hear her crying.

"Karen, what is it?"

"We can't right now, Vanessa, we can't pay for uniforms. Actually I was going to pull her out of choir next month—we just can't pay for it right now, not with Christmas coming."

Cassie backed away, guilt and fear tightening her chest. What was happening? Were they that poor? What else would have to go? Voice lessons too?

She settled into her seat in the car and stared out the window, waiting for her mom to reappear. When she did, she looked much calmer, though her nose and eyes were still red.

"What was that about?" Cassie asked, hoping her mom would tell her. "What happened?"

"Nothing." Her mom sniffed and pulled away from the building. "I got it all worked out."

"Got all what worked out?" Cassie prodded.

"Your uniform. It's taken care of."

Cassie leaned back in her chair, hoping that meant she got to stay in choir.

ꙮ

"Cassie, I need your help with dinner," Mrs. Jones said.

Cassie put down her homework and wandered into the kitchen, glad for another opportunity to ask her mom about what happened in choir. "Sure."

"Drain this, please." Mrs. Jones gestured to a bowl of steaming water on the counter.

Obliging, Cassie carried it to the sink and dumped the contents into the strainer. "What is this?" she asked, staring at the small brown clumps.

"Bulgur wheat."

"What is that?" Almost the shape of rice but fatter, the light brown lumps snuggled together in the strainer.

"Here." Mrs. Jones put a spatula in her hand. "Stir the onions, please."

Cassie turned away from the sink and sauteed the veggies on the stove. Another pot of water vented steam as it came to a boil. "What's for dinner?"

"Spaghetti." Her mom returned to the stove and dumped

the contents of the strainer into Cassie's saute pan.

"Whoa!" Cassie exclaimed, leaping back as the water reacted with the grease and sizzled out of the pan. "Why did you put that wheat stuff in here?"

"Because it's taking the place of the hamburger." Her mom dumped a handful of seasoning on it. "Keep stirring."

A little leery this time, Cassie approached again and stirred the wheat with the onions. "This is going on our spaghetti?"

"Yes. It will taste just like meatballs when we add the sauce. Trust me."

Cassie had serious doubts about this.

Her doubts were confirmed half an hour later as everyone sat down to dinner. Bathed in the tomato sauce, the clumps of wheat really didn't look much different than hamburger. Cassie didn't say a word, not about to give away what it actually was. If everyone else was fooled, so much the better. She watched her siblings pile the sauce and Parmesan cheese on top of their noodles. Emily took a giant bite, slurping the noodles into her mouth. She chewed, her jaw working, and frowned.

"The meat has a funny texture," she said.

"Yeah," Scott said, taking a drink. "It's kind of popping in my mouth."

Cassie took a bite. The chewy granules, while imitating quite well the appearance of meat, came nowhere near the texture or flavor. "It's pretty good," she said, because she wasn't sure what else to say. And it wasn't bad.

"I like it," Annette said, though she had skipped the sauce and just put Ranch on her noodles.

"What's wrong with it?" Mrs. Jones said. "It's just spaghetti and sauce."

Mr. Jones didn't say a word, just shoved another bite in his mouth.

"There's nothing different about the meat?" Emily said, shooting a glance at Cassie.

Cassie shrugged.

"It's food," Mrs. Jones growled. "Eat it and be grateful."

No one said another word about the meat though the rest of the meal, but Cassie couldn't help wondering. Were they so poor now they couldn't buy hamburger?

"I've taken on a paper route," Mr. Jones announced.

"A what?" Scott asked.

Cassie pictured what she'd seen of paper routes in old movies. Boys her age riding bicycles through a neighborhood, usually with a dog riding behind them, tossing papers onto the neatly manicured green lawns. She'd never noticed her dad reading the paper. "How can you do that?" she asked, trying to replace the young boy in her mind's eye with her father. "We live out in the country. You're going to throw papers at our neighbors? From a bike?"

"Well, that's not quite how it works anymore," her dad said. "Not everyone takes a paper like they used to. So I'll drive the car and toss papers from the car window." He grinned like it was funny, but Cassie didn't think it was.

"Isn't that a job for little kids?"

Her dad's grin faded. "No. It's a way to supplement income for anyone who needs it."

"Can we help?" Emily asked.

"Everyone will have to help," Mrs. Jones spoke up. She scrubbed her hands over her face. "All the papers must be delivered by five in the morning."

Five in the morning. Cassie's mind got stuck on those words, and she felt a sick knot of dread forming in her stomach. The very thought made her nauseous.

"Not a lot of people take a paper these days," her mom continued, "so your dad can handle it during the week. But on Sunday, the workload triples. So one of you will take a turn each Sunday to help him get the papers out on time."

"Starting when?" Cassie asked, her mind already calculating when the next Sunday would be. Just three days away.

"I had my first day this morning," her dad said. His mouth quirked like he considered smiling, but couldn't quite get it. "So on Sunday, Cass, you'll go out with me. I'll show you the ropes."

The knot of dread hardened into a rock. "No way, Daddy. I can't get up that early. I can't do it."

"Everyone has to help," Mrs. Jones said, her voice clipped. "You wanted to know what you could do. This is it. What do you expect, Cassie? You're the oldest. Do you think it's easier on Annette to get up and help with the route?"

Cassie looked at her little sister and the guilt simmered beneath her consciousness, but she shoved it down. "I have school. I have homework. I have responsibilities."

"Not on Sundays, you don't. You'll have plenty of time to get home and changed before church."

More complaints were on the tip of her tongue, but she knew they didn't matter. The faces of her three younger siblings stared at her, waiting to see what she would say. It wasn't fair. If she refused, if she got out of this, so would they. And then her mom and dad would have to carry this burden on their own. But why should she have to take on a paper route when that was her dad's decision?

We all decided to keep the soccer store, she reminded herself.

She swallowed hard and nodded. "Okay."

"It's only once a week," Mrs. Jones said, her tone softening. She got up and walked her plate to the sink, where she rinsed it. "We'll get through this."

⟨flourish⟩

Though Cassie had taken to eating lunch in the library lately, the weather this week was too gorgeous to stay inside. Farrah invited her to eat on the back lawn with Riley and Emmett, beneath the red and gold leaves of the oak and maple trees. Cassie joined them on the benches and stared up at the blue sky, framed by the colorful foliage. The air held only the mildest nip, just enough for her to appreciate her long-sleeved shirt.

"The weather here is nicer than Texas," she commented. "In Texas it stays hot for a long time. And I don't remember these colors in the fall."

"Hm," Farrah said.

"Why do you eat in the library every day?" Riley asked. "We never see you anymore."

"Because she doesn't eat," Farrah said.

"You don't eat?" Emmett frowned at her. "Why?" His light blue eyes trailed her from her face to her feet, as if searching for clues.

"I eat!" Cassie exclaimed, her cheeks flaming. She hadn't realized anyone noticed. "I just prefer to do so privately."

"Then where's your lunch money?" Farrah said, looking up from her cheese sticks.

"I don't have any," Cassie said, holding up her sack. "I brought my lunch."

"Go on, then," Farrah challenged. "Let's see you eat it."

Her friends stared at her, waiting, and Cassie opened her

bag, humiliated by the attention. She pulled out a baggie of crackers, another baggie of freeze-dried bananas, and a baggie of raisins.

"You call that a lunch?" Farrah said, her tone mocking. "That's not enough to feed a humming bird."

"My mom packed it," Cassie said, opening her crackers and taking a nibble. She didn't want to admit it was all they had, so she said, "She's really encouraging me to be healthy."

They all gave her suspicious looks, but they didn't bug her about it again.

Cassie's eyes wandered away, searching for a source of subject change, and she spotted Luke stepping out of the cafeteria doors. "Luke!" she called, waving.

He spotted her and paused, sack lunch clutched in his hand.

She stood up and walked to him. "Come each lunch with us."

"Okay." He followed her back to their track of grass.

"Hey, guys, this is Luke," Cassie said, dropping down next to Farrah.

"Yeah, we have a class together," Farrah said. "But I've never seen you at A lunch, Luke."

"I switched lunch schedules last week," he said.

Cassie berated herself for staying in the library. She would've noticed Luke right away if she'd been out here. She hoped he hadn't been eating alone. "You'll have to eat lunch with us from now on."

"Thanks, Cassie," he said, offering a small grin. The pink scar around his eye wrinkled when he smiled.

Cassie patted his hand and ate her raisins.

When the bell rang, they all stood and gathered their trash.

"Bye!" Farrah went around and hugged them all. "Have a

great Thanksgiving! See you guys in a week!"

"You too!" Cassie squeezed her tight, then waited for Riley so they could walk toward the math building together.

"What are your Thanksgiving plans?" Riley asked.

"We'll just be home this year." Some years they went to her cousins' house in Georgia, but not this year. "You?"

"Same." Riley bobbed her head. "We'll be at church on Sunday."

"That's great." Cassie meant it. She enjoyed seeing Riley on Sundays, and it seemed to be bringing them closer together again. She waved as the reached the school doors. "See you later!"

Chapter Twenty-Nine
Hot Ink

Cassie prepared herself the best she could Saturday night for her first paper route. She had to admit that a part of her was slightly curious, maybe even excited, to see how this would go. What happened during a paper route?

"I'll wake you up a little before three," Mr. Jones said to her.

Cassie sat on the couch reading a book, about to go to bed even though it was only seven o'clock at night.

"Wear something warm because it's cold when we're out there tossing papers," he added.

"Okay," she said, slipping her bookmark between the pages and closing her book. Downstairs, the video game her siblings played whined and whistled as they blew things up. She stood and stretched. "Guess I'll head to bed now."

"See you soon."

Cassie put on the black tracksuit her dad had gotten her from the store. It fit nicely around her frame and warmed her body. She jumped into bed and snuggled into the blankets, ready for this adventure. She closed her eyes.

But sleep wouldn't come. She tossed around for a bit, then opened her eyes and looked out the window. The wind blew the trees outside, which danced in the moonlight, the leaves still clinging tenaciously to the branches. Thanksgiving. Christmas. Cassie considered the money she'd saved up from lunches before her mom starting sending a sack lunch. Did she have enough to get nice gifts for everyone?

The TV turned on in the living room, a high-pitched kids' show that carried all the way to her bedroom. Cassie pulled out her phone and flipped it open. Not quite eight o'clock. She scrolled through her contacts, wanting to text someone. Talk to a friend. She went back to the beginning of the list, her heart panging at the sight of Andrea's name. Their friendship had been so solid. How could Andrea have let it slide away? Cassie closed the phone and stared at the moon, blinking back the tears that threatened.

"Cassie."

The hall light turned on, and Cassie flinched, squeezing her eyes tighter to filter out the brightness.

"Cassie." Her dad's voice came again, and someone shook her shoulder. "Come on, sweetheart, it's time to get up."

Get up? Dimly Cassie realized she had fallen asleep. She rolled out of bed, stumbling like a zombie. Mr. Jones caught her and steadied her.

"I'll be in the living room," he whispered. "Come out when you're ready."

"Okay," she murmured. She felt around for her glasses and slipped them on, then stepped into a pair of shoes. Careful not to wake her sister, she closed the door to the bedroom and tiptoed to the living room.

Mr. Jones stood up and gave her a sympathetic smile.

"Ready?"

She nodded.

"Let's go."

The newspapers were not in the van. Mr. Jones explained that he had to pick them up every morning before he could drop them off.

"Today I really need your help," he said. "Not only do we have three times as many people to deliver to on Sunday, but the Sunday papers come with a special insert. So first we pick up the paper, and then we pick up the insert. Your job will be to get the inserts into the paper."

"Okay," she said. She was more awake now, more alert, even though her head ached and her eyelids felt like sandpaper.

Her dad pulled the van into a convenience store. He opened both of the side doors, then ran inside. A moment later he came back, another guy in tow. Both of their arms were laden with stacks and stacks of papers.

"Cassie," her dad said, dropping a pile in the middle row of seats, "you're going to want to sit back here. You'll work while I drive."

She undid her seatbelt and climbed into the back. The other guy dropped his pile next to the first pile, and they both went back in. Within minutes, every visible spot around her in the van had been taken up by newspapers.

"Feel this, Cassie," Mr. Jones said, stopping beside her seat. He handed her one of the papers and put her hand on it.

"They're warm," Cassie said, surprised. "The paper is warm."

"Hot off the presses." Mr. Jones showed her how many pages to count. "Open it up. Then you take this one." He grabbed up one of the thick colorful papers from the seat beside her. "Stick it inside."

"Got it," she said, flexing her fingers. The cold November air poured in from the open door, negating the warmth from her tracksuit. Even the freshly minted papers didn't warm her hands.

"Do thirty of those for me right now. I need to leave them here in the box."

"What box?" Cassie asked, creating a new pile on her lap once she had merged the two papers.

"Outside the gas station." He pointed to a red metal stand. "People leave their money and take a paper."

She looked over at it. "It has newspapers in it already."

"Those are the ones that didn't sell from yesterday. I'll put them up front with me and take them home. If we clip the dates, I get reimbursed for them."

She knew that word. It meant he'd get money back. "Why would they give you money for the papers that didn't sell?"

"Because I bought them, Cassie, and if they don't sell, I can get my money back."

She paused mid-motion, paper half lifted between her fingers, and looked at her dad. "You bought all these newspapers?"

"Yes." He laughed. "That means all the money I get today belongs to us."

She finished doing the insertions, and her dad switched out the papers in the metal box. He dropped a bag of coins on the dash and grinned at her.

"Pay day," he said. "I need twenty more for the next gas station. Can you have those ready?"

"Yes." So far this wasn't too hard.

They went to all the gas stations in the immediate area, switching out the papers. Each time, Mr. Jones dropped another bag of coins on the dash.

"The next one's the last gas station before we start doing houses," he said as he drove. "Just keep doing the inserts, as many as you can."

She didn't bother responding, just worked as quickly as she could, sliding the two papers together for her father. He took her next twenty to the box, and Cassie kept doing the inserts. She glanced up when he got back in and waited for the expected drop of the bag of coins. Nothing. No papers from yesterday, either.

"Did you sell out? Where's your money?"

Mr. Jones hung one hand over the steering wheel and shook his head. "Someone took them."

"Took what?"

"The papers." He sighed. "It happens. Someone puts in the quarters, opens the box, and takes all the papers."

Cassie gasped. She hadn't realized that could happen, but of course it could. The papers operated on some kind of honor system. "What do you do?"

"Nothing." He put the car into drive. "We don't get reimbursed if we can't turn the old paper in. We just have to eat that money."

Cassie pursed her lips together, feeling a stab of indignation. Her parents were working too hard to be cheated out of a few coins by dishonest people.

Delivering to houses turned out to be much more work than dropping into the boxes. After getting the inserts together, Mr. Jones showed Cassie how to roll the papers into a cylinder and wrap them with a rubberband. Then he tossed them out at the houses. Cassie worked quickly, placing her rolls in a pile on the console next to her dad so he could grab each paper and toss it without missing a beat. The air blew in from his open window, and Cassie shivered. She turned up her heat vent, but nothing diffused the freezing wind that licked her face and hair.

By the time they went home, exhaustion pulled at every muscle of her body. She collapsed on the couch, too weary even to walk to her bedroom. Mr. Jones disappeared into the kitchen.

Cassie's fingers didn't want to uncurl. She lifted a hand to her face. Black. The skin was coated in a sooty black layer, leaving only the ridges of her fingerprints exposed. "What is this?" she murmured. Her head throbbed and her eyes ached, but she forced herself up and dragged her feet into the bathroom.

The same sooty blackness streaked her face. She traced her finger across her forehead, leaving another streak. "Ink," she said, understanding dawning on her. The black ink of the paper coated every thing.

Cassie turned on the warm water and lathered her hands and face with soap. After a good scrub, she'd gotten rid of the blackness. But now the sleepiness weighed her down. Cassie dried her face off, then pushed herself to her room and collapsed on her bed.

☙꧁꧂❧

Cassie held the notepad and pen in hand, following along behind her mother as Mrs. Jones turned glass jars and Number Ten cans around and studied the various contents in the downstairs pantry. Odd items like pickled beets and freeze-dried onions stared back at her.

It had been two days since her first paper route run, and she still didn't feel like she'd recovered. But there was no school this week, and she hoped that tomorrow she could sleep in as late as possible to make up for it.

"Write this down, Cassie," her mom murmured. "We can make a stuffing with the beets and onions. I just need cornmeal."

Cassie wrote it down. Just because it could be done didn't mean it should be. "Doesn't sound very appetizing," she said.

"It's Thanksgiving. We should be grateful for what we have."

Cassie made a face. "Are we even going to have a turkey?"

"Well, of course. We have money for a turkey. But I want to see what else I have before I buy anything."

Cassie nodded, only slightly pacified.

By the time they finished their list, they had instant mashed potatoes, freeze-dried corn, and wheat rolls on the list. Oh and the beet-and-onion stuffing.

"So we'll buy a turkey," her mom said, the skin around her eyes tight. "And eggs and cranberries. And one pumpkin pie."

"What about an apple pie?" Cassie said. "And sweet potato casserole? And cheese balls and pickles and olives?"

"We don't need all of that this year," Mrs. Jones said, shaking her head. "We're lucky we have most of what we need right here."

Luck was a matter of opinion.

The doorbell rang upstairs, and Mrs. Jones started past her. Cassie followed, arriving at the top of the stairs in time to hear the conversation.

"Hi, Mrs. Jones? I'm Mrs. Lark, Scott's teacher over at Walker?"

"Oh," Mrs. Jones said, her tone startled. "Hi. Do you want to come in? Is everything okay? I didn't expect you."

"No, and I'm very sorry. I hope this isn't an intrusion. I should have called. I hope you're not offended."

"Offended? Of course not. What is it?"

Cassie peered around the corner. The teacher wrung her hands together, looking mildly flustered. Her short graying hair bobbed around her shoulders, fine lines around her mouth and eyes.

"Well, you see, Scott told us that your husband is unemployed and you have no food."

"Oh!" Mrs. Jones cried. "No, no, he has a job. We have a store, and we have food."

"So you don't need anything?" Mrs. Lark looked uncertain. "Scott's lunches have been—sparse."

"No, we—" Mrs. Jones' words faltered. "Things are tight, but we're fine."

Mrs. Lark smiled, her features softening. She pressed a hand to Mrs. Jones'. "It's okay to not be fine. I talked to the other parents, and we wanted to help. So we brought you a Thanksgiving dinner."

"You did—what?" Mrs. Jones' hand went to her chest, her words faint.

"I'll get it out of the car." Mrs. Lark walked back to her vehicle, and Mrs. Jones did not move.

Cassie hurried after the teacher. "Let me help you," she said, joining Mrs. Lark at her trunk. She gasped when the trunk opened. Her fingers flew over the boxes and cans. "Stuffing. Cranberries. Pumpkin pie. An apple pie! We'll have an apple pie!" She turned toward the house. "Mom! There's an apple pie!" Cassie gathered up the food in her arms and hurried to the front door. Mrs. Lark came behind her, carrying a turkey.

"I don't know what to say," Mrs. Jones said. She held one hand to her face, and tears streamed down her cheeks. "I never expected this. I had no idea."

"I'll just take this into the kitchen." Mrs. Lark let herself into the house and deposited the food on the table. Cassie did the same.

"There's just a few more things," Mrs. Lark said, and Cassie went with her to get the rest.

When they finished, Mrs. Jones hadn't moved from the doorway. "Thank you," she said, still crying. "Thank you, thank you."

"You're welcome. Happy Thanksgiving." She patted Mrs. Jones' hand and went back to her car.

Cassie returned to the kitchen and started sorting food. "Mom! A turkey, pie crust, pie filling, apple pie, eggs! Everything!"

"It's wonderful," Mrs. Jones agreed, her eyes moist.

"Crackers. Peanut butter. Stuffing. More peanut butter. Jelly. More peanut butter." She glanced up at her mom. "Do you think Scott told them how much he likes peanut butter? There are five jars here."

Mrs. Jones laughed, a short sputtering sound. "I don't know. Maybe." She squeezed Cassie's shoulders. "We certainly have a lot to be thankful for."

Chapter Thirty

Reason for the Season

The leaves finished their lazy descent to the ground sometime at the end of November, and by the time December rolled around, all of Springdale, Arkansas, looked like a barren, dead wilderness. Empty tree branches reached into the sky like bony fingers, streets and houses visible for a mile through the skeletal structures. Cassandra Jones' eyes drifted upward longingly, missing the warm days of sunshine and the plethora of green foliage that was the Ozark trademark for most of the year.

"Winter's coming," her sister Emily huffed beside her, rubbing her hands together vigorously as they walked home from the bus stop.

It was definitely cooler, but not yet cold. Cassie glanced behind them at their younger brother and sister, Scott and Annette, taking their time as they hopped over leaves and fallen branches.

"That means Christmas is coming," Cassie said, keeping her voice low. There were burdens she and Emily carried as the oldest children, and she didn't want the younger ones to overhear. "What do you think we'll do?"

"Who will do?" Emily asked, blinking her eyes in evident confusion.

Cassie sighed. Sometimes she forgot that Emily was only ten and didn't know all the family secrets Cassie did. "You know, because we have no money."

Emily had to know that much. The whole family did. They knew her dad had quit his job over the summer to open a soccer store and work full-time. They knew the soccer store wasn't bringing in enough money, and that's why Mrs. Jones had gone back to work as the breakfast manager at Wendy's. They knew that hadn't been enough and her dad started a paper route to compensate, and they all had to pitch in on Sundays to help him with the increased subscribers. Even their classmates knew there was trouble, eyeing their sparse lunches suspiciously and donating food for Thanksgiving dinner.

Emily chewed on her lower lip, her eyes focused somewhere in the distance. They turned onto the gravel driveway, almost to the house. "I don't know. I guess I don't really need anything for Christmas this year."

Cassie nodded. That was the answer she expected from all of her siblings. "Well," she whispered, shooting Emily a smile, "I've been saving my money. All my allowance, even my lunch money. I've got a hundred dollars. That's twenty dollars for a gift for each person. Even Grandma." Her dad's mom lived in Fayetteville but didn't really like the grandkids. She came around sometimes for holidays or when needed, but usually they didn't see her.

"So we'll have Christmas after all," Emily said, a relieved

grin crossing her face.

Cassie bobbed her head, feeling sagacious and wise. She might single-handedly save Christmas.

The topic got brought up on Saturday when Mr. Jones hauled out the boxes of Christmas decorations. The excitement was palpable as he put the tree up, and Cassie helped her siblings find the ornaments to stick on the bare green branches.

"I can't wait," Scott, her eight-year-old brother, said. "Christmas is my favorite. I'm going to ask Santa for an Avenger, a Transformer, a Batman . . ."

His list went on, and Mrs. Jones let him prattle for a moment.

"Well," she said, finally interrupting his animated litany, "Christmas is going to be a bit different this year."

"Different how?" Scott said, trailing off, a wary look crossing his face.

Mrs. Jones glanced at her husband, and Mr. Jones spoke up. "We're going to put a lot more focus on Christ and what the season means this year," he said.

"And not on presents?" Annette asked, her voice small. She looked worried.

"Not on presents," Mrs. Jones affirmed. "You'll still get some, I promise. But that's not what I want you to be thinking about."

Annette scrunched up her six-year-old nose in concentration, then relaxed and nodded. "Okay. I like that."

"Me too," Cassie said, exchanging a knowing glance with her sister Emily. "The more we focus on Christ, the more it will feel like Christmas."

"So with that in mind," Mrs. Jones said, opening up a

nativity box and handing it to Cassie, "what can we do to put the focus on Him?"

Cassie knelt in front of the coffee table and carefully began arranging the porcelain figurines. She paused on the tiny figure of the Christ child in his manger, the golden hay all around him. "We could do kind things for each other all month," she said. "Give gifts of love instead of money."

"As if we were giving gifts to Christ," Emily said.

"I love that idea," Mrs. Jones said. "How about each week, you pick one of your siblings and do nice things for them. Don't tell them it's you. Then the week after, pick a different sibling. By the time Christmas gets here, you will have done nice things for all three of your siblings."

Cassie nodded, her heart tender just with the idea. It would be a very special Christmas.

And she still had money to buy gifts for everyone.

Cassie decided to start her acts of love with Scott, since he was her most difficult sibling. He was in charge of the trash and feeding the cat. Sunday morning, Cassie got up and fed Baby Blue, then she set out a bowl of cereal for her brother (*sans* milk, since he probably didn't want it soggy), and made him a piece of toast with peanut butter. He loved peanut butter. Then she went back to her room to get ready for church.

Scott didn't say anything about it the whole way to church, and she suspected he hadn't even noticed. But it didn't matter. She felt good about her efforts, and it was a simple thing she could do every day.

Riley was at church. She'd been coming more lately, and she waved at Cassie. Cassie waved back, then sat with her family.

After the sermon, Sister Stathos, a tiny woman with dark curly hair, came and sat in their pew. She struck up a conversation with Mr. Jones. Every Christmas she brought over a big batch of delicious, fresh gyros, and Cassie hoped she'd bring some over this year also. She joined Riley to go to Sunday school and forgot about Sister Stathos until after church, when her mother mentioned her.

"I've got some interesting news," Mrs. Jones said, turning around to face them as they buckled themselves into the car. "You all know Elek, Sister Stathos' son?"

"Sure," Cassie said. She'd seen Elek several times in the soccer store. He always came around to talk to her dad, since he loved the sport and he was a referee now. He was four or five years older than Cassie, but always extremely polite and friendly.

Mrs. Jones glanced at her husband, then faced the kids again. "He's going to come and live with us for a few months."

That piqued her interest.

"Why?" Emily asked, beating her to the question.

Mrs. Jones lifted a shoulder. "He just is. There's a lot going on in his life, and his mom thinks our family will be a better influence on him."

Cassie could read between the lines. His friends were causing him trouble. "Cool," was all she said.

"Yeah," Scott said. "It's like I'll have a brother for a bit."

Cassie liked that. She'd always wanted an older brother.

Elek moved in that evening. He had his own car, and he hunched his broad shoulders under his backpack, keeping his eyes down and nodding respectfully to everything Mrs. Jones said. His thick dark hair, curly like his mom's, bobbed into his face with each head movement. He was so quiet. Cassie and Emily followed him to the guest bedroom, keeping up a steady stream of chatter while Mr. Jones showed Elek the bathroom and closet he could use.

"Girls," Mr. Jones said, finally turning to them, "that's enough. Give Elek some space."

Elek lifted his head and gave them a quick smile, his brown eyes crinkling pleasantly before he dropped his gaze again.

"Do you think he's in trouble?" Cassie asked Emily as they trooped back to their room, her curiosity getting the best of her.

"What kind of trouble?" Emily said, her eyes widening.

"Oh, I don't know." Cassie shrugged. "Friends. Gangs. Drugs."

Emily sat on her bed and rested her chin in her hand. "I don't think so. He's too nice."

Cassie didn't argue with her, but she imagined someone could be nice and still be in trouble.

Chapter Thirty-One
Jaded Eyes

Elek didn't say much all evening. Cassie hoped to chat with him a bit the next day, but he left in the morning for the high school before the bus came and didn't get home until it was time for dinner.

"How was going back to school for everyone?" Mrs. Jones asked as she served dinner.

"Boring," Scott said, and Cassie giggled, for once agreeing with her brother.

"Tough it out. You only have to endure three more weeks before Christmas Break," Mr. Jones said.

"This soup is wonderful," Elek told Mrs. Jones. "What is this leaf?" He fished it out with his spoon.

"Oh, that's a bay leaf," Mrs. Jones said. "Don't eat it. It just gives flavor."

Elek crinkled his brow, his dark wavy hair pulling forward on his forehead. "I don't eat it?"

"Well, it's just not good."

"Can I try it?"

Mrs. Jones shrugged. "Sure, if you want."

Cassie put down her spoon to watch as Elek stuffed the leaf into his mouth. He chewed, his eyes narrowing in concentration, his mouth working around the spice. Then he opened his mouth and pulled out the bent, mutilated leaf.

"You are right," he said. "I shouldn't eat it."

Everyone laughed, and Cassie grinned.

"Scott, don't forget to take out the trash tonight," Mr. Jones said. "The trashman comes while you're at school, and I don't want to have to do your job."

Oh, right. Cassie gave a little jolt. She had to remember to help him this week.

She waited after dinner as Scott gathered all the trash in the house into one giant bag. As soon as he put it down to tie it off, Cassie came into the kitchen.

"I think Mom wants you," she said, totally lying. "She's outside in the garden."

"There's no garden right now," Scott said, his brows knitting together. "It's too cold."

That it was, but it would get Scott out of the way long enough for her to take out the trash. "I know, it's weird. Just go check."

With a shrug, Scott left the trash behind and trudged down the stairs.

Cassie grabbed the trash bag and hurried to the garage door. Behind her, the door to the guest bedroom opened, and Elek came out.

"What are you doing?" he asked her.

"Taking out the trash for my brother. But I don't want him to know that's what I'm doing." She huffed as she lifted the bag into the trash bin.

"I'll help," Elek said, joining her.

"I can do it." She hit the button to open the garage door.

"I know. But you're being nice. I want to help."

She shrugged and let him take the other trashcan, then they hauled both out to the curb. Elek closed the garage door behind them when they came into the house.

"Thanks," Cassie said.

"You're welcome." He gave a nod, looking all reserved again, and disappeared into the guest room without another word.

Cassie hoped he would warm up to them. She really wanted him to act like part of the family, not a guest.

⌖

"They're handing out schedules for next semester on Friday," Emmett said as everyone sat down Tuesday afternoon. "I hope we all still have lunch together."

"That would be nice," Luke said, still a bit timid with them.

Cassie dropped her eyes, her own hopes fluttering in her throat. She hadn't spoken to Miles, her crush of almost two years, since that disastrous day in the gym last October when Andrea laughed about Cassie's crush on him. It would be amazing if she suddenly had lunch with him. She didn't have any proof that Andrea had told Miles about her crush, but she didn't trust Andrea. Her former best friend had morphed into a stranger.

Farrah couldn't stop talking about the skiing trip her family was taking for Christmas. It sounded like more money than Cassie's dad would make in a month, so Cassie did her best to tune her out. Instead she turned to Riley.

"Guess what? Elek moved into our house Sunday."

Riley nodded around a bite of gooey mozzarella. "I saw

your parents talking to his mom. Why did he move in?"

Cassie pulled out her crackers, glad she had cheese to eat with them today. Yesterday her mom had made peanut butter cracker sandwiches, and Cassie did not like peanut butter. "I guess he's going through a hard time. His mom wants us to be a better influence."

"It's probably gang-related," Riley said, noddy sagely.

"Probably," Cassie agreed. She sighed and nibbled at her cracker.

Riley noticed. "Want a cheese stick? I still have three."

Cassie did want one, and her stomach echoed that desire. She'd spent the past six months dieting, and very successfully. Ironic that now that she felt comfortable enough with her weight to eat normal food, her family had no money for it. "I'll just eat one. Want a cracker?"

Riley wrinkled her nose. "No."

Cassie laughed. She didn't really want them, either.

Friday morning, there was a table set up by the school office with signs underneath it. Cassie got into the line for kids whose last names started with A-J, her heart pounding nervously. She had thought she didn't care. She'd already submitted the classes she wanted, so she could guess her schedule, just not the order. Or who with.

Who with. She realized that was the part she worried about. Miles. And if she dared admit it to herself, Andrea. She missed her best friend. She would give anything to have a class with her, for a chance to rebuild their friendship. But what if Andrea only ignored her, just let the space between them grow? She wasn't sure she could bear it.

She got to the front of the line. "Cassandra Jones," she said, and held her breath while they looked for her schedule.

"Here you go," the aide behind the table said, handing a slip of paper to Cassie.

Cassie scanned it quickly. English, math, geography, social studies, choir, teacher helper, study hall. Of course it didn't list any of the kids in her classes. She put it away, disappointed. Nothing had been resolved.

Ten minutes later, she realized she should not have put it away, because every person she ran into wanted to see it. Turned out she had lots of classes with friends, but everyone kind of merged together, and she wished she'd bump into the only two people who really mattered.

"Let me see your schedule," Riley said at lunch, and Cassie handed it over. She would still have two classes with Farrah, as Farrah had checked it this morning.

"We'll have social studies together," Emmett said, leaning across the table to look.

"We'll have math together!" Riley said, excited.

"What do you have instead of art?" Luke asked.

Cassie handed the paper to him, letting him scan it.

"Study hall. And you get to be teacher helper. Lucky," he said.

"I know," Cassie said. She'd felt honored when her life prep teacher had asked her to be an aide during spring semester. It meant she considered her an exemplary student. She turned to Emmett. "What about Miles? Do you know his schedule?" Then she tore her eyes away, her face warming, afraid she'd been too bold.

"He showed me, but I don't remember," he said.

"Want me to find out for you?" Farrah asked, her eyes twinkling.

"No," Cassie said shortly. This was not something to joke

about.

☙〜☙

By Friday, Cassie had run out of nice things to do for Scott. She noticed someone had unloaded the dishes for her and cleaned up her bookshelf, and it tickled her pink to think of one of her siblings going out of their way to make her day better. She stopped at Elek's bedroom after choir practice and knocked on his door.

"Come in," he called.

She pushed it open and found him sitting at the desk, studying a textbook. He turned his serious brown eyes to her.

"Do you need something, Cassie?"

She came in and sat on the edge of the bed, kicking her feet. "I'm trying to do nice things for my brother this week, but I can't think of anything else to do. I've done his chores, made him food, set out snacks. What else is there?"

Elek lifted his eyes to the ceiling, thinking about it. "Maybe you could clean his room? Put away his laundry?"

None of those ideas were particularly exciting, but she guessed that was why it was service. "Yeah, I could clean his room. Thanks." She hopped off, but before she closed the door, she turned back to Elek. "Are you doing all right?"

"Yeah." He nodded. "It's very nice of your parents to let me stay here."

"We like having you here."

"Thank you, Cassie." He gave her one of his rare smiles.

Cassie smiled back, then hurried off to clean Scott's room.

☙〜☙

The next two weeks passed in a blur of pointless tests and then unabated excitement as the days pushed closer and closer to Christmas. On the last day before Christmas break, she hugged all of her friends at school and wished them a merry Christmas.

Cassie rode home with Riley after school so she could attend the Girls Club Christmas party.

"I've never done a progressive dinner before," she said, excited. She bounced around in the car with Riley and Janice.

"Me neither," Janice said. "I think that's the point. It's special because it's rare."

The progressive dinner meant they'd stop at different houses for each part of the dinner. First was Leigh Ann's, then Maureen's, and finally it ended at Jaiden's. For the first time all month, Cassie quit worrying about her schedule and next semester. Instead, she decided to enjoy the good food and her friends.

Leigh Ann's mom had set the table with green glasses, green plates, and lots of green holly. But it wasn't the decorations that drew Cassie's attention. Underneath the tall Christmas tree, giant boxes wrapped in shiny paper and huge bows covered the tree skirt. She tried not to compare it to the bare tree skirt at her house and focused instead on the beautiful spread of food Leigh Ann's mom served.

But the same thing happened at Maureen's house, and the worm of comparison swelled into envy. *It's okay*, she told herself. *We don't need lots of presents to have a nice Christmas.* She mostly believed it.

Cassie braced herself before they walked into Jaiden's house for the last course, dessert. Today she was splurging on her food, and she had no intent on of stopping now.

But there was no preparing for the plethora of Christmas gifts, so many that they spilled out from under the tree and lined the wall leading into the hallway. The other girls laughed and teased Jaiden as they climbed over the boxes to get to the kitchen. But Cassie's throat was a hard knot. All these gifts, just for two children? How fair was that?

Trisha, Jaiden's mom, brought out individual plates of flaming pudding, and the girls squealed with delight. Cassie only picked at hers, suddenly without appetite.

Riley nudged her. "You're not eating."

Cassie gave her a smile, trying to act casual. "I'm not very hungry."

"You look sad," Riley whispered. "Aren't you having fun? It's Christmas."

It's Christmas. Cassie looked at the other girls, giggling and hugging and smiling for pictures. Nobody else was moping over what they didn't have.

"Girls," Margaret, Maureen's mom and the Girls Club leader, said, clapping her hands to get their attention. "Trisha and I have a small gift for each of you also. So before you go, make sure you come and get the one with your name on it." She pointed to a row of gift bags, overflowing with treats and trinkets.

Leigh Ann plopped beside Cassie with her phone out. "Smile!"

Cassie barely got a smile on before Leigh Ann leaned in close and snapped a selfie. Riley pressed in on the other side, and Leigh Ann took another.

"Merry Christmas!" Leigh Ann said, giving Cassie a hug.

"Merry Christmas," Cassie replied, her icy heart melting a little.

"Merry Christmas!" Janice was next, smothering her in a giant hug. "I put a card for you in your gift bag."

"Thank you," Cassie said, touched and a little embarrassed.

She hadn't gotten anything for anyone.

The doorbell rang as parents began to arrive to take their daughters home. Cassie spotted her mom, and she said bye to the other girls before grabbing her bag and hurrying out.

"How was it?" Mrs. Jones asked.

The cold air chilled Cassie, and she shivered as she sat down and pulled her seatbelt across her shoulder. "Great. I have friends." She really did, and that knowledge warmed her. She also had a family that loved her. She wouldn't trade those things for two dozen wrapped boxes under the tree.

Chapter Thirty-Two

Merry Merry Merry Merry

During the first week of Christmas vacation, Cassie focused on doing service for Annette, which was super easy because Annette's chores were simple. Cassie put away the shoes and straightened the books in the dining room, two of Annette's chores. Next week would be chores for Emily, which would require a little more creativity, since they shared a room.

She looked toward her parents' closed bedroom. No one else was around. She stepped down the hall and knocked on the door. "Mom?" she said. "Are you in there?"

"Come on in, Cassie."

Cassie opened the door and pushed into her mom's room. Mrs. Jones looked up from where she sat on the bed and smiled, though her eyes looked tired.

"Hi, Cassie," she said. "Did you have a good day?"

Cassie sat down in front of her mom, noticing the pile of wrapped boxes. "What are these?"

"Christmas presents. What do you think?"

Cassie arched an eyebrow. "I didn't think we were having

any."

"I said Christmas would be small, Cassie," her mom chided, though she kept her tone mild. "Not non-existent."

"Oh, well." Cassie smoothed the bed covers. "I've been saving up my money and want to go Christmas shopping. I have enough to get a gift for everyone. Can you take me tomorrow?"

Mrs. Jones tilted her head, studying Cassie. "You have money you want to spend for Christmas?"

Cassie nodded. "I have twenty dollars for each person. Wait." She frowned. "What about Elek?"

"He's going home tomorrow to spend Christmas with his family. Then he'll come back after the new year."

"Oh, okay. So can you take me?"

Mrs. Jones gave a brief smile and pressed Cassie's hand with her own. "I think that is lovely. I'll take you tomorrow."

◦ֶ୨ৡৡ৹

Cassie had never been so happy to spend money, though the twenty dollars didn't go as far as she had hoped. For Annette she bought a coloring book with a set of markers; for Scott she bought a Transformer; for Emily a set of weaving looms with rubber bands; and for her parents, she put the money together and purchased a set of solar lights for the front yard.

Even though it wasn't much, she wrapped each present with care in her mother's room and then carried them to the living room and placed them under the tree. The sight of twice as many presents filled her heart with joy.

Emily stepped into the living room behind her. "You did it," she said, wonder in her voice. "You bought the extra presents."

"Yep." Cassie looked toward the baby Jesus nativity. Had He noticed? She looked at Emily and smiled, filled with the secret knowledge that she would be doing Emily's chores for the next few days.

6~~~°

Christmas morning.

Cassie's eyes shot open. Outside, the sun was cresting on the horizon, beautiful ribbons of pink and purple layering on top of orange, a hint of blue beneath it. She heard Annette's and Scott's voices coming from the living room, already getting into their stockings.

"Emily!" Cassie whispered. She sat up and put her glasses on, then blinked at the clock on the dresser. Almost seven in the morning! She'd slept in! "Emily, wake up! It's Christmas!"

"Christmas!" Emily bolted up. "Christmas!" She jumped out of bed and stumbled toward the door.

Cassie ran after her. She knocked on her parents' door as she ran past. "It's almost seven! Come on out!"

The two girls raced to the living room. The rule was they could get into their stockings but not touch the presents until their parents got up. Cassie's gaze moved to the tree, and she noted with surprise all the presents under it. Her gifts were not the only ones there. While it wasn't as full as previous years, it was far from empty. Then she turned to her stocking. The sock was stuffed to the brim, just like always. Cassie sat down and emptied it. A banana, an apple, an orange, a bag of nuts, a new toothbrush, and lots of chocolate.

"It's Christmas, guys!" Mrs. Jones said, coming out of the bedroom. She shook her hand through her short dark hair, smiling. Mr. Jones came behind her, yawning and rubbing her shoulder.

"Merry Christmas!" Annette said, jumping up and hugging everyone. Emily joined them, and Cassie followed, and soon the whole family was wrapped up in a hug.

"And we have presents!" Scott said, turning his face excitedly toward the tree.

Mrs. Jones caught his arm. She cupped his face and stared into his eyes, smiling at him. "But that's not what really matters here, is it?"

Cassie thought back on the days she had spent doing chores for her siblings, thinking of ways to help them. Serving them had not just made her feel good inside; it had made her reflect on the love she felt for them also. "Nope," she said, a gooey warmth filling her chest. She shivered with delight. "That's definitely not what matters."

Episode 5: Coming Up Empty

Chapter Thirty-Three
Story Pitch

The second semester started with an unnecessary amount of fanfare. Cassandra Jones weaved in and out of the students, hurrying to her English class. This class was the same as last semester and would have mostly the same people, unless someone switched into it from elsewhere. She said hello to Jimmy and Nicole and Leigh Ann as she slipped into her seat, then paid attention as Ms. Talo began class.

"We'll skip introductions and jump right into the lesson. We have a new book to read, and you'll be doing a project on the book when its done. Kind of a like a book report, but much more in depth."

Cassie took notes on her words, the mechanical pencil dancing across the paper, but her mind was elsewhere. Would she have any classes with Miles? Maybe math. Cassie had switched math classes, so there was a chance he'd be in her new one. Probably not in her teacher helper class, but maybe study hall!

"And don't forget," Ms. Talo said, drawing Cassie's

attention back to her, "the Market Fair is coming up. You and your partner should have solidified what you are making. Take the next ten minutes of class to sit and discuss what you'll be doing."

Cassie turned around and met Nicole's wide blue eyes. The two of them were partners and had batted a few ideas back and forth, but they hadn't yet decided on anything for sure.

"What are we doing?" Nicole mouthed at her.

Cassie waited as a few kids pushed past her chair, then got up and crouched beside Nicole. "I have no idea. I didn't even think about it over break. I thought you would have something!" Nicole was the smart one, always coming up with clever, innovative presentations.

Nicole looked sheepish. "If it doesn't involve movies, I'm kind of out of my element."

"I'm so not creative," Cassie said, her heart rate quickening. What were they going to do? "My mom does crafts. I'll talk to her at home. Maybe she can help."

"I'm sorry," Nicole said. "I'll see what I can do, too."

The bell rang, and Nicole stood, shouldering her bag. "We'll figure it out tomorrow, okay? We still have plenty of time."

"Yeah," Cassie said, though she didn't share Nicole's confidence.

She lingered for a moment by her desk, and then with a start she remembered second hour was her wild card class. It was the one where she wasn't sure who would be in it. Quickly she grabbed up her binder and hurried down the hall to the math wing.

"Good morning, Cassie!" Mr. Adams boomed when she walked in.

Cassie smiled, taking comfort in the sight of her favorite

teacher. "Good morning."

"Cassie!" Riley popped out of a desk and waved her arm up and down, as if afraid Cassie might not see her. "Come sit with me!"

Cassie's eyes scanned the classroom for a more inviting offer, but didn't see any other friends. No Miles. "Sure." She settled in next to Riley and tried not look disappointed.

Lunchtime arrived, and her heart sank as her chances to have a class with Miles or Andrea diminished. She scanned the cafeteria as she plopped down next to Emmett, Farrah, and Luke. No Andrea or Miles. She sighed and unwrapped her carrot sticks.

She thought things would get better at least in choir, but the first day of class was a total joke. It was a girls' chorus, so no chance of seeing Miles. Most of the girls were eighth or ninth graders, since the seventh grade choir met during first hour. Cassie couldn't take it then because of her English class, which was only offered first hour.

Ms. Berry took roll and then spent the entire time laughing and talking with another teacher. She ignored the class of students as they got louder and louder. The girls shrieked and gossiped, going through each other's purses, trying on make-up, doing each other's hair. Cassie couldn't remember the last time she'd felt so out of place. No one spoke to her as she sat in her chair, and that suited her just fine. She pulled out her math homework and began plugging away at the questions.

When the bell rang and Ms. Berry dismissed them, Cassie only had two questions left. She worried about what she would do in study hall and then remembered she still had her geography homework.

She quickened her step as she made her way to the life

sciences building. It really was an honor that Ms. Prose had asked her to be a teacher helper. She'd done well in her life prep class, sure, but she hadn't thought she'd done that well.

"Hi," she greeted Ms. Prose as she walked in.

"Right on time," Ms. Prose said. She fluffed her short dark mass of curls and directed Cassie to a room in the back. "Normally, I'll have you in here, grading papers, filing assignments and stuff. Since this is the first day of the semester, though, I don't have anything. And sometimes that will happen. Do you have homework to do?"

"Um, yes," Cassie said, caught off guard.

"Good. You might want to bring a book also. Grades come first, and I don't want anything in here to get in the way of your studies. If you have an exam or something important coming up, let me know."

"Okay," Cassie said. She sank into a chair and waited until Ms. Prose left. The teacher's voice carried into the small room as she addressed the students, and Cassie wished suddenly she was out there also, ears perked and taking notes, ready to learn. Instead she pulled out her math book and stared at the last two questions.

By the time she got to study hall an hour later, all of her homework was done.

This is great, she told herself. *I have lots of reading time.* She pulled out her book and started reading.

The next day was almost exactly the same. Except this time, when Cassie sat down at the long table in study hall and pulled out her book, she wasn't quite as excited. If every day was like this, she would need a lot more books.

☙❧

"Okay, girls," Ms. Berry said in choir on Wednesday. She

cleared her throat and clapped her hands, trying in vain to quiet a classroom of girls that had not been told to hush so far this semester. "Girls. Girls!"

She managed to get their attention the last time. Cassie stuck her finger in her text book and closed it, ready to pop it open again in a moment and finish her assignment. The other girls around her lowered their voices, the conversations slowly dropping off.

"So I had most of you last semester," Ms. Berry said, "but we have a few new faces this semester. I'd like to go ahead and do a range test with each of you. I'll have you come up in groups of two, okay? And this will probably take the rest of the week. I'll just play a scale and you sing to it until it goes too high or too low. Let's start over here with the sopranos."

Cassie opened her book again, turning back to her homework. She sat with the sopranos, but closer to the middle of the classroom. It would take awhile to get to her, and she could get most of this done by then. She could tell from the whispers around her that many of the girls were nervous to sing the scale in front of each other.

"You're all gonna do great," Alice, a ninth grade girl with velvety black skin and short kinky hair, said. "We done this lots before."

"Easy for you to say, Alice," a cute blond with pens in her hair said. "You've got the highest range in here." Others seconded her opinion, and Alice smiled, her teeth white against her charcoal skin.

"That don't make y'all any less important. We're a team."

Cassie examined Alice curiously. She hadn't realized there was a hierarchy in here, or that some might be considered better than others. So this was the leader of the sopranos.

She returned to her homework, and it was a full fifteen minutes later before Ms. Berry said, "Cassandra Jones. Christy McGarrah."

Sticking her sheet of paper into the book, Cassie stood up and walked down the risers. Beside her, a solemn-faced eighth grader moved stiffly to the piano.

"Hi, girls," Ms. Berry said when they arrived. She gave them kind smiles. "We'll start with middle C and go up, then work our way back down."

Up until this moment, Cassie hadn't felt nervous. But now she was suddenly keenly aware of her classmates staring at her back. She blew out a breath and positioned her feet the way Ms. Malcolm, her voice teacher, had taught her.

Ms. Berry began to pluck out the notes, and Cassie forgot to think about the other students as she concentrated on matching the pitches. Beside her, Christy McGarrah kept pace as well, though her voice was much more timid. The scale continued up the piano, and Cassie's throat opened with the higher notes. Christy dropped out, but Ms. Berry kept playing, so Cassie kept going. Her voice trilled, echoing through the small choir room. Then Ms. Berry let the fingers of one hand clink on the piano while she thrust the other one in the air.

"Yes!" she crowed, making a fist. "We have someone who can hit high C!"

Cassie glanced around, realizing suddenly that the entire room had fallen silent. Then the girls began to clap and cheer.

"You can sit down now, Cassie, Christy," Ms. Berry said. She smiled and called out the next two names, and Cassie made her way back to her chair, her face growing hot.

"Wow, you can sing," one of the eighth grade girls said. She scooted over, making room for Cassie. "She went higher than you, Alice."

Cassie grabbed the edges of her chair and sat down on the hard plastic.

"You okay, Alice?" another ninth grader asked.

Cassie looked at Alice and found the older girl staring at her, her mouth gaping. A single tear drifted down Alice's face.

"You can sing better than me," Alice said. "I've been replaced."

Immediately the girls settled about Alice, crooning and clucking like a bunch of old hens, rubbing her back and trying to console her. But in between comforting words to Alice, they snuck smiles at Cassie and winked at her.

Alice finally quieted her sniffles and looked at Cassie. "You sing good, girl. You the queen now."

"Thanks," Cassie said, a bit uncomfortably. At the same time, though, her ego grew, filling her chest like a hot balloon.

By the time Cassie stepped into study hall, the balloon of pride had morphed into a knot of dread. Another hour with nothing to do. She had no homework left; she'd completed it in sixth hour after making copies for Ms. Prose. Already this week she'd read an entire book, and she didn't feel like starting another, even though she had one in her bag.

With a sigh, she selected a table and dumped her binder and purse on it. The study hall monitor came in, told them all to get out something to do, and sat down to play on his phone. The students weren't allowed to have electronics, or Cassie might actually pull hers out and text people.

A kid in front of her crossed his arms on the desk, stretched out his lanky legs, and laid his head down. Cassie yawned. She could try taking a nap also. She copied his posture and dropped her head on her arms. She closed her eyes, but sleep evaded her. Someone coughed. Another kid tapped his pencil on the table. Someone else scooted their chair back, the legs screeching across the linoleum. Even the clock ticked loudly as the second hand made its way around the clock face.

Cassie opened her eyes and sat up. Opening her binder, she pulled out a piece of notebook paper and tapped her eraser against it. She hadn't done too bad in art with drawing subjects and people. Glancing from time to time at the boy sleeping in front of her, she started to sketch him. He didn't stir the entire time, but no matter how she tried, Cassie couldn't capture his image. After twenty minutes, she gave up and put the paper away. Instead she pulled out a new sheet. Across the top, she wrote, "Farrah."

Then she frowned. When her friends wrote her notes, they drew her name in big bubbly letters with beautiful designs. Cassie erased the name and tried to make a bubbly F, but instead it came out looking like a deformed marshmallow. She grimaced and subsisted. Maybe the A would help.

It didn't. It looked like a blown-up pyramid with a wedgie. Erasing it, Cassie scooted the letter closer to the F and tried again. When it didn't improve, she crumpled up the paper and threw it away. Regular letters it would be.

Her note to Farrah was so boring Cassie was afraid to give it to her. A glance at the clock showed there were still seven minutes of school left. With nothing else to do, she pulled out a notebook paper and wrote a note to Nicole. She folded both notes into little squares and wished she knew how to fold them into pretty shapes.

The bell rang, and Cassie charged to her feet just as quickly as Sleepy-head at the table in front of her. Inwardly she heaved a sigh of relief as she hurried out to the buses. She'd survived one more day of study hall.

But she couldn't survive a whole semester of this. Something had to change.

೨ᴥ৩

Cassie gave Farrah and Nicole their notes early in the morning and waited all day for them to write back. If they did, it would give her something to do in study hall.

As sixth hour drew to a close and it neared the time to go to seventh hour, however, Cassie realized they weren't going to. Not that she blamed them; she knew the notes had been boring.

Seventh hour started with its usual lack of luster and acclaim. Cassie pulled out a few new sheets of notebook paper and contemplated who she should write notes to today. Who was likely to write her back? Riley. Who else?

Cassie wrote Riley's name across the top of the page, but after that her mind went blank. What should she say? She really had no idea.

The words from a church song came to her mind. Erasing Riley's name, Cassie wrote out, **walk Beside Me.**

Why had she written the words to a song? What was she going to do now, write down the verses?

No, she realized, she wasn't going to do that. Unexpectedly, an idea came to her. A story idea. A story about a girl and her three best friends who ended up in the wrong place at the wrong time, and the only thing to get them through the trial was their faith.

Cassie fairly trembled with anticipation. She folded her notebook paper in half, opened it up, and wrote at the top, **Chapter One.** Closing her eyes, she formed images in her mind's eye of the four girls. She blinked, a smile on her lips, and immediately began drafting the backstory for these characters.

Chapter Thirty-Four
Bookworm

Now that Cassie had an outlet, the writing became an obsession. She filled page after page with her story in study hall, but the fifty minutes in there wasn't enough time. She found herself hurrying to first hour so she could sit and write before the bell rang, and then hurrying through her assignments so she could write some more.

"Everyone get with your partners," Ms. Talo said the third week of January. "The Market Fair is in two weeks. You should have your products decided on and priced. I'm sending out an expense sheet, and I need you all to fill it out."

Cassie looked up from her notebook paper where she had just started writing chapter five. The four girls had been taken to an abandoned house in Canada and just discovered a skeleton in the basement. She heaved a sigh, annoyed at the interruption. Whatever was happening in her novel was much more interesting.

"What are you doing?" Nicole asked her, sliding into the desk Jimmy had vacated so he could meet with his partner.

"Nothing." Cassie put the paper away. She hadn't told anyone yet. She wasn't quite sure how they would react.

Nicole's eyes followed Cassie's hand as she slipped the paper into her binder. "You're always writing on there. Are you writing notes?"

"No." Cassie didn't bother with that anymore. No one ever wrote her back.

"What is it, then?"

Cassie hesitated. She tapped her pencil on her desk, first the lead and then the eraser. "Promise you won't tell?"

Nicole's eyebrows rose, and a smile pressed itself to her lips. "Promise."

"I'm writing a book."

Nicole's eyes widened. "Really? Like a real book?"

Cassie nodded.

"Wow, I've never met someone writing a book! Can I see it?"

Cassie's eyes turned toward the folded sheets of paper in her binder. "Um, no. It's really rough. Maybe after I type it up."

"That's so amazing." Nicole looked impressed. "Does Ms. Talo know?"

Cassie shook her head. "You're the first person I've told."

"So, so cool." Nicole tossed her head and turned back to the expense sheet. "Okay. So what did we finally decide?"

Cassie had, at least, met with her mom about crafts and come up with a few things. The last time she and Nicole had talked, they had a few solid ideas, and Cassie had felt more sure about narrowing it down. "I've got three things I'm going to make. One, these really cool necklaces out of magazine pages. Two, my mom taught me how to make beautiful baskets out of cardboard boxes and crepe paper. And three, little twirling sticks."

Nicole lifted her gaze from where she wrote on the paper. "Twirling sticks?"

"Here, I made one." Cassie flipped to the back of her binder, where she'd stuck the stick weeks ago after she painted it. "See? It's a branch that I broke, but it wasn't a clean break. The top part curves around, like a pinwheel." Cassie pointed out the curly-cue piece of wood at the tip. "Then I painted it. Now watch." She stuck it between her palms and spun it. The painted curly-cue danced through the air, leaving a bright streak of blue in its wake.

"Yeah, that's kind of cool," Nicole said. "But who's going to buy it?"

"Anyone. It's just fun."

"Maybe for second graders. But we're in junior high."

Cassie furrowed her brow. She looked down at the twirling stick and realized the fatal flaw in her thinking. "I guess I thought people would buy them for their younger siblings." She couldn't picture her fellow seventh-graders sitting in class and twirling the little painted sticks around.

"Well, they don't cost much to make, right?" Nicole said. "We could have a few there."

"Yeah." Cassie shrugged it off. "What about you?"

Nicole gave her an apologetic look. "I can't think of much. I'm just going to make brownies."

"Hey, everyone likes brownies." Her own stomach growled in appreciation of the chocolaty treat.

"Yeah," Nicole said with a laugh. "So let's price these things out."

Tuesday after school, Cassie rode with Riley, Janice, and Maureen to their Girls Club meeting. Riley bounced up in down in the car, excited.

"I can't believe they're going to let us into the back of the restaurant," she said. "We'll be like the actual cooks! We might even learn new skills!"

"They won't actually let us cook," Margaret, Maureen's mom and club leader, said. "We'll just watch. You have to have a special food handler's permit to cook for other people."

"That's okay. At least we'll be able to see how they do it!"

Cassie did her best to tune them out. She had her notebook paper open in front of her, though her pencil bounced and jolted every time the car accelerated or braked. She sighed. Right after Girls Club, she had choir. Tomorrow voice lessons would keep her busy. And yet she was desperate to finish chapter five.

"What are you doing, Cassie?" Janice asked. Janice had short brown hair and a round face, and she'd always been nice to Cassie. They didn't have any classes together anymore, and Cassie only saw her at Girls Club, but she liked her.

Still, she hesitated before answering. She'd finally told Farrah and Riley what she was doing, but they had reacted with far less enthusiasm than Nicole, making Cassie fear most people wouldn't appreciate her efforts. "I'm writing a book," she said finally.

"She's always working on it," Riley said with an eye roll. "She hardly even talks to us anymore."

"What's it about?" Janice asked.

Cassie gave her a smile. "Four girls who get lost in the woods. They end up being taken to this old house, and it turns out to be a murderer's house."

"Oo, sounds creepy!" Janice said.

Cassie's courage grew under Janice's interest. "Would you like to read it?" she asked, holding out the first chapter.

"No!" Riley groaned. "We're not here to read your book."

Whether Janice would have or not, Cassie never found out. Margaret parked in front of the restaurant and ushered the girls out.

Cassie closed the car door and wrapped her arms around herself, shivering in spite of her sweater. January and February were the coldest months in Arkansas, and she couldn't wait for the warmth to come again. She glanced longingly behind her at the car, wishing she could stay in it. It was warmer, and she could work on her book.

She trudged along behind Janice and Riley and they met up with the other girls, but Cassie's mind kept going back to the imaginary world she was creating. Girls Club was just one more thing that took her away from it. *I don't want to do this,* she realized. She couldn't give up choir or voice lessons, and her dad needed her in the store too much to stop helping out. But Girls Club she could let go of.

⚘

The activity was only mildly interesting. Cassie watched her mom cook meals every day; learning how someone produced mass amounts wasn't that exciting. The pasta and bread they sampled after was tasty, but not enough to make Cassie glad she'd come. She stayed quiet in the car afterward as Margaret drove her to the community center for her choir practice.

"Here you are, Cassie," Margaret said, coming to a stop in front of the building. Other kids were also getting dropped off.

"Thank you, Margaret," Cassie said. She put her hand on the doorknob.

"Did you have fun at Girls Club?" Margaret asked. "You've been awfully quiet."

Cassie looked at Janice and Riley in the back seat, who were both staring at her as if waiting for an answer. Even Maureen, sitting up front with her mom, swiveled her head around the chair. No way was Cassie going to admit anything to them. Instead, she put on a big smile.

"Yeah, I had a great time!" she said. "So much fun! Thanks for the ride." She waved and closed the car door, then let her smile drop off as soon as she turned her back on her friends. If she had any say in the matter, she would never go to Girls Club again.

RyAnne, the tall brunette who looked two years older than Cassie, was being dropped off at the same time. She paused and waited for Cassie, though Cassie couldn't imagine why. They were not friends. RyAnne usually hung out with Samantha, a quiet eighth-grader. Cassie remembered her from the choir rehearsals the year before, and RyAnne was arrogant, superior, and condescending. To make matters worse, she actually had a terrific voice.

"I think I've found my first husband," RyAnne announced as if they were in the middle of a conversation.

"Really?" Cassie spared her a glance before opening the doors to the art center.

"Yes. He's got all the money I need. Then when we get divorced, I'll take half of it. My second husband won't have to be rich, but he needs to have prestige."

Cassie paused and turned around, blinking in surprise at RyAnne's words. "Your second husband? You plan to get divorced?"

"Oh, yes. Why stick with only one when you can try

multiples? After I divorce my second husband, I'll marry someone foreign and go live in another country."

Cassie had never met anyone who actually wanted to get divorced someday. And not just once, but twice. She shook her head and let go of the door. RyAnne could let herself in.

Cassie settled herself in a chair in the back row next to Kendra, another second soprano, and opened her black binder. She surreptitiously opened her school binder and pulled out the chapter she was working on. She settled it next to her music with her pencil close by. She sang every time Ms. Vanderwood called on the sopranos, but as soon as she turned her attention to the other parts, Cassie whipped out her pencil and worked on her chapter.

༄

Cassie waited until dinner was over and she had finished loading the dishes before she approached her mom about Girls Club. Mrs. Jones was in her bathroom, washing her face with a rag.

"Mom?" Cassie said. She stepped up to the counter and picked up the facial cream. She examined it before setting it down again.

"Yes, Cassie?" her mom said. She swiped a cotton ball over her face and eyed Cassie. "Do you need to wash your face?"

Cassie lifted her face to the mirror and examined her reflection. She'd lost a lot of weight in the past six months, and her cheek bones stood out in high relief under her brown eyes. But the glasses obscuring her face hid her features. She couldn't even see if she was pretty; washing her face wasn't going to make it better.

Stay on course. "No, that's okay." She cleared her throat. "I don't want to be in Girls Club anymore."

Mrs. Jones paused with her hand next to her eyes. One eyebrow arched upward, and then she settled back on her heels. "Why? You've been in Girls Club for seven years. You've always loved it."

She'd prepared herself for resistance. "I joined when I was five. I'm twelve now. Almost thirteen. It's just not as fun as it was. I don't have any good friends in it. And I'm so busy. There are other things I want to do with my time."

"Have to agree on the busy part," Mrs. Jones said. "It will be one less thing for me to worry about if you don't want to do it."

Cassie nodded. She held her breath, sensing her mother's willingness.

"Why don't you finish out the month, just to be sure," Mrs. Jones finally said. "If you still want to quit in February, I'll let you."

"Thank you," Cassie breathed. That was fair. She went back to her room, wishing she had time to do something besides start working on her Market Fair products. She knew she wouldn't be changing her mind.

Chapter Thirty-Five

No Fair

Each night after dinner, Cassie worked on her Market Fair crafts. Tuesday, Wednesday, and Thursday only gave her a few hours, since she had activities right after school. But Friday she had plenty of time, and she began to feel the pinch of panic. Each basket took her at least an hour. At this rate, she would only have six or seven done before the fair.

As long as I have other crafts, that will be fine, she told herself. And she would have others. She could make the twirling sticks very easily.

She sat at the kitchen table measuring crepe paper and carefully weaving it around the box late into the night. Elek came in around ten to get a snack, then bade her good night and went back to bed. Her parents had gone downstairs to watch a movie. Cassie considered joining them. Certainly she could watch a movie and do this at the same time.

A screeching noise outside caught her attention. She paused and listened. The noise began again, starting with a low, threatening growl, followed by a loud screeching yowl.

Cat fight! Their cat, Baby Blue, must be fighting with something. But what? Cassie bolted out of her chair and ran for the front door.

Sure enough, Baby stood with her hackles up, as if on tiptoes, every piece of hair standing straight on end. She shimmied sideways as she faced off a big, fluffy, black and white cat.

"Baby," Cassie said, trying to get in the middle of the two cats. They simply danced around her, as if she were rock or some other inconsequential object.

Then the black cat lunged, and Baby's paws shot out in defense, her mouth emitting the loud, threatening scream. The other cat got in a good whack at Baby Blue's ears. Baby hissed and lashed out, scratching at the black cat, who growled at her.

"Stop it!" Cassie screamed, frightened now. She grabbed Baby Blue, but the cat turned on her, lashing out blindly. Cassie cried out as the claws cut into her hands. She released the cat and jumped backward.

With Cassie out of the way, the black cat attacked. It leaped on Baby Blue's back and dug its teeth into the scruff around her neck. Baby Blue screeched and tossed her head, but she couldn't shake her attacker. Cassie clutched her torn hands, hot tears running over her cheeks. What could she do? If she got in the middle of them, she'd get scratched up even worse.

"Cassie?" Elek appeared in the doorway where she'd left the front door open. "What is it?"

In answer, Cassie pointed at the fighting cats. "They'll hurt each other!"

Elek took one look and disappeared into the kitchen again. When he returned, he had a broom in his hands.

"Shoo!" Elek shouted, and then he yelled out a few more words in a language Cassie didn't understand. He hefted the broom and brought the straw end down on the black and white cat, thumping it several times. The cat's ears flattened, and it climbed off Baby Blue and streaked into the night.

Cassie tried to pick up Baby Blue, but the cat retreated, pupils fully dilated and fur still on end.

"It's okay," Cassie crooned. She held out a hand, trying to earn her trust. "Let me see you."

"Stay with her," Elek said. "I'll get her some water. She'll be fine."

Cassie continued whispering to Baby, and by the time he returned with a bowl of water, Baby Blue was letting Cassie pet her.

"Is she hurt?' Elek asked, putting the bowl in front of her.

Cassie worked her fingers through the fur, searching for cuts or blood. "I can't find anything."

"I'm sure she's okay."

"Probably." But Cassie didn't feel right about leaving her outside all night. "I'm going to take her to my room."

"Will your mom like that?"

Cassie didn't intend to ask. "I'll set up a kitty litter." She scooted closer to the cat and managed to scoop up Baby Blue before she could run off.

The cat trembled in her arms, and Cassie held her tight. Tears rolled down her cheeks as she thought of the cat fight, of how her mama cat could have been injured. Cassie's hands burned where the claws had sliced into them, but she ignored the throbbing pain.

"Are you all right, Cassie?" Elek asked, following her into the house.

"Yes." Cassie sniffed and wiped her cheeks. More tears tumbled down after. "I'm fine."

Elek hesitated, and Cassie could tell he wanted to help some more but didn't know what to do. "Okay," he said finally. "Good night."

"Thank you," Cassie called after him, feeling a surge of gratitude.

He waved and disappeared into the guest bedroom, closing the door behind him.

◦⁓⁕⁓◦

Baby Blue cuddled next to Cassie all night, but by morning she was anxious to get outside. Cassie let her out and watched anxiously for the offending cat, but only black kitten, now an adult cat himself, came over to rub heads with her.

Baby seemed okay, but Cassie's fingers hurt so badly that she couldn't put her baskets together. Instead she made the twirling sticks and promised herself she'd have time during the week.

Each day left Cassie more and more anxious. She didn't have a chance to work on her book all week except during study hall, and not even much there. She'd actually had to study for a few upcoming exams. The characters and the story haunted her thoughts, and she grew more and more frustrated every moment that she didn't get the chance to write. She only had six baskets made. She carried the supplies with her to Girls Club, to church, even to choir, and wove the paper around the cardboard boxes every spare second.

By Friday evening, she had nine baskets. That would have to be enough.

She spent all day Saturday putting together beads made of magazine pages. First she cut the sheet of paper into long triangles. Then, starting at the wide end, she wrapped the triangles around a toothpick before gluing the edges. At first she found color coordinating pages, like all blue or all yellow, to make beads of that color, but as the hours slipped by and her fingers cramped up on her, she didn't even care, and instead made strips of paper from pages that had nothing but writing on them. Her head pounded, and she massaged the skin between her eyes.

Scott came into the kitchen and picked up several of her beads. "What are these?" her younger brother asked.

"Don't touch," Cassie snapped, snatching the beads from his hands.

"Sorry." He sat down across from her, watching.

Cassie rolled a strip around a toothpick, securing the bottom tightly so she could wrap the skinny side around it. She lifted her eyes. Scott was still watching. She heaved a loud sigh and put the toothpick down. "Can you go away?"

"Why? I want to see what you're doing."

She gritted her teeth. "That's exactly why. You're distracting me."

"I'm not doing anything." He picked up another bead, annoying in a way only an eight-year-old brother could be.

"Put that down!" Cassie shouted, slapping at his hand.

"Cassie." Mr. Jones walked into the kitchen at that moment, a basket of laundry in his arms. He frowned at her. "Don't yell at your brother."

She took a deep breath, then another, blinking back sudden tears. "I can't think with him here. I have to get this done." She held up the thirty or so beads she'd put together so far. "This is only enough for like three necklaces!"

"Scott, leave her alone," Mr. Jones said.

"I'm not doing anything!"

"You're bothering me!" Cassie said.

"Cassie," her dad said, that warning note in his voice.

Scott tilted his head and looked at her, then his finger darted out and tapped one of her drying beads.

"Just go away!" Cassie shouted.

"Cassandra!" Mr. Jones roared. "Go to your room!"

"What?" she sputtered. How was this her fault? She gestured at the glue, the toothpicks, all the cut magazines. "I have to get this done!"

"Not right now, you don't."

"Fine!" She threw her chair back hard enough that it banged into the wall behind her. She stomped out of the room, letting the tears of frustration roll down her face. She stopped short of slamming her bedroom door, though, knowing it would bring both parents down on her. She sat on the floor in front of her bed and sobbed at the injustice of it all. She pulled out her crepe paper and contemplated making another basket before giving up and letting it fall to the carpet.

Chapter Thirty-Six

Hiss Hissy

The incident with Scott and her father was not brought up
for the rest of the day, and Cassie spent most of Saturday night
making beads. She wondered how many necklaces she might
need. Twenty was a good number. She doubted she could sell
more than that.

Sunday morning came too early, and Cassie pulled the
blanket over her head as she heard her mother rousing the
children.

"Cassie," Mrs. Jones said, pausing next to her bed and
shaking her shoulder. "Wake up. It's time to get ready for
church."

Cassie pulled the blanket down and blinked up at her
mother, bleary-eyed. Her head pounded, the headache from
yesterday still taking up residence. Her weighted eyelids
pulled closed again, and her mother gave another shake.

"Wake up," Mrs. Jones said.

Cassie had no choice. She stumbled from the bed and found
a dress to put on. She'd worn this same dress for her sixth

grade graduation. At the time it had clumped together awkwardly around her waist, fabric trapped by the bulging skin, but now the white dress with lavender flowers draped her loosely. She tightened the ribbon belt, then decided that looked wrong. She let it out, and it draped around her hips.

"Get breakfast," she heard her mom saying to the other children. "We need to go."

Cassie put her glasses on and ran a brush through her long unruly hair. She looked awful, like she'd died and only partially come back, her skin paler than usual and her eyes bloodshot and puffy. Shoes, she needed shoes.

She was still on the closet floor searching for her other white shoe when Mr. Jones yelled, "Everyone get in the car!"

She groaned. So much for breakfast. And shoes. And fixing her hair. Even though it was still freezing outside, she grabbed the first matching pair she saw: flip-flops. Then she ran into the kitchen, picked up an apple, and hurried out to the car.

Nobody commented on her shoes in the car, but she doubted anyone saw. She sat in the back of the van and took a few bites of her apple, then leaned her head against the window.

The next thing she knew, the van had come to a stop in the car parking lot. Cassie climbed out of the van and dragged behind her family. A hollowness sat in the chest, leaving her heavy and empty at the same time. She didn't pay any attention to the sermon. She just kept thinking of all the things she had to do, all the things she wanted to do, and all the things she wouldn't get done today.

The sermon ended, and she trudged to Sunday School.

"Cassie, what's on your feet?" Tyler Reeves stopped abruptly in front of her, his eyes trailing down to the flip-flops she wore.

Cassie looked at the blue-eyed, brown-haired boy. Last year he'd been chubby, but like Cassie, he'd lost a lot of weight this year. He'd become rather cute, and Cassie's face warmed just from talking to him. But he was a jerk. She'd never forget the way he treated her last year when she missed the basketball during the game. And he always found something to tease her about, some way to make fun of her.

"Flip-flops," she said stiffly. "Lots of people wear them."

One eyebrow quirked up, and he smirked. "Yeah, in the summer. It's only February."

"I was hot."

He snickered. "Trying to start a new fashion wave?"

Two girls from the youth group, Michelle and Sue, came over, apparently drawn by Tyler's antics. Usually they ignored Cassie.

"What's going on?" Michelle asked, loudly popping her gum.

"Where's Jason?" Sue asked, spinning around and looking for Tyler's older brother.

"I was just admiring Cassie's chosen footwear," Tyler said, gesturing at her feet.

Cassie wished she could disappear. Or at least vanish everything from the ankle down.

"I'm going to class now," she said, turning around. She ignored them calling after her, the giggling that followed. She made a detour instead to the bathroom. She sat down in the stall and wrapped her head in her hands. She would just wait here until church was over.

Cassie stared out the car window the whole ride home. Her siblings chattered and showed off the pictures they'd made in class, then asked Mrs. Jones what was for dinner, and Mr. Jones told them they'd have a family meeting before they played games that night. Still Cassie didn't speak up. Somehow she had to get through the next week, and then it would be Friday again and she could finish making these necklaces.

Then it would be over . . . and maybe she would have time to write again.

"Cassie, what's wrong?" Mrs. Jones asked at dinner.

Everyone else happily spun their spaghetti noodles around their forks, but Cassie had no appetite.

"Nothing," she said.

She didn't miss the look her mom sent her dad.

Mrs. Jones sent them all to get pajamas on before the family meeting and game night. Cassie did as told, swapping out her flowery white dress for a baggy t-shirt and flannel pants.

A light tap came from the door. Cassie pulled the shirt over head head just as Emily pulled open the door for their visitor.

"Oh, hi, Daddy," Emily said. "Come on it."

Mr. Jones did. He side-stepped the pile of clothing by the door, wrinkling his nose slightly, then sat down on Cassie's bed. "Emily, do you mind giving me and Cassie a moment of privacy?" he said.

"Sure." Emily bounced out.

"What is it?" Cassie asked.

He gestured at the spot next to him on the bed. "Come sit."

Cassie hesitated. She wasn't feeling touchy-feely, but she couldn't exactly say no. So she scrambled up onto the bed next to her dad.

"Are you okay, Cassie?" he asked, his tone all gentleness. "You haven't seemed like yourself lately."

Immediately yesterday's indignities rose to the forefront of her mind, and along with them, the tears. "I'm not acting any different! It's everyone else who's treating me like I'm doing something wrong."

Mr. Jones held up a hand to calm her. "I'm just trying to talk to you."

Cassie took a mental step back. She was overreacting, and even she could see it. "It's just—everything—I don't know!"

He watched her, his clear blue eyes patient, and Cassie tried to find the words for her concerns. "I have so much to do. I can't keep up! It's this Market Fair I'm working on, I have to get all these crafts done, and I hate it! I hate making crafts! And Ms. Vanderwood keeps sticking me in second soprano even though I'm a first! I sing first soprano! Even Ms. Berry at school recognized my voice for how high I can sing!" She paused for a breath, but then started right back in.

"I'm so sick of Girls Club. It's boring, I'm not really friends with anyone, I have other things I want to work on. I'm always in trouble with Ms. Malcolm because I don't practice, but when do I have time? I want to write, I just want to write my book, and there's no chance to do it! And the kids at church, they make fun of me, they're mean to me, I wish we went to a different congregation!" She thought of Elise and Tesia, the girls she had befriended at church camp over the summer. They lived in Rogers and went to the Rogers congregation. Hot tears pricked her eyes again. She missed them. Why weren't they closer to her?

"And—and—and—I can't even find my shoes!" she sputtered. There. She'd said it all. Drained, Cassie dropped her head into her hands and cried.

"That's a lot on your plate, Cassie. What do you mean about

writing a book?"

She lifted her head, cheeks warming. She hadn't meant to toss that out like that. "I started writing a book at school. I really love it. But lately I haven't had time to work on it, and it's making me crazy." Crazier would be trying to explain how writing had become her happy place. The fictitious characters she'd created were her closest friends.

"I think that's great. So what can go? What can we take off your plate?"

Cassie exhaled, a huge sense of relief filling her. He was taking her seriously. "Girls Club," she said instantly. "I don't want to do it anymore."

"Done," Mr. Jones said. "You don't have to go."

Her lips spread into a wide smile, and it felt as if light filtered into her soul at those words.

"Anything else?" he asked. "How are you with working at the store? Helping out with the paper route once a month?"

"That's fine," Cassie said hurriedly. The last thing she wanted was to increase the burden on her family. "I can do that."

"You mentioned the community choir, voice lessons. Should we let one of them go?"

Cassie settled back on her hands and studied the ceiling. Not voice lessons. As much as she hated disappointing Ms. Malcolm, she loved the private one-on-one teaching time too much. And even though she wished Ms. Vanderwood would put her on first soprano, she couldn't quit singing just because of that. They were a huge commitment. Twice a week for the choir and once a week for voice. "I can't give them up."

"When is this Market Fair?"

"In a week," she said. "And then I think things will calm

down. It's just really stressing me out. I have to make so many things for it. And I don't like making things."

"You should ask your mom for help."

"I did. She's the one who gave me the ideas."

"Ah." He nodded. "Well, even with taking Girls Club out of the equation and knowing Market Fair will be done in a week, there's something more we need to do."

"What?" Cassie asked, curious. This talk had gone far better than she'd expected. What more could he do for her?

"I think it's very important that you have some quiet time in the evenings, all to yourself. You can read your scriptures, pray, write in your book, whatever you want. But you need that down time. And no homework. We'll probably set a time each day, and even if the other kids are involved in another activity, you'll need to remove yourself to another room and take your time out."

Half an hour of mandated silence with nothing to do but read or write. Cassie closed her eyes. Sounded like a dream.

"Can you do that?" he asked.

Her eyes opened. "Absolutely."

Chapter Thirty-Seven

Good-bye

"So it's February," Farrah announced at lunch as she popped open a can of soda.

"Yes," Cassie said, grimacing at the salad in front of her. She didn't need another reminder that the Market Fair was right around the corner. What she really wanted was a slice of Farrah's pizza. Or some of Emmett's chocolate muffin. "We know."

"So," Farrah said. She gave a little huff. "Don't you know what that means?"

Cassie, Riley, Luke, and Emmett stared at her. Cassie raised an eyebrow, waiting for an explanation.

Farrah gave another sigh. "Valentine's Day!" she said. "Aren't you guys excited to see who wants to give you a Valentine?"

Cassie pressed her lips together and didn't say a word. She already knew no one would give her a Valentine. Still, a little piece of her heart couldn't help wishing she'd get one from a certain boy. . . .

Emmett scoffed. "Of course you would be thinking about Valentine's Day. I can tell you right now, guys just don't care. Right, Luke?"

Luke ducked his head, his cheeks turning a rosy color. He mumbled something, but Cassie didn't understand the words.

"We'll see about that," Farrah said. "Just to prove you wrong, I'm having a Valentine's Day party on Friday. And you're invited." She settled back in her chair with a smug smile on her face.

"A party!" Riley exclaimed. "That sounds great!"

Farrah scowled at Riley. "I didn't even invite you."

Riley's face fell. "Really?"

Farrah's brows lifted and her lips pulled down, and then she smiled brightly. "Just kidding. Of course you're invited."

Emmett laughed. Cassie looked at him, wondering if he had seen what she did. But neither she nor Emmett brought it up.

"So?" Farrah said, turning her attention to Cassie. "Are you coming?"

Cassie remembered the Christmas party she'd gone to in sixth grade. It had been her first boy/girl party, and she had not enjoyed it at all. The guy she liked hadn't come, and the host's boyfriend had followed her around all night. "I can't. I have the big Market Fair on Monday. I'll spend all weekend working on it."

Farrah smacked her on the back of the head. "It's not this weekend! Next Friday. Say yes."

Cassie considered. Market Fair would be over by then. Maybe this party would be different. They were older now, after all. "I'll ask my mom. I'll see what she says about it."

☙❧

Five days before the big Market Fair, Cassie sat down with

Nicole to finalize the booth.

"You should have purchased all of your supplies by now," Ms. Talo said, handing a sheet of paper to each group. "Use this sheet to fill out all your actual expenses. And then make an estimate of the amount of hours you've put into this. When it's all over, you'll be able to see how much you made per hour. Market Fair is on Monday. If you have anything left to make, do it this weekend."

"I should've done what you're doing and baked cookies," Cassie said to Nicole.

"Yeah, but at least you've been able to get a head start." Nicole started filling out half the information on the sheet. "I have to bake brownies all weekend long."

"How many will you make?"

"Two hundred, probably."

Cassie nodded, but her heart sank a little. In comparison, she didn't have a lot to offer.

As if reading her mind, Nicole asked, "How many of your crafts do you have?"

"Well, let's see." She stalled, hoping the numbers would magnify if she took her time. "I've spent nearly ten hours making baskets so . . . Nine." She forced a smile, but Nicole only nodded and wrote it down. "I hope to do five more this weekend, though," Cassie said. "And I have ten necklaces. More by Monday. And about thirty twirly things."

"Okay." Nicole continued filling out the sheet. "So by Monday, you expect to have fourteen baskets and, what, fifteen necklaces?"

"Yes." Cassie nodded. "That sounds about right."

"Great." She passed the sheet over to Cassie. "I'll let you write down how much they cost and how many hours you put into them. And we have to figure out how much we'll sell things for."

Luckily Cassie hadn't spent a lot of money. She calculated up the crepe paper and the toothpicks. The magazines had just been lying around the house, and the cardboard boxes constantly showed up on the front door. The paint she'd found downstairs in her mom's craft box. Mostly it was just time. She'd spent way too long making these things.

"I think I'll sell each brownie for two dollars. Does that sound good?"

"Yeah." Cassie nodded. "Sounds great. Do you think I can sell my baskets for ten?"

"You can try, at least."

Cassie wrote it down. "And the necklaces for seven. The sticks for a dollar." She added up her potential profit. Even if she sold everything she'd made, plus everything she hoped to make this weekend, her profit wasn't quite three hundred dollars. She frowned. That hardly compensated for her time.

Maybe it wasn't too late to do cookies.

⟡

"You make the best soup, Mrs. Jones," Elek said at dinner Monday evening.

Mrs. Jones laughed and shook her head. "It's just an autumn stew. Nothing special."

"No, it's very good." Elek dug his spoon around and came up with a leaf. "What's this?"

"That's a bay leaf," Cassie said, recognizing the herb. She'd helped her mom cook often enough that she was starting to know her way around the kitchen. Which was more than she could say last year, when she and Emily totally butchered the food they tried to cook for their parents.

"Can I eat it?" Elek asked.

"Well, you could," Mrs. Jones said. "But I wouldn't recommend it. It's just for flavoring."

Elek looked at her like he didn't quite believe her. Then he plucked the leaf from his spoon and folded it into his mouth. Cassie pressed a hand over her lips, concealing a giggle. What was he doing?

Elek chewed for a moment while everyone around the table stared at him. Then he pulled the leaf out of his mouth, now a wadded up bunch of broken plant.

"You're right," he said. "It's not great for eating."

Everyone laughed, including Elek. Then his smile faded.

"I hope you won't be upset," he said, "but I've decided it's time for me to move home."

Cassie's spoon dropped from her hand and clattered to the table. "What?"

Her mom shot her a look. "Are you sure, Elek? I thought your mom wanted you to finish out high school with us."

He bobbed his head, his dark eyes not quite meeting anyone's. "You have all been very kind to me. I need to start living again. I left things a bit of a mess. I need to put them back in order."

Hot tears filled Cassie's eyes. "But we love having you here!"

He looked at her and gave a small smile. "I love being here. You are all family to me. But I feel like I must go home."

"Well, if that's how you feel," Mr. Jones said, drawing the focus to his end of the table, "we support you. I'm sure your mom will be happy to have you home."

Elek nodded. "I'll go home after church on Sunday. If I can stay here that long."

"Of course," Mrs. Jones said with a warm smile.

Cassie turned back to her soup. She fought to keep from crying, starting at the carrots and celery floating in the dark broth. She'd gotten so used to his presence.

⁀ᚾᚱᚾ⁀

Even though Cassie worked feverishly all Friday night and all day Saturday, she only managed to complete four more necklaces and two more baskets. She had seriously considered the cookie thing but decided against it. She'd put way too much energy into these crafts to reject them now.

She didn't feel like watching a movie with the family after dinner, and she was tired of making crafts for the day. Instead she took their dog, Pioneer, and went outside. She sat on Elek's car and stared at the stars, appreciating the nip in the February air. She couldn't stay up too long because tomorrow was her newspaper day, and getting up at two a.m. was never easy for her.

Pioneer trotted around the trees in the front yard before returning to the front door of the house. Then he sat down and stared at Cassie, waiting for her to come let him in. She considered it but decided she wasn't ready to go in yet.

The door opened, and Elek stepped out. "Cassie?" he called.

She straightened. "Here," she said.

He walked down the porch steps and stopped in front of his car. "What are you doing out here?"

She shrugged. "Just thinking."

"Are you okay?"

"Yeah. Just . . ." She sighed. "I didn't think you'd be leaving any time soon."

He joined her, sitting on the hood of the car beside her. "I'm sorry if I offended your family."

"No, no!" she exclaimed. "It's just, I think of you like a brother. I enjoy talking to you."

"And you and Emily are like my little sisters. I will miss you."

Cassie tilted her head and looked at him. "So why are you going?"

He exhaled and lifted his eyes to the sky. "I have a family also. My mom and my brother need me. He's all alone now."

"But I thought you needed us." Her throat ached. "Why did you move in here?"

"I needed to get my thoughts in order, Cassie. Now I have. It's time to go home."

Cassie nodded without saying a word, though inside she felt like a family member was moving away.

After church on Sunday, Mr. Jones helped Elek move his two bags from the Jones' van to his own car. Then they shook hands.

"I'll never forget what you did for me," Elek said.

"You are welcome in our house anytime," Mr. Jones said.

Elek shook each family member's hands in turn. Cassie lingered behind her siblings, wanting to be last. Finally Elek took her hand in a firm grip and offered her a smile.

"You are strong, Cassie," he said. "They all look up to you. Don't be afraid of who you are."

She smiled and nodded, appreciating the words. Then she climbed into the car with the rest of her family.

Chapter Thirty-Eight
One Plus One

Mrs. Jones helped Cassie load up all the baskets into the back of the car Monday morning. "These turned out beautifully, Cassie," she said. "I bet you sell them all."

"I hope so," Cassie said. She stuck a finger in her mouth and bit around it, the long-conquered nail-biting habit reemerging with her nerves. "What if no one likes my stuff?"

"That's not going to happen. Get in the car, and I'll get the others."

Since Cassie wasn't riding the bus, Mrs. Jones didn't make the other kids either. But that meant Cassie had to sit, rather impatiently, as Mrs. Jones drove them to Walker Elementary first. Cassie watched her younger siblings run out of the car and into the front doors, feeling a pang of longing. She hadn't even realized how good she had it last year. Miles had been in her class, and he talked to her every day.

And she had Andrea.

She shook her head, physically removing the thoughts. She couldn't go back to that time, even though she wanted to.

Mrs. Jones pulled behind the junior high gym, where the students were setting up their booths for Market Fair. Cassie grabbed several baskets and looked for Nicole.

"Cassie, over here!" Nicole shouted, giving a wave. Cassie smiled and waved back, then joined her at their booth. Small plates of chocolate brownies covered the table, all wrapped in cellophane with a price tag on them.

"Wow, you made so many!" Cassie exclaimed.

"Your baskets are beautiful!" Nicole picked one up and admired the woven crepe paper design.

"Thanks."

"There are a few more baskets in the car," Mrs. Jones said. "Shall we go out and get them?"

"Right," Nicole said, giving a nod. Her fluffy blond hair bounced around her. "I'll help."

They brought all the baskets in, and Mrs. Jones helped them set up a cute display with baskets, necklaces, and brownies. The only thing that seemed out of place were the twirly sticks, and Cassie hesitated to put them out.

"Just put out a few," her mom said, seeing how she held one indecisively in her hand. "If they sell, put out more. If they don't, no harm done."

"Okay." Cassie nodded and placed a handful around the brownies.

"Looks great, girls, let me get a picture." Mrs. Jones stepped in front of the booth, and Cassie leaned into Nicole with a smile.

"Lovely," Mrs. Jones said. "Okay. I'm heading home, but call me and let me know how it went!"

Cassie sat down in the chair behind the booth, her leg bouncing up and down with nerves. "I can't remember how long this lasts."

"Seventh grade is first," Nicole said. "I think they come in at nine. We have like an hour to set up. Then eight grade at ten, and ninth at eleven. Then it's over and we clean up before lunch."

Cassie glanced around at all the other tables set up as booths. It hadn't occurred to her that the older kids would be participating, though she supposed it should have. She saw a pair of ninth grade girls across the aisle setting up a booth with Hershey kisses. A play on words, maybe?

"Now we just wait." Nicole pulled out a small plate and grinned. "And eat a brownie." She offered one to Cassie, and Cassie took it. One brownie wouldn't hurt.

"These are really good," Cassie said, closing her eyes in pleasure at the intense flavor.

"Yeah, so if they don't sale, I won't be complaining much." Nicole laughed.

Cassie shook her head. "These will sale." She looked at her baskets with a trace of worry.

A little after nine a.m., the first group of seventh graders shuffled in. Cassie's heart rate ratcheted up, and she felt her throat close up. The kids roamed past her and Nicole, their eyes scanning the table before moving on.

Cassie exhaled as the group filed past. "No one bought anything."

"Yet," Nicole said, sounding confident. "They're smart. They want to go around and look at everything first. Then they'll come back and buy what they want." She opened another brownie and smiled around a bite of chocolate.

"I'm sure you're right," Cassie said, though she wasn't sure at all.

The next group came in before the first group had left, and then a third group, and soon the gym was full of milling students. Several made their way back to Cassie and Nicole's table.

"Brownies look good," a girl with long brown hair said.

"Hi, Cassie," Farrah said, grinning broadly. "How are sales?"

"Oh, great!" Cassie said, faking enthusiasm. "Great so far!"

"Oh, good!" With a wave, Farrah moved on, and Cassie's heart sank. Not even her friends were buying her baskets.

"I'll take a brownie," the girl said, and she handed over two dollars. Another girl joined her, and Nichole sold four more brownies.

"I like these baskets," a teacher said, pausing to pick one up. "What a clever idea."

"Thanks," Cassie said, sitting up straighter. "My mom came up with it."

"How much?"

"Ten dollars."

"I'll take one."

"Thank you!" Cassie jumped up to handle the exchange of money. "Pick any you want."

"I like this pink and green one. The bow is really nice." Hefting her basket, the teacher moved on.

"Cassie!" Nicole squealed. "You sold one!"

"I did." Cassie smiled, straightening her shoulders with pride. "And your brownies are a total hit."

The brownies continued to sell, but not the baskets. She sold a few necklaces, though no one even picked up the twirly sticks.

"Hi, girls!"

Two hours into the fair, Mrs. Jones' enthusiastic voice rang out behind them, and Cassie turned around, relieved to see her mother.

"How's it going?" Mrs. Jones asked.

"Pretty good," Nicole said. "Ninth grade should be coming in soon. I think I've sold about forty brownies. Cassie's sold a few things too."

Cassie forced a smile and tried to look excited. "Yeah. A basket and a few necklaces."

"Hmm." Mrs. Jones surveyed the display. "How much are your baskets?"

"Ten dollars."

"Let's drop the price to five. And the necklaces?"

"Seven."

"Let's say they are five also and they get a free twirly stick with each purchase."

"Want to write it down?" Nicole asked, holding out a sheet of paper and a pen.

Cassie finished making the changes just as the ninth grade classes began to enter.

"Free twirly stick with each necklace purchase!" Mrs. Jones exclaimed, tossing one at an older boy.

"What?" he said, taking a step back in confusion. The girls beside him laughed.

"This is cool," one of the girls said, picking the stick off the ground and stepping to the table. "How does it work?"

"It's a stress-reliever," Cassie said, improvising. "A mental distraction. You just rub it between your palms, like this, see?" She demonstrated.

"And I get one free with a necklace?" The girl leaned over to examine one. "What are these made of?"

"Magazines," Cassie said. "Environmentally friendly. My way of recycling."

"Totally cool! How much?"

"Five dollars," Cassie said, and she held her breath.

"I'll take one." The girl fished her wallet out of her purse and forked over the money.

"Brownies too?" The boy had joined them, and he picked up one of Nicole's bags. "I'm starving."

"Those are two dollars," Nicole offered.

For the next fifteen minutes, a small swarm hovered around their table. It seemed everyone wanted one of Nicole's brownies, and the students couldn't resist a free item. Cassie sold almost all her necklaces and even five baskets.

Finally the crowd thinned, and a few moments later the last of the kids trickled out of the gym.

Ms. Talo came through, clapping her hands. "And that's it, everyone! Great job! Clean up your things, tally up how much you sold, and we'll discuss the next time I see you in class! As soon as you finish putting away, get to your expected destination!"

"That was really fun," Nicole said, packing away what was left of her brownies. "I've only got seven left."

"And we only ate three of them," Cassie teased, in much better spirits now.

"Thanks for your help, Mrs. Jones." Nicole turned to Cassie's mom. "You really brought a crowd."

"Yes, thank you," Cassie echoed, fighting back the instinctive urge to be embarrassed. "People started buying things after you showed up."

"No problem," Mrs. Jones said. "I'm so glad I was useful."

Cassie and Nicole filled out their expenses and profit sheet before they left the gym. They took their time packing up, joking with other kids and comparing results. By the time they made it to the cafeteria for lunch, Cassie was in high spirits.

Turned out Market Fair was the highlight of the day. Fourth hour passed slowly. Ms. Berry had a big concert coming up with her select choirs, the ones that kids actually had to audition for, and so she didn't make the girls in fifth-hour choir do anything. She sat behind the piano organizing her sheet music, occasionally yelling at them to quiet down.

Cassie found this all incredibly boring. She had a science test on Thursday and knew she should study for it, but there would be time for that later. She got up and went to a chair on the highest riser, scooting herself against the wall and away from anyone's prying eyes. Then she pulled out her latest chapter. This was the one where the main character, Joyce, realized that her friends were depending on her to make contact with their families, to find help for them.

Her pencil flew over the paper as she pictured Joyce, similar to Cassie with long dark hair and brown eyes. But Joyce was smart, sassy, confident, and beautiful, all things Cassie wished she were. Even when faced with terror and horrible men, Joyce kept her head. She would do whatever necessary to protect her friends.

Cassie tapped her pencil to her lips and let out an exhale. Joyce also had a circle of three best friends. Four girls who loved each other like sisters. What Cassie wouldn't give to have a group like that.

꧁ ꧂

On Tuesday Cassie and Nicole turned their expense report in, and Cassie couldn't even begin to describe the burden that lifted off her shoulders. Market Fair was officially over.

Not only that, but she felt a huge sense of liberty as she walked to the soccer store after school. Normally, she'd be tracking down Riley so she could ride with her to Girls' Club. She was done with that. She no longer had to force herself to go to a boring activity with people she didn't connect with.

"I'm here," she said as she let herself into the store.

"Hello, sweetheart," Mr. Jones said, looking up from the register. "How was school?"

"Great." Cassie went behind the register and put away her binder. "Things are much better now. Market Fair is over. I don't have to go to Girls Club. I can concentrate on music and writing." As she said those words, Cassie realized how those were the two things she was passionate about.

"And how's your book coming?"

"Good." Cassie smiled. "I've finished chapter eight now. I've even shown it to some of my friends."

"What are you going to do when you finish with it?"

She shrugged. "I don't know. Type it up. Maybe try to get it published. Wouldn't that be cool?" She could picture it now. *Twelve-year-old child genius, youngest author ever*. Of course, she better hurry because she'd be thirteen in less than a month.

"Well, if you need any help, just let me know."

"Thanks, Daddy."

Chapter Thirty-Nine

Party Pooper

Farrah wouldn't stop talking about her Valentine's Day party.

The closer it got to the weekend, the more she talked about it. Cassie considered herself lucky to be invited, since she was no one's best friend and definitely not in any popular groups. Other than that, though, she didn't pay much attention. She probably wasn't going to the party, anyway.

And then Farrah mentioned that she had invited everyone from Student Council.

Miles was on Student Council.

"Did you say you invited everyone on StuCo?" Cassie said, interrupting Farrah's diatribe before school.

Farrah tossed her shoulder-length blond hair and shot Cassie a smug grin, the scar on her chin crinkling. "Yes. But I don't know who's coming yet."

Cassie turned to face the hallway as they left the locker hall, a hopeful anxiousness stirring in her stomach. Maybe she would go to the party. A flurry of mixed emotions flooded her. Excitement that maybe she and Miles would finally get a chance to talk, dread that Andrea might have said something to him about her, hope that maybe he felt the same for her as she did for him, and embarrassment that she could even be thinking about him that way when he'd never done anything to lead her on.

"I got RSVPs back," Farrah said at lunch on Thursday, waiting until she had her friends' attention. "Don't you want to know who's coming, Cassie?"

Cassie's stomach folded in on itself. She knew why Farrah was asking. Farrah had discovered Cassie's crush on Miles, and though she didn't tease her about it, she did take every chance she could to mention him, since they were on Student Council together.

"I don't really care," Cassie said, feigning indifference. "I'm sure I'll be fine with whoever is there."

Farrah smiled, a knowing twinkle in her eyes. "Oh, I know you want to know about this one. Miles will be there."

A hot flush warmed Cassie's face, and she hoped she wasn't blushing. She glanced surreptitiously at Riley to see if she caught the connotation, but Riley had already turned back to her French fries.

"Oh," Cassie said. "That's great. Miles is a nice guy."

Farrah giggled. "So I've heard. Although I might not know him as well as you."

Cassie lifted her eyes to find Emmett watching her very carefully. She looked away, afraid he would read something on her face. Emmett and Miles were good friends.

Luckily the subject was dropped, and Cassie spent the rest of the day trying to brainstorm the next chapter of her book. She hurried through her homework in choir, and was a bit annoyed when she actually had to grade papers in Teacher Helper. But as soon as study hall came along, the only thing she had to do was write. She hadn't had a chance all week because of today's science test, and now that it was out of the way, she could focus on her writing.

At least, that was the plan. Oddly enough, her mind kept wandering to Farrah's Valentine's Day party. That anxious knot formed in her stomach whenever she thought about the guest list. She shook it off and forced herself to write a chapter.

By Friday, half the school was talking about Farrah's party.

"I think I'll have about a hundred people there," Farrah said as she and Cassie went to third hour together. "I'm not sure what my parents will think. They told me I could have twenty."

Cassie choked back a laugh. "I think my parents would disown me."

"No," Farrah said. "You'd have to do something much worse, like get pregnant or something."

The thought of pregnancy dredged up thoughts of the act necessary for someone to get pregnant, and Cassie couldn't help the heat that prickled up and down her skin. "I would never do that," she said.

"Someday you will," Farrah sang out. She opened the classroom door and slipped inside, and Cassie followed, trying to purge her mind of Farrah's words.

For once, Farrah didn't mind Riley's chatter at lunch, and the two of them talked nonstop about the evening's party.

"You are coming, right?" Farrah asked Emmett and Luke.

"Oh, I don't know," Luke said, looking slightly alarmed. "Who will be there?"

"Only friends," Farrah reassured him.

"Maybe," he said, focusing on opening his milk carton.

Farrah turned her attention to Emmett. "Emmett?"

"How could I miss it? Sounds like even my parents will be there," he teased, and Farrah laughed.

"Not," she said. "Cassie? Your parents said yes?"

Cassie bobbed her head, avoiding all eye contact. If she looked at Emmett, she was afraid he'd see the naked hope in her eyes that she and Miles would have a moment . . . just a chance to sit, talk, to see if the connection between them still existed.

Or maybe the connection had only been in Cassie's head.

The closer the hour hand got toward the evening, the more anxious Cassie felt. She tried to distract herself with reading and homework, but only one thought kept marching through her mind: *Tonight I'll be at a Valentine's Day party with Miles.*

So much expectancy hung on that thought that Cassie wanted to vomit.

She hurried through her chores at home and then sat on the computer to type up a chapter, focusing on something besides who might be there.

"Are you sure you want to go to this party, Cassie?" her mom said as she came downstairs to put something into her craft room. "You look rather sick."

Cassie grunted. "The last party I went to was really boring. But Farrah said Miles will be there. So will half the school. What if he doesn't even talk to me? That would be worse than if he didn't go at all. Maybe I should just stay home."

Mrs. Jones laughed, and then pressed her lips together. "I don't know, Cassie," she said. "Looks like you have some tough choices in front of you."

Cassie cocked her head to the side, certain her mother was

somehow making light of her dilemma.

A distant, high-pitched noise caught Cassie's attention, and she turned away from her mom to listen for the sound. Mrs. Jones didn't seem to have noticed.

"Do you still like Miles?" she asked.

Cassie didn't even get the chance to say how obvious the answer to that was before she heard the noise again. It came from outside, drifting through the basement walls, and sounded like a scream.

It came again, a blood-curdling scream of pain. And in that instant, Cassie identified the voice.

"Annette!" she said, bolting for the stairs.

Her mom was right behind her, and when they got to the living room they saw Emily also racing for the front door.

"It's Annette!" Cassie cried.

Emily flung the door open. Cassie ran down the porch steps, shading her eyes and searching for her youngest sister. Her heart plummeted when she saw her.

Annette stood in the shade of a few trees, just yards away from the house. Dancing around her, barking fiercely as he tried to protect her, was Pioneer. But the smaller dog could do nothing against the bigger black dogs that leapt at Annette, snagging her in their jaws.

Annette screamed again, hands protecting her face. Mrs. Jones took off, screaming even louder, clapping her hands and charging at the dogs. Theirs heads whipped around, and they backed away when they saw the raging mother.

Cassie recognized them. A few years ago, she'd tried to deliver something to the neighbors across the street, and their two dogs had held her hostage until the owner came out and found her.

Mrs. Jones reached Annette and gathered her into her arms before hurrying across the yard. The dogs didn't chase her but sat back on their haunches, tongue hanging out, as if they were nothing more than innocent bystanders. Emily stood behind Cassie on the steps, her face ashen.

"Emily, get Pioneer into the house," Cassie ordered.

"Where are you going?" Emily asked.

"To the neighbors." With that, Cassie took off down the driveway.

She didn't get far before she saw the dog's owner coming up his walkway. The old man wore his usual overalls, and though he walked with a plodding gait, Cassie could see he was trying to hurry. She ran up to him and joined him as he continued up to the street.

"Your dogs," she panted. "Your dogs attacked my sister."

He spared her a quick glance, his brow furrowing slightly. He didn't say anything, but he walked a little faster.

Mrs. Jones sat on the porch swing with Annette in her lap. Annette sobbed, her six-year-old frame trembling and shaking. Mrs. Jones cooed at her as she ran her hands over her body.

The dogs hadn't moved from where Mrs. Jones had left them. When they saw their owner, they both leapt to their feet and started forward.

"Stay!" the man commanded, and the dogs settled back again. He turned his attention to Mrs. Jones. "Look, I don't know how they got out. They're still just babies, see, only two years old. They were just playing."

Mrs. Jones' head shot up, and fire snapped in her eyes behind her glasses. "Tell that to my daughter!" she shouted. "Your dogs mauled her! She's been bitten, there are punctures everywhere!"

"The dogs have had their rabies' shots—" the man started.

"Is that supposed to make me feel better?" Mrs. Jones screeched. "What if he'd gone for her face? Her throat?" She shook her head, tears glistening on her cheeks.

"I'm sure he was more interested in your dog—"

"*Our* dog, on *our* property. If you can't control your animals, get rid of them!" She stood up, lifting Annette with her. "I'm taking her to the ER. Cassie, stay here and watch Scott and Emily. Your dad's meeting me at the hospital."

"Okay," Cassie said. Now that her adrenaline rush was fading and her heart rate returning to normal, she had to swallow past a lump in her throat. Annette looked so frightened, and in so much pain.

"I'll come too," the man said.

Mrs. Jones looked like she wanted to argue, but then decided against it. "Put your dogs away first," she snapped.

"Call me," Cassie said. "Let us know how she is."

Mrs. Jones got Annette all strapped in the back and settled into the driver's side. "I will, sweetie. She's going to be fine." She started the van and backed down the driveway.

Cassie shuddered and went into the house. She kept hearing Annette's screams in her head, the panic, the fear. She wished Elek still lived here. She needed someone to help hold her together right now. Instead, she had to hold everyone else together.

"Okay, guys," she said with forced cheer, closing the door tight behind her, "let's make some dinner and watch a movie. It's Friday night."

⚬⤜∽

Mrs. Jones called Cassie's phone about an hour later.

"I'm on my way home," she said.

"How is Annette?" Cassie asked. She cleared the soup bowls from the table and loaded the dishwasher, a nervous energy pumping through her veins. She'd spent the past hour alternating between frantic housework and sudden bouts of worry. They'd eaten ramen for dinner, and Emily had taken Scott downstairs to watch a movie, but Cassie had seen the concerned glances Emily sent her.

"Mostly fine. A few of her puncture wounds were deep, but she didn't need stitches. A couple of shots. They're keeping her a little longer. I'm coming home to get some things in case I have to spend the night."

Cassie exhaled and leaned her head against the refrigerator, relief rushing through her. "I was so worried."

"I know. Why don't you go get ready for your party? I'll take you when I get there."

Party? For a moment Cassie's mind blanked, and then she remembered. The Valentine's Day party! "I don't feel like going to a party."

"You should, Cassie. It will be good for you, distract you."

"I'm not sure," Cassie said.

"Just get ready. We'll discuss it when I get there."

Cassie hung up her phone and went to her room to survey her closet. Valentine's Day. Didn't that require something red? Cassie found a red t-shirt, but it was nothing special, not a baby tee or even a V-neck. She paired it with blue jeans and examined herself in the mirror. She looked frumpy. Another search of her closet revealed a red sweater in the back, but it was covered in sequins and sparkles and looked like it was made for a seven-year-old.

Well. It would have to do.

Cassie pulled the sweater over her head and made her way to the bathroom. There she scowled at her reflection. What could she do to make herself look less like a fourth-grader? She brushed half her hair up and left the other half down, but she still didn't look like a sophisticated seventh grader going to the Valentine's Day party. Frustrated, she took all her hair down again and put on a red headband.

"Are you ready, Cassie?" Her mother appeared in the bathroom doorway. Weary lines surround her eyes, her nose still pink from the crying fest she'd had earlier. "I have to get back to the hospital. I need to take you now."

"You don't have to take me at all," Cassie said. "I look awful. I don't even want to go."

"Just come, Cassie. I don't want to argue with you. You'll be sad if you miss it."

Cassie couldn't say for sure, but she suspected her mom might be right. Sighing, she grabbed her purse and headed after her.

"Emily, you're in charge," Mrs. Jones called down the stairs. "Your dad will be home soon."

Once they were in the car, Cassie asked, "So how is Annette? What did they do to her?"

"She really is okay. They probed the wounds to make sure there was no dirt inside and they gave her a couple of different shots, which she didn't like. She's doing much better. They wrapped her whole body up in gauze."

Cassie tried to picture her little sister covered in bandages. "And the dogs' owner?" Cassie looked at her mother. "Did he meet you at the hospital?"

"Yes. And he finally apologized. He even offered to have the dogs put down."

"Put the dogs down, as in, put to sleep?"

"Yes, but I don't think it's because he felt bad so much as because we can sue him for what happened. I told him we would talk about it, but as long as he keeps his dogs fenced in, I don't think they needs to be put down. They don't have any children; those dogs are their babies."

Cassie could understand that. But she couldn't stand the idea of the dogs somehow getting loose and hurting someone again.

They arrived at Farrah's house, and Cassie swallowed back another bout of anxiety.

"You're a little bit early," her mom said. "Just hang out with Farrah until I come get you, okay?"

"Right." Crapola. No one arrived early to a party. Cassie put her hand on the door handle and pushed the car door open,.

"Have a nice time, and call me later!" Mrs. Jones said.

Farrah opened the door when Cassie knocked, her face brightening. "You made it after all!" Then she took a good look at Cassie. "What's wrong? Have you been crying?"

Cassie bobbed her head, swallowing back a fresh torrent of tears. She saw a few other kids lingering in the kitchen and hallways, but only about five people. Lowering her voice, she said, "My sister was attacked by a dog today. She's in the hospital."

Farrah's hand flew to her mouth, and she gasped. "Oh no! Is she okay? What are you going to do?"

The tears came now, an automatic response to Farrah's sympathy. "She's okay, really." Cassie wiped the tears, trying to brush them aside. "It was just really scary. I keep hearing her screams in my head."

Farrah gave Cassie a hug. "Well, I'm really glad you came.

We'll have a lot of fun anyway."

Half an hour later, Cassie knew she would not.

Most of the girls arrived in droves before the boys, and by the time the party started, there were about thirty girls and seven boys. Farrah tried to get things going with some music for dancing, but with so few boys, there wasn't really anyone to dance with. Soon the girls began clustering into the same groups they belonged to in school. Farrah mingled with one of them, joining up with a couple of kids from Student Council.

Cassie looked around to see if any of her friends were there. Riley hadn't come, in spite of her earlier excitement. She spotted Emmett and headed his way, grateful for at least one person to hang with.

And then she saw who he was talking to. Sometime in the past twenty minutes, Miles had slipped in, unnoticed by Cassie. Now he stood next to Emmett, laughing at something someone said.

Cassie's heart melted. He looked so adorable, the way his hair spiked up in the front and the way his eyes crinkled behind his glasses when he laughed. Had being on StuCo changed him? Was he as funny and friendly as he'd been last year?

Cassie turned away. No way was she going to burst into the middle of their group just to talk to Emmett. She glanced around the living room and kitchen, teeming with students holding paper cups filled with apple cider punch. Half the girls wore cute red dresses with black slacks underneath, and the other half wore sexy low-cut shirts that showed off their skinny bodies. Cassie glanced at it her own sparkly sweater and baggy jeans.

Nope. She certainly was not going to say hello to anyone. In fact, it was better if nobody even noticed she had come. Finding the bathroom, Cassie pulled out her phone. She knew her mother was at the hospital and she didn't want to bother her, so she called her dad.

"Hello?" Mr. Jones said. "What's up, Cassie?"

"I'm at this Valentine's Day party," she said. "Mom probably told you. Anyway, I'm ready to come home. I'm tired."

"Oh, okay. Your mom said the party didn't end for another hour. Are you sure you don't want to stay a little longer?"

"There's nothing to do here except eat," she said, trying to hide her desperation. She needed to leave *now*. "It's pretty boring, and I'm exhausted. Can't stop thinking about Annette. I don't want to party. I want to sleep." It wasn't exactly true, but there was a lot of truth to it. She felt overwhelmed with emotion, a sadness that radiated throughout her soul. Though it had very little to do with her little sister.

"Well, I'm in the middle of stuff here. I'll come get you in half an hour."

Cassie swallowed. "That's fine." She closed her phone and stared at the bathroom door. What now? Should she go out and risk somebody seeing her? Or should she hide out here in the bathroom?

Hiding in the bathroom won.

Cassie would've stayed in the bathroom until her father arrived, but soon other kids were knocking on the door, needing to use it. So she vacated it with a brief smile and hid herself in Farrah's room. Only when she heard the front door open and her father's voice roaming through the music did Cassie hurry toward the entryway.

"Are you okay?" Mr. Jones asked when he saw her.

"Fine," Cassie said, shouldering her purse and avoiding making eye contact with her classmates. "Let's just go."

"Cassie?"

To Cassie's horror, Miles suddenly appeared in the kitchen doorway, looking at her. She blinked at him, wishing she could shield her body with her hands.

"I thought Farrah said you would be here." Miles smiled, the friendly, open expression on his face as achingly familiar as Cassie remembered.

"Oh, I am, but I'm just leaving."

Oh," Miles echoed. "Well, it was nice to see you. I don't bump into you much anymore."

"Yeah," Cassie said, waving her hand. "School kind of keeps us apart. But I think about you a lot." Immediately she cringed at her words. Thought about him a lot? Why would she say something so revealing?

Miles' cheeks turned pink, visible even in the dim lighting. "That's nice," he said. "See you in school."

"All right," Cassie said, shoving her father out the door and closing it behind her before he could say another word.

The cold air did nothing to calm the heat in her face, and Cassie pushed her hands against her cheeks, wishing more than anything that she had never come to this party.

"What was that about?" Mr. Jones said. "Is that boy someone special to you?"

"No," Cassie said shortly. "He's just a friend. And I don't think about him all the time." At least, he had been a friend before today. Cassie doubted Miles would ever talk to her again.

⚭⚬

Cassie didn't see Annette until Saturday morning. She sat

on the couch reading when Annette walked in the front door with Mrs. Jones, who had spent the night with her in the hospital.

Cassie took one look at the gauze covering every inch of Annette and burst out laughing. "You look like a mummy!"

Annette smiled. "You should see what's under my bandages. Daddy nearly passed out when they started checking me."

Cassie could imagine that. Her father didn't have the strongest stomach. He had handled it well the year before when Cassie got bit by a snake, but only as long as he didn't have to watch them draw blood.

Mrs. Jones carried a vase of flowers. She set them on the dining room table and brushed her hands on her pants. "We are lucky the dogs are up-to-date on their shots. Could have been worse if we had to worry about that too."

"What are you going to do about the dogs?" Cassie asked.

"I left it up to Annette." Mrs. Jones looked at her youngest daughter. "I guess she didn't want to put them down."

Cassie also looked at Annette. "Why not?"

Annette gave a big smile. "Because they're just dogs. And the neighbor promised he would put up an electric fence to keep them in. As long as they can't get out and hurt other people, I don't care if they are alive or dead."

"That is very pragmatic of you, Annette," Mrs. Jones said. She rubbed Annette's head affectionately, one of the only parts of her body that wasn't covered in gauze. "I know they are very grateful that you are so forgiving."

Cassie's eyes never left her sister, and though she knew Annette was trying to be forgiving, she could tell from the waver in her smile that Annette had a lot of healing to do still.

Chapter Forty

Quitter

"Are you coming to Girls Club tomorrow?" Riley asked at lunch. "You didn't come last week." She bit into one of her mozzarella sticks, the gooey cheese going everywhere.

"No." Cassie nibbled at the edges of her sandwich. She couldn't bring herself to spend money on something as greasy and unsatisfying as mozzarella sticks, even though they looked delicious. "I quit Girls Club."

Riley dropped her cheese and gasped. "What?"

Cassie nodded. She'd managed to avoid telling Riley, but everyone was bound to find out soon enough. "Two weeks ago was my last time. That's why I wasn't there last time."

"Good for you." Farrah nudged her with her shoulder. "It didn't seem like you liked it that much anyway. You said all the girls were snobs."

Riley's brow furrowed, and Cassie felt the heat rush to her face.

"We are not!" Riley exclaimed. "Is that what you think of us?"

"No!" Cassie said, rushing to save face. "It's just sometimes I feel like I'm not a part of the group. Everyone talks around me but not to me."

"That's because all you want to do is write your book," Riley said.

"Well, it's pretty important to me right now!" Cassie said, feeling sensitive.

"We were talking about your book last week," Riley said. "Janice said she wants to read it. And everyone started asking questions about it."

"Really?" A little spark of hope flared in Cassie's chest.

"Don't you want to come tomorrow? Bring a few pages for us to read?"

The prospect was tempting. Cassie was ready to get eyes on her book, ready to hear what her peers thought of her story. But Girls Club always had some other activity planned. "I don't think that's what everyone wants to do."

"I want to," Farrah said.

"Me too," Emmett said, watching the exchange with a hint of amusement in his eyes.

"But me first," Riley said, jumping in and frowning at Cassie. "Come tomorrow with your pages."

"I don't know," Cassie said, her hesitation returning. "It was so nice last week not to have that many activities."

"What about Camp Splendor?" Riley challenged, striking where it mattered. "You can't go if you're not in Girls Club."

"I can't?" Cassie hadn't gone to the summer camp last year, but the previous year she had, and she loved it. This year, since she wouldn't be doing soccer camp, she fully intended to go to Camp Splendor. "Why not?"

Riley shrugged. "That's just the rules."

"Well, that's pretty dumb," Farrah said. "They should let everyone go."

Riley shrugged again, not meeting Farrah's eyes.

"I'll talk to my mom," Cassie said. "See what she says."

❦

"I thought you wanted to be done with Girls Club," Mrs. Jones said, her forehead knitting in confusion as she pulled the towels from the dryer.

"Well, I did." Cassie took the first hot towel from the top and folded it. "But Riley said they missed me. And I thought maybe I misjudged them. So I might give it one more chance."

Mrs. Jones heaved a sigh. "You are so confusing."

Cassie's face warmed. "I don't mean to be."

Her mom waved a hand. "It's fine. You've only missed one week. If you want to go tomorrow, we'll just keep doing it."

"Great!" Cassie put down the towel and started from the laundry room.

"Where are you going?"

"Oh." Cassie paused, her hand in the door jamb. "Well, Riley said they wanted to read my book. So I thought I'd type up the first chapter and bring it to them tomorrow."

"Hmm." Mrs. Jones nodded. "Fine. But help me fold these towels first."

❦

Cassie could barely contain her anticipation as she walked down the seventh grade hallway, the folder with the typed up pages clutched under her arm. She spotted Farrah goofing off with a few boys and grabbed her arm, dragging her away.

"What? What is it?" Farrah asked, shooting one more glance at the boys before focusing on Cassie.

Cassie held out the folder and beamed.

Farrah looked down at it, blinked, then looked back at Cassie.

Cassie sighed and gave it a little shake. "Take it!"

"Oh. Okay." Farrah took the folder and opened it. "Walk Beside Me. By Cassandra Jones," she read out loud. Then her blue eyes grew wide. "Is this your book?"

Cassie nodded, a smile breaking out across her face.

"'Chapter One.'" Farrah squealed and gave a little jump. "Can I read it?"

"Yes," Cassie said, clutching her hands together. Her heart thumped harder. She stuck a finger in her mouth and chewed around the nail, watching Farrah as she read through one page, then turned to the next. Cassie tried not to speculate what Farrah was thinking. The first chapter was pretty short.

Farrah finished the last page and lifted her eyes to Cassie. "Wow! It was so good! You wrote this?"

Cassie's heart leapt with glee. "Yes! Did you like it?"

"I can't wait to read the rest!"

The warning bell rang, and Farrah pulled out her phone. "I've got to go. Thanks for letting me read it! Let me know when you print the next chapter!" She waved and hurried off to class.

"I will," Cassie said, unable to wipe the grin from her lips.

❦

"All right," Cassie said as she slid into lunch beside Farrah and Riley. She waved the folder at them. "I've got the first chapter right here. Ready for tonight."

"Oo, I want to read it first!" Riley said, snatching it from her.

"I already read it," Farrah said, a smug smile on her face.

"What?" Riley shot a glare at Cassie. "When?"

Cassie opened her mouth, but Farrah spoke first.

"This morning. Cassie found me before class and asked me to read it."

"I wanted to make sure it was good enough before I showed it to everyone," Cassie said defensively.

"And it is. It's really good. You're going to love it." Farrah sat up straight and rocked a little, a gleam in her eye. "I can't wait to read chapter two."

"I'm going to read it right now." Riley opened the folder and took out the first page.

Cassie glanced at Farrah, who winked at her.

"Why did you do that?" Cassie asked her after lunch as they walked down the hall. She once again had her first chapter tucked under her arm, after Riley read it and sang its praises. "It just made her mad at me."

"Riley is only motivated by jealousy," Farrah said. "She wants to feel important. If I've done something she hasn't, she has to do it too."

That did sound like Riley. Cassie considered all the fights they'd had in grade school. "How did you know that about her?"

"I have a sister." Farrah grinned knowingly. "See you later. And I want that next chapter tomorrow!"

☙❧

Girls Club was at Trisha's house. Cassie didn't care too much for Trisha. They'd had an altercation back when Cassie was new to Arkansas, and though more than two years had passed, they'd never developed a close bond. They tolerated each other and remained cordial.

Cassie rode with Riley, who talked nonstop about her first chapter, telling her mother, Mrs. Isabel, again and again what happened.

"It was so amazing, Mom! And Cassie wrote it!"

"That's nice," Mrs. Isabel said. "Now remember, you're here for Girls Club, not Cassie's book."

"I know," Riley said, but Cassie didn't comment. There was only one reason she was here.

"Everyone wash your face," Trisha said as they entered. She handed a hot, wet rag to the girls. "We're going to go over facial care today. Next week we'll talk about make-up."

"Guess what?" Riley whispered loudly as they all lined up at the bathroom. "Cassie brought her first chapter!"

"Oh, great!" Janice exclaimed. "I've been anxious to read it!"

"I've already read it." Riley puffed out her chest. "It's really good."

"I want to see it," Maureen said. "Where is it?"

"We're not here to read books," Jayden, Trisha's daughter, said stiffly. "We're supposed to be washing our faces."

No one paid her any attention. The girls circled around Cassie, wet washrags in hand.

"Where is it?" Janice asked.

"Is this a project for English class?" Leigh Ann said.

"It's in my backpack," Cassie said, suddenly shy in the face of all this attention. "It's not for class. Just for fun."

"Who writes a book for fun? Only Cassie!" Maureen gave her a playful shove.

"Girls," Trisha said. "What's taking so long?"

The circle dispersed and the line reformed in front of the mirror, but a warm tingle tickled Cassie's neck. There really was interest in her book. Maybe she would stay in this club one more year.

໑ๅ๛

There was no time Tuesday to type up chapter two, since

Cassie went straight to the community choir after her club meeting. And Wednesday was voice lessons, followed by church. Thursday she worked the store and then went to choir again.

At least she had Friday.

"It's a good thing I have no social life," she grumbled to herself. The television played in the room next to her, but Cassie sat with her back to it. Too easy to be distracted. She did pretty good in her keyboarding class, even if she wasn't the best typist. It took her an hour to get two more chapters typed up.

Monday morning was a fight to see who would get them first. Farrah and Riley both crowded around her locker.

"I only have one copy," Cassie said apologetically.

"I'll take it," Farrah said.

"You read first last time!" Riley complained.

"I'm a faster reader. You can have it at lunch."

Cassie couldn't help feeling pleased as she watched them argue over her book.

Riley tossed her head and stomped off. Farrah started to put the papers in her binder, but Cassie stopped her.

"I need it for first hour," she said.

"Oh. I'll just read it real quick, then." She rested against the lockers and scanned through the two pages. "Awesome, Cassie," she said, handing them back. "I gotta go, okay? Chris!" She waved down a boy and hurried off with him.

Cassie tucked the pages away, a little doubtful that Farrah had actually read them. But she shrugged off the worry.

"Leigh Ann," she whispered in English class, poking the girl next to her, "I brought a few more chapters."

"Oh, good, I waited all weekend!" Leigh Ann said, and she

took the chapters from Cassie.

"What are you girls doing?" Ms. Talo asked when Leigh Ann handed them back after class. "You're not sharing homework, are you?"

"No, no, of course not!" Cassie said.

"It's her book," Leigh Ann added.

"Book?" Ms. Talo asked. A few of her classmates lingered nearby, listening.

"Cassie's writing a book," Leigh Ann said with a toss of her thick brown hair. "We've been reading her chapters as soon as she gets them typed up."

"Really, Cassie?" Ms. Talo looked at her with an expression mixed with admiration and surprise. "How long is it?"

"Um." Cassie shuffled her feet. "I'm not sure. I'm on chapter fifteen. Maybe seventy pages?"

"When you finish it, I would love to take a look." Ms. Talo smiled at her.

"Sure—yes—of course," Cassie said, stumbling over her words. She took her chapters back from Leigh Ann and hurried out the door.

"See, now even the teachers want to read your book," Leigh Ann said, falling into step beside her. "I only finished two chapters. Can I see it again tomorrow?"

"Yeah," Cassie said, a little relieved she wouldn't have to type any more chapters for awhile. As flattering as it was, she suddenly felt a brand-new pressure: to make sure each chapter she wrote pleased her peers. And where was she supposed to find the time to type if she was also writing—not to mention, doing her school work?

Perhaps she shouldn't have told her friends. But she had to admit having their approval felt nice. She couldn't help hoping that maybe Andrea or Miles had heard something about her book. She straightened her shoulders and walked a little taller, just in case they were somewhere in the halls where they might see her.

Episode 6: Branching Out

Chapter Forty-One
Soccer World

With the advent of spring, the weather began to get nicer. Cassandra enjoyed this time a year for two reasons: the warm sunshine and her birthday.

"Your science teachers and I have been discussing a new idea for you seventh graders," Ms. Talo said on Monday morning. "We had the idea to have a week of outdoor school as soon as the weather gets warmer. How would you like to have school outside?"

There was no question about it. All of the students were in favor. The clamor began at once, everyone excited to say their thoughts about an outdoor school.

"When will it be?" Nicole asked.

"Well, we are still discussing the details, but we expect to do it after spring break. Maybe the first week of April."

"And where will it be?" Cassie asked. Before she got her hopes up, she needed to make sure this would be somewhere interesting, and not just in the courtyard behind the school.

"There is an excellent science study and observation center

at Lake Fayetteville," Ms. Talo said. "That's where we plan to do it. Now, everyone pull out your book reports." A flurry of groans filled the room, but Cassie didn't mind. Her book report had been the easiest part of this weekend. She waited her turn to give her report and then sat down again, wishing every class consisted of nothing but book reports.

Nothing exciting happened in any of her other morning classes. She ran into Luke after fourth hour, and together they walked to the cafeteria.

"Hi, guys," Luke greeted as he sat down at the table.

Cassie smiled at him, pleased with how much he'd warmed up to them. Just a few months ago he'd been shy and reticent.

"Cassie's birthday's in a week," Riley announced, plopping down at the table with her typical mozzarella sticks and a side of carrots.

Cassie glanced at Riley, surprised she had the courage to bring it up. She and Riley had an awkward history surrounding Cassie's birthdays. One year Riley just didn't show, and the next year she didn't come because she was mad she hadn't been invited to spend the night.

"Sweet." Farrah texted furiously on her phone and barely glanced up, the grease coagulating on her pepperoni pizza. "What are you doing for it?"

"I don't know yet," Cassie said. "Something small." Against her will, her thoughts wandered to Andrea, her former best friend who had come to all of her birthday parties since Cassie had moved to Arkansas. If Cassie asked her, would Andrea come this year?

"Who are you inviting?" Riley asked, taking a bite of her carrot stick. Her eyes never left Cassie's face.

Cassie shifted. Her family had a tradition of only inviting

two friends. If she could get Andrea to come, that only left room for one other. She couldn't decide with Riley and Farrah both sitting next to her. "I don't know yet."

"Well, you better decide." Riley snapped off the end of another carrot stick with her teeth. "Your birthday's this Saturday."

Cassie bobbed her head. Riley kept better track than she did.

Cassie saw Andrea before fifth hour. No longer in glasses, her hair sleek and styled and her clothes fitted to show off how much weight she'd lost, Andrea hardly resembled Cassie's old best friend. Cassie took slow breaths to calm her racing heart, and told herself to just walk up to her and invite her. But Andrea was giggling and poking a tall eighth-grade boy in the stomach while her new friends, Amity and Cara, stood by laughing. Then they walked past Cassie without even noticing her, and the opportunity passed.

Tomorrow, Cassie told herself. *Tomorrow I'll invite her.*

After school Cassie walked over to her dad's soccer store where she worked several days a week, a little exhausted from trying to beat the traffic on the busy streets.

"Hey, Daddy," she said, heading for the stockroom in the back.

"Hey," came the reply. He looked up from the screen-printing machine, donning a bright blue and white soccer jersey. "Did you know we offered the soccer league a discount to put all of the numbers on the backs of the jerseys?"

Cassie shook her head. "I didn't know. That was very generous of you."

Mr. Jones grunted. "Yes. Very generous. But they took their business elsewhere, ordering from an online company instead."

"What?" Cassie exclaimed. "Why would they do that?"

"I don't know." Mr. Jones heaved a sigh. "I would like to think it's simply that they got an offer too good to refuse, but I'm starting to think maybe they don't like me. "

Cassie scoffed. "That's ridiculous. The Fayetteville league has been using you for all their soccer things."

"Yes, and that's why I think it might be personal. I'm offering the same discount to both Springdale and Fayetteville leagues, but Springdale is taking their business elsewhere even though the store is right here. I have customers that come in from Missouri, from Oklahoma, even Kansas, but I can't get the people right here in Springdale to shop at my store."

His frustration was evident in his voice, and Cassie felt bad for him. "The store is still pretty new. Maybe people are just used to shopping elsewhere."

Mr. Jones tossed his hands into the air. "We are trying so hard to make money here, just to break even. But I can't compete. I can't compete with the prices of Walmart or Target, even though my store offers much higher quality products. And I'm offering them so cheap that I'm hardly making anything."

Cassie said nothing. She wasn't even sure what to say. The store, her dad's dream, seem to be going down the drain. And it was sucking the family with it. She hated the paper route that her parents did in the mornings, hated that her mom had to work early hours at a fast food joint. She didn't even enjoy being at the store anymore because hardly anyone came in.

"There's a big tournament in two weeks. I doubt I'll get any shoppers. Everyone will probably buy what they need online."

"I'll work the shop for the tournament," Cassie volunteered. Her dad looked at her and sighed again. "Never mind. I'm being all gloomy. Help me price these shoes, will you?"

Cassie pasted a smile on her face. "Sure." She picked up the pair of shoes and ran the sku under the scanner. The retail was almost two hundred dollars. She knew her dad wouldn't charge the full retail price, but still—who was going to buy them?

She marked the shoes and set them on the shelf, all the while wondering why they kept at this store.

꩜

Today I'm going to talk to Andrea, Cassie told herself as she lay in bed Tuesday morning.

But somehow talking to Andrea wasn't any easier Tuesday than on Monday, and Cassie found her stomach knotted from her second day of failure as she rode to Girls Club with Riley. They practiced putting on eyeshadow and lipstick without looking like clowns.

"Any more pages of your book, Cassie?" Leigh Ann asked. "I love it so far."

"Me, too," Janice said.

Cassie pasted on a smile and tried to bask in their praise. "Not yet. But soon."

She forgot all about how poorly the soccer store was doing, about her friends reading her book, even about finding the courage to talk to her former best friend, when she got to the community choir.

"We're going to put together a musical production," Ms. Vanderwood said.

The group of singers met her pronouncement with dull stares. That was nothing new. Every time they practiced, it was for a musical production.

"But this one will be special," Ms. Vanderwood continued.

"We'll be performing it for elementary schools. For two days, we'll do four performances a day while schools take field trips to see the musical."

Cassie's eyes widened. Now *that* was something new!

And not just for Cassie. The other singers leaned forward, expressing the same excitement Cassie felt. Performing! For other kids! Classes taking field trips to come see them!

Ms. Vanderwood let them chatter for a moment, and then she clapped her hands. "Let's get to work, shall we? We only have two months until the first performance. That's less than sixteen practices."

They quieted as Ms. Vanderwood struck a chord on the piano, but not before RyAnne said, quite loudly, "I'm sure I'll have a solo."

Cassie's mood soured. RyAnne was probably right. And Cassie would be stuck singing second soprano.

ॐ

On Wednesday Cassie stepped onto the bus determined to ask Andrea the moment she got to school.

It's now or never, she told herself. *My birthday's this Saturday.*

She waited outside on the sidewalk until the warning bell rang before first hour. Just as Andrea said goodbye to Amity and turned to flounce away, Cassie darted into her path.

Andrea's blue eyes widened, and she halted. "Cassie! You startled me."

Cassie gave a brief smile, her heart racing a hundred miles a minute. Why was she so nervous? "I just wanted to see if you could come over this weekend for my birthday."

Andrea gave a small squeal. "Your birthday? I'd love to! What time?"

Cassie's heart lifted. Right out of her chest and into the air above her, hovering somewhere just beneath the ceiling. "Really?" If only she'd known it would be that easy! "I'll text you!"

"Great!" Andrea reached over and gave her arm a squeeze. "See you later!"

Cassie couldn't stop grinning all through first and second hour. She cornered Farrah in third hour.

"Farrah, want to come over on Friday for my birthday?"

"Of course." Farrah opened her binder and waved a red card at Cassie. "I was waiting for the invite. Just in case, I have your birthday card right here."

"Keep it till Friday." Cassie lowered her voice. "Don't tell Riley, okay? I'm not inviting her."

"No worries there."

Cassie hoped she wouldn't, but Riley brought it up at lunch.

"Did you decide who's coming to your birthday, Cassie?"

Cassie pulled on her earlobe and focused on something in the cafeteria just behind Emmett's head. "Um, no, not really."

"Isn't it this Saturday?"

Cassie didn't look at her. "I'm not sure I'm gong to do anything. Maybe I'll just hang out with my family."

"Oh, okay." Riley sounded disappointed. "Well, call me if you change your mind."

Farrah's foot nudged Cassie's under the table, and she felt her face warm even more. She lowered her eyes to her sandwich and hoped she didn't look guilty.

☙❧

As soon as Cassie got off the bus after school, she called Andrea. It rang and rang, and then went to voicemail.

"Andrea, it's Cassie," Cassie said, though surely Andrea still had her number programmed into her phone. "Call me, okay?

We can talk about my birthday." She still couldn't believe Andrea was coming. She felt hopeful, jittery. Maybe this was just what they needed to reconnect and become best friends again.

Andrea hadn't called back by the time Cassie left for voice lessons. Ms. Malcolm made her silence her phone, and then she took it away when Cassie kept slipping it out of her pocket to check it.

"Focus, Cassie!" Ms. Malcolm chided. "Now it's time to sing!"

Cassie let out a loud sigh to display her displeasure, then she did her best to forget about Andrea.

After voice Mr. Jones took Cassie to church for youth group. Cassie snuck off to the bathroom and called Andrea again. This time, to her immense relief, Andrea answered.

"Hi!" Cassie breathed out.

"Hey, Cassie," Andrea said. "Hang on a sec." She must've covered the phone with her hand, because for a moment her voice was muffled. Then it cleared up. "What's up?"

Cassie ran her fingers over the hard metal wall of the bathroom stall. "I was just calling about my birthday. Can you come over around five on Friday?"

"Sure," Andrea said. "That sounds great."

"Perfect!" Cassie said, not even realizing she'd been tense until her body relaxed. She heard laughter on Andrea's end. "Who's over there?"

"Oh, just Amity and Kitty," Andrea said. "I've got to go, but I'll see you Friday!"

"Sounds great!" Cassie hung up and left the bathroom with her head high.

Cassie hurried through the halls when she got to school

Thursday morning, racing toward the front entrance so that she could find Andrea. She saw her immediately, sitting on a bench with Cara, both of them looking down at a smartphone and giggling.

Cassie took a deep breath and told herself not to be nervous. Andrea had said yes. That meant they were friends. Cassie could talk to her. She pushed through the crowd of students around the bench and went around to the back of it. Tapping Andrea on the shoulder, she said, "Andrea."

Andrea and Cara both turned around to look at her.

"Oh, hey," Andrea said, standing up. "I'm glad you found me. I need to talk to you."

Oh. Cassie's chest tightened. She told herself not to be alarmed, but experience warned her to react otherwise. She followed Andrea over to a less crowded section of the outside wall.

"What is it?" Cassie asked.

Andrea sighed and looked down the grassy field. "I can't go to your birthday party."

Cassie's heart plummeted. She'd known, deep inside, that it was too good to be true when Andrea said yes, but it still hurt. "Why not? My mom can pick you up. You won't have to drive all the way to my house."

Andrea shook her head, avoiding Cassie's eyes. "I forgot we're having a special dinner with my grandma that night. It's really important to her, so I have to be there."

For some reason, Cassie doubted her words. When they were best friends in sixth grade, Andrea would never have lied. But this new Andrea seemed so different. She cared too much about her hair, her boyfriend, her jeans. Cassie knew Andrea's friends had been over the night before. After Cassie called Andrea, did they tell Andrea not to go to her house? Did they concoct a plan so that she would be able to say no?

Cassie decided she didn't really want to know.

"That's fine. You weren't the only person I invited, so it won't matter if you're not there."

"Who else did you invite?" Andrea asked, curiosity tinging her voice.

Would that make a difference? "Just a couple of my friends from student council." Cassie lifted her chin. "Have fun at your grandma's dinner." She turned and made her way into the school building before the hot tears could find an exit.

Chapter Forty-Two
The Great Outdoors

Farrah came over by herself Friday night. She and Cassie spread their sleeping bags in the downstairs living room and turned out all the lights except for one lamp. The two of them stayed up watching the old black-and-white version of *Invasion of the Body Snatchers.*

"That was so boring," Farrah said when it was over. "To think, that's how people watched everything. With no color and slow action."

Cassie should have realized Farrah wouldn't like it. It hurt her heart to know she had no friend who really understood her. "Yeah. Different world than today."

"Anyway." Farrah leaned over in her sleeping bag, a sparkle in her eyes. "Have you talked to Miles since the Valentine's Day party?"

Ugh. Cassie didn't even want to think about that moment last month at the party, when she opened her big mouth and told him she thought about him all the time. She rolled over, putting her back to Farrah. "No. I don't think we'll ever talk again."

"Why not? He asked about you in StuCo yesterday."

Cassie wavered in her decision and swiveled her head to look at Farrah. "He did?"

"Yeah, asked why you left the party so quickly, if everything was okay. I told him about your sister. You should really talk to him yourself."

Cassie considered it, and then she remembered what she'd said to him. She shook her head. "I can't."

"Cassie!" Farrah chucked a pillow at her. "You're being stubborn."

"Just tell him I said hi." She handed the remote control to Farrah. "You pick this time. Just find something for us from streaming."

Farrah scrolled through the online choices, but Cassie's mind wandered in the direction of their previous conversation. Did Miles really wonder about her? Or was he just being nice? With guys like him, it was so hard to tell.

❦

Cassie's dad woke her up early, shaking her while she slept bundled up in her sleeping bag.

"What? What is it?" she asked, her eyes still sticky from dreaming. Her head lolled to the side and she saw Farrah, her face peaceful as she slept.

"You offered to help me with the store during tournament. That's today," Mr. Jones said.

Cassie sat up enough to look out the window. The sun was up, at least, with a beautiful blue sky framing it. "Okay, yeah."

"Wake your friend. We'll take her home."

Cassie couldn't help feeling lame as she reached over and nudged Farrah. "Farrah, wake up."

Farrah cracked one eye open. "Hmm?"

"Come on, I have to take you home. My dad needs me to work the store."

"Take me home?" Farrah pulled the sleeping bag over her face. "It's too early!"

Cassie fished around the living room floor until she found her phone. "It's almost eight. Not too early."

Farrah yanked the sleeping bag down again. "Don't you know the definition of a slumber party? It's when we slumber!"

Cassie giggled. "We did. And I'm really glad. But now I have to go to work."

Farrah crawled out of the bedding, grumbling under her breath. But she shot Cassie a smile to let her know she was just teasing.

Half an hour later, after they'd deposited Farrah at her house, Mr. Jones pulled into the soccer store.

"I'll have you man the store, Cassie. Call me if there are any issues." He hopped out and unlocked the front door.

Cassie trailed him as he deactivated the alarm. "Wait, you're not staying here?"

"Nope." Moving in a flurry of rushed activity, he went around her to the cash register and began counting the bills. "I have a booth set up at the soccer fields. I'll be selling things and taking orders."

Oh! Now that sounded like fun. In the middle of the action —in the middle of all those boys. "I could do that part," she said, trying not to sound too hopeful. "You can man the store. That would be easier, right?"

He shook his head but didn't stop counting. Then finally he shoved all the bills in the drawer and closed the register.

"They might ask questions you don't know the answers to. Here, pretty much all the inventory is right in front of the customer's eyes." He patted her on the head. "Good luck!"

And with that, he was gone, leaving Cassie alone in a store that didn't even open for another hour.

Good thing she'd brought the book she was writing.

Cassie laid the notebook pages on the glass table top and dove into the world behind her book, getting behind the mind and eyes of Joyce, her heroine. After days of near starvation, her characters had finally found salvation—in the form of unexpectedly cute teenage boys. One of whom, of course, was very interested in Joyce, the smart and witty main character.

The chime above the door sounded, jerking Cassie back to the present. She placed her pencil on the paper and looked up as a family walked in. The two younger boys, faces still red and sweaty from their game, immediately went to the shoe rack on the back wall.

"Hi, welcome to Soccer World," Cassie said, putting on her best airline-stewardess smile. "Can I help you find anything?"

"We're just looking, thanks," the woman said with a wave. The man didn't even glance toward Cassie.

She shrugged it off and went back to her book. The door opened again, and a woman with a young girl came in.

"Welcome to Soccer World—"

"Thanks," the woman said. "I need an insulated water bottle that won't spill, and quickly. Her game is in ten minutes."

"Sure." Cassie hopped off her stool and came around the counter. "We've got lots."

Two more people came in while she was explaining, and she waved her hand and yelled hi so they'd know she was the employee. She hurried back to the register when customers began lining up with their purchases. Several more walked in, keeping up a constant chiming at the door, and Cassie thought maybe she should prop it open.

"We saw your booth at the soccer field," an older man, probably her dad's age, said. "We thought we'd check the store out."

"Thanks for coming by," Cassie said. She handed him his bag and started ringing up the next person in line.

"This is a great store," the first woman who'd come in with the two boys said. "We need something like this in Conway."

"Oh, this store's the best," another man said, glancing up from where he browsed the jerseys. "We stop here every time we're in town. We live in Oklahoma."

"You guys should advertise more," the woman said to Cassie. "We live here in Springdale, and I'd never heard of you guys."

"I'll tell my dad," Cassie said. "Thanks for coming by."

The traffic didn't let up, and Cassie's spirits rose. Maybe this was a turning point for the store. Maybe all these people would go home and tell their coaches and teammates about the great store in Northwest Arkansas, full of high quality and customizable soccer gear.

Mr. Jones came back to the store after noon to check on her.

"Games go until five o'clock. Are you good?"

"I'm good." Cassie gave him a thumb's up sign. "I can handle it here."

"I brought you food." He laid a hot meatball sub in front of her, and Cassie's stomach growled appreciatively. He glanced around at the half a dozen people milling about the store. "Been busy?"

"You wouldn't even believe it." She grabbed up the

sandwich and took a bite. "We're pretty empty right now. I think everyone left for lunch. They've kept me on my toes."

His eyes lit up. "That's fantastic! It's been pretty good out on the fields also. I'll check back with you in a few hours, all right?"

"Yep."

Things picked up again around two in the afternoon, and Cassie stayed busy until nearly six. Mr. Jones still hadn't come back, but Cassie knew the closing routine. She turned the sign off and locked the door, then opened up the register to start closing it out.

The door unlocked and swung open, and Mr. Jones walked in.

"What a day!" he exclaimed.

"Tell me about it." Cassie finished counting out the money and set it into the bank deposit bag. "I even sold a friendship bracelet."

"How much did we make?"

"I've only added up the cash, but that was more than a thousand. Plus the checks, which I didn't add up either, and the credit cards."

Mr. Jones wasn't listening. He was already checking the transaction history, his lips moving as he counted to himself. Then he looked up.

"Three-thousand four-hundred and fifty-two dollars!" he exclaimed, his cheeks flushed with excitement.

"Wow!" Cassie exclaimed. "That's great!"

He held both fists over his head and danced in a happy circle. "Great day. I brought in about a thousand from the soccer fields, also."

"Does this mean the store's going to be okay?" Cassie asked.

"It's going to start making money now?"

That stopped his happy dance, and his smile faded a little. "It only means today went well. We need to bring in three thousand a day to keep this place in the black. Not three thousand a week."

"Oh." Then things weren't looking up, after. "But everyone was so receptive, so complimentary. It has to mean they'll come back. Maybe business will really increase now."

"Maybe."

❦

Cassie had almost managed to forget about how Andrea brushed off her birthday—until she saw her in school Monday morning.

For a moment Cassie wavered at her locker, eyes on the back of Andrea's head as Andrea laughed and giggled with her new friends. Laughing and giggling. Did she take anything seriously anymore? Cassie had a vision of herself striding up to Andrea and yelling at her, telling her what a lousy friend she was. How Cassie didn't want her friendship now anyway.

But Cassie's shoulders trembled, giving away her vulnerability. She would do anything to be Andrea's best friend again. Cassie faced her locker, the tears stinging her eyes a lousy second to the ache in her heart.

Ms. Talo sent home a reminder sheet with a checklist of all the things the students would need for outdoor school in two weeks. The outdoor school would be Wednesday, Thursday, and Friday.

"Remember," Ms. Talo said, "this is only for seventh-graders in the advanced classes. So most of your friends aren't going."

Cassie understood. She didn't mention it to Farrah and Riley at lunch, though she was desperate to talk to Emmett about it. He wasn't in her advanced English class, but she knew he was in advanced math.

Not Miles. He had decided not to take any advanced classes this year.

Cassie handed the paper over to her mom when she got home, and Mrs. Jones read over it.

"This reminds me of when I was a kid. My school in California was mostly outdoors. We had such nice weather. It just made sense for us to utilize the outdoors."

"I'll need a packed lunch each day," Cassie said, studying the sheet. "We'll meet at school and then bus out to Lake Fayetteville."

"You'll also need lots of water and a towel in case you get wet. And sunscreen."

Cassie rolled her eyes. "I won't need sunscreen."

Cassie rested her head against the car window all the way to church on Sunday, her eyes closed, pretending to be asleep. When the car gave the soft jerk that meant they'd come to a stop, she opened her eyes.

"There's Riley," Mrs. Jones said.

Cassie grabbed the headrest in front of her and used it to haul herself to her feet. Sometimes Riley could be very annoying, and Cassie didn't always want to hang out with her at school. But seeing her at church brightened Cassie. She didn't have any church friends, and sometimes she didn't even want to come.

Riley saw Cassie, and she gave a tentative smile. Cassie broke away from her family and ran over to Riley.

"Come sit with me," Cassie said, grabbing Riley's arm and tugging her into the chapel.

With Riley by her side, Cassie was more engaged in the sermon than she ever had been before. She didn't dread going to Sunday school, where she usually sat by herself and didn't talk to anybody. She didn't even dread seeing the cute boys, who often ignored her as if she were invisible, or worse.

"So what did you think?" Cassie asked when church was over.

"I had fun," Riley said. "So tell me about Jason. He's really cute."

Cassie snorted. "Yeah, he is cute, but he's a jerk." She'd never forget the way he'd treated her last year during basketball.

Riley arched one eyebrow. "That's too bad."

"Yeah," Cassie agreed. "Seems like all the cute ones are jerks."

"Hey, I know," Riley said. "Come over Friday. We can have a sleepover."

"Sure," Cassie said, surprised at the genuine stirring of excitement in her chest. "Sounds like fun."

Chapter Forty-Three
Survival of the Fittest

The following weeks were busy for Cassie, as she had extra rehearsals with the children's choir. And she and Riley hung out at school and church, making Cassie feel like she had a close friend again. It didn't take away the hurt and longing she felt every time she saw Andrea at school, but it gave her a blue-gold ray of hope in her heart. All she'd ever wanted was a best friend.

The morning for outdoor school arrived, and Cassie's mom handed her a packed lunch, looking harried and tired. Cassie wasn't sure if she'd come home early from her Wendy's shift or hadn't left yet.

"Do you have your sunscreen? You'd hate to get sunburned," Mrs. Jones said.

"It's only April!" Cassie's skin tended to darken in the sunshine, not burn. She couldn't remember the last time she'd had a sunburn.

"Make sure you have water, then."

"I've got it."

She got on the bus with her siblings and played it cool, trying not to show how excited she was for outdoor school. As soon as the bus arrived at the junior high, Cassie got off and headed for the gym, where the paper had specified for the students to meet. She opened the door and was greeted with the noise and smell of dozens of seventh graders crowded on a sweaty gym floor. She walked in, searching the faces for her friends. She saw Jaclyn, Nicole, and Leigh Ann, and they waved her over.

"Isn't this exciting?" Leigh Ann said with her usual enthusiasm. "I can't wait!"

"I'm very curious what this will be like," Nicole said. She had a bottle of sunscreen in her hand and was applying the pink cream to the fair skin of her face. "I hope it's not boring."

Cassie looked at Jaclyn, the quiet girl with the olive complexion and dark curly hair who had sat next to her every day in art last semester. "What do you think, Jaclyn?"

Jaclyn smiled, revealing a deep dimple on her left cheek. "It all sounds good to me."

Nicole bumped Jaclyn's shoulder. "When do you ever disagree with anything?"

"I do!" Jaclyn said. "I disagree with lots of things."

"Like?" Nicole asked.

Everyone fell silent, eyes on Jaclyn as she struggled to come up with a response.

"Well—I just do!"

Ms. Talo and Ms. Prose stepped into the gym. Ms. Prose blew a whistle and waited as all eyes turned to her.

"Are you ready for outdoor school?" she yelled.

"Yes!" the kids shouted back.

"Then let's stand up and get on the bus!"

Ms. Talo stepped forward. "Before the stampede starts! On your way to the bus, I will hand you a number. Hold on to it. That's your 'family' at outdoor school. When we get there, you'll need to join up with your family group. You'll do all the challenges together."

"Great, and I thought we got to pick out own groups," Leigh Ann sighed.

Cassie hadn't thought about groups at all. But if they had to do groups, she'd rather do it this way. If someone else had to pick her, she'd be picked last for sure. And with good reason. She was the worst at sports or brain puzzles. She felt bad for whoever's group she'd be on, because she was sure to make them lose. She waited in line to get her number, then took the square of paper from Ms. Talo and sat by Leigh Ann on the bus.

"What number did you get?" Cassie asked.

"Number two. You?"

"Four." Cassie forced a smile. She hoped someone she knew would be in her group.

During the twenty-minute drive to Lake Fayetteville, the kids chatted excitedly, trying to figure out who else was in their group. But there were four buses, and the groups were all split up.

As soon as they got to Lake Fayetteville, the buses dumped them out. The teachers gathered them together.

"OK!" Ms. Talo said. "I want everyone from Group One over here with me!"

Cassie's heart sank a little more. She wanted to be in Ms. Talo's class. Maybe she would be with Ms. Prose, a teacher who Cassie also liked a lot. She watched as her friends Janice and Nicole joined several other kids in Group One.

A male teacher who Cassie didn't know stepped up next. "Hey kids!" he said, waving his hand above his head goofily. This was followed by several cheers from students who knew who he was. "I've got Group Two!"

Ms. Prose stepped up next. "I've got Group Three."

So much for that. Finally Ms. Murphy, another teacher Cassie didn't know, stepped forward to call Group Four. Cassie glanced around to see which of her friends would be joining her. She recognized Jaclyn and Emmett. Perking up a bit, she waved at them, and they waved back as they joined her in Group Four.

"What do you suppose we'll do now?" Emmett asked.

Jaclyn shrugged. "I'm sure we have some team project to do, but who knows what."

"Group Four!" Ms. Murphy came around to the front of their small group. She was a short woman with thick brown hair that ran just past her shoulders. She always looked stern, as if waiting for the opportunity to yell at someone, but Cassie's friends said she was nice. "We are about to participate in a group challenge," she said. She pulled out a bag of yellow mesh jerseys. "Everyone put these on."

While they donned their colorful new outfits, Ms. Murphy said, "This is survival of the fittest. Anyone know what that is?"

Emmett raised a hand and blurted, "It's when everyone except the strongest dies."

"Exactly." Ms. Murphy clasped her hands. "You are about to become a part of the food chain. Imagine that all of this—" she gestured to the meadow around them— "is a savanna. There are lions, hyenas, elephants, and gazelles. Who's the top of the food chain?"

"Lions," Cassie said.

"Right. And the bottom?"

"Gazelles," Emmett said with a snort. "All they are is food for the big guys."

Ms. Murphy eyed him, then said, "Well, let's hope they can be more than that, because you guys are the gazelles."

"What?" a boy Cassie knew as Jack exclaimed. "So we're already the losers?"

"Well, let's talk about this." Ms. Murphy pleated her fingers together. " Are gazelles extinct?"

"Obviously not," another girl said.

"But if the lions all want to eat them, how are they surviving?"

Cassie considered the question. "Maybe there are more gazelles than the lions can eat."

Ms. Murphy nodded. "Could be. Do they have any defenses?"

"They're fast," Emmett said.

Ms. Murphy pointed a finger at him. "Exactly. In a few minutes, guys, you, along with the lions and hyenas and elephants, are going to be let out into the world. Your goal is to survive. The predators will be in red jerseys, while you and the elephants are in yellow. All the lions or hyenas have to do to kill you is touch you. Once touched, just drop to the ground and play dead. If you make it to that tree with the red paint, you survive." She indicated a tree across the meadow, several hundred yards away. "And as the fastest gazelles, you'll go on to reproduce the fastest gazelles, and so on, with each generation becoming faster than the previous."

"So all we have to do is run?" Emmett asked, clearly not intimidated by this.

Ms. Murphy nodded. "As fast as you can."

Run? Cassie bit her lip to keep from groaning. She hated nothing in the world as much as she hated running. This could not end well.

Ms. Murphy pulled a roll of name tag stickers out of her pocket. "Put these on your back."

Cassie took one and stared dubiously at it. The word "GAZELLE" was written across it in giant letters.

"I'll put it on you if you'll put mine on me," Jaclyn said.

Cassie didn't want to. As long as she didn't, she hadn't committed to this game and she hadn't opened herself up to the possibility of being the most unfit. But there was Jaclyn, already peeling the backing off and sticking it on Cassie. Without a word, Cassie stuck Jaclyn's badge on her jersey, also.

Ms. Talo stepped into the middle of the clearing. "On the count of three, I'll blow my whistle to release all the animals. You know the rules. Ready?" She scanned the group of students, and most of them nodded back. "All right. One, two, three!"

The shrill whistle blew out across the meadow.

"Run!" Ms. Murphy cried. "Run as fast as you can!"

Cassie didn't need to be told twice. She took off running as if a fire chased her. She didn't dare look back or around her lest she lose time.

Her sprint started out really strong. She was almost on Emmett's heels, keeping close pace with him and Jaclyn.

And then, out of nowhere, someone barreled sideways into her, knocking her to the ground.

"You're out," Connor Lane said, standing above her and laughing, his blue eyes mocking.

Cassie shielded her eyes and looked up at him, a mixture of loathing and humiliation warming her. Connor had been on her soccer team last year, and he'd taken every opportunity to tease her and make her feel inadequate. Unfortunate now that he should be the one to take her out.

But he was already gone, looking for some other gazelle to knock over. She sighed and brushed the grass off her pants, hoping the rest of the games wouldn't have such an obvious outcome.

𖥔

They played the game twice more, but Cassie never got the opportunity to survive and reproduce.

"Sure hope it's not an analogy for my life," she grumbled to Jaclyn, who giggled.

The groups split up for two more classes before gathering under the pavilion to eat their sack lunches. Cassie found Nicole and Leigh Ann and sat with them.

"Learning about photosynthesis out here is a lot more fun than in the classroom," Leigh Ann said.

"Except we all learned about photosynthesis in the second grade," Nicole said. "It's hardly exciting or noteworthy now."

"Well, I always forget what it is," Leigh Ann said with a sniff.

"What's next?" Cassie asked. Luckily none of the other activities had been physical, and Cassie found herself enjoying the early spring sunshine and the chatter of wildlife.

"I think Ms. Prose said we're going on a scavenger hunt. We have to pair up with someone. Fun, right?" Nicole said.

"Oh," was Cassie's only response. Scavenger hunts often involved riddles and cute little hints that made sense to everyone except her. They were more her sister Emily's style.

But if she had a good partner . . . "Want to be my partner?" she blurted at Nicole.

Nicole's cheeks flushed. "Oh, I can't. I'm actually partnering with Jimmy."

A boy? Both Cassie and Leigh Ann turned around to scan the pavilion for him.

"Guys!" Nicole hissed, slapping the table in front of them. "Don't stare! He asked. And he's, well, cute." Nicole's face flamed, the red streaking up her cheeks and into her blond hairline.

"And nice," Leigh Ann said, tossing her poofy brown hair over one shoulder. "Good choice. Right, Cassie?"

"Absolutely," Cassie said, jumping right in. "Couldn't have picked better myself."

"Maybe we should have picked him," Leigh Ann said.

"That's enough!" Nicole shot daggers with her eyes, and Leigh Ann fell silent, though she giggled. Cassie looked at her and giggled also.

"We don't need to be partners with Jimmy, though," Leigh Ann said, hooking an arm through Cassie's. "We'll be partners."

"Yep," Cassie said, sharing a smile with Leigh Ann.

They weren't surprised after lunch when Ms. Talo told everyone to partner up.

"Come on, partner," Leigh Ann said, sidling up next to Cassie. "Let's see how we do on the scavenger hunt."

Ms. Talo passed around a sheet of paper and a plastic bin to every pair of students. "On the scavenger sheet is a list of clues to help you find the items you will need to collect from nature," she said. "When you find these items, put them in your bin. After you get back, I'll check your bin and see if you were correct. The first team back with all the right items gets a prize!"

Cassie scanned the scavenger sheet quickly.

"It doesn't look too bad," Leigh Ann said, peering over Cassie shoulder. "Find the tree with the white bark. Bring back one branch with leaves on it. Simple."

"I don't know what tree has white bark," Cassie said. "Do you?"

"We don't have to know it," Leigh Ann said. "We have our booklet of wildlife and plants they gave us on the bus. We just have to look it up."

"Oh, right," Cassie said. She's completely forgotten about that booklet. "I'll go get mine. It's in my backpack."

She returned a moment later with the small booklet full of identifying information for trees, bugs, and animals.

"Great," Leigh Ann said. "Go to the trees section. Let's find a tree with white bark."

They quickly found a handful of trees with white bark, but narrowing it down to trees indigenous to Arkansas was a little bit harder.

"I think it's a birch," Cassie said.

"I think so too," Leigh Ann said. "Now let's find that tree."

With the book to help them, it didn't take the girls long to find several birch trees. And then they were able to find item number six, a shell of a cicada, still sitting on the tree trunk. They added that to their bin. They located a nest of tree worms waiting for warm weather so they could hatch, and so on down the list. They even found the squirrel droppings, although neither one of them wanted to pick it up and stick it in their bin. They opted for taking a picture instead.

"Just the mushroom left," Leigh Ann said.

"I found lots of mushrooms," Cassie said, surveying the ground around her. "None of them turned into a ball of dust when I stepped on them, though."

"When we do find one, we have to be careful not to break it."

Leaves rustled behind them, causing both girls to whip around in surprise.

"What was that?" Leigh Ann said. "I didn't see a squirrel."

The rustling continued, moving through the undergrowth of bushes and leaves around their feet. Cassie backed up, her eyes scanning the ground, trying to find what it came from.

"There!" Leigh Ann shrieked, pointing. "Snake!"

Cassie's eyes followed Leigh Ann's finger, even though she didn't want to. Slithering through the grass was a long, thick black snake. Cassie's mouth opened, and an ear-splitting scream escaped her lips, even though she didn't recall telling herself to scream. Panic jolted through her limbs like electricity and she turned around, racing through the trees, running as fast as she could. She heard Leigh Ann on her heels, heard other students shouting, and belatedly realized she was still screaming.

They reached the pavilion in the meadow, and Cassie climbed onto one of the tables. Only then did she sit down and wrap her arms around her knees, trembling.

"Cassie! What happened?" Ms. Prose drew near, her eyes round and full of concern.

"It was a snake," Leigh Ann panted, doubling over and resting her hands on her knees as she tried to catch her breath. "Cassie, I thought you said you couldn't run."

"Yeah," said Emmett, coming out of the forest to join them. "You ran so fast, I thought your hair was on fire."

Cassie straightened up as her trembling subsided, and she giggled. "I guess I kind of had a reaction."

The commotion had drawn most of the other students out of the forest, and they gathered around Cassie.

"That's understandable," said Janice. "Since you were bit by a snake two summers ago, I think we all understand why you might freak."

"You were bit by a snake?" Emmett said. "I didn't know that! What happened?"

Scavenger hunt forgotten, Cassie spent the next five minutes giving the brief version of when she was bit by a snake. After her week-long stay in the hospital, she definitely have an aversion to the reptiles

"Well, I'm glad nothing happened this time, Cassie," Ms. Prose said. "Let's see everyone's scavenger hunt results!"

Cassie glanced at Leigh Ann. "We didn't quite finish," she told the teacher. "We found everything except the mushroom."

"Considering you returned early because you were being chased by a snake, I think that's pretty good," Ms. Prose said with a smile. "In fact, you two were the first ones back."

Cassie gave a relieved smile of her own. At least this project haven't been in a complete failure.

Chapter Forty-Four

Dancing Queen

The first two weeks of April, the community children's choir rehearsed Monday, Tuesday, and Wednesday, all in preparation for their all day performances on Thursday and Friday.

"I won't to be here tomorrow," Cassie reminded Farrah and Riley at lunch on Wednesday. "Or Friday."

"Why not?" Farrah asked.

"Cassie has her big choir performance," Riley said. Now that she was coming to church on Sundays, Riley was extra nice and extra supportive of Cassie's activities, from singing to writing. "She missed girls club on Tuesday because she had extra long rehearsals."

"But why do you have to miss school?" Farrah asked.

"Because we are performing for other schools," Cassie said. "We are their field trip. You know, like when we take a field trip to see a play? Only they are taking a field trip to see us."

"Cool!" Farrah said. "Too bad you're so busy. I haven't seen much of you lately. Last week you were gone for outdoor school, and this week you have music stuff."

"I have," Riley said. "I get to see her at church on Sundays."

"Oh?" Farrah raised an eyebrow. "Does that mean I should start coming to church with you, Cassie?"

Cassie perked up at the idea. It would be so much fun to have a group of friends at church. "Sure! I can even come pick you up!"

Riley frowned. "I don't think you'd like it much."

Cassie rounded on Riley. "But you said you like it."

"Yeah, but we're the kind of people that go to church."

As much as Cassie knew she could argue that point, she was more concerned with how the comment might have offended Farrah. But Farrah only laughed.

"Yes, Riley, I'm sure you're so much better than me at going to church."

Silence reigned at the table. Even Luke and Emmett focused on their trays of food, picking at the green beans.

"Well," Cassie said, putting on a smile," "you guys have fun at school without me! I'll see you on Monday!"

⟲⟩⟩⟩°

Wednesday's practice was even more grueling than the previous two days had been. Miss Vanderwood got onto the second Sopranos over and over again about staying on the right note. And then she didn't like the way the girls in the front row were doing their dance, and she made Cassie and her group do the farmer's dance so many times that Cassie thought her hamstrings were going to explode.

By the time Cassie rolled into bed Wednesday night, her feelings were a mixture of excitement, anticipation, anxiety, and dread. This would be fun, but she also could not wait for it to be over. She didn't have any solos or exciting parts, but all of the singers were part of the moving mechanism that would make the performance work.

Thursday morning, Mrs. Jones woke Cassie up before she left for her work shift at Wendy's.

"Cassie, come on. You have to be at the community center at six in the morning."

Cassie could barely open her eyes. She squinted them enough to look at the clock on her phone. It wasn't even five yet. "Why are you waking me now?"

"Because you need to get ready. Put on your costume, do your hair. Your dad will take you in about an hour."

"Okay. I'll get ready." Cassie moved the blankets off her legs and made a great show of sitting up and putting her feet on the ground. Her mom left the room, and Cassie sat still until she heard the front door close. Then she laid back down. Just a few more minutes of rest.

Cassie woke again to find her father standing over her, shaking her.

"Cassie," he said. "Your mom said she was going to wake you up. It's time to go, and you're still in your pajamas."

"What?" Cassie bolted up right, her heart rate suddenly skyrocketing. She's gone back to sleep! She couldn't even believe it. She's only meant to sleep for a few more minutes, not an hour. She threw herself out of bed, launching toward the bathroom. She could hear her dad saying something, but she didn't listen. She brushed her teeth and combed her hair at the same time, doing neither very well. Where were her clothes? And this hair, what was she going to do with it?

She ended up just throwing it into a ponytail and tying a ribbon around it. She found her flannel shirt and the loose overalls that went with it. Then she took a make up pencil and drew large freckles all across her cheeks and nose.

Perhaps too many. When she finished, she looked like she had a weird version of the chickenpox.

Mr. Jones laughed when she stepped out of the bathroom. Cassie scowled at him, and he stopped.

"You look great," he said instead.

She harrumphed and didn't respond.

Cassie was one of the last ones to arrive at the community center. She got out of the car and ran into the lobby, where she saw Ms. Vanderwood already organizing everyone into sectionals.

Ms. Vanderwood shot her a disapproving look. "Cassie, you're with the second Sopranos in group two."

Cassie already knew this, of course, because they had been practicing their groups for the past week. But she didn't say a word, instead joining the other second sopranos doing the farmer's dance.

Ms. Vanderwood led all of them behind the stage to a series of dressing rooms. "Remember after the farmer scene, everyone will come back here while RyAnne and Samantha have their solos. When they finish, everyone will come back onto the stage for our last encore. Then we'll go backstage, and you have about one hour before the next group arrives."

Andy raised his hand. "What if they don't ask for an encore?"

"We won't wait for them to ask," Ms. Vanderwood said. "We have one prepared, and they're going to get it. Let's hope you do well enough that they want it."

"How many schools are coming today?" Kendra asked.

"There will be four schools today and four schools tomorrow," Ms. Vanderwood said. "The first school will be here at eight-thirty. It's just a little after six. Line up on the risers and let's rehearse."

Singing at six in the morning. Cassie followed the other singers like a zombie. This was an abomination.

They ran through the skit for the next hour and a half, and then suddenly it was eight o'clock.

Ms. Vanderwood clapped her hands. "Okay everyone, backstage. The first schools will be here in about half an hour. I'm going to close these curtains and I want everyone in the dressing rooms in the back. Keep your voices down when you're not onstage."

They filed off the stage, and nerves replaced the exhaustion in Cassie's soul. She was tired of this skit, she was tired of singing, she was tired of being here. And yet, an excited energy ran through the singers, rejuvenating Cassie and wakening her body. They stood in their lines with an electric tension surging around them. It wasn't for practice this time; it was the real thing.

The low murmur of voices drifted backstage as students filed into the auditorium.

"I can see them!" Chris, a red-headed sixth grader, whispered at the front of the line as he peered through the gap between the curtain and the wall. "Lots and lots of people!"

Cassie's heart beat a little faster. What if she went on stage at the wrong time? Forgot the dance?

Ms. Vanderwood walked onstage and the murmur quieted down. She introduced the choir and then everyone clapped. She stepped behind the curtain.

"Places!" she hissed.

They were already in place, in their lines, ready to dance onstage. But her obvious tension only added to Cassie's. She drew in deep breathes, running through the dance moves in her head.

The music started and the curtain raised. The choir sprang into action like a hydraulic force relieving a load. Cassie followed Kendra, moving her arms and spinning and singing all in a fluid, choreographed motion. Cassie's nervousness abated. All of the practicing was paying off. She knew this performance without even thinking about it.

Sweat dripped from her brow and down her shirt, but she couldn't think about that. She ignored her burning hamstrings as she squatted her way through the farmer's dance. And they jumped and leaped and oh, it was hot!

She froze in her assigned position as the music faded. The curtain fell, and Cassie filed off the stage with the other singers. In the audience, she could hear the cheers and loud calling from the kids who come from the schools to watch. An adrenaline high rushed through Cassie, and she stood backstage with the other singers, a smile dancing over her lips. What a thrill performing was.

The sound of RyAnne's solo filled the corridor behind the stage. A hush fell over the audience, and Cassie felt the stirrings of jealousy in her chest, quickly extinguishing the euphoric feeling of success.

"Why does RyAnne always get the solos?" she asked Kendra, who stood in line next to her.

Kendra shrugged. "I think it's because she's a really good singer."

She was that, but Cassie couldn't believe that was the only reason. Cassie was a good singer too, as was everyone else in the choir. "I think she's Ms. Vanderwood's favorite. She gave her a solo part in the Christmas program too."

"I don't know," Kendra said. "I'm just glad she didn't pick me."

Cassie wished she had been picked her. RyAnne and her friend Samantha thought they were the best in the choir, and even though Samantha was quiet and didn't brag to everyone, RyAnne was insufferable.

Chapter Forty-Five

Gossip Girl

Thursday finally came to a close, and just in time. Cassie didn't think she could open her mouth and sing another note. One day down. One to go.

"Well, how did it go?" Mrs. Jones asked when she picked Cassie up around four.

"It was great," Cassie said. "But exhausting. I could not do this every day."

"Even performers don't do this every day," Mrs. Jones said. "They'll perform for a week, and then take a month off, and then perform for a week."

"Really?" She considered that. "I guess that wouldn't be bad." She wondered if she had it in her, to be a professional performer. Her throat felt a bit strained from the constant singing, and the routine had become monotonous. Maybe if she had an important part like RyAnne. . . .

The one silver lining was no choir practice after school.

When Mr. Jones dropped Cassie off at six o'clock Friday morning, she was ready, at least, and with a lot fewer freckles on her face.

"Hi," she said, joining Kendra in the huddle by the risers.

"Just in time," Kendra said. She wore heavy make-up under her eyes, but it didn't camouflage the weariness. "We're about to practice."

"Again? Seriously?" As if doing it four times—no, five times, if she counted the warm-up—yesterday hadn't been enough?

Kendra just grunted in response.

The day started out as an exact repeat of the day before. They crowded in the dressing rooms at lunch time, everyone opening the sack lunches the community center had provided for them.

"Come on," Kendra said, standing up. "The older girls are in room B."

Cassie supposed being a seventh grader made her an older girl. There were kids as young as fourth graders in the choir. She followed Kendra into the other room.

" . . . And he said to me, 'just close the door,'" Samantha was saying. She barely glanced at Cassie and Kendra as they came in. "I was sitting there in my bra and underwear, and he totally caught me off guard. So I closed the door."

Cassie froze where she was in the door frame, enraptured by Samantha's story. Sitting in her bra and underwear—with a boy in the room?

"And this was at your family Christmas party?" RyAnne said, peeling the wrapper off her sandwich. Her brown eyes flicked upward to Samantha for a moment before she focused on her food.

"Yes. Everyone was downstairs except us. He told me to stand up, so I did. Then he came over to me and started kissing me. And, well." Samantha gave a helpless shrug.

Cassie couldn't listen to any more. She slipped out of the room, her mind buzzing with confusion, trying to sort together what she'd just heard. She found a vacant room and sat down, eyes unseeing as she opened her sandwich.

"Cassie?" Kendra stepped inside and sat next to her on the floor. "What are you doing?"

"Did you hear what Samantha said?"

Kendra shrugged. "Yeah. So?"

So? Cassie cocked her head and leaned closer to Kendra. "I think she—Samantha—I think she had sex." Her lips puckered as the word left her mouth, and heat rushed to her face.

"Oh, no," Kendra scoffed. "Why would you say that? I'm sure it was nothing like that."

"What was it, then?" Cassie demanded. "She was in her underwear. With a boy in the room. And he kissed her."

"Yeah, but she didn't add any details after that," Kendra said.

"Probably because we can figure it out!" Cassie hissed. Her ears rang with the certainty of her words. This would be the first person she'd talked to who had actually *done it*.

"Five more minutes for lunch, everyone!" Ms. Vanderwood's voice carried through the corridor. "Finish up and gargle warm water before the next group gets here!"

Cassie turned away from Kendra and ate her food, but her brain burned with forbidden knowledge and curiosity.

She completely forgot about the conversation as they launched into their next performance of the skit. She even forgot how tired she was of the songs and dances as the children in the audience cheered and chanted for them. She beamed as they sang the last note and held her pose, arms outstretched and chest heaving. A smile pushed at her mouth. Maybe she could do this as a job.

During the break they had between schools, Cassie hurried to the restroom to wash her hands and get a drink. Her hand smelled like mustard from the sandwich earlier. As she stood there looking at her reflection and fixing her ponytail, the bathroom door opened, and RyAnne came in.

"I need to talk to you," RyAnne said without preamble.

Cassie looked at her surprise. Even though she had met RyAnne a year earlier, the two of them didn't talk. They were not friends. "Yeah, what is it?"

RyAnne cleared her throat and give a toss of her dark brown hair. "So Kendra told me what you're saying about Samantha. You should know that really hurt Samantha's feelings. She can't believe you would say something like that about her."

Cassie's heart began to pound as she interpreted RyAnne's words. She felt a flash of betrayal that Kendra would tell Samantha what Cassie said. But that was less important than her own offense. "That's not what I meant," Cassie said, scrambling to cover her tracks. "I was just wondering what happened."

"You don't know the whole story," RyAnne said. "What happened that night really upset Samantha. It was one of the worst nights of her life. For you to go around saying something like that, when you don't know all the facts and you obviously don't know Samantha, it really hurts her. You need to stop talking that way."

Cassie could tell from the heat behind her eyes that she was very close to tears. "I'm sorry. I wasn't talking about her to anyone except Kendra."

"That doesn't make it okay," RyAnne interrupted. "You

shouldn't talk about her to anyone."

RyAnne was right. Cassie felt ashamed of herself, and her stomach twisted guiltily. "Okay," she said, hating to admit to RyAnne that she'd been wrong. She turned and walked out of the bathroom, not saying another word.

They still had twenty minutes before the next performance. Cassie stood out in the corridor away from the others, sick to her stomach at the thought that she had spread a rumor about someone. She hadn't meant to, but she'd spoken out of turn. She knew what she needed to do, though the thought made her palms sweaty with anxiety.

Cassie checked all the dressing rooms until she found Samantha, sitting in a chair with a group of students and laughing at a joke. Cassie came in and placed herself directly in front of Samantha.

"Can I talk to you?" she said.

"Sure," Samantha said. To everyone else, she said, "Can you give us a minute?"

The other singers left the room, casting curious glances at Cassie and Samantha. Cassie cleared her throat and launched right into her apology. "I'm sorry I said something about you to Kendra. I never meant to start a rumor. I was just kind of thinking out loud."

Samantha shook her head. "It's okay. You shouldn't have said anything about me. You came in in the middle of a conversation and thought that you had the right to comment on it."

The tears pricked Cassie's eyes. "I know. I didn't have any right to say anything. I'm really sorry."

"I thought we were friends," Samantha said.

Cassie had no idea why Samantha thought that, as they had

never had a conversation together before. But still, she clung to her apology. "I'm really really sorry. I promise I'll never do something like that again."

"It's fine. You should just be really mindful what you say. If you don't know everything."

"You're right," Cassie said, because she didn't know what else to say. Other than telling Samantha over and over again that she was right and Cassie was sorry, there was nothing else to do.

Samantha smiled. "Then let's not worry about it. Kendra said she wouldn't tell anyone else, but I'm glad she told me. I hate to think if you had told someone besides Kendra."

Cassie followed Samantha out of the room, the shame from her indiscretion taking all the joy out of the upcoming performances.

"I didn't," Cassie said. "And I won't."

Samantha stood. "I believe you. We better join everyone else in line before it's time to get up there."

Chapter Forty-Six

Escapism

Ms. Vanderwood ordered pizza after the performances were over as a celebration. Cassie kept to herself, not talking to Kendra or anyone else, still humiliated that she had unwittingly started a nasty rumor about someone. She'd also learned that she couldn't trust people. Something she'd said in private to a friend had made its way back to the original speaker.

"Did everything go okay today?" Mrs. Jones asked when she picked Cassie up.

"Yeah," Cassie said. She didn't offer anything more.

"You sure?" Her mom frowned at her. "You seem down."

Cassie didn't want to go into detail of her shameful error. "Good as can be expected."

"Do you want to talk about anything."

"Nope." She let the "p" pop between her lips, giving just enough emphasis to end the conversation. Her mom got the hint and didn't say anything more.

Cassie shut herself in her room when she got home, pulling

out the handwritten pages of her book. She hadn't had the
chance to work on it for two days, and she needed to enter
Joyce's world. Even though it was fraught with danger and
betrayal and tension, it was safer than her own frailties right
now. Joyce was strong and confident, kind and forgiving. She
would never judge someone wrongly like Cassie had.

By Saturday she felt better, managing to put the incident
behind her. She typed up a few pages of her book, glad to
have an outlet for her emotional distress. She remembered that
Riley had read all the pages so far and gave her a call.

Ms. Isabel answered and put Riley on the line.

"I typed up another chapter," Cassie said. "Do you want to
read it?"

"Has anyone else seen it yet?"

"No." Cassie thought that an odd question. "I haven't even
printed it. I can bring it to church tomorrow."

"Sounds great. I'll see you then."

By Sunday morning, most of Cassie's stresses had faded to
the background. Their big performances were over, which
meant the community choir should be calmer for awhile. And
she had someone who really enjoyed reading her book.

She found Riley in the foyer before church.

"Here are the pages," Cassie said, handing them over.

"Thanks." Riley folded them in half and put them in her
purse. "Have you seen Jason yet?"

"Not yet. But he'll be here. His family always come."

"Okay."

Cassie eyed her, wondering why she was asking about
Jason. But Riley didn't say anything more about it.

Her family sat with Cassie's during the sermon, and then
they split for Sunday School. Jason sat with Michelle and Sue,

and the three of them flirted like crazy. Cassie noticed the way Riley's eyes followed him, but he ignored her just like he did Cassie.

"I'll get these pages back to you tomorrow," Riley said when church let out and they headed back to their cars. "I haven't had the chance to read them yet."

"Of course," Cassie said, though she was anxious to hear Riley's thoughts on the chapters. "See you in school."

"See you."

The relief Cassie felt about the performances being over quickly dwindled when she realized she hadn't been to school for two days, and not only did she not have her assignments done, but she wasn't even sure what they were. She had forgotten to go around to her teachers and get her assignments before the performances started. She knew she had a test on Monday in science, but without being in class, she didn't feel adequately prepared.

"You're back!" Farrah squealed when she spotted Cassie Monday morning before school. "How did the singing go?"

"Great," Cassie replied. She switched out her books for first hour, holding on to her science book so she could study in between classes. Anxiety made her rush, her hands nearly dropping her books as she juggled her binder.

"Have you typed up any more pages?"

"Yes," Cassie said without turning. "Just two more."

"Awesome! I want to read them."

"I have them." Riley arrived on the scene, tossing her short blond hair and grinning smugly. "I got them first."

Farrah looked at her, unfazed. She didn't even blink. "I'll read them when you get done, then."

In spite of her anxiety, Cassie choked back a laugh. Riley did everything she could to make Farrah feel second-best, but Farrah never even took the bait.

"I gotta get to class, guys. Big test in science today," Cassie said, checking the time on her phone quickly.

"See you at lunch," Riley said.

"See you in geography," Farrah said.

Cassie waved, and they went their separate ways.

She didn't hear much of what Ms. Tali said in first hour. Instead she opened her science text book in her lap and studied the pages. Her heart pounded hard in her chest, warning her that she hadn't prepared properly.

"How's your book coming along, Cassie?" Ms. Talo asked when first hour ended.

"Pretty good," Cassie said, stuffing her assignment in her folder and standing. "I didn't really work on it last week, but I will this week."

"Don't give up on it," Ms. Talo said. "It's easy to start a book, but very few people ever finish one."

Cassie hadn't considered that. She wondered if she hadn't been giving the book enough priority lately. "Don't worry, I'll get it done. I've got several chapters typed up now, too."

"What are you going to do with it when you get it finished?"

"I want to get it published."

Ms. Talo beamed at her. "Fantastic! I'll help you. I told my daughter about it, and she wants to read it. Do you have any pages with you?"

"Sure!" Riley might have Cassie's newest chapter, but she kept the others in her binder, just in case someone wanted to see them. She pulled out the first three chapters and handed them over.

"Great. I'll let you know what my daughter thinks."

Cassie beamed all the way to second hour. Once there, however, the reality of being behind on assignments crashed over her. Mr. Adams told them to pull out their homework, and Cassie sat next to Riley and tried not to feel out of place as everyone graded their own work. Everyone except her.

❧

"Here's your chapter back, Cassie," Riley said at lunch. "It was great."

"I'll take that!" Farrah snatched it from Riley before Cassie's fingers even touched it.

Emmett laughed. "Is this something I should be reading? I'm starting to feel left out."

"Oh no," Cassie said, her face warming. "It's definitely a story for girls."

"I like to read," Luke said. "What's it about?"

"He might like it," Farrah said. "It's adventurous with kidnappings and murders and skeletons!"

And romance. But Farrah hadn't read that far yet, so Cassie kept her mouth shut. "I finished page one hundred today," she said instead.

"How many chapters have you typed up so far?" Emmett asked.

"Just eight. I'll try to type up another one this week."

"I've never known an author before." Farrah put the pages in her purse. "When the book comes out, you have to sign a copy for me."

"Of course I will." Cassie straightened, more pleased than she could express with the thought that someday she might have actual copies of books to sign.

Cassie entered fourth hour all a flutter, scared to death for this test. But as she looked over the multiple choice questions, her heart rate slowed down.

I know these answers, she told herself. *I studied this.* She'd scanned over the pages in first hour in a panic, but as she read the test questions, she realized she'd learned the material in class before her break for choir. She finished the test quickly and turned it in. Then she sat down at her desk. Her mind was settled now, the churning in her stomach calming down. She could think about something else. So she pulled out her story.

Page ninety-eight. Her handwriting had gotten much smaller now, more compact than in the beginning as she tried to fit more and more words onto a single page. Excitement warmed her at the thought of reaching one hundred pages. She pulled out her pencil and began to write.

Chapter Forty-Seven
On the Range

"Girls, I have an announcement to make," Ms. Berry said, clapping her hands to get everyone's attention in choir. It took several tries before they looked at her.

"On the first week of May, I'll begin scheduling tryouts for my select girls' choir, Unison. If you want to try out, put your name on this sign up sheet. That might seem forever away, but it's only two weeks, so start thinking about it!" She handed a clipboard to the row of girls nearest her. "That's all. You can go back to your chatting or whatever it is you were doing."

Cassie dropped her eyes back to her notebook paper as the conversations resumed, but out of her peripheral view, she watched the clipboard make its way through the rows. Her heart pounded a little harder with each hand that passed it onward, as if the clipboard were her actual tryout. She had to make this select choir. No way could she do this joke of a class another year.

She gave up pretending to write and waited for the clipboard arrival. It fell into her lap, and she gripped the pen.

She scanned the names of the other students who had signed up. Only a handful of eighth graders and one other seventh grader. Cassie signed her name at the bottom of the list, her heart skipping a beat. Ms. Berry always said she was such an excellent singer. Certainly Cassie would make this choir.

The next two weeks were a flurry of activity as every teacher seemed determined to fit in one last project before school ended in May. The children's choir still had meetings, also, although now that the school performances were over, the practices were much more relaxed.

And then May arrived, and with it the flutter of excitement as students began preparing for their upcoming grade.

"I'm trying out for cheerleading," Farrah said. She opened her grape soda and guzzled it.

"Me, too," Riley said. "Dance Team also. I've been practicing with Michelle. She's already on the team."

Michelle went to church with Cassie, and now Riley, though she had never been friendly to Cassie. Maybe if Riley made Dance Team, that would change.

Farrah nodded, for once her eyes approving of Riley.

"Not me," Cassie said, not at all disappointed she hadn't joined the pep club this year. She'd known when she didn't join that she precluded herself from ever being a cheerleader. Fine with her. She had no interest in dancing for anyone.

"But I bet you're trying out for Unison," Riley said.

"Yes," Cassie said, her stomach twisting up again at the thought. "You?"

"Yes." Riley took a sip of her chocolate milk. "I'm sure you'll make it."

Cassie's face warmed under the flattery. "You, too."

"Of course you will, Cassie," Farrah said. "You're an

excellent singer."

"Want to come over after school Friday?" Riley asked.

"Sure!"

"What, no invite for me?" Farrah said, sticking her lower lip out.

"I can only have one friend over at a time," Riley said.

"I was only joking," Farrah said. She smiled at Emmett across the table. "I'm going to Emmett's house."

"Wh-what?" He choked and sputtered on his sip of soda, and the girls laughed.

That afternoon, Ms. Berry posted a list with each person's tryout day. Cassie trembled when she saw her tryout was on Friday. That was both good and bad: good because it gave her one more day to prepare, and bad because it meant she wouldn't get it over with quickly. She saw Riley's name on the list for Friday also, as well as Janice and a few other friends.

When Cassie walked into voice lessons with Ms. Malcolm on Wednesday, she had an objective.

"I need your help," she said, dropping her bag and looking at her teacher in the mirror on the front wall of the studio.

"What is it?" Ms. Malcolm asked.

"Friday I have tryouts for school choir. I need to practice."

"What do you try out with? A song?"

"I don't think so. I think we just sing a scale. Ms. Berry didn't give us a song to prepare or anything."

"Well, if it's just a scale . . ." Ms. Malcolm shrugged. "We sing one of those every day in your warm up. That shouldn't be hard."

"Can we just . . . I don't know, practice one?"

Ms. Malcolm's mouth twitched, and Cassie got the funny feeling she was trying not to laugh at her. "Why don't we go ahead and warm up? I'll record the lesson like I always do, and you can take it home, practice it anytime you want."

"Okay." She hummed the note Ms. Malcolm played, and then she sang the scale on an "ah," just as she did every Wednesday in her lesson. Ms. Malcolm took her all the way up to high C and then back down to middle C.

"Make sure you warm up with that scale before your try out," Ms. Malcolm said. "Hum it, at least. It will really increase your range and strengthen your tone."

Cassie nodded, pressing her lips together.

"And don't be so nervous. You're going to do great."

Cassie woke up with a knot of fear in her stomach Friday. It rolled and pitched so feverishly that she was afraid she'd be sick. She found Riley at the lockers before school.

"Are you nervous about Unison tryouts?" Cassie asked.

Riley nodded. "I think I'm going to be sick."

"At least you'll get yours over with sooner," Cassie said.

Riley had choir first hour, so that was when she'd try out. Cassie had to wait until fifth hour.

"You're still coming over after school, right?" Riley asked.

"Yes," Cassie said. "Just like I told you." Cassie had been ditched too many times to do that to someone else.

Her nervousness increased as each hour passed. By lunch time, the nausea was so strong she couldn't eat. She only had fourth hour to get through, and then she had her tryouts.

"Well?" She greeted Riley as soon as Riley sat down at the table. "How did you do?"

Riley shrugged. "I don't know. I think I did okay."

Farrah gave Cassie's arm a squeeze. "Don't even worry about it. I've heard you sing. You'll do great."

As fourth hour ended and Cassie made her way over to the music building, Cassie sure hoped Farrah was right. She didn't feel nearly so confident.

She passed the piano on her way to the classroom. Ms. Barry had moved it into the hallway, along with a music stand. Cassie walked into the choir room and took her normal seat. The chatter continued like always, as if Cassie were the only one nervous about these tryouts.

"All right, girls," Ms. Barry said. "I'm going to start calling the names out one by one for those of you who are trying out for Unison. If you're not trying out, I'm asking you to keep things to a dull roar in the here, please."

Cassie pulled out her story and tried to concentrate, tried to enter the fictional world she had created and not worry about the tryouts. But she couldn't. The more she waited, the harder her heart pounded. Her stomach twisted, jostling and threatening. Her foot tapped out a quiet beat, searching for some way to relieve the tension. Four girls went into the hall and returned, one at a time. Cassie strained her ears to hear them, but no sound percolated into the choir room. Five girls. Six. And then—

"Cassandra Jones." Ms. Barry stood in the classroom doorway, smiling at Cassie.

Cassie put down her notebook. She stepped forward, holding onto the chairs in front of her to keep from losing her footing. She followed Ms. Barry out into the corridor.

"Hi, Cassie," Ms. Barry said. She slid behind the piano. "You don't need to be nervous. This is going to be much easier than you think."

Cassie took a deep breath and tried to smile, but her hands were shaking.

"Let's start with a warm-up, shall we? Just sing the scale for me."

Exactly like Ms. Malcolm had said. At first Cassie's voice quavered as she went up the notes, but her confidence grew in the familiarity of the exercise. Her voice got stronger and louder the higher they went, until Ms. Barry started the descending scale.

"Very nice, Cassie. See? Nothing to worry about. Now, pick up that sheet music and sing it to me."

Cassie lifted the sheet of paper from the music stand. Her panic dissipated when she saw the song, "Happy Birthday."

"Really?" She arched an eyebrow.

"I had to pick a song everyone would know," Ms. Barry said.

Cassie sang the song, relaxing. Ms. Barry knew how to make her feel at ease, anyway.

"I'm going to take it up a key, Cassie, so keep singing." Ms. Barry played the new key chords, and Cassie launched into the higher transition of the song. Ms. Barry played a higher chord, switching keys again, and Cassie sang again. She felt her throat trying to close up on the highest notes, and she opened her fingers, stretching them in an effort to hit the notes.

"Thank you, Cassie," Ms. Berry said, placing her fingers on the piano keys. "I'll have the results posted on the doors tonight."

That was it? Cassie wanted to ask questions, to ask how she'd done, but instead she only nodded. She returned to her chair in the classroom, exhaling loudly. At least that was over.

༄༅

Riley waited for Cassie at her locker, and then the two of

them walked to the pick up circle.

"Well?" Riley said as her mom pulled up to the curb. "How was your tryout?"

Cassie plopped down into the back of the van and gave what she hoped was a confident grin. "I think it went really well."

"Really?" Riley opened the passenger side and climbed in, then swiveled to look at Cassie. "Did Ms. Barry say something?"

Cassie shook her head. "No. Not really. But it was exactly like I practiced, and I think I did well. I guess we'll see."

"Yeah, I guess so. My mom is going to drive by later tonight to see the list."

Cassie's stomach knotted in on itself at those words. It was one thing to think she'd done well, it was another to have to test the theory. "Oh, that's great. At least we won't have to wait until Monday to find out. How soon until you think they'll post the results?"

Riley shrugged. "Ms. Barry said sometime tonight. My mom will probably check after dinner."

Cassie would be home by then. Her family lived too far out in the country to drive back to the school just to check the results,. "Can you call me as soon as you know? And tell me if I made it?"

"Of course," Riley said. She made a sad face. "I hope I don't make it and you not. It would be really sad if I were in choir without you."

What an odd thing to say. "Yeah. Or vice versa."

Riley nodded, looking contrite. "That's a more likely scenario."

An awkward silence descended over the two of them.

Cassie poked at a hole in her shoe.

Nothing more was said during the drive to Riley's house, and the topic wasn't brought up again. They played on Riley's computer, watching cat videos and laughing, and Cassie pretended like the choir results weren't the only thing on her mind. But she was very aware that as soon as Mrs. Isabel dropped her off at home, she was driving back out to the school to check the results. Mrs. Isabel cooked biscuits and corn for dinner, but by then Cassie could only pick at her food. The results were probably posted.

Finally dinner ended, and Riley and her mom took Cassie home.

"Call me as soon as you know something," Cassie said as she grabbed her backpack and hopped out of the car, hoping she didn't sound too desperate. She wished she could drive to the school right now. Her heart pumped out an anxious beat, unable to calm itself.

"Yeah, sure," Riley said with a wave. Then they drove off, and Cassie let herself into the house.

Her family had turned on a movie downstairs, typical for a Friday night. She joined them, telling herself not to check her phone every five minutes. She did anyway.

An hour went by. She checked to see if she'd missed a text from Riley, but she hadn't. Surely Mrs. Isabel had already checked the Unison list. What did it mean, that Cassie hadn't heard anything?

Cassie could only think of one thing: she hadn't made it.

Chapter Forty-Eight

Select Choir

Cassie waited until nine o'clock before calling Riley. More than two hours had gone by. She tried to tell herself she could wait until Monday, but the anxiety was eating her alive. She had to know.

Riley answered on the third ring, sounding bored and tired. "Hello?"

"Riley? It's Cassie." Cassie gripped her phone tightly in one hand, trying to keep her voice calm.

"Hi."

Hi? That was it? Didn't Riley have anything else to say to her? Cassie tried to play it cool. "What are you doing?"

"Getting ready for bed. I have cheerleading tryouts tomorrow."

"Oh." That explained a little bit. Maybe Riley was too stressed or tired to think about calling Cassie. "Did your mom go look at the results?"

"Results?"

Cassie shifted one foot, glad her impatience didn't show.

"You know, the choir try outs?"

"Oh, right, yeah. Yeah, she went."

Cassie exhaled, wanting to reach through the phone and shake Riley. Couldn't she be more excited? Why was she acting this way? Unless . . . Maybe Riley didn't make it?

"Did you make Unison, Riley?"

"Yeah, I made it."

Well, there went that theory. "Did I?"

"Yeah."

"Riley!" Cassie exclaimed, unable to contain herself any longer. "You were supposed to call me!"

"Sorry. I forgot."

Cassie shook her head, perplexed. She'd planned on shouting, screaming for joy, jumping up and down and giving Riley a virtual phone hug. This reaction was so anticlimactic, so disappointing. "Well, thanks. And congrats."

"Yeah, you too. I'm going to bed now."

"Good luck tomorrow," Cassie added.

"Thanks," Riley replied, her voice completely devoid of emotion.

Cassie hung up and stared at her phone for a minute. Then she pushed herself off the bed and went to her mom's room.

"Mom? I made Unison."

"You did? Cassie, congrats!"

Now she had someone to hug and jump up and down with.

༄

Saturday morning arrived, and Cassie went with her dad to help him work on the store. She texted Farrah and Riley early.

"Good luck!" she told them both. And then she chewed on her fingers while she waited to hear how tryouts went. While she knew how badly they both wanted to make cheerleading, a part of her feared what would happen to their friendships if they did. It was something she couldn't relate to, something she couldn't be a part of.

Farrah texted her a little after eleven in the morning. *All done. Waiting on results.*

How did it go? Cassie responded, her fingers hammering out the keys on her flip phone.

Lots of people. Don't know.

That didn't sound like Farrah's usual optimistic response. Cassie tried Riley next.

Done with tryouts?

Cheerleading, came Riley's reply. *I have Dance Team in an hour.*

How was it?

Great. I think I was better than most girls.

Cassie arched an eyebrow, surprised at the difference in tone from her two friends. *Awesome.*

Saw Andrea there.

Cassie supposed that shouldn't be a surprise. Andrea and all her friends were the perfect cheerleading type. *Cool. Good luck with dance! What if you make both?*

I'll have to choose.

Even through the text message, Cassie could imagine the smug gloat in Riley's voice. Was she possibly that good? How should Cassie know? She'd never watched Riley dance.

When will you know?

All the results will be up by 5.

Cassie left off the texting on that note, telling herself she had nothing to worry about, for better or worse, for a few hours.

The store was quiet. Soccer season had just about wrapped up, and nobody seemed interested in buying things for the fall season just yet. Taking advantage of the moment, Cassie pulled her notebook from her bag and began writing the next chapter.

Her mom stopped by around two o'clock, and Mr. Jones let Cassie go home with her.

"How was the store today?" Mrs. Jones asked.

"Pretty slow," Cassie admitted. If the store was supposed to keep them afloat, it wasn't doing such a great job.

"I was afraid of that," Mrs. Jones said with a sigh.

They drove the rest of the way in silence, with Cassie's mind drifting pleasantly back into the fictional world of Joyce and her friends. She hadn't decided if they would be rescued in this book, or if there should be a second book. She kind of liked the idea of a sequel.

Her mom put her in charge of cutting onions and peeling potatoes in the kitchen, but Cassie's eyes kept darting to the time above the stove. Would her friends go check the results right at five or wait a little bit? Her heart pounded with each passing minute, and she peeled the potatoes with a fast slicing motion.

"Toss those in the pot of water when you're done, Cassie," her mom said, taking the onions from her.

Cassie threw the potatoes into the pot and waited. And waited.

The potatoes finished cooking, and she still hadn't heard from either of her two best friends. Frowning, she drained them and began mashing them while her mom browned hamburger with the onions. The food smelled great, but she had to know what was going on.

"I'll be right back," she said, slipping away. Taking a deep breath, she called Riley first.

"Hey," Riley answered, though her voice sounded raw, and she sniffled loudly.

Crying. Cassie knew it the moment she heard it. "Are you okay?"

"I didn't make it." Riley cried harder, sobbing into the phone.

Cassie felt the stab of disappointment for her friend, tainted by a guilty relief. She ignored the latter. "Either?"

"Either one." Riley sobbed.

"Oh, Riley, I'm so sorry."

"Farrah didn't make it either," Riley added, triumph tinging her voice now.

Cassie should have known Riley would check. She had to scope out her competition. Which reminded Cassie. "What about Andrea?"

"No. She didn't make it either."

Cassie closed her eyes and let out a silent breath. She didn't know why she still cared, but if Andrea made cheerleading, it would've been one more nail in the coffin of their friendship. And as much as Cassie hated to admit it, she still had hopes in reviving it. "Are you going to be okay?"

"Yeah. At least we have Unison together."

"Yeah," Cassie agreed. "I'm gonna call Farrah, okay?"

"Sure." Riley hiccuped. "See you at church."

Farrah answered before the first ring even finished.

"Hey, Cassie," she said breezily.

"Hey," Cassie said. "Riley told me. I'm so sorry."

"Oh, it's fine. What is it but a stupid club? They don't want me, I don't need them."

Cassie smiled to herself. That sounded like Farrah. "You sure you're not sad about it?"

"Sure, I'm sad. Basically they just told me I suck as a dancer. But I don't. I just got nervous. Better luck next year."

"You'll do great," Cassie said. "It's one more year where you get to hang out with me."

"Yep," Farrah said. "Well, I gotta go eat dinner. But we'll talk Monday!"

❧

Monday all anyone could talk about was who made cheerleading or Dance Club, and Riley's eyes reddened every time it was mentioned. Farrah honestly didn't seem to care. Cassie learned that all of Andrea's friends, Cara, Amity, and Kitty, had tried out, but none of them made it. The evil part of her felt a stab of vindication.

But by the end of the week, all of the tryouts had been forgotten, replaced by only one thought: one more week of school.

The beginning of the last week of school held nothing but torture in the form of exams and finals for the seventh graders. But by the last day of school, the teachers had relaxed and pulled out the candy and movies.

"I can't believe seventh grade is over," Farrah said at lunch.

She, Cassie, Riley, Luke, and Emmett all sat outside on the grass, enjoying the sunshine pouring down on them from overhead. Half of the seventh grade kids also milled about on the lawn, everyone taking advantage of the liberating, fresh feeling in the air.

Cassie bobbed her head in agreement. A lot had changed since the beginning of the year. She'd lost her best friend, but she'd gained new friends. She'd also discovered new talents and gained confidence in herself.

"Next year will be easier," Emmett said. "We won't be the

babies anymore."

"Let's just hope we all have lunch together," Riley said.

Cassie glanced at her and felt that familiar twinge of panic. What if they didn't? What if she had to start over again and find new people to eat lunch with?

Emmett shrugged. "It won't matter if we don't. It's not like we'd quit being friends because of that."

"Yeah," Luke added, looking fiercely certain.

"We would just find new people to eat with," Emmett continued.

Cassie pushed her shoulders back. Emmett was right. Real friends stayed friends, even without lunches and classes together.

She didn't like to admit it, but that probably said something about Andrea.

Farrah let out a deep breath. "Well, I'm so glad you guys can find friends no matter who's at your lunch table, because next year I won't be."

Cassie turned her head to her, as did Riley and the boys.

"Why?" Cassie asked, confused. "You don't want to sit with us next year?"

Farrah pasted on her brilliant smile, the scar on her chin dimpling. "My parents are getting a divorce and I'm moving with my mom. So, new school. Looks like I have to find the new friends."

Cassie blinked at her, surprised at the ache of emotion building in her throat.

Farrah scowled at her. "Don't look at me like that. No tears allowed, okay?"

Cassie reached over and wrapped her arms around Farrah's neck. Farrah patted her arm and then pulled away.

"Enough's enough. I just wanted to tell you guys so you don't wonder where I am next year."

Cassie looked down at her crackers, fighting hard to reign in her tears. First her friend Betsy moved away, then Andrea quit being her friend, and now Farrah was leaving. Was this how every year would be?

Emmett gave a little cough. "Riley, what are your summer plans?" Emmett asked.

"I've got Girls Club camp," Riley said. "And I'll visit my grandparents."

Cassie lifted her head, pleased with the subject change. "I'm going to Girls Club camp too," Cassie said. "Maybe we can go together. And church camp." She wouldn't mind church camp nearly so much if Riley came.

The bell rang to signal the end of lunch, but nobody moved.

"Well," Farrah said, brushing her legs and finally standing, "everyone's got my phone number. If I don't see you over the summer, then *hasta luego!*"

"Until next time," Riley said, rising as well. She hugged Farrah, then Cassie.

"Until eighth grade," Cassie said. She made sure to hug Emmett and Luke also, her face warming as she pulled away. She wondered if she would hug Miles, if he were around.

"Later," Emmett said.

Cassie hugged Farrah extra tight. "It's been a good year, thanks to you."

"I'm not gone for good," Farrah said. "We'll be in touch."

Farrah's news put a damper on the rest of the day, but Cassie tried not to dwell on it. She hurried to her locker after school so she could empty it and still catch the bus.

"Hey, Cassie! I was hoping to find you. I never see you here after school."

Cassie froze with her hand on top of her notebook, just about to yank it out of the metal compartment. *Miles.* She rarely came to her locker after class since she had everything with her before study hall and went straight to the bus from the cafeteria. She turned slowly, her heart pounding anxiously in her throat. "You were?" she squeaked.

He rested his shoulder against the locker beside her and smiled. He'd matured over the school year, shooting up a few inches and getting a new pair of glasses. But still the same friendly brown eyes. "Emmett told me you made Unison. Congratulations. You've always been such a good singer."

"Thank you," she said, hardly believing he and Emmett had talked about her.

"I made the boys' choir. So I guess I'll see you at concerts and stuff next year."

Yes. Yes yes yes! But all she could do was nod.

He pushed away from the locker. "My mom's probably waiting outside. Want to walk with me?"

She shook herself, remembering where and when she was. "I can't. My bus will be leaving soon. I better go."

"Sure." He nodded with another smile. "Have a great summer, Cassie!"

He was half a step away before Cassie managed to say, "Miles!"

He stopped and turned to face her.

"Congrats on making the choir. I'll see you next year!"

He bobbed his head and waved before continuing on. Cassie grabbed the rest of her books and hurried down the hall, a smile pressed into her lips. She'd survived seventh grade, the worst year ever for her. Next year had to be better. She would make it better.

And she wouldn't let Miles slip away from her this time.

Available now!
Southwest Cougars Year 2: Age 13!

Seventh grade was the year Cassandra lost it all: her crush, her social status, and her best friend.

This year she's taking it back. Starting with summer camp, where she intends to employ her new queen bee skills and become the most popular girl in the woods.

There's just one thorn in her side, and it comes in the shape of her elementary school friend: Riley. Will she shake Riley off for good or find another way to become Queen Bee?

About the Author

Tamara Hart Heiner is a mom, wife, baker, editor, and author. She currently lives in Arkansas with her husband, four children, a cat, a rabbit, a dog, and a fish. She would love to add a macaw and a sugar glider to the family. She's the author of several young adult suspense series (*Perilous, Goddess of Fate, Kellam High*) the *Cassandra Jones* saga, and a nonfiction book about the Joplin Tornado, *Tornado Warning.*

Connect with Tamara online!
Twitter: https://twitter.com/tamaraheiner
Facebook:
https://www.facebook.com/author.tamara.heiner
blog: http://www.tamarahartheiner/blogspot.com
website: http://www.tamarahartheiner.com
Thank you for reading!

17706776R00227

Made in the USA
Lexington, KY
20 November 2018